D1407738

BRILL AMONG THE RUINS

BY *Vance Bourjaily*

The End of My Life
The Hound of Earth
The Violated
Confessions of a Spent Youth
The Unnatural Enemy
The Man Who Knew Kennedy

BRILL AMONG THE RUINS

A NOVEL

Vance Bourjaily

NEW YORK *The Dial Press* 1970

The lines quoted on page 166 are from the poem "Elm" in *Ariel* by Sylvia Plath, copyright © 1963 by Ted Hughes. Reprinted by permission of Harper & Row, Publishers, Inc.

Library of Congress Catalog Card Number: 72–103436

Printed in the United States of America

First Printing, 1970

THIS BOOK IS DEDICATED TO

Jim Silberman

My use of archaeology in Part Two is not scholarly enough to warrant a formal acknowledgment to Charlie Wicke, who read the manuscript out of sheer good nature and made those technical corrections necessary, I hope, to keep it from being irritating to devoted professionals like himself. I thank him.

Among those I most respectfully hope not to irritate are Richard S. MacNeish and John Paddock, whose work is mentioned in the text. Scotty MacNeish generously spent a couple of days showing me sites near Tehuacan. John has been my teacher, my supervisor in the field, and my friend for many years; the opinion ascribed to Gary Pederson in the text of John's book, *Ancient Oaxaca*, is one held by many of his colleagues.

Most of the other books and periodicals I raided are mentioned in the text in one way or another. An exception is *Meso-American Notes* and its successor, *Bulletin of Oaxaca Studies*. I owe debts to both.

Chuck Barker of Iowa City read the book with attention to its treatment of the legal profession, made some useful suggestions, and, like Charlie Wicke, was good-natured about the rest of it.

V. B.

PART ONE

1

The Nile splits at Cairo, Egypt. The Damietta branch goes east, and the Rosetta west.

On this west branch, near a city then called Rosetta (pop. 32,800, and now renamed), was found in 1799 the famous black basalt stone inscribed in three alphabets which taught European scholars of the nineteenth century A.D. to read the language of Egyptian scribes ( )s and courtiers ( )s of the nineteenth century B.C.

The three alphabets were hieroglyphic, demotic, and Greek.

Hier- means sacred, a glyph is a symbolic figure. Hieroglyphic was a pretty slow way to write.

So in addition to their language of sacred pictures, the s had a kind of cursive they could scratch along in called hieratic. Demotic, the second alphabet on the stone, was a simplified, thus popular, form of hieratic.

Greek was, and is, whatever it is to each of us, but those educated nineteenth-century Englishmen, Frenchmen, and Germans could read it like we read Dick and Jane, when they weren't busy shooting cannon at one another under Wellington, Bonaparte, and Gebhard Leberecht von Blücher.

Today in the gazetteers Rosetta is called Rashid. This seems to be the preference of contemporary Egyptians, in their gray suits and red fezzes, their Hamitic hearts still brooding over the ancient, Pharaohnic error of letting Moses' people go, 2,300 years ago, whatever the plagues and provocations.

Before it was called Rosetta, Rashid was called Bolbitine, a place name which no longer appears on any maps, even in parentheses. If it hadn't been for the stone, we might surmise, the place name Rosetta could have disappeared as well by now. As it is, it survives, if not on Egyptian maps, then, like many other Asiatic and European place names, on maps of the United States of America.

But does it? And is it the good old scholar's key to ancient times which is commemorated? Research will tell.

The atlas locates a Rosetta, population 350, in Wilkinson County, Mississippi. It is in the southwestern corner of the state, about thirty miles from Natchez, on the Homochitto River.

But an inquiry, addressed to The Mayor, Rosetta, Mississippi, mailed January 30, 1969, was returned unopened from a nearby town called Crosby.

There is only one other Rosetta listed. It is in Johnson County, Arkansas, in the mountainous northwest part of the state, about sixty miles from Fort Smith on the western border.

A similar inquiry to its mayor, mailed on the same date, written in typewriter, the script of American scribes and courtiers of the twentieth century A.D., received the following reply in demotic, postmarked from a town which must be nearby but whose postmark cannot be read. It looks like this:

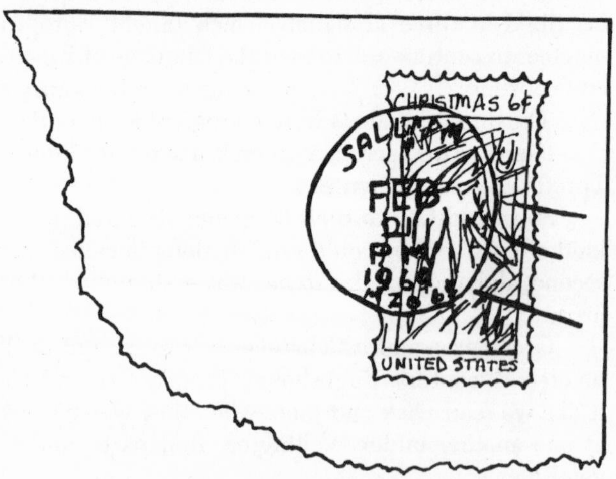

The letter reads:

Rosetta is a community, it was at one time able to support a school, P.O. & a store. Now it has neither. Only three families live in a 3 mile radius. When the P.O. was established the first Postmaster was Mrs. Rosetta Allen.

They named the Post Office after her. I do not know the date it was established. It has been discontinued about 35 years.

Thank you, unsigned Sir or Madam. There's nothing like a little research to smudge a point, but if there are no Rosettas left, we are free enough to invent one for ourselves.

We'll put it in southwest Illinois, on the Mississippi River, and number ourselves, like the present population of Rashid, 32,800. We'll put ourselves twenty-one miles east of University City, where we sometimes go for culture, across and a little upstream from Cape Girardeau, Missouri, where we sometimes go for candlelight and wine.

This puts us an hour north of Cairo, Illinois, where we sometimes go, in a businesslike way, to shoot Canada geese.

Mid-American businesslike. Easterners don't understand. They think we socialize in order to do business, but really we do a little business in order to socialize. Of course we take it off the tax, but to ask a truthful question, what the hell other friends do we have or occasions to spend time with them? Cairo.

Bob Brill, the lawyer, who can shoot a Browning magnum 12 at a high goose better than anyone else in town, doesn't go there any more. Cairo is hardly north at all of Memphis, Tennessee, which has four different Holiday Inns, for Christ's sake.

Though University City is larger, Rosetta is the county seat of Alexandria County. College kid needs a wedding license or to spend a night in jail, he comes over here for it. Cattle are traded here; farmers served in two ways. Honest and dishonest. There is light, smelly manufacturing. There are marginal oil wells nearby, and even a marginal oil millionaire, renamed Robert E. Lee Trump. That's right, he was born Cesar Trumpanek, his dad was a miner; putting the name change through court was one of Robert Brill's first jobs. Not that the information is especially crucial to Brill's story; it's just that we've been playing with names. Which is how life starts.

2.

Now: Midnight Friday. Brill awake in his cups, beside a perfumed lady sleeping. Brill imagining himself seventeen years old, in conversation with a cousin named Felix, then nineteen, who was dead before he reached twenty.

What is life? Well, that's something they've got for people who don't watch television. Be serious, Felix; what about art? Sheeyit. What about history? All right: only never was ever is.

You can take a flaming frig at the moon, Cousin Felix.

Felix does. Astronauts complain. Brill sleeps.

3.

Through the quiet, cool, and dark of four A.M. in mid-October, Robert Brill, six foot three, sandy-haired and warmly dressed, sculled a low, peculiar boat, moving it softly away from, and then turning parallel to, the bank of a minor oxbow of the Mississippi River, on his way to hunt ducks.

He carried with him a Winchester 28-gauge side-by-side double, a yellow dog, and a hangover so mild as to be almost pleasant.

He'd have brought a large, common-sense, and much less graceful gun had another human been along, to avoid technical debate and the possibility of appearing to show off.

The dog, which he called Unk, would have been left behind as well, a second reason why it made Brill happy to be going out alone. He'd have had no trouble finding five or ten more.

He sang, *"Oh, the man bone's connected to the dog bone,"* and said: "Isn't it, Unk?"

Unk was using all the space forward in the boat designed for two more men. Each would have been on his back, nearly lying down, head and shoulders braced against a slanted thwart board and feet sticking into the bow under a spray shield. The shield had slits in it for peepholes. Concealed in this way, with a third man lying behind, shoulders against the transom and sculling, gunners could move in among ducks on the water, the birds seeming to take the craft as no more menacing than a drifting log. Once within range, all three would sit up at the same moment and fire in three directions as the birds flew off.

In Brill's cabin on the small bluff, below which he had untied the scull boat, three people were sleeping whom Brill had been careful not to wake: they were his friend Martin Habib, a movie-theater owner of Lebanese parentage and Nicaraguan upbringing; a lady they called B.S.L.; and an airline stewardess whom Martin had met returning from a business trip and brought from St. Louis for the hunting weekend. Her name was Edith.

Martin Habib didn't hunt but last night Edith had said to Brill: "You get me up to shoot those ducks, you old Bobby, you hear?"

Now, moving through the black water, him old Bobby said to Unk: "Airline stewardesses used to be tense, smart, slim girls, didn't they?

With upper middle airs. They're calmer now and plumper. More like waitresses than mistresses."

When in doubt sit; Unk sat.

This morning, going into the bedroom in the cabin to wake Edith, Brill had found the room warm, a lamp on, and the man and woman stretched out asleep, naked and reversed, Martin's head on the girl's soft stomach, Edith's left arm still under Martin's thighs. The scene was not without a certain sweetness, in Brill's view, except for the evidence that the girl had not taken time to wash off her makeup before it got underway. Because of this detail it seemed most tactful to turn out the light and leave, stocking-footed, affectionate, and a little horny.

The third person in the cabin, whom he and Martin called B.S.L., which stood for Big Shy Louise, was a nice, somewhat arch woman who worked as a sorority housemother in University City, twenty-one miles away.

Big Shy Louise liked time in the morning to get herself together, and would have been painfully confused at being waked before four, hurried into her clothes and into a duck boat. Big Shy Louise had been unusually passionate and enduring the previous night, and while Brill had felt obliged to oblige, she'd left him with what he thought of as a crick in his pecker this morning.

He shifted his position, to put the crick out of friction with his hunting underwear, and smiled, and sang, and talked to the dog—all very quietly—as he came out of the oxbow onto the big river.

4.

It was still night, more than an hour until sunrise.

At thirty minutes before sunrise he might load the gun, for it would then be legal to shoot.

The river water was still black, and the stumps in the shallow part through which he was sculling hardly separable from it, so that now and again he bumped one gently.

Good enough reason not to use a motor, if you needed some reason other than liking the quiet.

The stars, bright through holes in the clouds when Brill started, were disappearing now, and the clouds moving in a wind which must be strong up there, though it hardly rippled the river yet. He looked back east and there was a promise of light, lying as a margin between land and sky.

Breeze started, just enough to rock the boat a little.

Something was moving above him, shadows of birds against the clouds. He guessed cormorants, but couldn't see well enough to know. He nudged another stump, and, in a parody of cause and effect, there was a splash out somewhere on the water, a big carp, probably, or a muskrat.

A lost cow, bawling on shore, sounded ambiguously like a bullfrog, but it was too late and cool for frogs.

The water was grading from black to gray as Brill came out of the area of stumps, into the edge of the Mississippi current. He turned to scull upriver, to get above his decoys, and a small flight of wood ducks went over him in the dawning sky, coming out of the oxbow, turning overhead, and cutting back toward the bank.

They were going, he judged, to Captain's Slough, a mile back from the river, where oaks dropped acorns into shallow water; and a long time since Brill had been there.

The wood ducks he recognized not by their appearance, for he could barely see them, but by the soft, hooting call-note of the males as they passed.

5.

Ask anyone in Rosetta about sculling ducks, and the majority will ask you back, "Doing what to them?" Still, there's quite a few of us will nod and tell you that the men who do it any more are damn fools, with the low duck limits we get these days: two mallards, one redhead or can.

You've got to have fifteen dozen decoys just to start, which is three hundred bucks right now, unless you're like Bob Brill the lawyer that inherited a barnful of them. Even those have to spend two good weeks in the fall, painting them up, and a couple more days rigging them and setting them out. And every time the wind changes, those decoys ought to be moved around. The old rivermen used to put their diver decoys on heavy chains, at intervals, so they could pick up one end at the buoy and move the whole set that way.

Pick up a couple of hundred feet of chain with your left hand and scull with your right? The old rivermen: long, funny, chunky forearms, coupled short to round shoulders and deep chests, just about the way bears are built, knew how to do it.

It's not just the work and expense, it's uncomfortable and risky. If there's weather enough to make a day fit to hunt, you're going to be taking spray and shipping water. There's been lots of men drown out of scull boats. Remember Armistice Day, 1957? For a couple of mallards.

Pete Canaday, who's a hot-shot hunter, shoots from pits and blinds, he was runner-up in the duck-calling contest at Stuttgart one year.

Pete once said: "Sculling is like standing in a cold shower with your clothes on, tearing up twenty-dollar bills."

Later Canaday admitted that he got that one from a girl he knew when he was on the West Coast, that he went sailing with, and said it about sailboat-racing.

Bertrand Russell once said: ". . . there were countless ages during which there was no knowledge . . . there probably will be countless ages without knowledge in the future."

We don't know where Russell got that one.

6.

There were 207 decoys in Brill's spread, two thirds of them divers, anchored in a raft in open water. The puddle-duck decoys—mallards, pintails, and widgeons—were set off at the shallow end near a sandy island. He watched the set as he sculled past, keeping the boat close enough to the riverbank so that birds sitting among the blocks wouldn't see him go by.

Each of his was anchored individually, but he was thinking, as he regularly did at this point in the trip, about the old men and their long chains. He must get one of those chains and learn to manage it, or that way of setting out might be lost for good from local use.

"How about that for a grave responsibility, Unk?" Brill said, sculling. "That cognac, dog. Still working here this morning. Make a big-time epistemologist out of you."

Tried to remember the eighty-six-proof profundities of the night before, as he'd lain awake beside Louise, and couldn't, though he did recall that Felix, the long-dead cousin after whom he'd tagged, growing up, had been in his mind when he finally went to sleep. At least he hadn't got up, as sometimes happened, to write fierce, thoughtful, barely legible notes, uninhibited by rationality, bottle beside him on the kitchen table, about the state of his household, his profession, and the nation.

A couple of hundred yards above the decoys was another shallow area with stumps in it. Brill stopped sculling there, dropped a hitch over one of the stumps to hold steady, and looked at his watch.

Five minutes more till legal shooting time.

More birds were going overhead, cormorants for sure this time. He watched the big, black, gooselike bodies, wondering at the way a dozen birds could fly like dancers, all wings stopping together to glide, all starting in again to stroke on the same beat.

He remarked to himself, and also told the dog, that he had not shot a wild goose yet this year, and that his family expected one for Christmas dinner. Cooked by three serious specialists—Brill, his fifteen-year-old daughter Trinket, his college-age son Cal—last year's goose had sure spattered grease all over hell.

The children's mother, Brill's wife Pat, was still pretty good around the kitchen mornings, but by midafternoon most days, last Christmas no exception, she'd drunk enough California sherry to go to bed for what was called her nap.

"My wife isn't just any drunk," Brill thought, too loyal to say it aloud to the dog. "She's a genuine wino."

The thought was not without tenderness and not without regret.

Shooting time had come, but Brill didn't load. The level of light was high enough so that he could make out individual decoys down below on the river, and now ducks went over him: divers. Bluebills, probably, at considerable but not impossible range, perhaps sixty yards, a flight of thirty. Short, rapid wing strokes, chunky bodies, they were such busy, urgent fliers you almost imagined them buzzing as they went.

Unk saw them and whined.

"Wrong ducks, boy," Brill said.

He watched the flight go over and past his decoys without pausing, which pleased him since bluebills were not what he wanted. He watched them go on down the river, low, and was pleased again because no shots were fired down the line. So far he had the river to himself this morning.

There were a half dozen other men in the area who put out decoys and used scull boats, but they didn't hunt much after opening weekend, some because they liked only the appearance of being hunters, not the reality of hunting, and others because they were old.

At ten minutes before sunrise, Brill had still not loaded his gun. He might, by now, have dropped a wood duck, and a second flight of bluebills had gone overhead, landing this time among his decoys. They'd be swimming around there now.

At the shallow end a duck rose on its tail in the water, shook its wings, and settled back, and he felt quite certain it was a mallard and that there would be other mallards with it near the sand island.

But he was enjoying the freshness of the morning, lazy if you like, and thinking about it, thinking that regardless of how polluted the water was, and the air, a night's sleep seemed to do the earth good, producing at least an illusion that all was clean and sane again.

"But don't drink it," Brill said.

Unk whined.

"You want action, do you, Unk?"

He wondered if the dog knew as he did that there were bluebills in the deepwater blocks, mallards in the shallow ones.

Unk was a big, yellow Lab, and had no more business in a scull boat than the 28-gauge Model 21. A man in a boat can more easily retrieve his own ducks than handle a large, wet dog, clambering back in. Brill had raised Unk to go jump-shooting with him. If he was mushheaded enough to let a dog's pleasure in it persuade him to bring Unk out on the water, he was nevertheless damned if he'd be bullied by a dog into sculling down for bluebills, or even mallards, when it was a canvasback he wanted.

There was one in the refrigerator at the cabin, which he'd shot last evening at sunset, and only a second like it would satisfy his image of what to serve Martin and the ladies for lunch though they would neither know nor care.

"When I was nine," Brill explained to the dog, "Dad and I and Felix got fourteen cans one morning. Five was the limit then, so we were one under. Mother couldn't cook worth a damn, and she was at her worst on game."

Unk's tail quivered.

"Maybe she could have cooked . . . fish from the ocean." Brill's mother had been an exchange student from Peru, when she'd met Brill's father long ago in law school. She'd gone back to Peru when Brill was ten. "The Humboldt current . . ." Brill veered. "One canvasback a day, two in possession. All we can have this year. People drain marshes . . ."

He decided to load, and as he did he heard, from the direction of the sand island, someone attempting to blow a highball on a duck call. He looked above the island and there were ducks in the air, mallards, which turned in alarm from the sound of the ill-blown call, and the dozen mallards which were in Brill's decoys rose, all at once, to join the flock in the air. There came nine shots, which meant three men with plugged automatics, and Brill felt he could hear dismay in the shots since the gunners must have been watching the birds in flight, unaware that there were others in the decoys.

The lowest bird in the rising group wheeled off, though, in a long, sailing fall, and Brill said:

"Two lucky, long-range pellets in a wing, Unk. Let's see if they've got a dog."

He watched the island and saw the three hunters appear and run to the edge of the water. They must have a boat over on the other side, by which they'd reached the island, and he thought he knew who they were: three Missouri men who'd got tired of waiting in a blind on their side of the island, and been on their way to see if they could jump birds out of his decoys when they saw the flight they'd called to. They had no dog; by the time they could have got their own boat, the crippled mallard would be long gone in the current.

"I guess you're the dog," Brill said to Unk, and cast loose.

He set aside his gun, rose to his knees to be able to scull faster, and started downriver, current and a growing breeze behind him.

He thought of some pretty uncouth things to say to the high duck shooters, when and if he delivered their duck, but as he reached the outside edge of the decoys and five canvasback went up with the bluebills he felt such an idiot for not having made a proper run, on the way to retrieve for the others, that his anger left.

He even felt more like laughing than cursing when one of the sports on shore took a hundred-and-fifty-yard shot at the departing divers.

Brill was beginning to breathe hard as he got below his decoys, into the area where the wounded duck had dropped, and was relieved when he saw it, swimming along with the curious appearance of serenity, of having been tamed by shot, which wing-shot ducks seemed to have.

A mallard hen; as he saw her she dived. Unk was up, poised, watching, quivering all over, and Brill breathed: "Stay boy," stopped sculling, and shouldered the gun. When the bird came up it was only ten yards away and he shot it quickly, holding on its head, before it could go down again, and said, "Fetch."

Unk's leap took him five of the ten yards and dog reached bird while she was still thrashing.

It was a good moment of a morning which had gone ridiculous to see the way the retriever handled her, turning the bird, treading water with his mouth open, waiting for the back to be presented, then darting his head forward to hold the body softly, wings trapped now, taking yet another second to arrange it in his mouth before he started back for the boat.

Brill took the duck, hauled his dog in, recovered his oar.

It wouldn't be all that bad to have a motor now, to save sculling back up to the island. Because the rising wind made the work harder, and he could hear the hunters yelling at him, apparently thinking he intended to make off with their damn duck, Brill's ill-temper at the men returned.

And then, hell, they were boys, three early-teen-agers, all decked out in new hunting gear, and for a sad instant, because his own son Cal had never cared much for hunting, Brill wished they were his to raise.

The nearest boy caught the bow of the boat, and Brill tossed the duck ashore thinking: Too late. Not too late, perhaps, in terms of the boys' ages, but too late in the century, not enough ducks left, too many hunters around, too frantic, too witless. Last, hysterical minutes of the lost game.

"How much does a dog like that cost?" The boy holding the boat asked, and Brill smiled at him and shook his head.

One of the others said, "That's not the duck we shot. We shot a mallard."

"It's a mallard, son," Brill said.

"I saw his green head," the kid complained.

"They come in two kinds," Brill said. "Male and female."

The first boy said, "Hey, can we go in the boat with you, mister?"

"My name's Robert Brill. Call me in Rosetta, if you'd like to go out. I'll take you."

"Can't you now?" The kid was ready to climb in.

"The wind is up and the water's choppy," Brill said. "We'd have a hard time getting back here."

The first boy, then, turning loose the boat, turning away, to his friends: "Boy, wait till I show my mom I got a duck."

"What do you mean? I got him," said one of the others. Most of the grown men Brill knew didn't hunt any better than that, or have much better manners either.

7.

Then, on his way back down the river, because there was no sense going back up to his sculling position if the kids were going to roam the island, he got his canvasback.

It was unexpected, and just as he wanted it.

There was a set of sculler's decoys in open water, off the mouth of the oxbow into which he would be turning. He was lying back, drifting in, watching the set, thinking that in order to cook duck for lunch he'd be lucky enough to get one of any variety now, when the cans came in.

They whistled over him from behind, left and descending, unmistakably big, fast, and noisy—gleaming off-white bodies, dark heads, and Roman profiles, for the beaks came straight out from the foreheads without indentation—and splashed without a pause into the blocks eighty yards in front of him.

Brill looked quickly, right, left, and behind, to be sure he wasn't in someone's way; but he had never seen another boat work these blocks, and didn't now.

Unk was down, hand-signaled, behind the spray shield, and Brill eased the oar, turning. He must work in slowly, disturbing the water as little as he could; he steered more than sculled, across and downwind, hoping the wind itself, which had been freshening all morning, wouldn't take him in too fast.

He risked a glance along the coaming, past the spray shield, and saw his ducks swimming there, fifty yards away now. He picked a tree on the long bluff below the oxbow, a tree he could see over the top of the shield, and lay back again, guiding obliquely on the tree, making a running calculation, not in his head but with varying pressures of his hand against the oar.

He passed a decoy in the stem of the set, an old hand-carved wooden one, and had time to admire it. It was tossing now in water which seemed quite disturbed, so he held back just a little more to steady the boat against what must be stronger current here.

He raised the Model 21 in his right hand by the pistol grip, holding its butt under his arm for now, and stayed crosswind, shipping a little water into the cockpit but not enough to worry about.

This was the moment for which he carried the little 28-gauge gun: in wind and current he could shoot it one-handed, keeping the boat in control with the other hand, ready to turn should the ducks swing far to one side.

He heard them now, current against duck bodies and a kind of clacking, and one duck giving a low little burring call, like someone rolling r's under his breath.

He looked along the coaming again and there were ducks almost under the boat, swimming slowly away, spreading right and left, not in alarm yet, simply letting the floating object by. Though he had seen it a thousand times in his life, Brill still felt wonder at getting in so close.

There were about two dozen of the canvasbacks, swimming irritably away, getting just a little nervous, when Brill shouldered his gun, picked his drake, and rose to a sitting position to start him. Instantly, the drake began a run to takeoff, short wings vibrating powerfully, and the others joined the movement.

Brill's drake cleared the water, came in sight above the spray shield in full flight, right to left and away. Brill, his little gun choked full and full so that he wanted to wait for the range to widen, held on it, body swinging at the drake's speed. The drake turned left a little, but it was as if it were hanging still in the air as Brill moved the gun a touch ahead and shot, knowing the lead and the moment without thought. The big duck folded and plunged, dead before it hit the water.

"Fetch, boy."

For practice, then—or as a salute to great flights past—Brill swung and tracked another, and could quite easily have had him, too, but did not fire. One canvasback was what he had asked of the morning, and all he would accept.

While he was reaching to help Unk back in the boat, canvasback aboard on the floor, the squall struck, a mean, sudden bolt of wind down the river that spun decoys and tore the boat away from the dog.

8.

One moment Unk was there, confident, forepaws on the coaming, master reaching for his shoulders; the next moment the boat was ten feet away and the dog striking water with his paws.

Unk righted himself and came swimming down. Brill held with the oar until the paws came up the side, let go the oar, and lunged to try to reach behind the dog's shoulders, and again the wind and current swept the boat away.

Brill threw himself back once more to the sculling oar, took it with both hands, rose to his knees, and turned toward shore. He called Unk to swim with him, and tried to work crosswind to get into the lee of the bluffs. Unk caught up and tried this time to crawl in by himself, letting water pour in, nearly tipping them.

"No, boy," Brill shouted. He couldn't let go of the oar again. "Come on, now," and he sculled away. For a moment the wind seemed to let up. Unk had swum up behind and Brill tried reaching into the water for him, across the stern. He couldn't hold.

On his knees in four inches of water now, and sculling hard, Brill saw that he was losing too much way, moving downriver too fast. Soon he'd be unable to reach the bank at a place shallow enough to make a landing, and he didn't think the boat and dog would last out a fast, two-mile drift past the bluffs to the next shallow place. He put extra effort into it, short, fast, lunging strokes, and could make some progress that way, across the wind, calling to Unk. The dog, confused, tried to climb onto the sculling oar and was thrown back.

Chain. If the decoys he was moving through were anchored with chain? He swung toward a decoy, let go the oar with his right hand, and plunged his arm into icy water, grabbing, taking a grip underneath where the cord was tied. For a moment they slid along, the decoy pulling slack in its anchor line; then he could feel it catch and hold, down below, strain, slip, find a mooring, and the boat slowed and stopped as Unk caught up again. The forepaws came over the coaming, hooked, and Brill made a wild stab with his free hand, got the dog by the skin on the back of his neck, and heaved. Unk was in the boat.

The wind wasn't letting up. Brill rested a moment, hanging tight to the decoy, dog pawing happily at his lap, shaking.

"Jesus Christ, dog," Brill said, chest heaving, pockets awash in the water he had to sit in in the boat bottom. "You'll get me all wet," and laughed in the wind's teeth.

They weren't out of it. Pretty quick now, before his hand got too numb to hold on, he'd have to drop his duck and drive his truck.

"Sit down, Unk," he roared, got back to his knees, turned loose, grabbed the oar, and started chopping water. He was crossing now toward the low end of the stump area, but couldn't gauge how far that kind of bottom extended before drop-off. The boat was wallowing, shipping a little water each stroke, so he hadn't much choice. When he saw stumps above him, he kicked off his short boots, took the stern line, looped it around his wrist and through his hand, and slid his feet into cold water.

Slid his rear down along the side of the boat, reluctant to go but aware that every second moved them toward deep water, if they weren't already there. Pushed off, sank for an interminable, scary moment, wondering if he'd even try to swim—sure, goddamnit, he would—wished himself back in the boat, kicked down with his feet, and felt, with enormous, close to hysterical, relief, his feet touch bottom and settle as the water reached his diaphragm.

Waded in, Bob Brill did, towing boat, dog, and duck after him, to shore. The bluffs started forty yards below where he crawled out of the river and, for a couple of minutes, collapsed, never letting go of the line.

2

Brill put Unk in the station wagon, started the motor, turned the heater on, cracked the window, and went into the cabin.

He left his boots and wet coveralls outdoors, told his teeth to shut up, and went in.

Martin and the airline girl were up and dressed. He was pleased not to see Big Shy Louise. She did enough mothering of girls all week, and while she might have liked the change of maternal care to a large, wet duck hunter, Brill felt the hunter could get along fine without it.

"Louise is dressing," Edith said. "Did you get some ducks?"

"Just one." Brill put it down by the cabin sink and went to the fire. "Nice, Martin,"

"I built it," Edith said.

"Nice."

"A little wet out there?" Martin asked.

"Little."

"You were mean not to wake me," the girl said.

"I'm a mean guy."

"It's a nice duck." She picked it up and cradled it. "Poor thing. If you only got one, it couldn't have been very exciting."

"No."

"Does this work?" Edith put the duck down and crossed to an old parlor organ, against the east wall.

"It was in the basement of one of the theaters," Martin said. He moved a pile of Brill's books off the organ seat. "Go ahead. Wheeze one out."

"We're drinking vodka and orange juice," Edith informed Brill, sat down at the organ, pulled out half a dozen stops, and started to pump.

When he had her playing "Bye-Bye Blackbird" with one finger, Martin nodded, turned, looked carefully at Brill and shook his head. He was a slim, dark, graceful man, with something of the melancholy look Brill saw in pictures of the bullfighter Manolete. He kept looking at Brill and as he did a white, self-deprecating, Lebanese-Nicaraguan smile gradually took over his face, and he walked quietly to the sink and gazed at the duck. Then he looked back at Brill, shook his head again, and poured out half a water glass of whiskey, lightly mixed with water.

He brought the drink to the fire, held it out, and Brill said: "Go to hell, Habib," and took it.

"Get scared out there today?" In a low, suggestive voice that excluded the girl at the organ.

"Damn right."

"What happened?"

"Got careless."

Brill took a swallow of the strong drink, letting it go down before he added: "Been on the river all my life, Martin. Suddenly seem to be doing things I'd want . . . someone else locked up for his own protection if he tried them. Taking Unk in the boat. I don't know. Kids out there today."

"Were there?"

"Stupid little know-nothing shits, they were taking better care of themselves than I was."

Martin made a small, tan fist and hit Brill on the arm; it looked as if it were coming softly, but in the last few inches Martin speeded it up, enough to jar.

"Never know where it's coming from," he said.

Brill grinned, Edith the one-fingered organist stopped playing, and cried: "Look who's here," and in came Big Shy Louise in a cloud of French perfume.

2.

It's an unwary President who names his favorite tune. For the next four years of his life—or eight—the poor bastard's going to hear "Home on the Range" or "The Missouri Waltz" played by everything from high school bands to symphony orchestras, everywhere he goes.

In Brill's view, Louise had made a similar mistake.

Early in her widowhood, when she'd first gone to work for the sorority, she had remarked carelessly that she loved French perfume. Since when half a generation of relentless little girls, passing the intelligence along, had loaded her with the stuff. She got it for Christmas and at birthdays, got it in the fall when girls came back from summer trips to Europe, got it from their parents at graduation time.

"I literally have a closetful," Louise would say. "And they always want to know, if I go out, what I'm wearing this time. They don't ever want me to wear the same thing twice, Bob, and they're so darling about it, I don't even dare give any of it away."

She was a big, dewy gardenia of a woman, always arriving helplessly in a wave of call-girl musk.

"What is it this morning?" Brill asked, as she came over wifelike for a kiss on the scrubbed cheek.

"*Fleurs . . . Fleurs du Mal,*" Louise said. "Isn't that awful?"

"Nice," Edith said.

"Do I hear a Russian accent?" Martin asked, bringing vodka and orange juice, and Brill excused himself to change clothes, pausing only to pick up a book. Reading maketh an empty bowel.

Coming back fresh-shaved, in khakis and camp slippers, he paused in the bedroom doorway to look at Louise, giggling by the fire with Edith, and thought fondly that in that whole three-story building of young girls, over in University City, Louise was perhaps the most girlish.

He put his book down on the hearth, got the duck, and another, milder drink, and joined them.

"Don't you want me to do that?" Louise meant pick the duck.

"I like to," Brill said, which was true. Once he'd said yes, to please her, and found when he got back from splitting firewood that she had heated water and scalded four plump little blue-wing teal to get the feathers off more easily. Anyone else he'd have told brusquely that that was no way to treat game. Louise, feeling a touch of female triumph at her shortcut, would have been crushed.

He began to pluck the breast feathers off the drake, a few at a time so as not to risk tearing the skin, enjoying the fire, only half-listening to the conversation.

Edith asking if Martin would really dare show all the same movies in the county seat town of Rosetta that he showed in his art movie house in University City?

Martin saying: Movies would get raunchier.

Louise asking: How could they? Oh dear. The girls knew entirely too much already.

Anthropology Today, which he'd set down on the hearth, saying "Edited by Sol Tax, from the classic 'encyclopedic inventory' . . ."

Brill picked on, comfortable in false domesticity. Only rarely could Louise find someone she trusted to stay the night with her girls. Generally she and Brill came to the cabin on hurried afternoons, inventing passion since there wasn't time to achieve it. It was nice to see how blue her eyes were in the morning light, nice that she and Martin, for they liked one another, could be together and relaxed.

The body feathers were off the duck, and he began working at the wings, saving the soft, miraculous down on the breast for last. When he did a duck, he did it all, taking the tough primary flight feathers one by one even from the outer joints of the wings, for he liked to see how the wing bones of a bird were articulated in the same way as forearm, wrist, and hand.

Now he took the down, burying his big, blunt fingers in it, pulling gently, dropping it as he had the larger feathers in a discarded shopping bag, and the canvasback drake was nude.

Nude as Miss Anne Heywood in *The Fox*, of which Louise was saying: ". . . of course girls feel that way about each other sometimes, but isn't it part of growing up? Of course we try to explain it to them . . ."

Edith said that there were these two senior stewardesses, when she was in training.

Anthropology Today said that one of the most distinctive and widespread traits of the Neolithic was the manufacture in mud, baked clay, stone, chalk, bone, or ivory of female figurines.

The author of that chapter, V. Gordon Childe, would hardly have been surprised, then, to learn that Neolithic Brill had just made a female figurine out of a canvasback drake, for Brill was now comparing the plucked drake body, the shape defined by smooth skin netted over with diamond-patterned lines, to Louise's nudity, apprehended and recalled. She was indeed a fine big duck, that lady, the same elongation and chestiness, tight-stretched and plumped out around the tail.

Edith? He glanced at the younger girl (". . . a passenger trying to get into the john, over Salt Lake, and they had the *door* locked! They couldn't even *wait* till San Francisco . . ."). Edith, naked, was a plucked quail, he decided, compact, gallinaceous, and lengthier of leg. Less waddle and more hop to her, thus would he not care to be locked in the *john* over Salt Lake *City plucking* such a neat bobwhite? Sure, but he was a one-girl-at-a-time guy, and faithful these days, with certain regrettable exceptions, to Louise. Whom he took pleasure in pleasing.

Yet Brill found himself in a mild state of general lust, and if it was not for Edith, neither was it for Louise. There was a curious desolation to it, something like that moment out on the river when, hanging onto the side of the boat, he thought for an instant that he'd gone too far downstream and would find no bottom he could touch.

That told him, sadly, what he wanted: it was to go home and make love to his own wife, Pat, but not as she was now, for the same pain that made Pat drink prevented anything robust in her circumscribed life. What he wanted was Pat as she'd been fifteen years ago, before Trinket's difficult birth and the operations that followed.

"How can it hurt if there's nothing left in there to hurt?" she asked once, but generally Pat was braver than that, more ironic than plaintive. The hollow tree lives, putting out leaves to tap the sun, cracking in the wind . . .

Bob Brill steadied the boat, raised the gun, and shot that revery one-handed.

"Come on," he said, loud and jovial, jumping up and into his Big Pig Farmer style: "Let's git out the han' trap and see can Miss Edith hit a clay bird in the ass with a scattergun, 'fore we all git bad drunk here this mornin'."

Martin said: "You two go ahead. Louise and I haven't held hands yet."

Louise giggled.

"Shall I show you where to squeeze her?" Brill put his hands on the nice solid shoulders, and Louise covered his hands with her own. Warm. Sure, this was his afternoon girl, his weekend girl when she could be. What he wished for her was simple, a happy marriage to someone nice, but meanwhile why not try to put a good day together?

There was a knock on the door.

Yeah.

Dislike at first sight: leaving the others by the fire, he went to the door, opened it, and saw through the screen a young man, all forestry cloth and Wellingtons and get-the-job-done, with a plat book in his hand.

3.

"Are you the owner here?"

"That's right." Brill opened the screen. My, see the keen blue eyes.

"We're going to run a survey through."

"Are you?"

"Thing is, we have to bring a truck into the drive."

"A truck." Look at the healthy, wiry hairs on the backs of those hands. The clean, strong fingernails. Plainly loved his scrub brush. Maybe even a little queer for it?

"Just a panel truck. Mind leaving the gate open for us?"

Do you get an erection when you scrub your nails?

"You don't have livestock do you?"

"Forty head of racoon," Brill said.

"Oh? Right. Well, we'll be starting this afternoon or Monday." The young man nodded, about-faced.

"Starting what?" Brill asked.

About-faced. Halted, one-two. "I explained that, sir. A survey."

"What for?"

"Oh. Well, it's for a pipeline. There'll be someone around, of course, to see you about paying for the right-of-way."

"Will there? Tell me, if you hadn't wanted the gate left open, would you have bothered to stop by? Or would you have just gone to work?"

"Well, I noticed you keep the gate padlocked."

"Notice the signs on the fence that say 'Posted' ?"

"Sir, we have a right to survey."

"Is that what they teach you in engineering school?"

"Look, mister . . ."

"Brill. Robert Brill."

"Say! Are you?"

"It says so in your plat book."

"Say!" It was the smile you learn from television, the big dazzler; you break it with the head rolling back and the arm rising. Irresistible. "I knew I recognized you. You came and talked to our class about city planning. Aren't you an architect?"

"No, I only talk about it."

"Mr. Brill, it's certainly a pleasure to meet you." He stuck out his hand. Brill shook it. "I'm sorry if I got off on the wrong foot here. But, well, I'm kind of new at the job and you folks that own land out here just aren't around during the week. I've tried hard to find you."

"I have an office in Rosetta."

"I didn't know that."

"Okay."

"Well say, as long as I'm here anyway . . ."

"Have your company write me a letter."

"You don't understand, Mr. Brill. This is a hurry-up job. We've got to get the engineering studies going. The pipeline's coming all the way from Birmingham."

Brill looked at him.

"Of course you'll be paid for the right-of-way. I'll bet you can make a good deal, but of course that's not my department."

"I don't sell rights-of-way."

"Then that's between you and the company. Shall I make a report?"

"Just say you weren't allowed to survey."

"We have to survey, sir."

"That's enough," Brill said. "No."

"We can always climb over the gate, you know." Twinkle. Who could resist boyish mischief in a good cause?

Brill could. "I'll tell Sheriff Siebert you said so."

"You wouldn't want to have to go to court about a thing like this, would you?"

"All right," Brill said. "I'll see you there."

"What are you, a lawyer?" The tone accused Brill of being less than a gentleman for withholding such discreditable information.

"Yes, and I've had enough of this."

But the young engineer was too right, too manly, too low in tar and nicotine, too utterly polyunsaturated, to be dismissed. "We have eminent domain, Mr. Brill. You ought to know . . ."

"I'll tell you what I know. I know that a great deal of unauthorized surveying goes on without permission these days, from planes and helicopters. My guess is you've already got your survey tucked away in your briefcase, and what you want now is to sneak in a few stakes for the main project."

"I don't have to sneak anything." The young man was breathing deeply. The young man was turning red. But the young man's strength to control himself was as the strength of ten, due to pure-heartedness. "Don't you understand? Nobody's going to hurt your land. We just clear a narrow strip, five rods, dig a small trench, lay the pipe, and cover it up. That's all. It's for progress, Mr. Brill."

"It's for erosion," Brill said.

"It'll carry natural gas by-products for industrial use. That means jobs for people. That's why we have the power of condemnation. When we fill it in we'll bring in fill, if you want, and tamp it, and seed it for you."

"Seed it with what?" Brill asked.

"Just whatever you want."

"How about morel mushroom spawn?" At least that stopped the young ass from talking. Brill went on: "Got some showy orchis roots in your panel truck? No? There's swampy land in there that woodcock like when they come through in the fall. You'd tile that out, I suppose, and drain it."

He was completely misunderstood: "If you want to buy the tile, we'll cooperate. But our pipe would have to go underneath."

Brill tried to think of something to say which would be within the limits of this young man's comprehension. Brill noticed he still had a drink in his hand and finished it. Brill smiled and said: "I eat engineers. They're so yummy good."

"What?"

"I pull them off their little orange bulldozers, and then they can't grub my trees and foul my water and fill my air with stink."

"Mr. Brill."

"Last engineer who came here just wanted permission to hunt quail."

The young man was backing away.

"And I'll tell you what I told him: You kill a thousand quail every time you pick up your pencil. Be too slow for you, doing it with a gun. Then I ate him."

The distance between them was now six feet. "What's the matter with you, man?"

Brill patted his stomach. "Too much engineer I guess."

"Thanks a lot for your cooperation."

Brill nodded and smiled and watched him go, righteous and angry. Brill found he himself was trembling with more anger than he'd realized he felt; faced the house, sought control; located it in a definitive paragraph in *Theory of Tactical Law* by Robert Brill, on which he'd base an explanation of his behavior for Martin and the ladies:

> There is only one way to react in a stupid-ass proceeding, and that is, every time they hit you, smash back at them insanely. You don't do this because your legal grounds are any good. It's how things work. If you can make it painful enough for them this time, maybe they'll go hit some other poor jerk next time.

Okay. Stepped back in the house, pleased to register the warmth, wanting a new drink, and saw Martin alone in the room.

"I'm a fairly bad bastard," Brill said. "Where are the girls?"

"Louise is in tears in the bedroom," Martin said.

"Huh?"

"She knows that boy. She thinks he saw her in here."

"Knows him?"

"He lives in University City. He married a girl from Louise's sorority. She went to the wedding."

"But he couldn't have seen her, could he?"

"I don't think so. But she won't believe it."

" 'Bye, Louise," Brill said, starting for the bedroom to offer comfort unacceptable.

And Martin, swift, soft, sad rhymer: "Bye-bye . . . Big Shy . . . 'Weese Pie . . ."

Twenty minutes after the young engineer's visit, Martin and the two women were packed and gone. Martin had to go through University City to get Edith back to St. Louis, and Louise emphatically preferred going with them to riding home with a fairly bad bastard.

The perfume was packed, and the satin, miniskirted negligee, so inappropriate to her that it was kind of sexy. "I'll miss you," Brill said, simple and sober.

4.

Alone in the cabin, he drew the duck and put it with the other in the refrigerator. The wind had gone down some, though it was still a cloudy day, a day that might clear or storm.

If you don't like the weather here, wait a minute—a day like this could bring new migrants in. Redheads, which came along just after canvasbacks. Ruddies? Brill wasn't sure just when they migrated.

There as a museum science man at the University who had asked Brill for a ruddy duck, or better still a pair, for taxidermy.

He decided to go out again in the boat. He got the 28 double down. He'd recently finished wiping it with oil. He changed the shells in his belt to trap loads: in case he did see ruddy ducks, he would try for a pair with small shot, though he'd shoot at nothing else.

Ruddies were never abundant, and it ran in his mind that they migrated earlier, perhaps at the end of September just after blue-wing teal. He also seemed to remember reading that there was a special, summer nuptial plumage—which would be what the museum man expected, and would be changed by now to something duller. He could have checked both these points in Kortner's *Ducks, Geese and Swans*, over by the organ, but didn't.

Deprived of a party, he wanted a sense of purpose, any purpose.

Anyway, he'd enjoy seeing what was on the river. Once he was out there it would clean him of emotion—the residue of emotion. It was a kind of pollutant, wasn't it? A man used emotion to fuel his machine, it left gums and tars and carbons. And caused cancer? Why wouldn't a man have his foot hinged right for kicking himself in the ass for a fancy like that one?

Call it plain residue, there was the loss of Louise, anger at the engineer, depression of knowing that the pipeline had the law on its side, and some fear and shame still left from the careless earlier turn on the river, too.

Ran that gamut in ten flat, found dry outer clothes, and put his boots on wet.

He stood in the doorway for a moment. His eyes went to the station wagon where Unk, seeing the gun, was scrabbling at the rear window and wagging his tail.

"You think I'd take you out again?" Brill asked.

He thought his way down the bluff, along the path to where the scull boat was, thought his way out among the stumps to the river and the great decoy spreads, starting five hundred miles away in Minnesota, going all the way down, thousands and thousands of imitation ducks, past Louisiana to the Gulf. More decoys in the world by now than real ducks, probably.

He walked quickly over to the station wagon and let Unk out.

"Come on, dog," he said. "We'll be all right, won't we?" Rubbed the head, feeling the loose skin move over a skull creased between the eyes, the crease becoming a ridge on top, becoming a knob at the rear, covering a brain no larger than a pear. "Won't we? What do you say, boy?"

3

Between five forty-five Friday, when he mixed the first martinis for his guests at the duck shack, and five forty-five A.M. the following Tuesday, when society caught up with him, Robert Brill drank two fifths of whiskey, a fifth of vodka, a little under a fifth of cognac, a couple of dozen shots of Whatever You Got, over private and commercial bars, and frequent cans of beer.

A feat of formidable endurance; an exhibition of prodigious metabolism; a demonstration of deeper disaffection than the community could tolerate.

Brill's come a long, rough way from the time when he was twenty-eight and the Mississippi flood was crested up at Rock Island and coming, and time was short, and somebody had to take charge of dike-building, day and night, sandbag-filling, evacuations, and Adlai Stevenson was governor, and he said: "Get Bob Brill. Get my big Indian, down at Rosetta."

2.

The eighty-hour drunk got its first recycling when Brill came in from his second turn on the river, after which there was nothing much he felt like doing except deal the whiskey, drink a hand of solitaire. There'd been no ruddy ducks out there, and by the time the water skiers made a pass, no ducks of any kind.

The whatter-whatters?

Water skiers. In October? At twenty-six damn degrees? I was almost willing to admire them when I heard the boat, saw it coming up the river, one girl driving and another facing backward, watching, which indicated someone behind on skis.

Then ugly came in sight, towed along and molded black from head to heels, what in hell was it? A skier, sir, wearing a skin-diver's wet suit to keep warm.

Grass my ass with sassafrass, what'd the hunter and fisherman think? We were supposed to have the river to ourselves and our own bad-tempered kind during some bleak season of the year?

Yeah.

Silt, raised in the wake, brought brown waves toward us that should have been white.

And I saw the three kid duck hunters on the sand island come out of hiding in the willows, and shake their fists; one even pointed his shotgun at the offensive boat.

It was a little far to shout to them, so I explained to Unk: hunters' equipment for three couldn't be worth more than $1,200. The water skiers' superior investment of a couple of grand for a ski boat and motor gave them a clear moral right to the river, didn't it?

I put that in the form of a motion, and hearing no disagreement, turned the scull boat toward home. On the way, I saw, floating among the stumps, the carcass of a bald eagle. It must have been eating dead fish, which must have been eating smaller fish, which must have been eating water insect larvae, which must have been eating protozoans, which must have been full of DDT, and I told Unk not to fetch it.

Said: Nevertheless, someone ought to knock that kid that pointed the gun half the length of the island.

At the cabin, he invited Unk in.

He built up the fire, mixed a drink and drank it, took a pull straight off the jug, and then mixed another drink. Sat down, with *Larousse Gastronomique*, to look for a picture of a duck press, a device he'd always wanted to own but could never really justify spending a couple of hundred dollars for; didn't reach the duck press: Went to sleep in his chair, his eye caught by the entry HARES.

"The hares of Beauce, Brie, and Champagne have golden coats, the color of ripe corn."

Enjoyed sleep, and a simple dream. When he woke, it was snowing out, big wet flakes, and the hares of Normany and Touraine . . . were usually small with tan coats, darker than those of Beauce, Brie, and Champagne . . . too dark to read.

And quiet. So quiet he could hear mice moving in the walls. Deer mice, probably, fixing indoor shelter now that winter was about to come, building nests of shredded paper and mattress stuffing in the dark, six-inch world that stood between this room and the weather.

He crossed to the light switch, didn't want it; went to the window instead and watched the fall of dusk and melt of snow.

He switched on a tape Martin had brought out, a young girl folk singer. Martin had made the tape at a meeting where the girl sang, voice and autoharp, sweet, clear, and reproachful:

Dirty old man of war,
Dirty old world of war.
A rusty gun on a greasy machine
Only the blood ever comes out clean . . .

That's where Brill's son was. Cal.

And it's mixed with dirt
Into sad red mud.
That's where the old man sends his love,
Dirty old man of war . . .

Let her sing. Drink to her.

I said to Cal: "What was wrong with Montreal?"

Cal said: "Nothing. It's all right up there."

"I wasn't looking for you back."

"I know."

"You change your mind about the war?"

"No."

"What's next?"

"Let them draft me. If they don't put me in jail for taking off."

"No. You weren't due for induction yet."

Cal was drafted, a conscientious objector, into the medics, and never said why he left the sanctuary. What bothered Brill was the thought that his son might not have had a reason.

Passivity in people was, to Brill, inexplicable and slightly scary.

I'll get my love away from you,
Before you turn him dirty too.

Cal's last letter from Vietnam said he was leaving the medics. The telephone rang.

Dirty Lyndon. Dirty Dick.
Pay your blood and take your pick.

The kids didn't make any distinction between Johnson and Nixon, but it seemed to Brill they were at least . . .

The telephone rang.

. . . different kinds of vulgarian. Johnson's vulgarity was deadlier; Nixon's more depressing.

Take a bug before next fall.
Air-cooled ride to Montreal.

We're ahead of you, song. Back from there. But I don't know why.

The telephone rang.

"Shut up." Brill showed the telephone a fist the size of its base. "Can't you see I'm trying to think?"

The miserable black lump of plastic and wire jangled at him once more, defiantly; he stared it down, and it stopped. He turned off the tape machine.

Where was he?

In the time of the dangerous clowns.

Brill stepped outside, closing the door behind him, stuck out his hand and let a big, soft flake of snow fall into it and melt. If Cal's mother had quit, so, in a different way, had Brill's own mother, Cal's grandmother.

Brill demonstrated once again to a respectfully silent world how a snow crystal, in spite of the icy perfection and beauty of its form, could be melted instantaneously by the warmth of the human palm, took his bow, went back inside, and fixed an evil drink.

Had he and his father before him—a man of tireless rectitude—made, without knowing it, impossible demands on the energy of the women they married? Good old family characteristic, like freckles and large feet? So that each Brill son was bound, by God, to go around feelin' (sometimes) jus' lak a motherless child?

Makes it pretty tough on a Brill boy in the army, when he has to admit that what he misses most is his father's apple pie, Chaplain.

Brill scratched, scowled, drank, and then tried seriously to counterpose two moments to see if they were parallel in any way:

Mother left the farmhouse. I was ten, Francie twelve, Elaine thirteen. There was a cab waiting, Daryl Simonson's cab. It must have been September, because school hadn't started. We were watching from Francie's room, in front of the house. We ran up there when Mother waved, told us to stay, and went out the front door.

Mother hadn't exactly said good-bye, but we knew she was going a long way away.

I said, "Did Dad say she could take a cab?" I knew cabs were expensive.

Elaine cuddled me sentimentally, which I didn't mind.

Francie said, "She's not really going to Peru."

And Elaine said yes, dummy, didn't she say so?

Francie said she could never understand what Mother said, exactly, and I guess we all felt that way. Maria Elena never learned much English, and Dad didn't want her to teach us Spanish. Fourteen years of that probably suited Dad all right; he wasn't much of a talker. But hell, maybe Maria Elena liked to talk?

No, in Brill's own marriage there was no moment like that, of course—not with Daryl Simonson's cab, and solemn children at the window. In Brill's marriage the lady was still at home, cherished to whatever extent she'd let herself be, by husband, son, and daughter. Cherishing back, sometimes, as best she could. What Brill wondered, and would never know, was whether Maria Elena had been, to begin with, high-spirited and even willful as Pat had been.

A moment?

No. Once, I was being boisterous, getting us ready to go out, ran out without my coat to start the car and warm it, ran back in to feed the dogs. Stopped to sing Trinket her lullaby—she favored World War II numbers, and especially one called "They Started Something, and We're Gonna End It." Then I tore into the bedroom to see if Pat was ready, and instead of putting on party clothes she'd got undressed and into her nightgown.

"Go ahead out," she said, and smiled. "My big ball of fire."

She was drinking milk punch, and said, looking rather cute about it, she'd just decided she felt more like a long night's sleep. We were supposed to go out dancing with Tommy and Martha at the River Club, but I canceled and stayed in. And Pat did just as she said: finished her milk punch and went to sleep.

Is that some kind of moment?

Other times she'd insist that I go out, Christ, pick out a tie for me, and once she asked seriously if it was all right, when she didn't feel like keeping up with me, and once I said no, it wasn't, picked her up, and carried her out of the house laughing and yelling, to take her to a movie I knew damn well she wanted to see.

No, Felix, for Pat Felucca had been Felix's girl. She didn't scratch my eyes out. She thanked me afterward, for Christ's sake, but declined to go again.

Then she stopped driving. Then she stopped leaving the house much during the day. Then, the hysterectomy, which was supposed to make her feel vigorous again. She had it and headed for the attic. Then the color TV, though she doesn't watch it if she's got a book to read. A couple of times a month Trinket and I go to the library to pick out half a dozen books for her, ridiculously intense about whether she'll approve of our selection, really excited when we take them home.

Then another operation, because the first one didn't get it all out. If that's the medical truth of the matter; damn it, all right, telephone. She just signed off, except for now and then when she feels she has to rise up to stand between me and one of the kids. Maybe she's right.

All right, telephone. All right.

This time he answered it, not unwilling to be interrupted.

"Tommy calling, Bob." Tommy Rebranch was Brill's law partner. "I'm sorry to disturb you in your hideaway."

"Not hiding at the moment," Brill said. "Go ahead."

"That St. Louis firm that's defending on the crop damage suit. They've been trying to call you here all day."

"That's what you get for going to the office on Saturday," Brill said. "My phone calls."

3.

Last spring one of Train Pacek's dual-semi tank trucks, on lease to a guy doing contract hauling for the army and full of some kind of chemical, is sneaking down county road A-14, the big trucks do it all the time to get around the state cop weight station on the highway. Fact.

Roy Ellender, he's a big, surrealistic corn farmer. Let us tell it; you don't know what the hell goes on out in the country any more. Roy works damn hard planting six hundred acres in May, and cultivating corn in June. And he works damn hard October, November, harvesting and fall plowing. So it's go, four months a year, day and night, and a cash flow of $75,000–$80,000 through his bank account; some years there's profit in it, some years loss. But a man with that kind of energy and used to spending money the way Roy's got to (he'll have $25,000 just in seed and fertilizer in a year), is going to do some wild stuff in the other eight months—try to raise trout by putting aerators in warm-water ponds; make trips to Russia and Black Africa. Know what he did? Built a pipe organ into his silo when he quit feeding cattle. Fact.

Roy's coming out his farm lane, on his big John Deere, moving a six-row cultivator across the road, you don't exactly do the minuet with one of those jobs behind, even on rubber.

Here comes the tank truck, bellowing at him, ninety miles an hour.

Power steering saved Roy's life. Rev and swerve and into the ditch, baby, while the truck tries to tear by on the road shoulder on the other side. Shoulder breaks in from the weight, truck flips down the bank eight feet and does a quarter turn, and plows forty feet of Reed's Canary Grass up by the roots before it stops sliding.

Roy's okay, he rode her down. Gets off the tractor, a little shaky, trots across the road, climbs up on the left-hand door of the cab. Opens it, and damn near falls in. Heavy door. He has to prop it open with his body to get an arm down for the driver to grab and haul out on.

Driver's all right, of course. You ever hear of one of those guys getting hurt in an accident?

Christ, they oughta have separate roads for big trucks, like they got railroad tracks. Load up one of those dual semis and what have you got? An engine and a two-car train.

Look out, the chemicals are leaking. The chemicals are leaking. Turning into gas.

Roy and the driver, scrambling off the side of the cab, driver yelling, "Haul ass," and finally he and Roy are running like hell up the lane when the whole thing explodes and knocks them flat on their faces.

We could see the smoke and hear the roar in Rosetta, seven miles away.

Gas, smoke, whatever it was, ruined about sixty acres of corn in the 240 Roy farms across from his home place, but what would happen, we wanted to know, if a truck like that started to leak in town some time?

Army says that's classified.

Roy Ellender says: To judge by his cornfield, it'd sure defoliate some men, women, children, cats, and dogs.

If Caligula went from 37 to 41 A.D., and Nero from 54 to 68, who in hell did they have between 42 and 53?

4.

Tommy Rebranch said: "They want to settle. Way it sounds, the lawyers for the hauler don't want to come down to court Monday for an eight-thousand-dollar suit."

"They want to settle over the phone?"

"Way it sounds. I keep having to tell them I don't know about the case."

"They mention a figure?"

"Said if I couldn't reach you, ask you to think about double the seed and fertilizer cost, that'd be forty-eight hundred dollars. I imagine they'd round off at five."

"Got a phone number?" Brill asked. Tommy read it to him. "Bet I get sixty-five," Brill said. He felt immediately dumb for saying it, not because he didn't think he could but because there was nothing to be gained by telling Tommy his intention.

Tommy was conservative financially, and there'd been a time when Brill was quite concerned with trying to loosen up the way the younger man operated. A drink of whiskey had tricked him into feeling that Tommy's education was still his affair.

"What does Roy expect?" Tommy now asked.

"He'd have signed a release for twenty-four hundred," Brill said. "If I hadn't stopped him. Roy thought maybe it was his fault."

He hung up, made a couple of notes, dialed St. Louis, and asked for the man defending the shippers.

"Bob Brill in Rosetta callin'," he said, easing cornpone into his voice. "How's weather up there in the city?"

"Well, fine, Bob." The other man was going to play, was he? "Mighty fine."

"That right? We've had her kinda windy down here, but I believe it's calmer now. Say listen, I'm sorry you couldn't get me before. Been outdoors most of the day . . ." He hoped that conveyed an image of the country lawyer spending Saturday on a tractor.

"Fine," his opponent said. "How do things look?"

"All right, I guess." Brill said it puzzled, as if this weren't a line of politesse he'd started himself. "Say, this is long distance. What was it you wanted?" Should have been ashamed of himself. Wasn't much. Principle: always originate long distance calls to negotiate, even if it means taking a number and calling back. The advantage of being the man who's paying for the call is worth the price of it.

The other man reached back for his opening pitch; Brill listened to just enough of it to be sure the St. Louis lawyer was properly off-balance, and decide that liability would be uncontested; only the amount was at issue.

Took a small sip of drink, and interrupted: "Well, look here. We're not all that unwilling to go to court. Mean to say, that's what your courts are for, isn't it? Settle disagreements, now, I don't mind telling you what I'm going to tell the jury . . ."

"Thank you, Mr. Brill."

"I think you're underestimatin' Roy Ellender's operation just a little." You're a big bully, Brill. "After all, we're not talking about some nickel-dimer in three-year rotation with a job in town, goes fifty percent in the program every year, looks to feed out his grain or seal it at support. Are we?"

"Well, um, no, sir."

Brill, you're a monster. "Why, Roy's been in continuous for six years here, gone dense population, thirty-inch rows. He's got white corn contracts, too; I'd say you're lucky the wind wasn't blowing the other way, over the white, wouldn't you?"

The other man gave in: "I'm not an expert."

"We're prorating farm overhead low in those figures I sent, and Roy's time too. Now, I don't know if you've seen the farm . . ."

"No, sir. Not yet. I haven't had the opportunity."

"Tell you what let's do." Fiendish Brill started to close the door of the Iron Maiden. "Why don't you drive down here tomorrow, and I'll show you Roy Ellender's farm. I want you to see that when we talk overhead, we're talking about automated drying equipment, and self-propelled picker-shellers and big diesel stuff." And a silo with a pipe organ in it. "Now what you do, take Route Fourteen south . . ."

"I was thinking we might get together tomorrow. Mr. Brill," the other man said hurriedly. "Why don't you come up here, and we'll have lunch at my club?"

"Have a little trouble bringing a picker-sheller in to show you at your club, wouldn't I?" Brill said.

"I'll accept your figures on overhead and labor provisionally," the other man said. "But surely Mr. Ellender's crop insurance will cover the actual cash loss."

"And that's all it'll cover," Brill said. "It won't pay for the crop that isn't there, in spite of what they call it. Way everything else's gone up and that crop insurance adjustment level lags back, maybe we ought to go on into court with it. Start talking effect of inflation and high interest on those cost factors . . "

With this the other man interrupted to offer five thousand dollars, and Brill, as if he hadn't heard, said maybe he ought to amend his suit, first thing. Ask the judge and jury for ten or twelve.

The man said six.

Brill said well, what the hell, he guessed he was willing to stick with eight and not amend his suit, if the other lawyer thought that was fair.

The St. Louis man said sixty-five.

Brill was tired of the game. He switched on a light, squeezed the telephone between ear and shoulder so that he could reach his glass and freshen the drink, and decided to reach climax.

"You tell me you're putting the check in the mail today, sir," Brill said "and we'll take seventy-five hundred. Roy Ellender might gripe a little, but I'll see he takes the pill. Or say, if that don't sound right to you, I'll clear things out and we can go ahead and have that conference on the farm tomorrow."

"Mr. Brill . . ."

"Why don't I fix that up? I'll keep Roy home from church, and get Bess Ellender to dress a couple of chickens and fry 'em up. Of course, if you'd rather, we could eat in town. Best Western got a pretty good dining room, hell, I eat there most every day . . ." Brill had never been in the place, Betty Ellender was never called Bess and kept no chickens, and Roy wouldn't have known where church was.

"No, no. Seventy-five hundred will be fine, Mr. Brill," the other lawyer said. "I'll send the check today. I surely will."

Brill believed in letting a negotiation end with the other party feeling he'd won the big points. *Saved my client $500 and court costs and the expense of a trip to the boonies,* the other guy could assure himself —and protected some Sunday ritual, golf and Bloody Marys maybe. 'Bye, St. Louis.

Brill felt cheap. Brill drank.

"Many of the hares of southern France are of fine quality, especially those of Perigord and Gascony, though these are seldom to be found in Paris."

Yeah, but he still felt cheap. Played the lawyer game again for what? To call up Tommy Rebranch and report? I said, and he said, so I said—Jesus Christ.

My dad said, "You don't negotiate with another lawyer. You negotiate with his client's representative. That's an important distinction."

So when Mother's representative came to adjust things, Dad threw him physically out of the office, my office that I use now, and locked the door so the man couldn't get back in.

I was there; that probably made him violent.

Brill sat in front of the fire.

5.

I was eight. The Depression came. Dad closed the house in town, moved us out to the farm, and rode a horse, Bay General, to town, to the law office, five miles every day.

And we had no cook, and only hired help sometimes with the farm work, and Mother went back to Peru.

Maria Elena. She lasted two years here of hard times that she didn't have to put up with. Her family never wanted her to marry an American Protestant and make a life away from Lima.

I think she was brave to try. Actually, she must have been extraordinary, to be a foreign student then, in 1920; came, I think, with her brother, who was studying engineering at the University. And what happened?

Whatever happened, it was in the nature of a family story which, abruptly, a family stops telling. She went home. We talked about her, Dad and Elaine and Francie and I, because at first it was just that she'd gone home for a visit.

In 1931, it must have been, Dad got himself appointed mission supervisor, and down we all went to Lima for a year.

I think she liked me, but I was terribly big compared to Peruvian kids, and brashly affectionate, and I realize now that I made her shy. But then I thought she was cold to me.

Probably partly because she must really have been cold to Dad.

Francie always claims to have liked Mother, but she's only a year older and can't remember all that much more than I do, or Elaine.

It was Elaine, anyway, who saw her in Peru, the only one of us who saw Mother after growing up, and Maria Elena's dead now; Elaine says that house was not so big and dark as we remembered it, but of course we didn't live there. Lived in an apartment, stayed in Mother's family's house sometimes, and she would not, would not, be Dad's wife again; and so he could not let her be our mother, I suppose.

Lima has big, dark houses, and carved wood and stone.

Felix, who was not related to her by blood at all, looked more like Mother, slim and dark (but blue-eyed), than I did, her big, clumsy son, even with brown eyes.

When we came back from Peru, Felix waited a day or two and then he asked me:

"Your mom coming back sometime?"

I said, "I don't guess so, Felix."

"Come on," he said. "Let's go practice on my unicycle."

Sonofabitch could ride that unicycle, and I got so I wasn't too damn bad myself, and Cal, Cal, by God, when we got her down from the attic and cleaned her up . . .

He didn't like where he had been, and where he was going, and so he threw another log on the fire, thought of driving home for supper, decided against it—he was not expected—and brought to mind a comforting fish.

I will sit here now and drink to yesterday, when . . .

At the age of fifteen he had caught, a couple of hundred yards from here, in the oxbow, a large-mouth bass weighing 12¼ pounds, which stood as a state record for nearly ten years.

Remember my fish first, take off my clothes, and go to bed for a long, long sleep.

I thought the stump had moved. Cast to the stump, a feeding station that I'd saved for last, a place where, if a good bass was caught one day, another would move in the next.

Had saved the place for last, moving the boat around the edge of the slough first, casting to the bank, getting and returning small fish. The little brown plywood rowboat, canoe paddle, warm, flat evening water. Dad's nine-foot Black Diamond Heddon, bamboo, walnut handle, with black windings, signed by the maker, and a new torpedo taper fly line Felix gave me for my birthday.

Felix and I used to give one another presents, that's not ordinary, I remember saving egg money to buy him a special pair of gloves he wore for flying.

Porky Pig said, "First team only," and unzipped her white flannel culotte, down the side.

No. Fishing: the lure was a hair bug, a deer hair crawdad tied by Nelson Cripps, one-legged riverman. Hollow deer hairs, tightly flared around a long-shank hook, then trimmed into a dense cylindrical body. Nelse left two bunches of hair long, toward the front, and then wound them tight with thread, halfway along, to create a joint, and then flattened and divided the ends and lacquered them into claws.

No, Peggy. Porky. Pretty Pig. Not now.

I showed Felix how Nelson burned shallow indentations across the lower back for tail sections, and Felix said, "God damn, kid. That's not a fish lure, that's a piece of sculpture." Felix never went fishing with me that summer, went every day on his motorcycle to U City, to the airport, turning

In our football equipment to the manager, and Little Porky had a sense of humor. Gary was manager, nervous as hell about what was going to happen, and Porky said, "Here, manager. How about checking in my suit?" and made him take the culotte and sweater. Funny sight, line of guys standing there, some with shoulder pads and all with erections, watching her take off her bra, those bouncy little teats, buddy, you better get off Porky now before you start saluting yesterday with an open fly.

The rod whipped so strongly that I raised my wrist to drop the hair bug lightly, and knew I'd made a decent cast. It landed by the stump, and little green dots of duck meat floated away in the ripples, each dot a tiny plant with an almost microscopic root trailing under it. Duckmeat. Floated away from my bug, leaving a cleared circle which was interrupted where its circumference reached the stump. And I waited, watching the lure in its black circle of water, so buoyant I never even twitched the line to make it move. Soft wind moved it, I was concentrating, I ought to get a strike and didn't want to miss this one, and there was a heaving of water by the stump so vast I didn't believe it.

Something bulging up to meet my lure, something huge, as if that stump itself were coming out, bottom first.

Drink to that moment; mystery and excitement. Thought I'd dislodged the stump, somehow, made two or three other fast, simultaneous guesses—scared a big snapping turtle, backhooked a carp—and then I felt a pull on my wrist and hand like an anchor sinking.

All the time I knew it was the biggest bass I'd ever had on and it frightened me.

It did. It scared hell out of me. Set the hook as hard as I dared, turned the fish away from the stump, and set it again. Had a five-pound tip on the leader, and my mind went over all the knots in the tackle, stopped at a frayed spot in the backing, and the fish ran. It ran along the bottom first, away from the stump, and I checked it a couple of times, trying to get it up, away from snags.

Lie there on the locker bench, Pretty Porky, your lovely lump of ass cozy cradled in foam rubber that was used to wrap the players' thighs, your springy tuft of public hair standing up and proud, a football helmet jaunty on your head, white sneakers and white socks and not another stitch, legs cracked, ready for the first, a smile that hides your secret motive unguessable to boys, thin, hard boys, fleshy, hairless boys, half-developed athletes, our yearning concentrated now in a line of penises attentive to your cracked legs but somehow diffident, lie there, thou still unravished bride of the unbeaten and untied Rosetta Stones, I've got a fish on.

It rose toward middle water and started toward the far shore, taking line fast through my fingers. I tried to keep an even pressure on, the rod tip up, but didn't see how I could hold him for long.

I wanted, as my arms ached with excitement and caution, just to see him, to coax him to the surface and know what he looked like before the leader or the backing broke. As I wished hard for this, the light boat lurched a little; the fish was starting to tow me. I reached for the paddle, holding the rod with my left hand only for a moment, and stabbed paddle into water with the right.

Made one sweep so that the pull of the fish wouldn't have to overcome all the inertia, found that the weight of the moving boat would keep the tension right, and made a new wish: not just to see the bass but to see it close, up at the side of the boat in the water; I didn't believe I could land it without a net and I had no net.

The line was all out, and some of the backing, and I knew I had to start recovering it soon before the frayed place came off the reel. The fish turned laterally, fifty yards away; it seemed like half a mile. I started getting backing, dropping loops into the boat, keeping the line tight, and the boat turned slowly as the fish did. Then for the first time, he came to the surface. He jumped and rode his tail across the water, and I was too scared really to look. I watched the rod tip whip instead, and got the rest of the backing in. Then it was line coming into the boat and the fish made his second run. This time I was ready with the paddle, and got the little boat in motion before the tug came, so that drag of line, tip, boat, was pretty well adjusted, and the fish began to tire.

But it was almost dark before I got him to the boat, and did something I'd never tried before, hooked the index finger of my right hand into his gill, holding the fly line tight with my other hand, right thumb into the mouth, and raised him from the water. He was heavy, I was arm-weary, and I had never seen such a thing.

A great, deep-bellied, slab-sided bass, wider at the thin part, just before the tail, than any other bass would be at the thickest, and broad as my hand across the head.

He was more than two and a half feet long, black and olive-green, and I said, "My God, bass," and watched him breathe and felt, more than anything else, like putting him back. Almost superstitiously. I was too young.

I kept him so that people would believe me; damn it. All right, Pretty Porky, now:

When Felix was done, the captain, I went over. The tuft of public hair, I noticed, flattened for a time, had sprung gaily up again, and she said,

"Get some, Blocker."

So I got a knee onto the locker-room bench between her legs, and then the other knee, wobbling, awkward, teetering toward her. She reached for something to balance me with, found an ear of Golden Bantam, slid it into warm butter, and popped it with one toss of the shaker.

Hands on my butt to steady me, she gave a nice little laugh for how easy it was. Then she let go and I rolled off onto the floor, and everybody laughed. Me too, lying there a moment.

Great. Scrambled up, jogged around the locker room, sparred with Felix nude, and then watched the next nine guys. By the time they were done, I would have gone for seconds, but she was up, smiling, teasing poor Gary, the valiant black tuft sticking out at him.

"Manager," she said. "Your team plays pretty good," and went over and pressed her bare, sweaty self against him. "Where's the girl's shower, Gary?" she said. "You don't 'spect me to take a shower with a bunch of boys, who knows what they might try to do to me?"

Gary was always so clean and neat; she stained him. That was before Gary and I were friends.

Brill poured whiskey, put on a log, found a legal pad, and wrote:

There are three possibilities: 1. Since Porky was from Gary's part of town, she did it to appall him. 2. She wanted Felix but couldn't have him singly. 3. Both boys were on her mind.

12 1/4 lbs.

She always smiled

6.

Felix's father, Uncle Ed, said: "Good Lord, boy. Is that a bass? I thought you were bringing in a moose head for a minute there."

Dad said, "I'll get the parcel-post scale. It's quite accurate."

Felix said, "Who called the paper? My dad, I'll bet. Not yours."

The taxidermist said: "You shouldn't have hit it over the head, son, to kill it. Another time, take your knife blade and go inside, through the roof of the mouth, to the brain."

The reporter who came to the office was Herbie Stoner. Still a reporter. Came to the office just last Wednesday. Photographer then, too. Old Herbie had some questions for young Bob "Blocker" Brill, sophomore standout for the Rosetta Stones where, leading interference for his cousin, Felix "Blitzer" Brill, he contributed so much to the success of last fall's Class B championship season.

"Was it the biggest bass you ever saw, Blocker?"

"Yes, sir."

"Did you have any idea it would be a state record?"

"No, sir."

"I imagine it's quite a thrill to have a state record, isn't it?"

"Yes, sir. I guess so."

"What advice would you give to other bass fishermen? Any tips on how to get the lunkers?"

"I . . . I guess not."

"Put up quite a fight, did he?"

"Yes, sir."

> "It was quite a fight," said young "Blocker" Brill. "And I've caught some monsters. He was a fighting fool, and it was the thrill of a lifetime to catch him."
>
> But when asked to divulge his fishing secrets, the young expert smiled wisely and replied, "No comment."

I can see that news story still, word for word, and the grainy photograph of me and a fish-shaped blur, and the game warden, Charlie Hagen it was then, who got into uniform and came over to the office to have his picture taken shaking my hand.

Good God, of course. Porky and Gary; and the bass, and that's why Gary did it, then: he and his little group, all juniors, I was a sophomore and they were hanging in the hall that day after the story came out.

"What do you weigh, Blocker baby?"

I didn't see it coming. It was a reasonable spring question for a high school sports editor, which Gary Pederson was, to ask a football player.

"One sixty-five about," I said.

"And that bass was twelve pounds? Some fight, huh?"

They all laughed.

"I once swatted the state record housefly," Gary said. "Boy, I'll bet he weighed a tenth of an ounce."

"Thrill of your lifetime, wasn't it, Gary?" said one of his boys.

"I was exhausted," Gary said. "I mean hauling a big heavy creature like that to the taxidermist . . ."

I said, "Excuse me," and walked on.

Abruptly Brill decided to go to the bait shop, where Nelson Cripps, one-legged riverman who tied the lure, still lived, and where the fish had hung on the wall for many years. And the deer-hair bug, fastened to the same plank of polished wild cherry wood.

The fish was no longer there, of course (Brill capped his bottle); it had long since lost its scales and been set aside. But he thought Nelson would have some lures like that, and he'd like to see and touch them, and Nelse (Brill uncapped his bottle and had a drink) might be lonesome and thirsty (Brill capped his bottle, called his dog, turned out the lights) of a Saturday night. Hell yes.

7.

Driving to the bait shop, whiskey bottle between his knees, Brill thought of the comfort: Nelson himself, deer-hair lures tied and finished with precision, sound of water swirling in the live tank. Smell of smoked fish. Hooks, leaders, sinkers, nets. Soft-drink cooler with beer illegally for sale in it: a time capsule big enough to walk around in.

Ever play serious football with a hangover?

He missed the turn to the bait shop, stopped, took a big, lip-smacking gulp from the bottle, and backed up, one-handed, holding the jug in the other. Made his turn, stopped, sixty yards from the shop.

Suited up, stands full of people, cheerleaders wheeling their powdered legs through the autumn air, and there I am with a dry mouth and shaky hands: big, rough, silly sixteen-year-old Blocker Brill, who only halfway likes the game, would as soon be out walking the edge of the woods with my Uncle Ed's dog Cozy, looking for quail. Or even home, reading biography books, the kind that make you laugh, by Lytton Strachey, Felix gets them at the library. Or shooting bumper pool. Or even starting to get drunk again, the way we did last night, and every Friday night, all this season—junior year for Blocker Brill, senior for the Blitzer.

Felix said we got too tensed up from a week of practice, overtrained, gentlemen, so we'd arrange for a pint of Old Mr. Boston Mint Gin through Mr. Nelson Cripps, one-legged riverman. Nelse'd buy it for us, and have one sweet swallow to repay himself, and go to beer for the evening, while we got stinking-punk drunk. Felix said we liked it better than the Friday night dating our classmates did, and whatever Felix said I agreed with.

"Wouldn't you care to be somebody's little play husband this weekend?" Felix would ask. "For ten French kisses and a squeeze on the sponge?"

I'd start to giggle.

Nelson would have hardly anything to say. He only watched, listened, and saw to it that we got home all right later. My cousin Felix could simply disable me with laughter, and he did:

"I think Old Mr. Boston just tastes one hell of a lot better than girlie tongue. 'Course, you probably like that girlie tongue."

I'd shake my head, recover, and gasp, "No. No fun in that, Blitzer."

"Will somebody please tell me, then? Anyone in the class, hah, do I see a hand? Where the fun *is* now . . . squeezing on that pink-tippidy sponge, through three layers of cloth, till you have got you a big, throbbing crowbar of a hard-on, and then you say, 'Thank you, dear,' and 'Forgive me. I was born bad,' and you say, 'Good-night kiss.' And for God's sake, you go home and goad your toad. What is it all that?"

"Quit it, Blitzer. I don't know."

"Flog your frog?"

"Please . . ."

"Break your snake?"

I couldn't answer, couldn't.

"Squish your fish, boy. Murdle your turdle . . ."

Then on Saturday afternoon, running out of the single wing, with me at blocking back, Felix at full, we'd play for the high school. For the town, I suppose. Obliged to.

It would be okay the first half, but I'd find myself starting to drag a little when we trotted off the field to rest. Look at Felix, and Felix would drop to his knees panting like a dog and crawl a step or two, and say, loud enough for the coach to hear:

"Hittin' powerful hard out there, today."

The coach was from the Deep South somewhere, and we'd mimic his accent:

"Lordy, yes."

"Fierce, fierce hittin'."

Coach taught history, too, but didn't approve of Lytton Strachey. We didn't approve of the coach.

In the locker room he'd be trying to keep us from drinking the quantities of water we craved by then, maybe suspecting, not wanting to know, why we did.

"That's enough uh that watuh, Brill."

"Oh, Coach, I gotta have me a little piece of watuh," Felix would say, and I'd start holding my stomach, trying not to laugh. "It's not like that pretty cooler never gave none to the othuh boys . . ."

Seeing him caress it, as if it were Porky Pig (who'd moved away from town by then, but the team remembered and I couldn't forget), I'd roll right off the damn bench. Again.

We scored. We backed the line. We were undefeated and untied for two seasons, and Felix could have gone to Notre Dame.

Brill faked a block on the charging end, took the tackle right off his feet with a low shoulder, and charged downfield, the car dashing after him, sixty yards to a touchdown at the bait shop door.

He could see old Nelse in there, dozing in front of television.

Brill let himself in, and Nelson woke right up, swung toward the door, hopped up and came over spryly, leg after cane. Nelson had a prosthetic leg that Brill had bought him, but he didn't use it.

"How do, Blocky," he said. He was perhaps the only person left around who still used the old nickname. "Where was you in fishin' season?"

"I came by once or twice," Brill said. "Carlotta was here." That was Nelson's daughter.

"I guess she said. You gettin any ducks?"

"A few. You want some?"

"Aw, no thanks."

"I got two cans in the car, all cleaned and ready."

"Got no one to fix 'em for," Nelson said. "Carlotta's away now." She taught school in Arkansas. "Use softer food myself."

"This soft enough for you?" Brill held up the bottle.

"Guess it would be," Nelson said, and they sat.

"How's Monroe getting along?" Brill asked. Nelson's son, a truck driver, was in prison for hauling stolen goods. "Does he write?"

"Never mind," Nelson said, savoring his drink. "You done your best."

Actually, Brill had gotten Monroe Cripps a light term, in view of the fact that Monroe wouldn't testify against his employer, Train Pacek.

"Drink up," Brill said, and asked about the fish. "Remember, you had it on a piece of cherry up over the counter?"

"Yep. There's some of it left. Outline drawed around what isn't there, out in the shed. You want to see?"

"No," Brill said. "But the bug that caught it. It was a deer-hair crawdaddy."

"Course it was."

"I'd like to see that."

"Fell to dust long ago," Nelson said. "Those lures, they'd last four, five years. Fish didn't tear 'em up first. Same thing makes deer hair float, makes it brittle. Hollow. Not like what we got now."

"No."

"Hell, these." Nelson reached under the counter and brought up a card of translucent, soft-plastic crawfish lures. "These'll last forever, Blocky."

"Yeah," Brill said.

"Look so real, you want to cook 'em."

Brill nodded.

"Don't cost but forty cents. You wanting to buy some?"

"I'd buy the deer-hair kind," Brill said. "Would you make me some?"

As he asked, he knew there was something wrong, something false.

Nelson didn't: "Got no call for them," he said. "Why hell, Blocky. I'd have to get a dollar and a half, two dollars. Used to take me half an hour to tie one right, and burn and paint it."

"If you want to make me some this winter, I'll pay three dollars apiece for all you make." Brill pushed on with it, but he knew what was wrong: he'd had this same conversation with Nelson Cripps before. Why should he, taking advantage of an old man's failing memory not to expose it, put them through the same set of demands and responses again?

Nelson shook his head: "I couldn't. Got no vise or anything now."

"Suppose I buy you a vise. And the hair and hooks and paint. And come watch you do it. I'd like to see how it's done."

"Truth is, I couldn't. Hands shake too much. Kind of . . . far-sighted. Not like when you and Blitzer'd come evenings."

"Have a drink, Nelse." Brill felt shame. That was it, of course; why he'd come. Been wallowing toward it all day. Nostalgia. Push the old man into it, and fall in himself. Goddamn nostalgia. He'd had him a philosophic drunk last night, moving toward a nostalgic drunk tonight, and Brill was considering how to check it when the new drink hit him and he gave in instead. "We had us some good times here, Nelson, didn't we?"

"Remember when you both went out to run the trotline with me some nights, before cold weather," Nelson said. "Bring home a mess of channel cat and your cousin always wanted me to clean one right away and cook it for him."

"He was a catfish eater, wasn't he?" Brill said. "There isn't anybody in the world can cook it like you, Nelse, with that pepper sauce."

"Next spring, I'll cook you some . . ."

"Next spring, we'll fish walleyes."

Part of nostalgia is to make impossible plans.

Not much later, when Nelson had gone off into an old man's nod and doze, so that talking to him wasn't much different from talking to the dog Unk, Brill said: "That Felix was a pisser, wasn't he, Nelse? Better than I was . . . he'd have been a hell of a man. We were going to practice law . . . Shit. He'd have been a drunk airplane mechanic."

Then later, bottle lowering: "Blitzer, what are we going to do about this drunk old one-legged riverman?"

Lower. "What are we going to do about this drunk old two-legged lawyer, for that matter?"

There was a scratching at the door. Nelson's cat. Brill let it in. "Hello, cat," he said. "Welcome to the hog wallow."

He caught the animal, held it for a moment, and said: "If you didn't bring any goddamn nostalgia with you, you're welcome to some of mine."

Then because he was standing, and the bottle almost empty, he put down the cat and picked up Nelson Cripps, who seemed hardly heavier. Carried the old man into the back room, put him on a cot, and took his one shoe off. There was no sock under the high-top shoe, and the ankle looked frailer, whiter, bluer-veined than Brill expected. He put the cane on a chair by the bed, pulled a navy blanket over Nelson, and the cat jumped onto it.

Brill went back into the store part of the bait shop, and on to the door. Months could go by, possibly whole years, without his thinking of Felix, who was killed flying at nineteen; and then the bastard ghost would come back and haunt a whole weekend. At least he hadn't brought his mother into the wallow this time.

He finished the last inch of whiskey, and then stood at the door, hanging onto the knob until he stopped tottering.

"Come on, Blitzer," Blocker Brill said. "We gotta game to play tomorrow."

8.

Don't tell Lawyer Brill, but as a matter of fact, we don't remember his Cousin Felix.

Would that have been Ed Brill's boy that had the Ford agency here for twenty–thirty years? Hell, we don't even much remember Ed, though he's still alive somewhere California somewhere.

If Ed Brill had kids, none of them lives in Rosetta. Or if it was just that one boy Lawyer talks about now and then (Felix?) and he got himself killed, well gawdamidy, think of all the boys gone from here in Worlwartwo. And Kawrea. And now Veetnam. The same as if they'd moved away and never come home.

9.

Fell, kicking horseweed, under the northwest window of the bait shop. Sat there till he got cold.

Remembered now, in waves of sardonic clarity which came and went, bitter toward his self-indulgence, Nelson Cripps' one visit to his office.

Nelson came last spring, didn't he, to make a will? "Leave the shop to Carlotta, cause she likes it," he said. "Truck and boat and nets, commercial fishing gear's for Monroe, so he'll have something to do when he gets out of jail. Not that he'll use it. Half belongs to Neal, but he don't know, Blocky, and I got no way to ask him any more. . . ." Neal, Nelson's old fishing partner, was in the Veterans' Hospital, "Only Spanish-American vet they got, Blocky. He don't see or hear no more."

"Neal has no heirs?"

"Just me," Nelson said.

I made the conventional remarks: that it was good to have a will, but should be many years before . . .

"No," Nelson said flatly, even a little aggressive if some young ass wanted to argue it with him. "I ain't going to live another winter, Blocky. Now I just ain't."

His wife of fifty-one years had died, just after Christmas, and Nelson said he wanted to make it through the summer when Carlotta'd be there with him. "But then," Nelse said, "you've seen a goose when it was paired, and the other one shot, stay on? The rest of the flock, it goes, but the one will stay, flying circles. Day after day, and I never thought he was looking for her. Not an old gander. He knows she's gone, don't he? He just don't know what else to do except fly circles, because it's like the exact thing that makes him know he's a goose is gone, ain't it? He don't cry. You never heard one of them honking. I don't know where they go at last, them old ganders. Off somewheres. They don't mate again, and they don't come by single either. When Reenie was a-dying, I thought about a goose like that a whole lot, and I knew I couldn't stand for her to die. I can't stand the grief another winter, Blocky, and I ain't goin' to try."

Cold, drunk, melancholy Brill, crawling out of the horseweed toward his car to drive two miles home through the empty, wanly lighted streets of Rosetta, at seven miles per hour. Brill the courage-bringer, life-renewing Brill.

4

Awake? At five thirty? What in the hell for? No, no, not duck hunting. This is the bedroom. That is Pat over there, sleeping. Come back, head, you glove-leather puffball.

Once Brill's eyes were open, the day was on, regardless of how much sleep he'd had, regardless of what kind of evening he'd spent. Had too much energy to lie back down again.

By a quarter to six he was up and dressed, prowling and growling through the kitchen, burned his hand on the coffeepot, cheered up when he remembered that, because it was Sunday, he was in for a perfectly atrocious day. Five inny-skinny clients to visit with, each to be told pretty much the same thing—we gotta amen your justamadeitup-come tax. Forms go off tomorrow, Let's us write an inny-skinny check.

Ah, there would be wailing and groaning, he thought with relish, from Miss Gibson, Mr. Habib, Mr. Ellender, Dr. Barragon, and Mr. Pederson. Screw coffee. Coffeepots burn people.

Found something to pour into a cup, first thing in the morning: cream and sugar? Just the way it comes, thanks. Nothing like a steaming cup of fragrant, fresh-perked vodka to send a man out his back door to the summer kennel. He let Unk out and the bird dog, Nevada, and the two pups remaining from Nevada's last litter.

The elegant Miss Gibson would wail high, yes, and she would indeed groan shrill and there were, were there not? certain things pending, not to say dangling, between Mr. Brill and Miss Gibson, come on, dogs, let's run.

The morning was warm. The snow hadn't lasted. Blue sky

coming, I said run. He took off across the lawn; there was nearly an acre of it, surrounded by poplars and planted with fruit trees. All four dogs gave chase, and Brill stopped short, dropped to his knees, and caught both pups in his arms. Nevada, her dugs still swollen with milk, sat and licked his eye.

"That's not fair," Brill cried, let go the pups, jumped up, and got Unk's retrieving dummy. He invented a game: he'd make Unk sit and stay, throw the dummy, and let the pups run after it. When they were halfway there, he'd tell Unk to fetch and the big Lab would barrel past the puppies, grab the thing and come in at a strutting high-headed trot with the young dogs chasing circles around him.

"Bob."

"Hi."

It was Pat, calling from the open bedroom window.

"Hey, you five dogs look like you're having a nice time."

"There's coffee," Brill said. "Shall I bring some up?"

Like the river, like the world, she was okay until the morning frost melted or, in summer, till the dew dried.

Black vodka with a coffee chaser. Tomato juice, that he'd canned out at the farm in August, to see how this year's was: damn good. Three waffles. Half a pound of country sausage. Saw a halfback slithering through the living room, Sunday paper tucked under the arm, and leapt from the table to throw a shoulder block and knock the rascal out of bounds at the sofa.

"Dad," Trinket protested, fifteen, leggy, and getting pretty.

"I'm glad you're a big tough boy, and not an inny-skinny girl," Brill said. "Who would I have to knock around?"

Two loafers to the stomach, and she pushed him away with her feet.

"I won't play football with you, I'm mad at you," she said. "Look." She held up the Springfield paper, first page of the state news section, and there he was again:

BRILL SAYS ABORTIONS CAN BE FUN

"Daddy did you really say that?"

"Sure," Brill said. "Suppose a rich young lady wants an abortion, Trink? She can get a dandy in London for a couple of hundred dollars at a good clinic, all very legal and a nice trip with it. Travel agents package it. A poor young lady in the same situation gets a bad, illegal operation near home, or loses half a year of her life waiting for a baby to come she can't keep, or goes off a bridge."

"The law discriminates," Pat said. "That's all Daddy meant. May I see it?"

"But why does it always have to be Dad that says things like that in the newspaper?" asked Trinket, who would hear about it at school.

"Because I'm Mr. Small Town America," Brill said. "Standing on the street corner in my galluses. I'm democracy in action. I'm the silent majority . . ."

"Because your father was state chairman of the Civil Liberties," Pat said. "And in politics once. And a reporter can always get him to say something outrageous."

"Come on, Squinket," Brill said. "Let's go fall-prune the fruit trees. I got an hour before I go start upsetting people."

"Call me by my right name, and I will," Trinket (Patricia) said.

A man should plant his fruit trees young, like Brill did, fifteen–twenty years ago—apples, peaches, apricots, pears, plums, and cherries.

Only two things: you might not like spraying, and if you don't you'll have marred fruit. Number two: every year some one of those trees will kind of swell up and damn near bust itself, giving you a ridiculously big crop.

What in the world you going to do with three and a half *bushels* of marred apricots, if your wife's not fit to can and you haven't got time?

But there's nothing prettier to see or sweeter to smell than a little mixed orchard, blooming in the spring.

2.

1. "A Brahmin child receives two names, one for common use, the other a secret name which none but his father and mother should know."

2. "Every (ancient) Egyptian received two names, which were known respectively as the true name and the good name, or the great name and the little name; and while the good or little name was made public, the true or great name appears to have been carefully concealed."

3. "Some Esquimaux take new names when they are old, hoping thereby to get a new lease on life."

4. ". . . a Caffre superstition that the character of a young thief can be reformed by shouting his name over a boiling kettle of medicated water, then clapping the lid on the kettle and leaving the name to steep in the water for several days."

From *The Golden Bough,* by Sir James George Frazer.

Now, 5. "Among the tribes of Central Australia . . ."

Just a minute there, Sir James George. Could we have your attention just a minute? Question from the floor, sir, okay?

Let's go back a little. If ESKIMO comes from the Cree, ASKIMOWEW (meaning "he eats it raw"), how come that Frenchiness in the way you form the plural? Sounds like you eat it raw yourself.

Can't blame Trinket (Little Pat) Brill. It's true. Her father's always saying or doing dumb-ass things that get in the paper, whether he means to or not.

"It's all right, Daddy," Trinket said.

3.

Stand in either bank and watch a farmer come in, we can tell you what he farms:

He's wearing working Wellington boots, a wide-brimmed hat, smoking a filter-tip and left a new, large mediocre car outside—a Buick, Olds, or Pontiac. Sits down at a vice-president's desk and waits. He's a cattleman. The vice-president will call him by his first name, and lend him one hundred percent of what he needs to buy some calves to feed, with a mortgage on the calves, provided he's got the feed, doesn't still owe on last year's note, and will pay the highest rate of interest the bank's allowed to charge. If he raises part of the calves he feeds, then he probably likes to drive that new car cross-country through the herd on sunny days; don't be surprised to learn his wife's gone back to work.

Next farmer: overall pants, a jacket, and galoshes. He chews a cold cigar that cost a dime, and came to town in a pickup. He shuffles up to the cashier window, an old hat in his hand, knowing he don't smell too good. That man farms pigs, and he smells grand to the bank—they'll lend him anything he wants on his signature, charge the lowest rate, and jovialize the conversation with scatological words, to make him feel at home; bankers are the very souls of tact, of *courtoisie*. (It doesn't make him feel at home; it makes him feel old, but hell, he looks old, from working that hard. Still he can hardly remember a time when pigs didn't have the farm paid for.)

Here's a farmer in a Sears leather jacket. What's he doing in the bank at all? Oh yes, he's going to deposit his pay check from pumping gas nights at a filling station in a joint checking account with his wife, who never did quit working—just took leaves when babies came. Forget him. He's a general farmer. A family farmer. He won't even try to finance a car here, he'll go to the installment credit crows and small-loan lampreys; they won't care a thing about the size of his farm or the shape of his mortgage, just want to know how long he's had that job working nights.

Long time, lamprey; can't seem to quit, crow.

Those are three archaic farmers.

If there's one kind of farmer complicated enough, ambiguous enough, confusing enough, exotic enough to be called modern, he'd be the big cash-flow man like we were talking about, a grain farmer like Roy Ellender, with a pipe organ in his silo, sitting on a lion skin, shooting a .357 special pistol at a white oak fence-post.

Bang.

In spite of the vodka eye-openers, Robert Brill had begun the day's drive-around fairly sober, his excitable nature calmed by tree-pruning with his daughter. It was not until he saw Roy Ellender, sitting on a lion skin, shooting a .357 special pistol at a white oak fence-post that it occurred to Brill that he was likely to be having another drink soon.

Watching Roy politely was a bearded black man in a gold and purple robe, whose name Brill didn't catch.

"Hello, Robert," Ellender yelled, swinging the big pistol around rather carelessly. "This here's"—he yelled some syllables. "Stayed with him in his town my last trip to Africa, showing 'em how to use pesticide. He's a chief."

"How do you do?" the black man said.

Brill shook hands.

"That's all the English he knows," Roy said. "Got two women in the house with Betty, a wife and some old girl from the State Department, traveling with them to San Francisco. Here," offered the chief his gun, pointed to the post he'd been shooting at. The chief smiled beautifully, bowed, said a sentence in French, and didn't take the gun. "He's too polite to shoot, but I know he's dying to. Have a drink, Lawyer Brill."

"No thanks," Brill said. "What's that you're sitting on?"

"Chief brought me a lion skin." Roy got up and put his arm around the black man. Brill thought the man looked dubiously at the big pistol in Roy's free hand. "He's got ten crates of lion skins in New York, trying to find a market for them here."

Brill couldn't say he wished the chief luck with the lion skins, or the pesticides either for that matter, but he smiled.

"Told the interpreter to tell him next time leave the skins, just bring heads," Roy said. "Isn't that right? Lot of people'd buy a mounted lion head to put on the wall, wouldn't they?"

"Maybe so," Brill said.

"Hell, yes." Still with an arm around the chief's shoulder, Roy raised the .357 and cut loose a shot that hit a staple or something in the target fence-post and went ricocheting off with a cinematic whine. "State Department wanted the chief to see Middle America," Roy said. "Here, Chief." Roy pressed the gun into the African's hand. "Take the safety off like this."

The chief shook his head, his eyes bugging just a little, and offered it to Brill with the safety off.

Brill jumped back, then, thoroughly alarmed, stuck out a hand cautiously, took the gun by the barrel and, as the chief released it, got the safety back on.

"Jesus Christ, Roy," he said. "I don't think your man knows what's happening here."

"Shoot it," Roy said. "If you won't have a damn drink, shoot my new gun."

Brill did, at the base of the fence-post. Saw dust puff two or three feet in front of it. Roy laughed, was pouring whiskey into a couple of glasses, and suddenly Brill had to laugh, too.

Couldn't stop. "I nearly . . ." He choked. "Roy, I—I nearly had a St. Louis lawyer . . . down here today . . . for chicken dinner in the country."

"What?" Roy asked. "Who? Come on now, Chief. Drink. Drink-um. Good."

His fear of the gun and the inexplicable laughing men, Brill guessed, made the poor chief grab the glass for security.

"That crop-damage claim," Brill said, explained, still tickled so that he kept chuckling in spite of himself at the image of the lawyer driving in about now. "Well, he settled high, Roy."

"Whoa-ho," yelled Roy Ellender. "You hear that, Chief?"

"Give you the bad news, too," Brill said. "Have to put your tax estimate up again."

"No," Roy yelled. "Get Mrs. Voosman, Chief . . ." The interpreter, apparently. "She's from the government. We'll keep her for a hostage, huh? Tie her to a post, gimme the gun Brill." He pointed to the fence-post. "Mrs. Voosman, okay, Chief? U. S. Government."

The chief struggled for a word. "Nice."

Wham. Wham. Wham. Roy shot three times. "Hear that, Brill? Thinks that'd be nice to do to Mrs. Voosman." Wham. "Got her."

"Nice . . . lady."

"Oh, boy." Wham. Wham. Click. "Out of cartridges," Roy said. "Hell, I'm sorry, Chief. Only got three boxes, had to shoot 'em out to get the cases, so I can reload. Use some hot powder this time, huh? Blammy, boy."

The shooting was over.

The big pistol was a throw-in, Roy explained. He'd bought it, three more fancy handguns, reloading equipment, ammunition, and a bench-rest for sighting them in, just to get his hands on that small, flat wooden box there.

"Gave three hundred and forty dollars for the rest of the stuff," Roy said, pointing to the box. "To get that there for sixty. Look here, Chief." Knelt and opened the box. "How about that?"

And Roy rose, holding at port arms a World War II, stamped metal machine pistol.

The chief said something rather shrill in French.

"I think he'd like you to put it away," Brill said.

"He doesn't need to worry, I got no ammo for it yet," Roy said. Shouldered it, crouched. "I'll get some, Brill. We'll have us a shoot up. Ack-ack-ack-ack . . ." The noise like a small boy, spraying panto-mime lead at the fence-post; Brill didn't know if Mrs. Voosman was still tied to it or not.

"You're a damn fool to own that, Roy," he said. "It's illegal."

"Wonder if it wouldn't take regular forty-five caliber ammo?" Roy said. "I got some of that, come to think . . ."

Brill said firmly that he'd take that drink now, thank you, Roy. A little shot of old machine gun, and pouring it did take Roy's attention off the war with Mrs. Voosman, and give Brill a chance to make sure his client understood: "You go firing that thing, someone's going to identify the sound, and you're going to be calling me from jail."

"Go to hell, Brill," Roy said, but he did put the gun away and write the tax check.

Brill wished the chief a pleasant visit to San Francisco, and drove off, beer chaser on the seat between his thighs, trying to imagine what the State Department had arranged out there: a look at the hippie colony, Chinatown, the Negro district, and perhaps a nice pro football game?

He was glad he'd packed the car carefully for today's trip—brief-case, twelve cans of beer, and the rest of his morning vodka bottle.

At Woody Barragon's place, which wasn't far from Roy's, he stopped and took a look first at the house, before he went in. It was a house he liked, a contemporary country house on twenty nice acres; the young physician had moved his family into it just three months before.

The young physician (said his pretty, sympathetic wife to the hulking, half-drunk lawyer, handling him with almost the humorous self-assurance of the well-married girl, but just an untidy hint, like a slip showing, of invitation) was in the greenhouse. He was transplanting (but then you might suppose Brill, a big, physical, dominant, good-looking ape, got a routine amount of that from most women) fig trees.

He was like hell.

Woody Barragon was in the greenhouse with his pants down, injecting himself in the butt with fifty milligrams of Thorazine.

"Damn you, Bob Brill," he said. "Now you know all my tiny secrets, don't you?"

"I might if I knew what Thorazine was," Brill said, reading the label on the rubber-stoppered bottle. "My last client told me to go to hell, and you damn me. I'm doing real good for Sunday."

"It's for hangovers," Barragon said, pulled his blue tweed pants back up, and fastened his beaded belt. "A condition you seem to be trying to cure yourself in a primitive way, to judge by the smell."

"I suppose," Brill said. It was a small, ready-cut, assemble-it-yourself-greenhouse, designed to be free-standing but in this case extending through the Barragon's kitchen door and sharing a wall. Two fig trees, each about three feet tall, were standing on the floor in small redwood tubs, next to a larger one.

"You going to put both your trees in the big one?"

"No." Woody Barragon looked gloomily at the big redwood planter, and the tartness left his voice. "I've been waiting five weeks for the garden store to get another sonofabitch like it." He picked up the Thorazine bottle and stared at that. "Care to drop your pants and take the treatment?"

"I'm not that bad off, thanks," Brill said.

"You ought to let me give you some Dexamil pills, anyway," Barragon said, and put the bottle down. "There's no reason for anybody to have a hangover any more. What is it, Bob?" He took a nervous skip to the kitchen door, closed it, spun around, and leaned his back against it, at bay behind his spectacles.

"Excuse me?"

"Stop torturing me, you goddamn sadist. What brings you out here? It's Willie, isn't it?"

"I'm sorry, Woody," Brill said. "No. It's just taxes. You better let that shot take effect."

"Oh."

"It's nothing to do with your friend Willie, and nothing to get upset about."

"Oh." Barragon came away from the door, beginning to look much brighter. "Ah-ha. Yes. Gave me a scare, having you appear in the doorway. Mountain of freckled flesh."

"That must have been a bad party last night," Brill said.

"Bachelors," Barragon said. "Of a certain kind. In University City. You know about that. My extraterrestrial life, but today I'm on surgical call."

"Will the Thorazine make you steady enough, if a call comes?" Brill had felt for some time that Woody reveled just a little more than necessary in the confidential nature of the lawyer-client tangle, and hoped to move the conversation away.

"It would just be traumatic stuff. Auto accident, Sunday knife fight, hunting accident. Something like that. We did so much of that crap in Vietnam, Bob. More of it in a week than you'd see in a lifetime of civilian practice. Drunk, sober, half-asleep . . ."

"I've got some figures here . . . ." Brill began.

"Did I tell you I met Willie there?"

"Yes." It was some sort of spillover, Brill supposed, from the secrets Barragon received in the doctor-patient throb.

"Love in the jungle."

"Woody," Brill said. "Why don't you join the damn Catholics, so you can go to confession?"

"What's the matter, don't you like earning your fee?"

"Not if you're going to talk about love," Brill said. "I gather there were Willies before, and there'll be Willies to come."

"Quite so," Barragon said. His Thorazine seemed to be working fine now. "In fact, after last night, I'd say the scholarship fund may need replenishing in a rather short time." Barragon's last boy, the one called Willie, who had followed him from Vietnam as far as University City, had been sent out of the state with money enough to keep him quite comfortable while he finished college on the GI Bill. Brill had arranged to have the funds paid no questions asked, through Gary Pederson, now a department head at the University, calling it a private scholarship.

"Next thing, you'll be wanting a tax deduction for it," Brill said.

"One-tax-mind Brill," Barragon said. "Well, why not?"

"Because the deal worked both ways," Brill said. "Calling it a scholarship was as much to protect Willie from the idea he was being paid off as it was to make your records look good. If you got yourself investigated, they'd question Willie, wouldn't they?"

"And you'd handle it brilliantly."

"Here, Woody," Brill handed him a sheet torn from a legal pad.

"This is the best figure I can give you. If we don't amend and increase the payment now, you'll have to pay interest and probably penalties."

Barragon said: "Old Uncle Snatch crying for more. Seven hundred grubbies."

"It'll buy one tenth of one percent of one small airplane," Brill said.

"I know, friend Brill. I know. A pursuit plane for happiness."

While Brill waited in the kitchen for the doctor to bring a check, Dotty Barragon came in. She was wearing slacks still, but it seemed to Brill she had changed her blouse to something softer. She offered to pour him a drink, gave it to him with ice, first cold one of the day, and stood a little closer than she needed to.

Brill, feeling very much between women, let it tingle, the young bosom of the woman brushing the middle-aged left biceps of the man.

"Stay for lunch?" Suggestive idea. "Sandwich?"

Brill felt like he'd be glad to stay for most anything, but the phone might not ring for Woody, and if it did, the kids might not nap for Dotty, and if they did, probably all he'd get was a sandwich.

"Pentagonal happiness." Barragon was back with a check and a filled-in prescription blank.

"The prescription's for Dexamils," he said. "Get it filled, and hang no more over, friend Brill."

Put his Barragon young arm around his pretty Dotty girl and smiled.

4.

About that redwood planter, good chance the young doc will never get it. Stores around Rosetta either can't get stuff, or won't, or something. Probably true everywhere, about goods.

About services, we aren't so bad off. Look in the classified: half a page of lawyers. Three pages of insurance men. Page and a half of real estate people. Six funeral directors.

Less than half a column of doctors, though, and we're lucky at that. Because we're close to U City and the med school, more doctors settle here. Take Doc Barragon, waiting for his planter. They say he's so brilliant he could have taught at Harvard. But he lives right outside of town, and practices here in Rosetta. He's a little strange sometimes, some people say he's a fag.

Who ever heard of a fag doctor? He was in Vietnam.

We got dentists coming out our ears.

(There's a road sign on the country road, on the way to town, between Barragon's place and the old Brill family farm. Altered:

Seems like the mind problem isn't one of width so much as one of depth, though. What would you say?)

Then there's the way Brill farms, which you might not believe. It's the family place he was partly raised on, and one of the best farms around, but the kind of rent he charges Kress Hartke is just about too weird. Kress has got to keep a farm chicken flock, silver-laced Wyandottes, listen to this, so Brill can have fresh eggs that haven't been refrigerated, and chickens that taste like bird—not (Brill says) like the plastic and cardboard supermarket chicken is wrapped in, which (Brill claims) gives the meat inside what slight suggestions of flavor it has.

Kress has to keep a Jersey cow, and sometimes Brill milks it but most of the time one of the Hartke boys, so there's fresh, raw whole milk at the Brill house. 'Course, Kress gets his milk too, but he'd damn sight rather buy it.

Kress has to keep a couple of steers on the grass, keep them till they're three-and-half, four-year-olds, hay them in the winter, before Brill will let him take them to the butcher; those animals never taste grain till the last few weeks, and then just enough to put a little shine on them, because Brill says where in the hell can you get those big old prime rib roasts where the rib bone's two feet long, and grass-flavored beef instead of that corn-fed stuff that all tastes like liver, full of the wrong kind of fat?

Brill gets loud about garden tomatoes, sweet corn, tiny young green beans, leaf lettuce, veal, lamb, pork—man, he'll bust furniture talking about what American meat packers have done to ham. *Perverts,* Brill says, *with their goddamn brine needles. They must get some kind of kick, sticking them into pig thighs. They certainly can't intend anything edible.*

(Brill's buddy, Doc Barragon, says every piece of meat and poultry you buy in this country is so full of stilbesterol, which is a male growth hormone, to make birds and animals gain weight faster, it's a wonder all our women don't grow beards.)

Well, that's what Kress Hartke and his family have got to do, along with farm—can and churn, plow garden, hand-feed—Christ, keep a spring open. Right. Brill even gets his drinking water at the farm, out of a pitcher pump in the kitchen. Goes by with five-gallon water jugs to fill, once a week.

Did you know there are sentimentalists in Texas who keep the longhorn steer from becoming extinct?

¿Did you know there are *culos* in Mexico who keep the ancient races of corn going, *Nal-Tel, pinche cabrón, y Chapalote?*

5.

Robert Brill walked into the old limestone farmhouse, water jug in one hand, vodka jug in the other, and the thought of phoning Beth Gibson in the middle.

He had timed his visit, as he often did on Sundays, for when the Hartkes, German Catholics, would be at mass.

Often he brought Trinket out and they rode, she on her pale buckskin quarter horse mare named Goldie, Brill on a huge, ancient red beast called McAlester, in a cavalry saddle older than Brill, Big Mac, Trinket, and Goldie added together.

Today was wet for riding, a little wet for bringing Trinket.

He dialed Beth, Rosetta's mysterious and exquisite spinster, who spent most of her time in Chicago but was home now. Not awake though. Her maid, her get this French Moroccan maid, said mademoiselle was in bed. Brill said to tell mademoiselle that he must see mademoiselle this afternoon, and would call back.

The maid said *oui, monsieur* in a voice that made monsieur squeeze his buttocks together. He knew a cure for the condition that ensued: he stuck his head under the pitcher pump, running ice-cold spring water through his hair and over his ears for a minute or two before he filled the water jug.

Since he had been thinking of his mother, something he seldom did, he wanted to look now at the housekeeping situation into which she had found herself demoted by the Depression, years before. The very young daughter of a large and elegant family, in what? High-spirited rebellion? Becomes a Protestant lawyer's lady in a strange but lively land, where her husband has land and position, and there are men to work the farm and women in the kitchen. And abruptly, after bearing three children, and with no preparation for it, the husband is doing farm work, cutting wood for the furnace in winter, riding horse-back to his law office to save on gasoline. And she has this house to keep, this cellar to fill with foods preserved, this kitchen from which to produce meals for a family. Probably it was brave of her even to try it for two years.

He walked, counting the steps, from the stove into the dim, cool dining room where the Hartkes never ate. It could not have been easy for Maria Elena, even with help; without help it was apparently not even a possibility. Yet Brill, sitting now at the dining table, on which the Hartkes had stacked magazines, curtains, boxes of Christmas cards, found he had very little idea why, for he didn't know what his mother's personality had been like.

When a kid is ten or twelve, he thought, parents are still generic, not individual, the large animals necessary to one's own, small animal survival. As well might the immature oppossum ponder its mother's personal charm, its father's wit, as a human child try the cruel exercise of analyzing characteristics in his parents before he is done relying on them.

Catalogues. Summer clothes. Unseasonal athletic equipment. Brill, ruminating, sucking so slowly on the lip of his vodka bottle he was hardly aware of an occasional drop rolling back along his tongue toward ingestion.

I asked her, what? She said. She looked. I was. He had, in fact, no particular recollections of Maria Elena, no scenes, no things said, no gesture or characteristic sound, only fragments: we made a white fruitcake. I brought her a scarf on Mother's Day. She was with me and Francie at the fair. In Peru we went to a restaurant on the Pacific beach.

If those twelve years were, in particular, forgotten, it was an article of twentieth-century faith that they could, with psychoanalytic help, be recovered. After which, would he know, or be, anything different?

"You want a nipple for it, Bob?"

"Huh?"

"Thought you might want a nipple for your gin bottle," Kress Hartke said. "Gawd, you were deep into it, weren't you?"

Kress stood in the kitchen doorway, grinning a dark-blue, church-suit grin.

"It's vodka. Want any?"

Pro forma question; Kress didn't drink, but he came on into the disused dining room, lifted a bolt of fabric off a chair, and sat down.

"Preached about you at church," Kress said.

"Me?"

"What you said in the paper, about girls having fun and getting abortions."

"That doesn't sound like what I said."

"You know how it is."

Brill had meant to get away before the Hartke family returned from church. Kress seemed to feel he had Brill at a disadvantage; perhaps he did.

"Was talking to Billy Boykin about the big bend in the creek?"

"You were?"

"Billy says, go ahead and straighten her. He don't care."

"Maybe I do," Brill said.

"It don't cost all that much if you look at it like new land bought," Kress said. "We'd spend seventeen hundred dollars and get better than six acres of good bottom land to farm—that's under three hundred an acre."

Brill shook his head.

"It's a bargain, way land is. It'd keep the water going straight past Billy's house, 'stead of cutting in on that low part of the curve."

"If nobody'd ever been allowed to straighten upstream," Brill said, "it wouldn't be cutting in."

"But they did," Kress said. "In about two dozen places."

"So now it's not a creek," Brill said. "It's a sewer full of silt, going to a silt river."

"Leaving the curve won't make it any better. Taking the curve out won't make it any worse. No use talking about how it used to be, Bob. When you were a kid, putting out trot lines for catfish, that's not . . ."

"I'm not going to talk about that," Brill said. "God, I must be a bore these days, Kress, if that's what I talk about. I'm not going to straighten the creek because of what anybody else does or has done. You tell me everybody else craps in his pants, it isn't going to make me start using mine that way."

"I didn't know you felt so strong."

What the hell. He was ready to go, but Brill indulged himself: the lecture. What they needed was a watershed project, money to go upstream and put the old meanders back in, slope and seed the banks, restore the marshes, reforest part of the flood plain, rebuild the natural ponds and potholes, and see the water start to clear; kill off the Asiatic carp, replant the native small-mouth bass, and in the spring see warblers in the brush like butterflies . . .

Kress shuffled and said that would sure be pretty, and Brill told him savagely not to hold his breath.

6.

Having beat up on Kress Hartke, a man too obviously dependent on him to fight back, Brill drove away, trying to think of some women and children to bully. There was, or rather would be, or rather would there be?, Beth Gibson; but later. He decided to go brutalize Gary Pederson, once his boyhood critic, later a halfway friend, now Rosetta's best-known man, the only man (unless you count Blink Gerolph, who played third base for the Philadelphia Atheltics) with a national reputation.

He was still getting those dumb flashes: the white fruitcake, the Mother's Day scarf, a trip to the fair.

To push them out, he called up, quite deliberately, another of the bait shop conversations with Felix, one which fit the present direction of his thought and travel, because Gary Pederson'd been there.

Junior year, Gary and Felix were seniors, I wasn't quite so dumb, and we used to take Gary to the bait shop sometimes. He'd drink just as much as we would. Felix liked him, said old Gary was the brightest boy in school.

"Bright like one of those straight-A girls nobody takes out," Felix said. "Partly. But he knows things, too."

God, we got Gary laughing that night till he was almost sick. ". . . gonna be twenty-two months, fourteen days," Felix said, "before you ever git to stroke the muskrat with you pinkie finker, Gary, and she's gonna act like you touched something she didn't know was there . . ."

"My heavens," I said. "What is that thing you just touched?"

"Jump like your finger was wired to a forty-four caliber, wet cell, booster battery . . ."

"I coulda swored I didn't *have* one of those."

"Twenty-seven-cell *hot*shot battery."

"I am so surprised and so ashamed."

"Lordy yes, bounce up in the air off the car seat, hit her little head on the roof, make the dome light turn on."

"Holding herself for dear life, just as tight as she can."

Poor Gary, what girl was it he was taking out? Kind of girl Beth Gibson was, but couldn't have been Beth. Beth was much younger. Anyway, Felix said we were good-mouthing her, and Gary got too drunk to talk, and hurt too bad to laugh, and Nelse made us quit, like we were trying to choke the boy to death with laughter.

7.

There are professors who live in Rosetta. Some seem regular enough, but all we really know about them is that they say they like living by the river, in a river town.

We know them casually, watch them curiously, and we roll their title on our tongues without knowing if the taste is sweet or sour. *Professor* is a real title, we suppose, but a weak one, probably, like the chickenshit nobility in Europe, little viscounts, baronets, and marmadukes.

"Had that professor that lives in the old Greene place in the store yesterday. Been married four years, and buying baby clothes. S'pose he just now come to that chapter in the book?"

Or, "Professor Hamill, the one with the beard? 'Bout set the street on fire trying to burn leaves when it was so windy Thursday. Believe they make 'em check their brains in at the Dean's Office when they quit work for the day."

"Hell, yes. Them brains works so hard, they have to cool 'em out ever' night."

We do not, selling a used car, say *Professor* with the relish for its effect on the buyer that we might have in saying, for example, that was *Doctor* Jameson's car.

Mysterious objects of uneasy fun, for whom we do not deeply feel the need nor wholly understand the function, though most of us heard them carry on for a year or possibly four, getting through or failing college, there are men around with titles some of us repose more confidence in (*Chief, Colonel, Father*) who say *Professor* as a word of accusation in these days of accompliceship in filthy, long-haired student riot, depravity, and disrespect.

Shut up, Coach.

Anyway, Gary Pederson's the one professor we can all call by his first name and all feel proud of. Can't we agree on that? Got wrote up in *Life* magazine.

8.

Gary and I were never friends in school. Felix took him up and we still weren't friends. Kind of a standoff. But the day Felix crashed, Gary was the first to call.

No. He was waiting when I got home from the field. I walked in and he was waiting there with Dad and Uncle Ed. Dad was trying to take care of his brother Ed, and he said to Gary:

"Can you stay with Bob, Gary?"

Gary said: "Yes, sir," and he stayed with me day and damn near night, except when I'd go to the hospital to visit Pat, for the rest of the summer.

Stood with me at my cousin's funeral; later, I suspect Gary was a little hurt that I didn't ask him to be best man when Pat and I were married.

Perhaps I should have; he was good to me that summer, and we were close. Mostly we spent the time collecting, which was what he wanted to do and I didn't much care what I did. We made surface collections of stone points and cores, and sometimes even potsherds, on every farm in the county where anything had ever been turned up.

And Gary made a deduction, I guess, from what we learned doing that; studied the county tope map and decided there should be stuff on the bluff below town, near the cave entrance.

So we made our little, unauthorized, amateur dig there. It must have been September, just before school started. Secret and serious, sorting over all the bits of stuff in what seemed to be a small mound. Putting things in separate bags. Gary thought we should come to a burial, but we didn't, and he decided finally it was a house site.

I suppose every paper Gary wrote senior year at school had something to do with Mississippian or Hopewell culture. Or Woodland? Things he thought were local, anyway. Christ, he took a couple of people from the University and the high school faculty around the county in the spring, showing them stuff; he's always had that flair for dramatizing what he does.

Which flair got a National Monument established eight miles down the river at Indian Caves, and in a funny way has turned Rosetta into a town of archaeology fans.

Though what he does is not often as exciting as being CAPTURED BY STONE AGE TRIBE in Brazil, and released to tell story to *Life* magazine:

> "As far as I can tell, my life was saved by a Polaroid camera," the ascetic, wispy-haired scientist said, though there are those of his colleagues who feel a certain saintliness of manner may have contributed equally to his preservation. But to go on with Dr. Pederson's story:
> "Anthropologists often carry two cameras, you know. One to make a record with, the other for instantaneous development so that the photograph may be given to the subject. Polaroids are a splendid tool, but I hardly anticipated the turn it would take.
> "After I had made and presented pictures to all the men, and they'd turned out to be very pleased rather than the reverse (as might equally well have happened), the head man scowled and reached for the camera.
> "I handed it to him, of course, case and all, and he gave a delighted shout, and hung it around his own neck! When they escorted me out, ten days later, Faroonu was still proudly wearing it and I suspect still is, the finest ornament in the jungle."

"Fine, Gary," I said. "That's a good yarn."

There was a letter from a movie company. He handed it to me. "Do you think these people can be serious?"

"I'll see if I can find out what price to put on it, anyway," I said. "And do what's necessary to get the copyright to this interview in your name."

MGM didn't make Gary's life story, but it was exciting for him for a while. At the end of the conversation he said:

"I really never expected the time to come when I'd need a lawyer, Bob."

"It's an age people reach," I said.

"Or perhaps a point of progress within the system?"

"Defeat by the goddamn system," I said. "Now you need help with your taxes. You want a good CPA?"

With a certain saintliness of manner, he put a hand on my arm, gave me a pleading look from his pale blue eyes, and became beyond doubt the crookedest, most exasperating tax client I ever hope to have.

A swallow for lucidity, another for resilience, brought Brill to the apartment Gary Pederson kept in Rosetta, a larger place than he needed, for Gary had been divorced some years before and spent much of his time out of the country.

I'll say this. Brill rang the bell and waited. He keeps us interested, even in his less dramatic achievements in Mexico. Partly it's because, being a department head, he's the ranking University man in town; partly it's through taking a local boy or two along on his digs when he can. Mostly, it's because he by God makes us invest. A good many people in this part of the state own a little piece of Gary's success.

That'll be the first question: Who do I know that might kick in a couple of hundred?

9.

"Who do you know who might like to contribute a thousand dollars, Bob?"

"When I get home I'll shake my daughter's piggy bank."

"What about Beth Gibson?"

"I'm going to see her later, but I don't think I'll ask. No reason why you shouldn't."

"Wouldn't she have the money? After all, Dr. Gibson must have left her quite comfortable, and I imagine she earns quite a lot doing those commercials, doesn't she?"

"I can't talk about a client's finances, for Christ's sake, Gary."

"Oh. Sorry. Is Bob Lee Trump a client?"

"Used to be. Haven't spoken to the man for five years. You never tried him?"

"I'd heard he was difficult, but recently people have been having some luck with him. Curly Hayes in Drama for one. Would you like a drink, Bob?"

"Thanks. Maybe in a little while," Brill said. Pederson drank very little. "What would you use the money for this time, Gary?"

"A new dig in Oaxaca. I'd like to make it a more extended season than University funds provide for."

Brill was looking at a page of bookkeeping. "This is the same one you raised foundation money for two years ago? For site survey?"

"Yes."

"Spent it all last year?"

"You're getting back to taxes, and not very subtly."

"Yeah. Would the accounting of how you spent it stand up, if a tax man looked it over?"

"Unless he made a field trip to Mexico, to investigate."

"What if he did?"

"Well, he'd find the hourly wages are lower than, uh, my accounts suggest. This is confidential, Bob."

"The Chicago papers call up to ask about it all the time."

"I juggle, like everybody. You know that. A two-hundred-dollar-a-week payroll for fifteen diggers looks reasonable. A hundred-dollar payroll, and a hundred dollars for bribes and illegally bought artifacts looks suspicious."

"Depends on what you do with the artifacts."

"They're for museums or for study."

"Never for resale?"

"Of course not."

"You don't give yourself a salary on the accounting."

"I have my University salary. Bob, do let me get you a drink?"

"Vodka," Brill said.

"Tequila?"

While Gary was out, Brill turned through the pages of *Indian Art of Mexico and Central America,* by Miguel Covarrubias.

"That's a beautiful book, and very sound archaeology," Gary said, coming back with a double shot-glass full of tequila. "Take it home if you like."

"Let's talk about lecture fees," Brill said. Roy sent him to hell, Woody damned him, Gary treated him like a cop with a curious weakness for books and booze.

"Well?"

He had to get rid of the glass; he drank it. "Gary, I have, wow, the impression you lecture ten or fifteen times a year."

"Shall I get you some lemon and salt? That's what they use down there for chasers."

"Just water," Brill said. While Gary was gone, he leafed through *Ancient Oaxaca,* edited by John Paddock.

"One of the best of the new books," Gary said. "It'll be really important, I think. Here." He gave Brill a plate with a glass of water, a slice of lemon, a heap of salt, and another shot-glass of tequila on it. "Take Paddock home, too."

"Gary, you only show six hundred goddamn dollars on this return in lecture fees."

"They're not all paid lectures. Another tequila?"

Brill looked at him.

"Bob, look. Some of these fees, well, the institution makes a report."

"The others?"

"Or withholds money. Those I list. Some of the others, they just hand me a check, like getting cash you know? So." He shrugged, smiled, wispy-haired, impractical. An academic innocent. Jumped up. "You know Vaillant's *Aztecs of Mexico*, of course. The great basic work." Over to a bookshelf. "It's not easy to get in hard covers."

"Gary, you have to report this stuff."

"I know, of course. But Bob, believe me. This work is all that matters to me. I spend a great deal of my salary money on it. I don't charge anything for all the dozens of hours of my own time I spend talking to individuals, recruiting, fund-raising . . ."

"That's not part of the tax problem."

"I make long-distance calls."

"Gary, we take those things off."

"I use my car . . ."

"I'm not the man who checks your return, Gary. I'm the one in the next cell for signing the return with you."

"I know. And I'm very grateful. Why don't I come and see you at your office sometime next week, and we'll go over it?"

"Because the amended return should be mailed tomorrow," Brill said. "And not reporting lecture fees could be damn serious. It must amount to somewhere around five thousand dollars, doesn't it? Gary, there's a man named Kristopoulous who directs the auditing of tax returns in this district. He's a walking computer; he's strict, he's fair, and he doesn't want you in jail. He wants you earning money and giving as much of it as possible to the government so they can kill more Asiatic children. You want to refuse to pay, okay. I'll argue anything with Kris but unreported income."

"I simply can't send them any more now than I've already agreed to," Gary said, as if there'd already been a negotiation.

"All right," Brill said. "We won't amend it now. But when we make out the final return, we're going to revise it and report all the income. What the hell, Gary, we'll list your bribes as expenses. I'll argue that with Kris with pleasure."

Gray promised that when the time came, they'd really work it over. Gary had been out of town all fall and wanted to see Brill, who accepted, and Pat, on whose behalf Brill declined, for dinner soon as possible, how about Wednesday? Gary thought Bob would like to see the eleventh volume of Dibble and Anderson's translation of Sahagun. It dealt with Aztec natural history, here, take it. Gary thought that, if Bob didn't mind, he would visit with Beth Gibson, wink, since Beth was in town and weren't they all three childhood friends? Did Beth sometimes speak with Bob about those days? But that lovely child, for heavens' sake, Gary hadn't seen her for years, how very foolish of him, wink, wasn't it?

Brill wondered if old wispy-head knew something, or could have heard something, and decided no, it was only that Gary came on as naughty about getting bucks for good works from people as another man might about copping a feel.

It wasn't until Brill was driving off, loaded with books and half-loaded with tequila, that he realized that, come income tax month, Gary Pederson would be off in Oaxaca, wherever that might be.

10.

Went home for lunch, and found himself so overwhelmed by simple pleasure he could hardly speak for it: Pat and Trinket had found the canvasbacks, got one out of the refrigerator to warm up to room temperature, and were waiting for him to get home so they could cook it.

Wouldn't have missed it for anything, yet he almost had missed it for nothing at all—for making a stop at the River Club, ostensibly to see if Martin Habib was there, but really to have a sociable drink with somebody, or nobody.

Sat in his chair, paper in his lap, just plain glowing, restraining himself from supervising his wife and daughter in the kitchen, unwilling to look at the paper because there was something in there which displeased that girl in the kitchen cooking his duck.

Gary asked me if I'd ever been to Mexico, and I said no, but that was not exactly true; and, if Gary'd thought about it, who knew better?

Speaking of being upset by things in the paper, poor Gary: I did get to Mexico first, in a way.

Start with the plane, how did we get the damn thing?

Crop-duster. It was a Curtis Robin, and been used for dusting.

Felix was one hell of a mechanic, and working for his father that spring at the Ford place, afternoons and Saturdays, late in the damn Depression, when Uncle Ed took the Curtis Robin in on trade.

Christ, he'd do anything to sell a car, my junior year in high school. Felix had to have that plane, and at two bucks an hour—high wage, but he was that good—figured he could get his father paid by the end of summer.

"You want to come work for the old man and help, Blocky?"

"Doing what?"

"Sweeping. Greasing cars. Helping out. I asked him, he'll pay dollar an hour."

"Credit on the plane?"

"We've got to get some cash. We need some parts, but not too many."

Felix had already sent off to the Curtis Company for a shop manual. "Sundays, we can use the garage. We'll take it apart and put it back together."

The idea was so completely Felix's idea of fun and excitement, he got me feeling that way and I spent a whole spring without watching the ice break up and the ducks come back. I never hunted morel mushrooms once that spring, and hardly even fished.

What the old plane needed was work on the motor mostly; the body was sound. And I didn't even know the names for most of the operations we went through; did we put in piston rings?

Made a trip to a junk pile somewhere around Memphis to buy a secondhand propeller off a junker, and some stuff for the controls, and got a whole bunch of tools thrown in.

We spent March and April taking it apart, May and June putting it back together, and in July, without either one of us having had a lesson, Felix read the instruction book through carefully, flew it, and then said it was my turn.

We were using a field at the home place where winter rye had just been harvested, and nobody paid a hell of a lot of attention to what we were doing.

The boys? They're playing with that old plane. Look up there. There they go.

After Felix did, I tried. I didn't have much feeling either that it was anything too different from the first time you drive a truck, or a tractor.

Of course, I had to be careful, but the controls were dual, and Felix was in the other seat; he wouldn't let anything happen.

It didn't. Lifting off, that was the damnedest thing. I looked down, over the side, and we were ten or twelve feet off the ground, and I shouted,

"Wowee," and probably damn near stalled it.

About tipped us over when I tried to land, first time. I was going too fast, and a wheel must have caught in a rut, not a very big rut, and slewed us, and there was a wing-tip dragging the ground before we righted back.

"Good, Blocker. Damn good, boy," Felix yelled when we stopped. "Now let's go get a flying lesson."

Sergeant Aydelotte. The army must have had him giving flying lessons to University boys? Something like that. He was a missionary, preaching left stick and right rudder to the heathens. We took our plane over on the flatbed farm truck, and Aydelotte just got up and came over when we drove in as if he'd been expecting us.

Checked it over with us for two hours, by God he must have been quite a mechanic too. Taxied it back and forth, listening to the motor. Finally he flew it, and came down and told us we'd done good work.

Then he gave us each a copy of a preflight manual and told us we had to pass a test on it before we could get in our plane again, or we could put the bastard back on the truck and take it away.

He came on tough, but he taught us to fly, Sundays, and stole government gas.

He'd never say it to Felix, but he'd tell me and I'd tell Felix: "Your cousin's natural as grass. I think he could fly anything."

Made me a little jealous.

That either explains why I did it, or was I just nutty and seventeen years old?

I remember events; motives I can only try to reconstruct with guesses.

I had those two heifer calves to sell, and the market was right and I had a buyer, Billy Boykin, so I sold. Had a hundred and eighteen dollars in dirty bills in my pocket out of Billy's coffee can. Couldn't deposit the money; it was Sunday.

The Sunday before, Felix had done his cross-country. Now I was supposed to do mine, fly three hours to outside New Orleans, get someone to certify my time of arrival, refuel, and fly back.

"You follow the maps, Blocky," Sergeant Aydelotte said. *Snag*, by God; that's what we called him. Snag said. "Even when you can look down and see the river and the railroad tracks, this is supposed to be a map-and-compass exercise."

"Then why don't you send me to Omaha, like you did Felix?"

"I don't want you gettin' lost, son." Snag was from New England. "Hell, what are you? Seventeen? Well now, after you've got your map and compass position, from figuring course and time, *then* I want you to look down and check yourself on the river and the tracks."

Made me mad.

So when I got outside New Orleans, I got some more charts from the freckled, red-headed man who ran the private part of the field. Told him I wanted to take them home to put on my wall for decoration. While he was putting in the fuel, I plotted a course over the Gulf, got in the plane, waved, and flew to Merida, Yucatan. Just like that.

Hours alone, cold, over blue water, finally over land, over jungle, and came in over a highway through the jungle; the wind had been blowing me south, so when I saw the highway, I automatically turned left. I don't think I had ten minutes' worth of fuel left when I landed.

And I still don't understand why the furor, the newspaper stuff: THE LINDBERGH OF ILLINOIS, for Christ's sake. Pictures. Me grinning, standing by the crop-duster. They wouldn't let me fly back. Put it on a railroad car up through Mexico, to Texas, and Felix and I went and got it there.

But what Gary minded: I'd gone to Yucatan.

That was his place, his Mayan dream place.

Perhaps it would have made it better if I'd told him, but I never did, never told anybody: I'd have gone on from Merida, if the consul hadn't cut me off. On down Central America, or as far as my hundred and eighteen dollars would have taken me, and I'd have made it, too. But I didn't know myself until I was out over the Gulf, having to piss so badly I finally just kind of hauled out and scrooched forward and squirted the side of the cockpit, I didn't know where I was going until I saw land, and thought: Good, that's the first leg of it. First leg of what?

I was flying to Peru to see my mother.

"Dad?"

"Trinket."

"The duck's ready."

11.

"You mean to say," Felix asked her, "that you were sitting there in the same room with me all through high school, and I never saw you?"

"If I'd had a spark plug sticking in my ear you might of."

"Listen to her backfire," Felix said.

Yes, that was Pat. Brill looked across the table at her, his wife now of nearly thirty years. She'd had some backfire to her then.

Brill wondered how much the airplane crash had damaged her, there and then, when she was just eighteen, how much of that carried over to weaken the body when the strain of childbirth was applied?

"Ladies, this is perfect," Brill said. "And I don't believe I ever said that about anyone's duck cooking before."

"Eighteen minutes in a hot oven," Pat smiled.

"I learned that like other children learn their prayers," Trinket said.

"You and the other children are both addressing endangered species," Brill said.

"Daddy."

"Your father doesn't think God's just dead," Pat explained. "He thinks God's extinct." But she spoke with irony, not fire—no backfire, frontfire, fire in the middle. Just irony. Brill was grateful for it, and took pleasure in provoking it. Even irony would start to fade now, as the shadows of the tall evergreens in the yard began to climb the west side of the house.

Brought up Catholic, Pat Felucca. Portuguese. Brown-eyed. Prettiest, sassiest girl. Felix's girl. Felix was getting ready to go off to MIT, and he flew her all around.

Hell, the Lindbergh of Illinois never could get the plane for more than half an hour.

Those two went to Chicago, Denver, St. Louis. Once they went to Tombstone, Arizona, because of a book Felix read about Billy the Kid.

But it was over farm ground, six miles from home, that they crashed. Hit by the wrong squall of wind, flying too low, they went into a concrete culvert nose first. Felix, in the front cockpit, never had a chance. Pat was trapped and hurt, and I worked with the hacksaw, breaking a blade; getting a new one. Making myself go slower. She moaned and then the doctor came and gave her morphine.

Sergeant Snag Aydelotte grabbed the hacksaw from me, but he was trembling too hard to use it, and I took it back again. We'd been following the plane in Snag's army pickup truck, watching them fly circles. Felix was teaching Pat; it was supposed to be her last lesson before she soloed.

"You ever think about going to church?" Bob Brill asked his wife.

Her hip was broken. God knows what got hurt inside.

Pat Brill replied to her daughter: "Our friend wants to know if I think of going to church," she said. "People think people with Catholic raising are hooked forever."

"Is that a myth?" Brill asked, curious to see if she would answer him directly, but she turned her eyes away.

Snag and the doctor and I lifted her out of the plane, and onto the ambulance stretcher. She was light then. Dr. Jameson took me away then; he wouldn't let me stay to help get Felix's body out.

Trinket said she didn't see why there was anything wrong with going to church.

Brill suddenly smiled at his wife, and, unaccountably, Pat smiled back. He was thinking, You were nothing but a pair of scared brown eyes on the hospital pillow; then, for months, while I finished senior year, you were so pretty on your crutches men stopped to watch you swinging down the streets in spring; I threw the discus at the state meet, you threw a crutch away and I tossed the other like a javelin; I had state record for the discus, but what was best was you could dance again.

In December, 1941, Robert Brill, nineteen, returned from the University of Chicago for Christmas vacation, failing every subject, and married Pat Felucca, who was twenty; joined the army, was trained hurriedly and sent to the Aleutian Islands to repel a Japanese counterattack that might have come at any minute for the first six months, any hour for the next six, any day, any week, month, year, decade, generation. Those tricky Japs (Brill cut the carcass of the canvasback, almost bare of meat, in half with poultry shears, offered half to Trinket, picked up the other in his fingers, and began to gnaw) might be re-arming secretly right now, to invade the Aleutian Islands while Brill's back was turned.

12.

The next two hours of Brill's Sunday were pleasant, too. He'd put a fair amount of time and thought into a proposed reorganization of Martin's holdings; the corporation that owned the theaters was going to show too much profit if they didn't raise salaries.

In the bar at the River Club Martin went over Brill's work, praising it, and Brill who had half-sobered up at lunch, sobered up a little more on some extraordinary unblended Scotch Martin had been sent. It was very old, straight malt whiskey, the kind that gets saved out when they hit it just right. There's never much of it.

Brill would have described himself as not liking Scotch, but had never tasted anything like this.

"This solves a lot of problems, Bob," Martin said.

"So does this," said Brill, holding up his glass to the light. "It tastes like dirt and golden dung. How often do I find anything new in the world to like?"

"I'm glad."

"I could dream atavistic dreams about this Scotch."

"Take the rest home," Martin said.

"No. I'd rather bum it from you, drop by drop. You want to sign the amended?"

"Let me read it through again."

"I've got to make a phone call," Brill said.

There was only one booth at the club. He waited outside it while a teen-age boy told another one, apparently, about a party in another town, at which "all the kids got stoned on grass, but I'd just palm it when the roach came by, and drag on a Philip Morris . . . no, man, I wanted to be large and able when poonie-time came, but the goddamn chicks there were too loose, had the bad giggles . . . I mean giggling all over, from the ankles up . . . man, you put your hand under a skirt it was like having it under the hood of a car with the motor running . . ."

Stolid with Scotch, Brill listened to the unchanged voice of youth, minding just a little, and when the booth was free, called Beth Gibson, wryly hoping poonie-time was coming for him.

Once again he got the French (Moroccan) maid, who told monsieur she was sorree, Mam'selle Geebsawn couldn't come to the phone.

Brill said it was important, a matter of business, and after a delay, Beth was speaking.

"Hello, Bob." It was a voice-lesson voice; several times he'd been sure he heard it coming over television in another room, gone in and seen that the soignée lady in the commercial Trinket or Pat had on wasn't Beth at all.

"Beth. Could you come by the office some time this afternoon?" It was a test question. It was hoped she'd say no.

She said no. "I can't. Not possibly."

"I do have to see you. About taxes. I've got to send off a check tomorrow."

"How much?"

"I need information you may have to look up," Brill said. Beth had capital amounting to a little over two hundred thousand dollars. She was the girl who had left Rosetta to become an actress in New York, and while she'd settled pretty much into doing television in Chicago, her professional earnings were neither insignificant nor uncomplicated. "Do you remember I wrote a month or two ago?"

"Oh yes. All right, I'll get the letter and look things up. Do you want to come by here?"

Yes, ma'am, yes, ma'am, yes, mam'selle. "Sure," Brill said. "Be happy to, Beth."

"But, Bob." Throb. "You won't be able to see me."

"I won't?"

"I'll be sitting in the dark."

"Um?"

"And if you tell anybody, I think I might shoot you, Mr. Brill."

Huh? Wowee? Poonie-time?

He went back to the booth, wishing he could talk to Martin about it. Every man his best friend's pornographer, but Martin, the only man in the world he might want to tell, was the last man in the world he could tell: not only did Martin live in Rosetta, but there was even a certain overlap between Martin's business world and Beth's. For in addition to his theaters, Martin was mildly involved with production, though in Cincinnati, not Chicago. From Rosetta, we look east for business connections.

Whatever Brill might, regrettably, have said to Martin anyway about Beth was well blocked: at their booth, sitting now, was Donnie Rebranch, younger brother of Brill's law partner and a candidate, about to announce, for the state legislature.

Donnie's group in town, which was fifteen years younger, had taken Brill and Martin up recently, Martin because he was a consistent contributor to political causes, Brill because he was supposed to have influence with the liberal bunch around the University.

And had once served a term in the legislature, declining to run a second time.

"Isn't there any chance of you running, Bob?" Donnie's test question. "I know a lot of people who'd work like hell for you."

"You're welcome to it," Brill said.

"You could have gone back," Donnie said. "What didn't you like about it?"

"It's boring," Brill said. "You like committee meetings? You like repetitious discussions?"

"Well, I suppose that's how the work gets done. The fun's out campaigning, isn't it?"

"You like saying the same thing over and over, all day long, with the same smile, to different strangers? Yeah, it's swell. Or the strategy part, those secret consultations with the funeral directors and asphalt contractors that turn up as precinct chairmen?"

"Will I have your support, Bob?" Donnie asked. "If you say yes, it'll be the moment I decide to run."

Brill said: "We got any more of that Scotch, Martin? Yeah, Donnie. I'll support you. Unless someone comes along I like better for it."

"Thanks." Donnie's intuitions were at least good enough so that he got up to leave. "May I assume you don't have anyone in particular in mind, Bob?"

"Just a type," Brill said. Donnie smiled. "If some really miserable prick comes along," Brill said. "In either party. That doesn't get along with anybody and doesn't want to, he's got my vote. They're the only guys that get anything done in legislatures."

Donnie laughed as if a joke had been made, posed for a minute, perhaps to make sure everyone in the bar registered whom he was talking to, and swung off.

"Well," Martin said. "What else for Sunday?"

"I don't know. Kid talking on the telephone. Upset me, looking at him. Thinking about Cal, in Asia. And me. Where were you, Martin? When you were nineteen?"

"Still in Nicaragua," Martin said. "All I could think of was getting across Costa Rica, into Panama, and joining the U.S. Army. For not very nice reasons."

"You wanted to get away from the Somoza boys, didn't you?"

"Yes, but not to be free. That didn't occur to me. To be rich."

"You couldn't get into the banana racket or something there, huh?"

"Only friends of Somoza. My uncle was; my father backed Sacasa, the man who lost. That was a family decision, when they first arrived. They would take opposite political sides always, so one brother would always be with the right people. And the winner would protect the loser. I thought a better way to be rich was to become a U.S. citizen by joining the army."

"Abou ben Alger," Brill said.

"I never connected fighting Somoza with fighting Hitler until the recruiter in Panama suggested it. I said yes, of course, and he was pleased. It made a little item for him in the paper."

"Yeah," Brill said.

"What's wrong?"

"I don't know. Do you realize every generation for the past seventy years in this country has been a war generation? A country can't live like a mother hog, eating her own little pigs." He grinned, and drank up. "Why hell, Martin," he said. "The Big Pig Farmer in the Sky will shoot her in the ass every time, won't he?"

Martin laughed. "If that's the sermon, I'm not putting anything in the collection box."

13.

Very well. Every man his own pornographer then? Driving off from the club, Brill warned himself against the wet armpits of anticipation, and tried hard to separate what he'd known of Beth for years and years, before anything happened, from what he'd learned, all in a rush, one long night of happenings in Chicago.

Delicate, mysterious, desirable, never-married.

Seven or eight years younger than Brill, he could remember Beth first as a vivid, oddly poised little girl in a fifth-grade play he'd had to attend for family reasons when he was a senior in high school. How can you already be willowy when you're only eleven years old?

Daughter, only child, of a widowed doctor, of a family as old in

Rosetta as the Brills were; growing up lonely, he guessed, in the pretty cottage where her father raised her. Some old money, and boarding school in prospect; eastern connections. What had she wanted?

To get out of Rosetta, probably; to be at home in New York, Paris, Rome. Known out there. Let each town send the world an actress; me.

Money is mobility. Beth had enough of that, so that by the time she'd finished boarding school and a year at Bennington, she didn't have to wait for the bald man to come along and say, "I hereby crown you Joan of Arc."

Coolness. Fragility. Some shimmer of inner strength but hardly any of sex. A conventionally musical speaking voice. A round, clear-featured, ambiguous face (is that girl mocking me?). Pretty, pretty hands. Those assets got Beth no further professionally than Chicago and television—people in Rosetta called each other up when they had seen one of her performances as the sort of door-to-door cosmetic saleslady who carries a three-hundred-dollar alligator purse, or exquisite hostess whose taste runs to serving instant coffee in a silver urn.

In the off-season she came to Rosetta and opened the pretty yellow clapboard cottage, the upkeep of whose paint, glass, and shrubbery was supervised in her absence, by Lawyer Brill. (Who only once used the place unauthorized, not for clandestine trysting but to hide a black boy who was on his way to Detroit after the rioting in Cairo, with officers after him who'd had an illegal tap on the phone of the Cairo lawyer who asked Brill's help. The cops used their warrant to check Brill's home, office, and cabin on the river, and Brill felt badly about the breach of trust involved in his hiding a fugitive in Beth Gibson's underground railway station, but good about the number of times he was able to say to the state cops, "He musta gone thataway." While the cops watched Brill, Martin picked the boy up and drove him out of town.)

Some pornographer. Brill was halfway to Beth's, stopped for a light, and the lady's pants weren't even on yet, much less off. He shifted, caught behind a big truck. They began to move again slowly.

14.

"The newest form of English diction is of course never written; the sense of that leisure-class propriety which requires archaism in speech is present even in the most illiterate or sensational writers in sufficient force to prevent such a lapse. On the other hand, the highest and most conventionalized style of archaic diction is—quite characteristically—properly employed only in communications between an anthropomorphic divinity and his subjects. Midway between these extremes lies the everyday speech of leisure-class conversation and literature."

That Thorstein Veblen's diction really swings, doesn't it?

No, really, Thorstein, all kidding aside, in making these death charts for our cities, we've learned to note as an early symptom how the poor damn middle class rushes to give up its elegant and archaic language, both in speech and in writing.

Even Big Anthropo can be imagined as communicating to his subjects in such terms as, "Beth Gibson, my daughter, b'lieve I'll just afflict you with twenty-three skiddoo of the giggy, 'fore I shuffle off this immortal coil to Buffalo."

Of course Thorse, old Norse horse, Big A's pretty busy and can't keep his slang quite as up to date as his afflictions.

Eggs were going all over at the end of it, and there was a flash, darkness on stage, louder music, and gobs of beaten egg began to fly out at the audience. We ran, laughing and screaming.

Beth grabbed my arm, I squeezed her wrist to my side. There was a big blob of egg in the middle of her forehead.

"I like happenings," I said, and covered her hand with my own. It was the first physical touch we ever exchanged, though I'd been seeing her in Chicago on business, or as a pretty companion for dinner or the theater, for nine or ten years.

Out on the street, while we'd been watching the program, they'd been having their own happening.

There were four private cars out there, including mine. The windshields were smashed clear out of every one of them.

Beth, who had just detached her hand from being held, with a firm smile and a cool pat, grabbed my arm again.

"Bob, Bob." She sounded not so much dismayed on my behalf as plain scared.

"It'll run without a windshield," I said.

She clung to the arm, pressed her face against my shoulder, and I think may have lost a tear or two.

"It's all right," I said. "If they're around somewhere, watching, don't let 'em see they've got to you. Come on."

Felt pretty silly, unlocking a car with no windshield in it, but our friends had neither unlocked it themselves nor taken anything out. There was a case of table wine in there, in the back. Odd.

The guy parked behind me was going back inside the building to call cops, but I couldn't see much point waiting for them. I left my name and address with him, cleaned the glass off the front seat, and started to drive Beth home. Right at the corner there was a loud bang on the roof, and I speeded up but caught a second before I got out of the free-fire zone.

"Kids on the roof, dropping bricks, Beth," I said.

"They could get on my roof, if they saw where we go."

"They'll be running like hell by now," I said. "Before the cops arrive."

"They might watch where we go."

"I'll drive you around first," I said. Beth's place was only four blocks from where the happening happened, but she hadn't wanted to walk, even with me for protection. "They aren't after us personally," I said.

It must have been like wartime, but I never really knew what wartime felt like, not in the Aleutians, not in Dutch Harbor. Maybe the Aleuts knew what war was there, but I never saw an Aleut. In 1840 there'd been 16,000 to 25,000 of them; in 1940, less than a thousand left; but it wasn't a war that killed them. They died of gentleness of the mind.

I finally pulled up in front of Beth's building, and she'd never once let go of my arm.

"It's silly, I know, but I'm afraid even to cross the sidewalk," Beth said.

"I think I can protect you from here to there," I said.

And of course, the street was deserted, though Beth was certain she saw someone put out a cigarette in an alley, down the way.

"Please stay with me a little while?"

"Beth, I would just love to," I said strongly, which brought a little flirtation back into her manner.

"My key, sir." She handed it to me.

In an early demonstration of the advantages of Russian over U.S. development for colonial lands, and vice versa, the Russians killed off the first half of the Aleuts, and sold us the rest of them. We bought them gladly and finished them off with real Yankee know-how.

I followed Beth up a flight of stairs, watching the nice movements of her rather sinuous body lilting upward, liking the way her head set back, chin lifted gaily, fair silky hair cropped short because she wore such a variety of wigs in her work.

I remember thinking that being locked in with a lady, if I was lucky enough to manage it, might be the only form of entertainment left available in Chicago.

I'd wanted to see the Black Hawks play hockey, but the hotel ticket-booth man said the game had been sold out for weeks; and because it was late, didn't think I'd have much luck at the arena.

"The scalpers start to get off the street with their dough while the crowd's still going in," my man said. " 'Cause there's muggers hanging around to try to catch the scalpers."

I tried to get a cab—it would have taken another half hour to get the car brought down from the parking ramp—but the driver didn't want to go out there. I went back to my room and was just going to call Beth when she called me, said some friends were presenting . . .

At the door of the apartment, she didn't hand me the key. This was a big special police lock, too complicated for a country boy to work.

"I was robbed twice," Beth said. "I'm lucky I wasn't home either time."

"What about your maid?"

She completed the double-key sequence; a bar fell away inside, and she let us in.

"The maid was out the first time. The second time the poor thing hid in a closet, and the men even opened the closet, looking for furs. They didn't see her, way in back. Poor, terrified thing; that's why I had this door put on. It's steel plate. Do you know what they did?"

She closed the door, went through the locking sequence.

"What?"

"One of them . . . defecated on the floor. In the middle of the living room. That's what upset her most, I think."

"You're living in a state of siege," I said, and Beth said she felt free enough to come and go during the day.

But she didn't go anywhere evenings any more unless there was someone to take her.

"When I work at night, the studio sends a car," she said. "Two drivers. One to stay with the car, one to come upstairs for me. Sometimes my maid and I are a little nervous about the one who comes upstairs."

She laughed. I laughed. She took off her coat and said, "Stay a while, Bob? It's early. Oh, but your car."

Out on the street were things that alarmed her still.

"I'll risk the car," I said. "If you'll risk the one who's come upstairs."

She said yes please. She made me a drink. She excused herself.

I always wondered how it started: the Aleuts, after 5,000 peaceful years, during which they had developed the most sophisticated of primitive civilizations (they were expert human anatomists, long before William Harvey), may have looked on the first Russians with hope and excitement, for Russian guns killed fur animals faster than stick-thrown harpoons, and the big Russian boats, held together with iron, must have looked like better protection from the old, cold, salty sea than kayaks and umiaks. Only gradually would they have realized that when the fur traders put men into the big boats to take and use as hunters on other islands, the traders could not be expected to concern themselves with whether the hunters returned.

Beth returned, Jesus-god, wearing a flimsy blond sweater, low-cut with seed-pearl embroidery, and insubstantial pink silk slacks.

"It's your costume for *Little Women*," I said, taking her hands.

"It's my temptress outfit," Beth said. "I don't want you running off." But she disengaged her hands, perched on a chair, not the sofa, and for the next half hour she flittered like an insect. Fixing more drinks. Showing me over a hundred photographs of herself (Fashion. Hand model. Character part. Ingenue. Nightgown, not very suggestive, for a mail-order catalogue. And all those ones in different wigs.) Letters from agencies and producers; telegrams: GOOD LUCK, BILL. GOOD LUCK, YOUR FRIENDS AT AVON. Put on music. Changed it.

Run for the roundhouse, Nellie. The brakeman can't corner you there.

After half an hour or so she was saying intimate things:

"I generally have two kinds of men in my life. At the same time, darn it. A sort of sweet, chess-playing, book-reading kind that I adore spending time with, but never let touch me . . ."

"I don't even play checkers," said the brakeman, looking for the correct angle of lunge. "What's the other kind?"

Nellie moved left. Beth smiled, and said: "Well, more masculine, I suppose. And less educated. Would that fascinate Rosetta? Do they talk about me?"

"They wonder why you don't get married."

"They'll never know," Beth said. Nellie eyed the brakeman; she perched warily forward in an overstuffed chair, and I made the first big move. Put down the drink, crossover, step in front so she can't stand up without bumping, sit on arm of chair, leg thrust out to block her rising, lean in and kiss her.

Beth sat quite still for it.

Then Nellie fluttered her eyes, slipped out from under my arm, neatly hopped my leg, and said, "Oh, I wish you weren't from home."

Then, as I straightened up and was considering, as a matter of fact, whether I wanted to play this thing out, Beth leaned up, kissed me, and said:

"Don't be a bear. There."

The brakeman stepped in, moved his big right arm under Nellie's armpit and across her slender back, his left across her butt, and walked the pore child two steps over to the roundhouse wall. Against which, having one thigh firmly thrust between hers, he humped her like a piston rod, nuzzling her neck the while.

She said, "Let's dance, Bob. Do you want to?"

Wanted it a little more romantic, did she? Glad to oblige. I let her go, kneel down, and change every record on the stack for the third time. I thought it would help her decide what to play if I were to place a hand on her shoulder, slide it down her back under the sweater, and undo the brassiere snap that I found down there. She rose and fastened it, as if unconsciously.

"Can you tango?"

Rudolph Valentino snapped his fingers, wove his big right arm under Nellie's armpit, his left across her butt, squeezing it this time as his hand went past, and tangoed the pore child two steps over to the tent wall. Against which, working until both thighs were firmly between hers, he humped her like a camel, correcting the bra strap situation once again.

When the record ended Beth put both hands on my chest and pressed, rather than pushed. It seemed to me I had her going, so I grinned and stepped back.

"I wish you weren't from home," she said again. "Don't you see?"

"I don't know where your home is, lady," I said, coming on silly. "I'm a Mohawk Indian from Philadelphia." Put my hand to my mouth "Wa-ba-ba-ba-ba-babaaa," and did a war dance.

It was not to be overlooked that on its last trip across the defenseless waif's rear end, the left hand had made a stop at what might be called grapefruit junction for a squeeze. There had been received at that time a report from the fingertips as follows: CHIEF MOHAWK INDIAN, PHILADELPHIA, PENNA. CAN REPORT LACK OF UNDERPANTS UNDER PANTS STOP EVEN FELT A STRAY HAIR STOP IT WAS CURLY STOP GOOD LUCK COMMA YOUR LEFT FINGERTIPS.

So when the new record started, Chief grabbum Little Redwing, pushum two steps against canyon wall, humpum like Bill Buffalo.

Beth slumped, I would have to say, when I stepped back from her after that record ended. I took her hand, meaning to lead her someplace more comfortable, but she shook her head, disengaged her hand, walked over to the big chair which had somehow become the maypole for our revels, and held onto the top of it.

Her breathing was irregular and her face pale. She looked exhausted, disoriented, older, younger, and five inches shorter. So of course I did the decent thing and let her recover; I did like hell. I stepped up to her as yet another record started, took her right hand in my left as if to lead her out dancing. Her left hand rose, automatically, to find its place on my shoulder, though her head was shaking no, and I quickly dropped my own left hand to her waist, closed in so her arms would stay up, and moved the left arm on around the waist till I could catch hers just below the elbow and hang onto it. I put my mouth firmly against hers until it opened, and stuck my right hand straight down the front of her slacks.

She jerked, trying to pull her mouth away, pull her left arm free, and close her legs tight all at the same time, but I had a finger pretty firmly in between the outer labia, and it seemed to me as I ran it lightly back and forth that I was in contact with the right point.

"Please." She finally had her mouth free. "Oh please, let go."

Did the decent thing again. Hoisted her onto the chair arm, just an inch or two, to distribute her weight less awkwardly, and kept the finger working. At that she seemed to relax for a moment, lubrication occurred, and the finger moved up inside her almost without my meaning it to. She squeaked, submitted—I'd have said responded—and suddenly was sobbing.

"Oh, for Christ's sake, Beth," I said, turned loose and let her slide away, into the chair.

The sobbing stopped. "Golly you're strong," said Beth, in Nellie's voice.

Wherewith the beast picked up the malnurtured, big-eyed packet of bones and went stomping around, looking for a damn bedroom, and the orphan pounded its furry shoulders with her tiny fists and said she didn't mean that.

I put her down on the sofa and inquired politely what the hell she did mean.

"Just," she said. "Just it's just exciting . . . for a . . . woman to feel a . . . man's strength."

I could play by that rule. I grabbed both her wrists in one hand, and stripped the pink slacks off, left ankle excepted, with the other.

She conceded? Like hell she did. There was squirming, there was pulling away of fingers, there was please-turn-out-the-lights, and when I got back from the switch, the pants were back up again.

"Please," she said. "Really, I mean it, Bob. I just love to neck. Like when we were in school?"

"If I'd necked with you in school, I'd have been arrested," I said.

To show me what kind of necking she meant, she opened my

pants, found a hot cucumber in there, and started to cool it with her fingertips.

I pulled her pinks back down again and she spread willingly, thinking, I guess, that we had a contract of mutual accommodation.

Decent to the end, I let her assume vigorously for about four seconds, then I took myself away from her, reversed, and rolled onto her. Her response was to lie quite still, while I tried to push in, raising her, spreading, guiding. It wouldn't work; I could not get my harpoon into the valuable, smooth-furred sea otter without her help. Or rather as it seemed I could, she stiffened, moved away, and covered up with her hand.

"It hurts, it hurts," she said, and the sobbing started again.

I sat up. Naked except for the sweater, which was pushed all awry, she sat up and put her arms around me, her head against my shoulder, one small breast pressed flat against my upper arm.

"You don't understand," she whispered. "I'm too small. I would, but it always hurts so much. Bob, it nearly cripples me."

"All right, Beth," I said. She was reaching for me again, and her face moved toward my lap, but I thought not. Virtue was going to triumph. I was leaving.

I stood up. She lay back, that one little breast showing under the sweater, pants on the floor now. She seemed crumpled together, not long and willowy but frail, small, pale, and exhausted. After each attack, if that's what they were, she'd seemed weaker, less able to resist, so that suddenly I thought: To take her now would be the next thing to necrophilia.

And the brakeman said: "Sure, buddy. And this is where we separate the men from the sweet chess players."

The Russians said there was still fur there, and I took my trousers off. Took my shoes and socks off. Took my shirt off. Got back on down there, lined up, lifted, and went in. I admit she didn't help, and that going in did seem to create some gasping and some squeaks, but I'd decided not to hear anything this time, not even sobs.

Surely that was how the game was played?

Once we were coupled, I can't say I lasted very damn long, but as I bucked and vented, it seemed to me she became less passive, and raised her hips to me in a small spasm of her own.

We rested. I whispered. She answered:

"Yes, damn you."

"I told you. I don't play chess."

"Do you mind?" She wanted me off? Okay. "I'll walk funny for a week."

I hadn't believed her, but it was true: Beth's small, and seldom used, and it hurts her every time.

I held her the rest of the night. In the morning I asked her about those masculine, uneducated types, and heard a parable: "I once knew a girl who had to get a movie job in Florida and had no money, so she hitchhiked. And almost every ride she got was in a big truck, and every driver who picked her up said the same thing: 'You're lucky it was me that picked you up, and not one of those other guys.' "

"You mean, they respect a lady's wishes?"

"Oh shut up," Beth said. "Yes. That's what I mean."

Though there were men who had come and gone, respectfully, and partially successful attempts at overcoming what Beth thought of as her physical handicap, I seem to have come closer than most to being her first regular lover. But with Louise, with the Funny Girls, with almost anyone else I can think of, once the first connection was made, the attitude seemed to be, Good. Glad that's over. Let's get this affair into gear.

Not Beth. I had to seduce her, or rape her a little, or whatever the act is, every damn time. She'd see me. She didn't avoid me. She would, in fact, claim to be in love with me. But each time we were alone, she'd try to stand me off, or, failing that, perform a divertimento. Sometimes she could, with her virtuoso embouchure, to which she adds one of the world's great articulative techniques, demonstrating, particularly in the accelerating glissando passages, a mastery of triple-tongue interpolations which seems to transfigure the instrument and transport the audience. . . .

These were increasingly uncomfortable thoughts to drive a car with. Brill banished them with a passage of sentiment:

Last year's girl. When, finally, there has been quite a bit of tenderness, and when it cannot really be expressed except as considerateness, because no enduring passion is permitted by circumstance (and if there is such a thing at all as enduring passion), then all the physical things are apt to reverse. I would go along with what didn't hurt her; she would insist that hurting didn't matter. And reversed psychically, too: I began to find her actress's vanity, the hundred photographs, somehow charming. And she to like my overbearing silliness.

We both liked playing roles, I suppose, and in addition I felt very protective. At the most intense time, I thought constantly about getting her to move back to Rosetta, where the streets (forgive me) were safe.

But then, twice, she did come to Rosetta, and would not let me see her here alone. For which, in retrospect, I must be grateful.

And then, I met Louise. Martin brought her to me. I stopped

making extra trips to Chicago. Beth sensed it all, and when I did go in and ask her out to dinner, she said she wasn't quite sure she wanted me to come up afterward. That suited me all too well, though of course I tried to pretend it didn't. I was all excited about Big Shy Louise; through with last year's girl.

At the end, were there Russians who regretted the dying of Aleut culture, the genocide of the people who knew human anatomy? Were there Aleuts, by then, who loved their executioners, and were hurt at being sold to other ones, however indistinguishable?

With my entrenching tool I excavated a little midden, covered with wildflowers, near a stream where grayling swam. You could catch them with a hook, a handline, and a piece of tan cotton torn from your GI underwear, beautiful slim fish with tall, improbable dorsal fins like iridescent sails.

There were a few small things in the midden, points, a simply carved bone, but I returned them all and buried them again.

The whole island was covered with wildflowers. Fifty centuries, at just under four generations a century, with a population which may have averaged 10,000 through the span, means just 2,000,000 of those gentle hunters lived, and died out, and are only the memory of a small race now, under the flowers.

15.

When he arrived at the small, pretty house where Dr. Gibson had had his practice and raised his only daughter, Brill was on the edge of sobriety. This made him feel unspecifically guilty, and perhaps inadequate to the situation he hoped might develop at Beth's. He thought of driving away, phoning her, and arranging to come by in the morning. He had a big swallow of vodka instead, things seemed better, and he went in.

The maid showed him down a short hallway, curtains drawn over its only window, to a bedroom door which was standing slightly open. The maid turned and went discreetly away.

"Hi, Beth," Brill said, putting his face in the opening. It was dark and curtained in the bedroom.

"There's a chair out there if you'd like to sit," Beth said.

"Can't I come in?"

"No."

"What's the matter?"

"Just stay where you are. Or find a chair."

"Okay." Brill leaned against the wall opposite the door, and said: "Do you have plague or something?"

Inside the bedroom, she laughed. "That's a laugh of pain," she said.

"Beth? What's wrong?"

"I hurt. I'm all puffed up."

"Shall I come back tomorrow?"

"I'll hurt tomorrow, too."

"Beth, what happened to you?"

He couldn't understand the reply.

"What?"

"I said, I've been peeled."

"What's it mean? I don't . . ." He was alarmed.

"Peeled. I had my face done." She laughed again, sounding quite cool and elegant. "What did you think? Some terrible Chicago street attack. Oh, Bob. Or the pangs of love, was that what you thought? No. I had my face done."

"I'm a country boy," Brill said. "I remember when you had your pretty teeth all filed off, and new pretty teeth put on. Is it something like that?"

"My teeth were a mess," Beth said. "Besides, you took it off the tax, or I wouldn't have told you."

"Is this another professional expense?"

"Of course. They put carbolic acid and stuff on your skin, and take the whole tired top layer off that way. And new, baby skin grows up to take its place."

Brill said, "Oooof."

Beth said: "Fifteen hundred dollars."

"Yeah. Okay. Paid the bill?"

"Yes."

"Well. That takes care of today's . . . business, then. That'll just nicely offset your income gain."

The voice from the dark room was enjoying its advantage. "What is it you're suppressing, Mr. Brill? Did you want to say, 'Sickening? Shocking? Barbaric?' "

"I don't know. Is it different from . . . oh, Ubangis, and their lip boards?"

"To want to look younger? Isn't that more human?"

"What else can they do?"

"Well, my grandmother had her lower ribs removed surgically," Beth said. "So she could lace her corset tighter, for a waspier waist."

"How much longer will you have to sit in the dark?" Brill asked.

"Ten days. Would you like to see?"

"I don't think so."

"Come on. Weren't you one of those kids who liked to look under other kids' BandAids?"

"No," Brill said.

A light went on then, in the bedroom.

"Bob?"

He couldn't.

"It's just, I didn't want the maid to be upset, but you're different. Come on, Bob. Look in at me."

"No, damn it." But he crossed the hall, put his hand on the door and opened it.

There was Beth's body in a smart dressing gown, sitting erect in a small, padded chair. There was no face. Beth's hair grew from a curiously powdered sphere, with Vaseline covering the powder, in which the eyes were nearly swollen shut and the other features only sketched on underneath.

"I can't smile for you," Beth said. "Till next week."

"God, Beth," Brill said, and went off down the hall, lurching the first step or two, followed by her pained laughter.

16.

Not long after he left Beth's Brill was almost in a fight. He was on his way to the cabin, where he proposed to leave off the archaeology books Gary Pederson had loaned him, when he passed a pickup truck parked along the road with surveying equipment in it. Then, just before he got to the gate at the cabin driveway, he saw, across his fence, a piece of red rag tacked to a tree.

He stopped, crossed the road, pulled the rag off, bent the nail out with his fingers, kicked down two stakes along the right-of-way ditch, breaking them off, got in his car, and turned around.

His adversary of yesterday, the young engineer, was just getting into the panel truck. Brill pulled in front of it, blocking it. There was another man in the right-hand seat of the panel.

The engineer closed his door on the driver's side, rolled down the window, and said:

"Hi, Mr. Brill."

Brill said: "You the party that nailed this piece of red shit to my walnut tree?"

The engineer said, "It wasn't. It was an ash."

Because of the possibility that the young sonofabitch was right,

Brill decided to smash his face in and tried to wrest the door open. The engineer, who had started his motor, put the panel truck into reverse, backed away onto the road, and drove off fast in the other direction.

Unwilling to go back and look again at the young tree, and being pointed in the direction of home, Brill drove home. Pat had gone to bed already. Brill and Trinket made grilled cheese sandwiches for supper in the waffle iron, something Trinket had read about in a newspaper cooking column. It worked, sort of; Brill held himself to beer while he had supper with his daughter; they discussed a high school war protest meeting, in which Trinket wanted to take part. It was to be in the evening, and after it the students would march downtown carrying candles. It frightened Brill, to think of his daughter doing this, but he said she could.

After supper he took the weekend's remaining canvasback down to put in the freezer and became upset with himself because there were still wild ducks in there shot, cleaned, and frozen the year before. Five pintails; they must have been set aside for some special occasion that didn't come off, but he couldn't think what it might have been.

Before he went upstairs again, he took every package of meat out of the freezer, sorted them, checked them over, and put them back in an order which seemed rational.

Trinket was in her pajamas when he went up, finishing homework. They watched the ten o'clock television news together; Brill tried to wake Pat to ask if she'd like to see it too, but couldn't get a sensible answer. Trinket went to bed. Brill went out to his car, retrieved the archaeology books and the rest of his vodka.

Meant to go to bed early, but leafed through the books and finished off the booze instead, about half a bottle.

Wrote:

> You destroy a people's land and culture, so the survivors have nothing left to belong to, they die out. What about a conglomerate race of wantons who systematically destroy their own land and culture, in what seems to be a compulsive form of national self-expression? Autogenocide, nanu.

and

> I care. I care very much. I am trying like hell to care. I wish I cared. Damn glad I don't care. (Check one.)

and

Don't give another inch, boys.

And hauled himself, hand over hand, up the banister, to bed.

This took place, probably: after he'd undressed, he got into bed with Pat who looked to him just as she had when he'd got back from the Aleutian Islands, but she woke and in waking changed in the dark to a creature of Vaseline and powder, and gave him directions for finding his own bed, Bob. Please?

5

Some damn little thing will happen so exactly dreamlike that a man can't believe it afterward, except he recalls words, spoken by someone, which he himself couldn't have invented, even in a dream.

For example: Monday afternoon, the phone rings on Brill's desk. He is much as we saw him yesterday, but dressed in office clothes, and has been tapering off the booze, having had no eye-opener in the morning, and only two stiff ones at lunch.

"Hello."

"Bob Brill. Is that you?"

"Yeah."

"Great to hear your voice, Counselor. How've you been?"

"Who is this?" Brill thinks he knows, but won't play games. Brill looks out the window.

"Oh, sorry there, Bob. It's Pete."

Brill is tempted to ask, *Pete Who?,* but that would be dishonest.

The window, since the Brill Law Office Building is only one-story high, is at street level.

"Hello, Canaday," Brill says.

In fact, it's practically on the street.

Pete Canaday says, "Bob, I'm down here at the courthouse. Did you know old Charlie Dean is sick?"

"Yeah." Charlie Dean is the county treasurer, no particular friend of Brill's or Canaday's, nor is Mr. Dean's illness likely to have anything to do with what's on Canaday's mind. Nevertheless Pete says:

"Well, Bob. Tell me. How bad is he?"

"How bad's emphysema?"

"Well, is *that* what it is? I swear, I had no idea . . ."

Here the dreamlike thing begins: Brill has brought to mind two faces: Canaday's, boyish and theatrical, projecting concern at the black pay phone on the wall of the courthouse corridor; and Charlie Dean's, turned sidewise on a pillow, wheezing. But Brill's eyes see two quite different faces looking in at him from the street: one is Martin Habib's, the other that of a tall, long-haired, floating girl, dressed in a kind of long, wine-colored coat that floats with her.

The window is closed, but he feels she is wearing so much perfume he can see it as a haze around her.

"What did you want, Pete?" Brill asks, staring out.

"I have to see you, Bob. Are you free?"

"I've got a meeting."

Now Martin Habib and the girl go slowly out of sight, head by head, as if they had looked into a cage together and were talking over what they saw.

"Can you put off your meeting a couple of minutes for me?" Canaday asks.

The unreal thing is not, of course, that Martin should be with a chick. Martin is with a chick every chance he gets.

"What's the bastard done now?" By *the bastard* Brill means Trump, the rich man Pete works for.

But Martin does not walk his chicks down the street in broad daylight at four on October afternoons, past the ninety-year-old Brill law office, for everyone in town to see.

"Look," Pete says. "I'll be right over."

Brill, wishing hard for Martin and the girl to float past his window again so he can get another look at her, becomes surly:

"You like geography, Canaday?"

"Do I . . . ? Excuse me?"

"There's a brand-new *National Geographic* on the table here. You can read it while I'm in my meeting."

"Bob, this is pretty urgent."

"There are usually some swell stories about South Sea islanders. Roasting pigs with bare teats."

Canaday misses his chance. Rosetta manners require that he say something like, *Well now, Counselor, you wouldn't want them roasted with brassieres on, would you?* And the Brill would laugh and give in. But Canaday tries wheedling:

"You can put off the meeting. Sure you can. Just for five minutes?"

"Wait, I'll get it." Big Brill, between women, reacting restlessly to the notion of perfume and the sight of his friend with a strange girl, moves over to pick up the magazine. Now he reads from the cover into the phone: " 'JUMBO AFRICAN FROGS'. Hey, here you go: 'ATLANTA, CITY ON THE MOVE.' I'll bet that's a good one."

What he really bets is he can make Pete Canaday express exasperation. Loses.

"Great, then. How long's the meeting?"

"Forty-five minutes."

"Come on, Bob. Please. I've got to get this straightened out."

Martin Habib walks briskly by the other way, alone. Alone?

"Forty-five goddamn minutes, Pete."

"All right. I'll be in your office when you come out."

"Yeah." Brill slams down, yanks out a desk drawer, grabs a bottle of cognac that's been in there untouched for about six months, and glugs down the inch or so of fire left in it. Flips for the wastebasket; misses. Kicks the bottle out of his way, crossing to the door, and in the doorway nearly rams into the levitated girl.

She has been floating in the shadow of his doorway, listening to and watching him, with big, wide, violet eyes.

She raises a hand as if to press it against his chest to stop his rush toward her, but doesn't quite touch him. Teeth over lower lip, she shakes her head.

"Oh, Mr. Brill." Now she touches his face ever so lightly. "Poor Mr. Brill," she says, purses her lips, turns and is gone, down the short hallway, around a corner toward the open front door. Disappears.

There is no perfume. None at all. Soap smell on lightly freckled skin.

Even in dreaming, it would never have occurred to this big, rumpled, sandy-colored, red-faced lawyer to think of himself as *poor Mr. Brill* for Christ's sake.

He shook it off. He decided that his irritation with Canaday had nothing to do with the girl, but was connected with the nature of the meeting.

It was a real estate closing, a routine exchange of a small farm—160 acres, no longer economic—for some money. Brill's clients, country people in Sunday clothes, wouldn't have minded waiting. They were used to it. They were the sellers, feeling as if they ought to be pleased. And soon there'd be another real estate closing, when their dough went into some wretched city property, and another farming family onto the city's day-labor welfare rolls. He was sorry for the kids, and sorry that the kids themselves would most likely be pleased.

It was going to be hard to be genial.

Who the hell were Pete Canaday and his rich man Trump to delay the beginning of this all-American process of deterioration, with its neatly spaced paychecks along the way for the lawyer, the doctor, and the undertaker?

Moreover it was not Trump; not a friend of Trump's especially; a mere imitation Trump, of whom there were several locally, whose representatives were buying the little farm. Imitators of Robert E. Lee Trump, drove Cadillacs, liked to appear at the River Club unshaven, and bought up farms for tax reasons. Trump, who owned ten or twelve farms by now, in different blocks, was an imitator, too.

He imitated what he thought Texas millionaires were like. Did Texas millionaires imitate what they thought God was like, a shrewd, smelly Little Man, trading for new power and glory every spring from General Motors?

2.

The meeting done, sale closed, Bob Brill shook hands all around and started back for his office, fairly pleased with himself and having forgotten the dream with the girl in it.

He had, on behalf of his clients and as smoothly as if it had really been agreed to months before, invented a timber and mineral rights exclusion and insisted it be included. There's oil around here.

Tommy Rebranch, his partner, was waiting by Brill's office door.

"Well," Tommy said. "How did Chick Taylor handle himself?" Young Taylor was a new member of the Rosetta bar in whom Tommy took a benevolent interest, having studied under Taylor's father in law school. "Does he make a good impression?"

"I shoved it up his tizzy," Brill said. "Real good."

"Hey, wait." Brill had started past. "You know who's in your office waiting?"

"Pete Canaday."

"Is he bringing Bob Lee Trump back to us?"

Long ago, when the partnership'd been new, Trump's affairs had paid the secretary and bought the groceries. There wasn't any rent; the brick building where Brill's father and grandfather had practiced law and managed farms before him was Brill's by inheritance.

"Trump? Coming back? Not to me he isn't," Brill said.

"Come on, Bob."

"You can have the sonofabitch if you want him."

"Take it easy on Canaday," Tommy said. "You don't always have to ride him, do you?"

"I wouldn't ride him if I had to walk the rest of my life," Brill said.

"You been drinking?" Tommy asked.

3.

"Canaday. What's on your mind?"

"Well, first." Canaday got up, smiling. He was young, tanned, light brunet, sincere-looking, athletic. He had a girlish mouth, a boyish grin, a manly handshake, and a womanly giggle. Brill always saw a headline when he looked at Pete Canaday, from a Sunday sports section, ten years earlier: "CANADAY'S MY QUARTERBACK," SAYS TEXAS COACH. The boy'd been exceptional in high school, got a big football scholarship, was a sophomore starter, and had bad luck with his knees. He was a first-rate golfer, so Brill heard. Brill didn't play the game.

Now Canaday was Robert E. Lee Trump's quarterback: "First, I've got a check for you."

"Yeah, that does come first."

"Five hundred dollars," Canaday said, handing Brill the check with something like a bow. "For services rendered, Rob Lee said to tell you. His mistake, Counselor, and many thanks."

Brill looked at the check. "Haven't you guys ever heard of interest," he said. "This thing been running six years."

"Think of it as having been in escrow for you," Canaday said smoothly.

"Sure. That's why I wrote it off my tax one year as a bad debt."

"I bring you Rob Lee's apology. He's been trying to tell you for six years: it's a beautiful house, he's grateful, sorry he lost his temper—but you wouldn't let him."

Brill shrugged. Six years before, when $500 meant quite a little more, Trump had still been Brill's client and had built an elaborate house. Brill had found a young Quaker architect in Chicago to design it, excited about the man's vision· Brill had once studied architecture himself, and became much too committed to the project. Had spent a couple of months, 125 hours in round figures, working at the site, supervising construction, because right after the plans were drawn, the Quaker architect had been jailed as a conscientious objector to the draft and refuser of alternate service.

So Brill had given Trump a bill for 125 hours at carpenter's wages, four dollars an hour, which Trump refused to pay. ("Who authorized you to do all that? Part of your job anyway, ain't it? Everybody's trying to take me. You did it 'cause your friend got hisself in jail, where he belongs . . ." Level-headed, temperate Brill told the man to get the hell out of his office.

(The only other result was that a couple of days later, one of the principals in a law firm as old as the Brill office phoned, a dignified older friend, to ask young Bob for a final bill for his legal services to Trump and suggested they work out a settlement on the building account. ". . . along the lines of fifty percent, Bob. I don't think I'd have any trouble getting him to go for that."

(Sensible, respectful young Bob replied, "I don't think you'd have any trouble getting him to go for his zipper either, if he had to piss real bad," and hung up.

(Brill had been appointed by a Republican governor as one Democratic member of a conservation study commission, on that older lawyer's recommendation. Brill was not reappointed when the commission was renewed.

(And Trump changed lawyers once a year.)

Brill calculated the interest. "Four percent was the bank rate then. I'm going to compound it annually . . ."

"Take it easy on us," Canaday said. "Let's play rules."

"What do you want me to do? Seven and a half percent, semi-annual? I'm giving you a break." He worked his calculating machine, something he enjoyed. "Yeah. One hundred and eight dollars and thirty-three cents."

Canaday hesitated, grinned, got out his checkbook, and began to write. "I wouldn't dare try this on Rob Lee. I'll pay it myself."

"Your ass must really be on the line," Brill said, sympathetic for the first time. "What's the problem?"

"We were coming in from dove hunting," Canaday said, signing the check, handing it over. "There goes my portable tape recorder."

"Thanks. How many doves over the limit, Pete?"

"The man thinks I should have been watching."

"How many?" The limit was twelve doves a day, but Canaday would have let Trump shoot his. They could legally have had twenty-four.

"Close to two hundred birds," Canaday said. "One seventy-nine to be exact."

Brill, disliking in himself the professional impulse to meet any man's anxiety with soothing words, said, more harshly than he meant to, "What the hell were you going to do? Feed them to the cat?"

Canaday laughed, shrill and placating: "Here's what I figured, Bob," he said. "There are three families living on Rob Lee's farms. They've got six hunting licenses among them. Rob Lee's and mine make eight."

"I always thought eight times twelve was ninety-six, but I can check that on the calculator."

Canaday laughed louder. The more you crowded him, the more he took it as a joke. "Sure, Counselor. Now, suppose we'd taken two days to get those doves. We could have possession limits, double the daily limits. That's one hundred and ninety-two."

"What are you waiting for?" Brill said. "Go shoot thirteen more doves." Laughter. "Okay. Who picked you up?"

"Bernie."

"Bernie Johnson wouldn't apologize and let Mr. Rob Lee Trump, sir, pass on when you did that arithmetic for him?"

"There was a federal warden riding with him."

Unprofessional Brill laughed, laughed hard; couldn't help it. "God damn, Pete," he said. "Oh God damn. What'd you tell the federal man?"

"I, well, tried to say all the birds but twelve were mine."

"You did?"

"They'd been following us. The bastards were sitting up on Daniels' ridge at noon, watching us. They watched Rob Lee shoot thirty-one doves all by himself over a rye field."

"Where were you?"

"There. Handling the dog. I hadn't even taken my gun out of the car, and they knew it."

"Well," Brill shook his head. "What do you need me for, Pete? You've got lawyers . . ."

"Wait," Canaday said. "We've had police court and posted bond. Two thousand bucks. Would that cover the fine?"

"The judge generally likes to get about ten dollars a bird."

"Rob Lee says forfeit the bond and forget it."

"He'd be a fugitive."

"If you could show up in court, plead him guilty, and pay up?"

"I'm not Trump's lawyer, Pete."

Canaday's mouth quivered, and Brill added: "Ask Tommy, if you want. He'll be delighted." He imagined Tommy sitting alertly in his room on the other side of the building, waiting to be called on.

"Rob Lee wants you."

Brill shook his head.

"He thinks maybe . . . once the federal boys are satisfied, you could work things out to get his license back."

"I doubt if it can be done," Brill said. "But Tommy can try."

"He doesn't know the people you know."

Again Brill shook his head. "Neither do I," he said. "There aren't any such people."

"There's got to be a way."

"Ten of them. All illegal. You guys can figure them out."

"What's the best, Bob? I know it doesn't sound important, but it is to me."

"Trump's got a St. Louis office. Make him a Missouri resident, and buy him an out-of-state license. Twenty dollars and fifty cents."

"Would that be legal?"

"No, but it'd be confusing. I think Bernie Johnson would agree to be confused."

"Hey," Canaday said. "Hey, sure. That's a wonderful idea."

"Tommy's full of wonderful ideas," Brill said. "Go talk to him, will you? I assume you can keep it out of the paper."

"Sure." Canaday got up, smiling his first genuine smile of the afternoon. Trump had bought the local daily several years before.

"Springfield? Chicago?"

Canaday winked, and Brill realized he was being naïve. The wire service stringer, and state news man for Springfield and Chicago, was also the editor of Trump's Rosetta *Herald*, the same Herbie Stoner who had, years before, interviewed Brill when he caught his record fish; and later, when he made his flight to Yucatan; and still came around, now and then, when instructed to.

"I'll go see Tommy," Canaday said. "If you insist. But you send us a bill, Counselor, you hear? Consultation and referral fee."

Brill stared at him. Didn't anybody ever listen to what anybody else said? "God, Canaday, you depress me," he said.

"The independent, uncorruptible counselor." Canaday was feeling much better. "You're an inspiration to youth, Bob. A little big in the gut, but inspiring. Been drinking on a little weight lately?"

Bob Brill smiled, picked up a legal pad on which he'd made some notes for a political breaking-and-entering case; kids protesting at the University. He connected a dictating machine, to write a letter from the notes.

"Okay, Pete," he said. He liked Canaday feisty a good deal better than he liked Canaday sucking.

"We'll have to send you a present," said Canaday, on his way.

4.

"Who in the hell was she?"

"She didn't tell you?" Martin smiled. Most afternoons, on his way home from his office at the Riverside Theater, which is farther from the river than his Northern Theater, which is a bit south of the Riverside, Martin stopped at Brill's office. Sometimes they went off together for a drink. Sometimes, as today, they finished whatever coffee was left in the secretaries' electric percolator.

Brill had decided to dry himself out.

"Her name's Gabby Light," Martin said. "I brought you a tape of her singing."

"She ain't the finest in the land," Brill said. "Graduate student?"

"Yes."

"Uncle Martin's new toy?"

"I'm not sure I'd know where to wind up one like that," Martin said. "Not that I wouldn't be willing to learn."

"She's too tall for you."

Martin smiled.

"Wouldn't you say?"

"When we measure girls," Martin said, "we leave off the head and legs. I don't see why she wouldn't work all right from bump to collarbone."

Brill said: "Where'd you get her?"

"Her father sent her to me."

"Nice."

"He's a foreign film distributor in Baltimore. I really saw her only once before today, when she came into my office and said she needed a lawyer."

"She didn't say why?"

"No, but she asked if I knew you and what you were like."

"Why not a U-City lawyer, I wonder?"

Martin shrugged. "We got to the outside door of your building. I was ready to bring her in and introduce her, and suddenly she stopped me. 'I'll just go in by myself now.' Then what happened, if ethics don't prevent your saying?"

Brill said: "Martin, there's a remarkable maneuver wild ducks make. A duck'll be coasting in confidently toward your decoys. Suddenly he sees something wrong, the sun off your forehead, maybe a red shell casing on the ground. And the bird stops. Just like that, in mid-air. It's called flaring. Its wings start going, it seems to stretch out and stand back, still out of range, and then, boy, it leaves. It was drifting in at fifteen miles an hour, about to be an easy shot, and in that instant it changes gear and direction and streaks off at fifty-five. That's what your friend Miss Light did. Flared on me like a duck."

"Mrs. Light," Martin said. "Judging by the ring finger."

"Didn't overlook a thing."

"She'll be back."

"What makes you think so?"

"She's a fan," Martin said. "When she asked me about you, she got all pleased and warm. Said not to tell you, which means I'm supposed to tell you, that she and another girl, when they heard you were in U City for some reason or other, used to follow you around."

"Sure they did," Brill said. "Happens all the time. Sometimes builds up to forty, fifty girls. Terrible nuisance."

After that the two men discussed the illness of Charlie Dean, the county treasurer, who was also Democratic party secretary.

Martin said Charlie had resigned, and they discussed who ought to have the party office. They did not say it specifically, perhaps because it was one of those matters which, while obvious, is not clear-cut, that this was one of the times when they would have to decide whether to deal with or oppose Train Pacek, the trucking man.

Train had the county voters pretty well tied up, in the smaller communities and the poorer city precincts. Martin could deliver that part of the Rosetta and U-City business community which didn't vote Republican, and Martin could raise money in it. Brill knew the University faculty, had some following among the students, and some among the farmers.

Train was popular with the courthouse office-holders they helped elect. Brill was not, because he turned up now and then as attorney for some student or indigent, and even more often in opposition to some piece of rezoning that would be good business for everyone. Martin was distrusted because he was close to Brill and had so flawless a reputation for scrupulous dealing that there obviously must be something wrong, somewhere.

The two boat rockers now agreed that the new party secretary should be a woman, from Rosetta rather than U City, and that Train could be allowed to designate her—it was unpaid work but carried some perquisites, like poll-watching and registering voters, which brought in occasional money.

"Unless," Martin said, "you think Pat might want it?"

It was not a serious suggestion, only a delicate way for Martin to ask how things were at home.

Brill shook his head.

"Be something for her to do."

"She doesn't want anything to do, as long as there's sherry on the shelf, and the library doesn't run out of books."

"I suppose."

They had this conversation from time to time, and Brill ended it as he often did with a remark which seemed just to him, though the context had long been forgotten: "It's not Pat's fault I'm a shit, Martin. More like my fault she's a drunk, I imagine." The phone rang.

Martin left.

The phone call was to remind Mr. Brill of a meeting of the county zoning commission. Brill had seen the agenda and felt no need to attend. He said he wouldn't be able to make that.

Tommy Rebranch came in to say thanks for the chance to do Trump's legal work. Partnership was not an accurate word for the relationship between the two lawyers, any more than the plaque on the building, THE BRILL LAW OFFICE, EST. 1848, was accurate. If Lambert Brill, born in New Hampshire in 1816 was admitted to the Illinois bar in the same year as Abraham Lincoln, a local legend which Brill doubted since Lambert had been seven years Lincoln's junior, Lambert's practice of law in Rosetta could have started in 1848—but in an office behind a store or in the parlor of a house. The brick building hadn't been built until one of Lambert's sons, the first Felix and Brill's great-grandfather, came back from the Civil War.

This being the situation, and Tommy not related to the family, there'd been no question of his becoming a member of the firm; but there'd been room in the building. Tommy offered to pay some rent, share the overhead; at that time they'd been friends.

Brill said, about Trump's legal work, that he'd advise Tommy to establish his fees in writing, and collect them in advance.

Tommy said, "Oh, let's grow up."

And Nadine, Brill's secretary, brought in a fifth of Jack Daniel's Black Label Whiskey in a sack from the liquor store, accompained by a pamphlet called *The Drinking Man's Diet,* inscribed to Brill by Pete Canaday.

"Here's an example for you," Brill said. "The big payoff for a half hour of unethical advice: an eight-dollar bottle of whiskey."

"I suppose you aren't going to drink it," Tommy said. "I suppose you're going to pour it down the sink."

"No." Who the hell said it was time to dry out? Mr. Daniels' pushed the plunger and saliva spurted into Brill's mouth as he worked the top off and caught the sweet-sour smell. "I don't think I will. Here, have a pull."

"No thanks."

"You must be entitled to half this fee, or thirty percent anyway."

Tommy shook his head. "I'm going to the Co-op meeting tonight," he said. "I've got to check the proxies. I assume I'm incoming chairman."

"That'll be pretty gay," said Brill, who had served a couple of terms as chairman himself; he raised his bottle to the Farmer's Cooperative board of trustee's incoming chairman, filled his mouth with whiskey, set the bottle down and rinsed the liquor through his teeth, swallowing slowly. "Yeah," he yelled when it settled. "Hey, I thought you and Martha were having a party tonight?"

"She can start without me. I can't miss the meeting."

"You work too much," Brill said.

"You drink too much," said Tommy Rebranch, doing his duty.

5.

As long as Tommy stayed, Brill drank from his bottle; the moment Tommy left, Brill got out a glass and mixed a drink with cold tap water.

Then he set himself slowly to reread a puzzling letter from his son Cal:

> . . . a kind of unreality about being in the Medics. I've applied for transfer, and even though I haven't had much weapons training, I think it will come through . . . Helicopters are amazing. Everyone here loves helicopters . . .

Brill didn't get it. He didn't know what was happening to his only son, and it was like not knowing what was happening to himself. In one of those late-night memorandums once, he could now remember writing about a time when Trinket was a baby and Cal four years old. Cal had come along and got in bed with him and Pat one morning, and he had thought: I love that girl baby in a particular way, but this boy—I look at his foot, sticking out through a big hole in the foot-part of his pajamas, and it's my foot; I look at his hand and it's my hand. Flesh of my flesh means the male child; the girl child is loved differently.

". . . Everyone here loves helicopters . . ."

Brill wrote on the bottom of the letter:

My own life has reached a kind of stasis, often pleasant, sometimes not, where I do a little good, a little bad, and a lot of indifferent. Grab the torch, boy; my arm's getting tired . . .

The phone rang, and he put the letter away. He thought of not answering the phone, for it was after hours, but when it rang again, he picked it up, working away at his second mixed drink now, and talked with Matt Palmer, a fisheries biologist who worked for the state.

Matt said there was evidence now that a small dairy in Wisconsin had polluted an Illinois stream, causing a major fish kill; could Brill help out in preparing what was going to be a ridiculously complicated damage suit?

Brill said, "I can't think about it tonight, Matt. I'm a little bit polluted myself," and heard someone walking lightly down the hall.

There was a knock on the door, and he said: "Come in," confidently expecting the floating girl. "Come in, Mrs. Light."

And in she came.

"Hello, Mr. Brill."

"Hello."

"Martin Habib said I should see you."

"Martin said I should see you," Brill said, and grinned. He was feeling pretty high already.

She sat. "I want a divorce," she said.

He kept grinning. "That's an idea. Maybe I should get one of those myself."

She looked startled. Then she said slowly, "You're Robert Brill, the lawyer."

He nodded.

"My mistake." She stood up. She pointed to the bottle. "Have a nice time," she said.

"Okay."

She was really quite nice to look at, her dress filmy under the wine-colored topcoat; pretty legs. Wouldn't a girl with legs like that want to have a drink with him?

"You don't do divorces, Mr. Brill?"

"Not after five o'clock," Brill said, raising the bottle. "Here."

It offended her. "God damn you people," she said, turning away. "Go to hell, Mr. Brill."

But when she reached the hall he heard her sobbing, and he thought: If I'd had one drink more or one drink less, I'd call her back.

It's dumb to misunderstand people willfully, assume about people.

I call her back. Felix is here. "Hey, Mrs. Light, here's my cousin

Felix. He does divorces after five o'clock. He's on the night divorce shift here . . ."

My mother looked more Indian than she did Spanish. Dark olive skin, and enormous, secret, brown eyes. What stories did she tell me, what songs in Spanish sang?

Flying.

"The Peruvians," Gary Pederson said, "are proud, weary, elegant people. Circumspect and kind, with manners but no force.

"If there is energy in Peru, it doesn't come from Lima. Lima has lived and died too many times."

What was Gary doing here? ("I saw the light. Am I intruding? Thanks, a very light one please.")

"Lima died a pre-Inca death, and the death of a great Inca city. Then it was the seat of the vice-regency and died again . . . now it's a museum and a memory and a slum . . . not like Mexico, where the feeling of energy is rising again . . .

"More like Damascus, I imagine. Or Baghdad . . . you know? A museum, a memory, a slum . . ."

"Or New York?" Brill suggested, which irritated Pederson, who seemed to feel he'd been misunderstood.

Gary demurred. Gary was a hotshot demurrer. Hotshot left.

"I know what I mean," said Boozy Brill to his beauty bottle. "It's a tragic goddamn city."

Rose up, went out of his office to the front door of the building, and shouted down the empty street after Pederson: "The only thing I like in New York is the goddamn pigeons."

6

Almost steady in the doorway, bottle in his hand, Brill considered with due care the fact that Martha and Tommy Rebranch were having a party, to which he was neither invited nor uninvited.

Though Tommy'd mentioned it, he'd pretty likely assumed Brill wouldn't come. But there'd been a time when the Brills and the Rebranches saw one another a lot and Brill, reaching back for that time, told himself that Tommy was a good old boy after all and ought to have a him a good dog.

Tommy was just now learning to bird-hunt, and very much wanted a pup from Brill's old setter bitch, Nevada.

Brill'd been evading Tommy's hints on the matter; Brill never sold dogs. Giving them was the only way to control what sort of life and use a pup might have.

There were two left from Nevada's litter, now ten weeks old. The big female which was going to look just like Nevada Brill had decided to keep, and the handsome little male he'd just liked too well to give away so far. Okay. For Tommy.

He rinsed a little whiskey through his teeth, reached back into the entryway and grabbed his big Stetson highroller hat off the rack. He hadn't worn or thought about it for weeks, but now he put it on, took a running start out the door, and jumped to the ground, clearing a flight of five wooden steps put there for the convenience of the lame, the halt, and the sober.

He got into his car, a Buick with power windows, lowered them all, turned on the radio and drove home singing loudly the words of

"Stardust" to a rock and roll tune, laughing and drowning out the singer.

The lights were on in the hall, the kitchen, and Trinket's room, reminding Brill that he'd forgotten about eating. He decided to sneak past Trinket, and if she caught him say he'd had a sandwich. He left the bottle in the car, and went tiptoeing into the kitchen to look for a box to put the puppy in.

Caught. Trinket was wearing pajams, and had her glasses on.

"Been reading?"

"What are you looking for, Daddy?"

"Box for the pup." He was careful to get the words out clearly. "Going to give that boy pup to old Tommy Rebranch."

"There's a nice big box in the cellar," Trinket said. "Wait, I'll get it." And, back in less time than it takes to hide a vodka bottle: "Aren't we keeping him?"

"I thought we'd keep the girl pup," Brill said.

"But he's so sweet. Can't we keep them both?"

"I'm not professional enough to train two dogs at once, Trinket," Brill said. He felt she was watching him very closely. He knelt on the floor by the box, took out his penknife, and concentrated on cutting neat, diamond-shaped air holes in the cardboard. Ever see a five-sided diamond? "Hey. We got some old towels?"

And when she came back with them: "Let's say the girl pup is your dog. Would you like that?"

"Are you going to train her to hunt?"

"Sure."

"I wouldn't ever take her hunting."

"I'd ask to borrow her from you."

Together they went out to the summer kennel to get the male. Trinket said it was chilly, and time her dog and its mother were allowed to sleep indoors, and could she name it Harriet? Brill said that silly girls in pajamas felt the cold air more keenly than furry dogs and that Harriet was a nice name.

Pup in box, box on front seat of car, Brill looked quickly and saw that the bottle was out of Trinket's sight; he'd got by the father-watch. He kissed her on top of the shiny head, so she wouldn't smell the booze now at the last moment, and told her to go on to bed now.

"Are you going to drink a whole lot tonight, Daddy?" Trinket asked.

Driving away, furious with himself for having lost a round with a fifteen-year-old, Brill decided he wouldn't. For him to come back soon, sober, before she turned her lights out, would mean a good night's sleep for Trinket, already trying to learn to live with the idea that her mother was alcoholic.

Brill spent the better part of the next hour parked three blocks from home, deciding on all this, playing with the pup in the box, and finishing his ill-got fifth of Daniels.

"Oh, huh," he said. "Okay then. Well, okay, Puppy Rebranch, you either turn my finger loose or bite it off all the way so I can have my hand free to drive."

His voice sounded thick to him.

There were a lot of cars parked along the street in front of Martha and Tommy's new split-level. He recognized a couple: Doc Barragon's station wagon, the Mustang of young Chick Taylor up whose newly-admitted tizzy he had lately stuffed the mineral-rights exclusion clause.

"Going to the ranch-style," Brill told the dog. "Where's our hat?"

Put the Stetson highroller back on, closed the top of the carton, and hauled the big box out, hearing the puppy's claws slide against the side, trying to steady the thing and keep it level. Went up to the door, set the box down, pushed the front door open, picked the box up, and marched in.

"Howdy, strangers," he yelled, in an atrocious cowboy twang. Twenty-two people stopped talking and looked at him. "I got some livestock for this ranch-style."

"Bob."

"Come on here, Martha," Brill called, as Tommy's wife, a thin, good-looking, rather insecure woman stood and took the first step toward him. "Come on and sign for this live pig."

"Bob!" Back then, toward the end of the friendly time, Bob Brill and Martha Rebranch had been on the edge of an affair. He'd stepped back. Now, when they met, it was as if Martha was caught forever in the moment of hesitation over whether she could risk reaching out for him, to pull him back and over that edge with her.

He carried the box toward her. Everyone was watching, so he made the announcement general. "I've been out to the farm, and you never saw cuter piglets," he said. "I just thought, I'll take a nice sow piglet in for Martha and Tommy, so they can get started ranching in their ranch house."

A couple of women laughed nervously. Martha was one, and Tommy said:

"Hey, Bob."

Pete Canaday said, "A real live pig, Counselor?" Pete had gone broke trying to run a man's store, before he got the job with Trump. This would be his first visit to the Rebranches, Brill guessed; no matter how little an hour may shine, you can always improve it some. . . .

"It isn't really?" a woman said.

A man from the Farmers and Merchants Bank, of which Brill was a director, said:

"Let's see her, Bob. What's she weigh?"

A man from the other bank, the Rosetta State, who didn't like Brill, tried gruffly to resume a conversation.

"Bob." Martha reached him. "It isn't really a pig?"

"Open it up. Open it up. Got some slops in the kitchen?"

"Here's your slops," Tommy Rebranch said, putting a drink in Bob's hand. Tommy guessed what it was, of course; Tommy was pleased. "Go ahead, Mart. Open the box."

Inside the puppy gave a short whine, Martha gave a nervous cry, a woman told another that the pig had squealed, and the other cried:

"Don't let it run out, Martha."

Brill was considered capable of anything by this group.

Martha undid the box, biting her lip, pulled her hand away quickly, then smiled when she saw what was inside, lifted out the pup and held it to her bosom prettily, cheek against its cheek. Cheers, squeals, house-breaking jokes. Namedropping: the Farmers and Merchants banker guessed it must be one of old Nevada's pups.

"Thanks, Bob," Tommy said. "I really appreciate it."

"Tommy." Brill sipped. "I can taste the water in here, and I can see the ice. Was there supposed to be something else?"

He stayed there half an hour. He was the only man at the party without a tie on.

He kept his hat on his head and tried to get things going a little, get people on their feet and music playing, flirtation talk instead of business and gossip; and suddenly, when the half hour was up, realized that it was lonely and unwelcome work. He patted Tommy's shoulder, squeezed Martha's hand, winked at the Farmer and Merchant in place of crossing the room to talk to him, and left the polite, sitdown party still holding his second glass, half full.

Stood on the lawn, looked at house. Settling back down now, free of Brillious obstreporations. Imagined voices: Martha's, saying, "Anyway, he meant to be sweet." Maybe Tommy's, "God, yes. But I'm worried about him." And the man from the Rosetta State Bank, maybe to Canaday: "Sonofabitch is tearing tonight. I hope no one gets hurt."

Brill shook his head. "What the hell is it they say?" he asked the house, container for the things contained. "Louder music, stronger wine, fuckheads . . ." He laughed, and drank, and then suddenly, quietly, tenderly: "Fuckheads. Poor damn neckties."

Finished the drink he had made himself, whiskey and ice, no water, set the glass down on the Rebranch lawn, plunged for his car, headed it for the River Club, changed his mind, drove by the White Way Tavern and on to Porter's Go-Go Lounge.

2.

Porter's is our lower middle class drink, dance, fight, and izza-pizza place. A business or professional man doesn't go there at all unless he wants to risk, for instance, taking a young secretary someplace for a drink. Honey, you better assume it's going to be a quick one, not an evening of it, because what your john is calculating is being recognized by someone who doesn't count, but you won't know that it's the mailman or the service station attendant saying, "Hi, there," so john's answered your unspoken point—that he's ashamed to be seen with you—and ducked it at the same time. Even so, he's not going to get involved in the crowd long enough so that it really registers—unless, of course, you've got the man going with the warm breath in the hairy ear and the warm hand on the glen plaid knee and the dizzy eyes and the addled voice till his judgment's turned to juice, throbbing and pressing in his vesicles.

You're that good, maybe he'll divorce his wife and marry you, and after that he'll take you not to Porter's but the White Way. He'll be a little older than the guys; they'll be the young ones, coming up in his part of our Rosetta world. Their wives will be the age you are, and either will or won't accept you, careful little bitches behind the friendly giggles. Bachelors hang at the White Way, Pete Canaday and his crowd. If you're going to dork around any after marriage, your first man, the one who gets what we call the marry-cherry, will probably be someone you meet at the White Way.

It better not be anyone you met at Porter's Go-Go Lounge, pretty.

After you've been married for a while, your trick will take you, as he does his present wife, to the River Club, if there's an occasion for having a drink out.

There are other taverns, bars, and clubs—forty-four of them, or one-and-a-half per thousand of our shuffling, guzzling, understimulated population.

3.

Brill wasn't looking for anything in particular at Porter's Go-Go, except another drink, some way to keep the evening going. At the River

Club would have been the same kind of neckties he'd left at Mart and Tommy's. At the White Way, some younger guy'd be apt to want to jockey with him. At Porter's he ordered a double whiskey at the bar.

Then he looked around for someone he knew to sit with, and was called over to join a table of five, presided over by M. Henry (Hankus) Harding, an auctioneer.

Brill ought certainly to have known better than to join an auctioneer on that particular evening, when sales of small farms were unhappily on his mind. On the other hand, he and Hankus Harding had never had any trouble before.

With Hankus were his partner, Blue Gesnecke (pronounce all three syllables), and a muscular country kid who worked for them, holding up items to be sold or circulating in the crowd, keeping the bidding orderly. There were also Blue Gesnecke's wife, Charlotte, and a girl who probably went home with M. Hankus, but sat in public with the kid.

Hankus said they were tired but celebrating; they'd had two sales today, both big ones. One starting at ten, the next at two thirty, and named the farms.

"Early for sales, isn't it?" Brill said. "When the corn's not picked?"

"Not an ear on either place," Blue said. "Both of them had their beans harvested, want to sell good tractors to the guys do have corn."

"Worked okay," Hankus said. "We got more for that big John Deere than you'd have asked on a secondhand lot."

"Hell of a lot more," said Blue.

"Sales come earlier ever year." Hankus knocked off a shot, sipped his beer chaser. "If you're going to quit farming and want to have a good sale, you better have it quick as you can, before cold weather. Hell, Bob, we been booked Christmas to November since last spring."

"Can't get over that John Deere tractor," Blue said. "Fifty-one hundred and fifty dollars, why hell. It couldn't have been a thousand dollars more than that new."

"I wasn't looking for more than thirty-two, thirty-three," Hankus said.

"Pretty near stopped there, didn't it?"

"See me clout that guy?" the kid asked suddenly.

"You did all right," Hankus told him.

"Of course, if a man wanted that particular tractor right now new, say to fall-plow with, he'd have to wait delivery awhile."

"That's the war in Vietnam," Hankus said, and Brill said:

"Clout what guy?"

"That Vietnam. Can't get good barbed-wire, machinery . . ."

Brill started to rise.

"There was a bidder started to squeal," Hankus said, soothing. Brill sat down again. "When the John Deere hit thirty-two and stuck there awhile. He was hollering I'd closed the bidding, that's all. See, just when I was gonna close it, I give the buy-bidder a look, see if she won't go up a little more . . ."

"You took a chance," Blue said.

"That's auctioneering."

"Clout what guy?" said Brill.

"Some farmer thought he'd got that big tractor bought cheap. I don't know the man, was it a Squiers, Blue? Once I got her moving, she climbed right up another thousand dollars." Hankus finished his beer, reached for the shot-glass in front of the girl, drank that, wiped his mouth, and challenged: "What do you care, Bob? It was just a farmer, wanted a big, dual, closed-cab tractor cheap. I don't blame him."

"I clouted him," the kid said. "Blue was coming over and the man was mad enough to try to go up and pull Hankus off the platform. So I swung short, my whole forearm right across the middle of his back, hard as I could, right across here, see? Where no one could see. He went forward and Blue had him, 'fore he really knew what happened."

"Oh, look, we made it all right with him, Bob," Blue said. "It took the grab and yell right out of the man. Yes, it was Squiers, Hankus. Donnie, farms over by Ingot. Showed him a four-row picker, it'll fit his old tractor fine, saved him a damn pile of money that way."

"Blue can talk to them," the kid said admiringly.

"And you can clout them," Brill said. "In the back."

"Hey, Bob," Hankus said. "I bid in a shotgun today I'll bet you'd like. Now listen. It's a beautiful old Damascus gun, I mean you wouldn't want to shoot it, 'cept with handloads, but it's the nicest piece of wood and decorating I've seen for a long time. Look here now, I bid it in at thirty-one dollars, and you can have it for just that."

"Now look, you shouldn't do that, Hankus," Blue said immediately. "Wait, wait, wait. There's gun collectors looking for those pieces, pay five and six times that and you know. That's what you bought it for, ain't it? Tell you what, let's get appraisal on it, 'fore you sell it to Bob, now. Be fair with me, now."

"Blue, I'm sorry," Hankus said. "Maybe I'm wrong and maybe I spoke too soon and maybe I'm not being fair with you, but damn it. By God. I did speak. I said it. And when I say a man can buy, he's got it bought if he still wants it."

They paused for Brill to say yes or no, and Brill said: "I'm talking to your clouter."

"What do you want with me, mister?" the kid said.

"How big are you, son?"

"Big enough."

"Now look here, Bob," said Blue. "This boy was just doing his job. He may not be too smart about it . . ."

"You this big?" Brill stood, six feet two and massive.

Hankus said to the kid: "Now, Mr. Brill's right, Sid. You can't expect to hit a man that way. That's not right. Now look here, Bob." Turning from Sid the Kid to Lawyer Brill. "If I thought he had that machine bought honest at thirty-two, here's what I'd do. I'd drive him that tractor over to his farm *now*, tonight, cold as it is, with the lights on, and pay the man who has it the difference out of my own pocket. You know I'd do that, Bob." Hankus hit the table. "And if you say I should, why Blue and I and this boy Sid will get right in that car and do it, and these ladies can sit here and eat the biggest pizza on the menu while we're gone."

Blue stood. "Will we take your car or mine, Hankus?"

Leaning into the table, on the balls of his feet, Brill said: "I asked your clouter how big he is?"

The kid stood, and Brill felt a joy at seeing that he probably came close in weight, ahead in muscle, though he might not have much reach. "This big, mister."

Hankus rose, pushing some money into Charlotte Gesnecke's hand. "Calm down here, Bob. I made you an offer . . ."

Jolly Blue said, "Fair, square and that's all she *had* to write." Blue accidentally had a pop bottle in his hand.

Brill said: "Farmers are my people."

A man at the next table, a farmer, rose and said: "What you got against farmers?"

The man with him rose and said: "That's Bob Brill."

Brill kept an eye on Blue's Coke bottle, and the kid said: "You keep pecking me, mister, you watch your ass."

Brill swung across the table and hit the boy hard, just in front of the ear. It was a wide, surprising blow; nobody thinks of a man with arms long enough to hit across a table. The kid went back into his chair, hard.

Brill ducked as he swung and caught Blue's bottle on his shoulder. It hurt.

Brill decked Blue, backhand.

Hankus, wiry, came up onto the table and jumped on Brill's back to bear him down.

Brill shrugged and Hankus spun off onto the floor.

Sid the Kid kicked the table at Brill; Brill caught it, and hurt his hand on the corner.

He laughed. "Come on," he yelled. "Farmers with me. Everybody else, watch your ass."

He backed away from Blue, rising again with his bottle, eyes like snake eyes, and backed right over kneeling Hankus, reprise of the oldest schoolyard trick. Brill went down, laughing; Sid the Kid tagged him as he fell.

When Brill got up again, the kid was facing him, no table between them, and swung. Caught Brill on the side of the jaw. Hurt.

"Okay, clouter," Brill yelled, seeing the two farmers, only ones in the place apparently, one holding the other back. Hell, they were the Reining brothers, Tom and Red.

Brill feinted another wild right hand and snapped in straight to the kid's gut with his left. Felt it go in and in and in, and the kid went back. Brill kicked the bottle out of Blue's hand, and himself caught a hard kick in the thigh from Hankus which spun him halfway round.

"Hey, Tom," he cried. "Hey Red."

Red Reining broke from his brother, decked a waiter who only happened to be standing in the way, and came bounding over, pushing away a man Brill recognized as a local concrete worker, sallow and strong.

Then Red was cracked over the head by another waiter, with a billy, and went to his knees; the waiter kept coming.

And here came the bartender, with a billy too. And Blue.

And Brill reached low, picked Blue right up off the floor, threw him into the waiter with the billy, and found himself confronting the bartender who looked tough.

The bartender circling, feinted with his short club, and Brill waited, to see if he could grab the thing. An arm came around the bartender's neck from behind. Red.

And a whoop, and here came Tom to help his brother, and Brill wrested the billy club away from the bartender and threw it somewhere where it made a nice crash.

And then the plumbers, carpenters, mechanics, masons, all the men with real right arms from incessant daily work with hammers, pipe wrenches, crescent wrenches, concrete hoes, were on them, and Brill realized that Hankus and Blue and the two women were hustling Sid the Kid out of there.

"Don't take the clouter," he yelled, and just then one of the good right arms caught him square across the mouth, and he went back from it, whack, into a rabbit punch, down to his knees again, hearing himself roar, lunged up and forward, butting his head into the nearest chest. Both hands working, several hands working into him, got a hard bang, waiter with the billy maybe, on his shoulder, leaped away, found himself in a cleared space for an instant, looking into the mild face of the waiter Red had decked who wasn't in the fight. Decked him again for good measure, and was borne down from behind, arms and legs pinned by half a dozen different men.

They turned him on his back, holding him, and the bartender was standing up there somewhere, saying, "You getting out of here, Mr. Brill? All right? Do I get the cops?"

"Okay," Brill said. "Okay. Tom and Red and me. Okay."

So the three found themselves on the street at midnight, sweat-soaked, shivering, and richly deserving a drink.

"Come on," Brill said.

At the White Way the Reining boys were uncomfortable, and Brill was unable to produce on his promise that he would fix them up with sweet, sweet stuff; the closest thing to sweet, sweet stuff at the White Way was Pete Canaday, stopping off for a nightcap on his way home from the Rebranch party.

Brill, hearing that the party was over, gave up on his secret intention of taking old Red and Tom over to meet some of those ladies there, wouldn't they have loved Red and Tom? Balked there, he tried to phone the Funny girls, but their phone didn't answer.

He asked the Reining boys if they wanted to go to the River Club, and they said no. They drove around then, looking either for Plain Jane, a whore whom Tom Reining said owed him some, or a trace of where Hankus and Blue might have taken the Clouter.

It seemed obvious to Brill that the auctioneer group would be glad for a chance to have a nice even fight, three to three.

Tom said he doubted that like hell.

While they were discussing this, Brill tried to park in front of a tavern where Plain Jane sometimes worked as a waitress; unfortunately the empty space had an invisible motorbike parked in it, and Brill sent the Yamaha sprawling. A college kid came out, aggrieved, and Brill wrote him a check for fifty dollars.

"I'm a goddamn menace," Brill said. "I'm sorry." He followed the college kid as far as the doorway to the bar, to look in, thinking it highly probable Mrs. Gabby Light, being from college too, would be sitting there waiting for something to happen.

She wasn't. However, it was necessary to go on in anyway, and have a beer, and assure the college boy with the dented Yamaha that he, Brill, knew himself to be the menace which in fact he was, and when he returned to his car, Tom and Red were gone.

At two thirty in the morning, Robert Brill phoned his friend Martin Habib from a five-booth farmer's tavern on the worst, or southeast, side of town. The place was called Hazel's, but there was no Hazel in charge there. Oscar was in charge, having bought Hazel out years before.

Since it was a weeknight, Brill was the only one left in the tavern and Oscar wanted to close up.

It took a number of rings to wake Martin, and when he answered Brill suggested reasonably that Martin get dressed, come to the tavern, and that from it they would go to Springfield where he, Brill, knew a couple of really nice girls who had an apartment, worked for the highway commission, and were always ready for a party.

Martin Habib took the position that, Springfield being several hours away, by the time they could reach it the two really nice girls would be getting up in the morning so that, whatever their disposition toward parties, they could hardly enjoy one and still hope to report for work to the highway commission that day.

Brill said he felt that girls getting up in the morning were fresh and dewy.

Oscar, the proprietor, said that Brill's friend's part of the conversation wasn't going to register very well if Brill couldn't hold onto the receiving part of the instrument, now dangling on its cord, and Brill assured Oscar that these particular girls in Springfield were always ready, consequently Martin Habib would be here soon.

Oscar said all right, but if Martin Habib didn't come right away he, Oscar, would take Mr. Brill home, okay?

Brill thanked him. Oscar began to clear his cash register. Brill went in the door of the men's room, found instead that it was the main door to the outside, kept walking steadily, got into his car, and drove away.

He went south out of town, in the direction opposite from Springfield. He turned west toward the river, got onto a gravel road, turned south again, stopped at some abandoned farm buildings, and walked among them.

He'd come here last when he was ten or eleven, he supposed, with two children named John and Joy whose family had been foreclosed. That day the family had borrowed a pickup truck from Bob Brill's father, their lawyer, and come to get what furniture was left in the house after the sheriff's auction. He thought of John, and especially of Joy, the three playing naughtily in the barn, motes of haydust in the sunlight, "Go on, let him," "He hasta kiss me," "You seen that in a movie," "I don't care. You want to Bob?" Yeah. Yes. Then, now, and forever Joy, tiny freckles like the motes of haydust on your pubic mound; clean, grassy smell; John laughing at my clumsiness; John afterward, companionable, taking a brother's turn; is that incest or young animals playing . . . ?

He saw by moonlight that what had been the roof of that barn, thirty years before, had fallen in. He picked up rocks and threw them up and into the remains of roof, wanting to hear it all fall down. He went back to the car to get a pistol to shoot the last window out, but entered the car instead, and drove on, closer to the river. Turned onto another gravel road, into a dirt one, at the end of which he stopped.

He got out, entered the woods, and walked two and a half miles through marsh and timber, without a track of any kind to follow and without the slightest hesitation, to a particular place on the edge of a body of shallow water called Captain's Slough.

A coon, hunting the edge for roosting shore birds, ran; that was the only sound. Robert Brill, an image in his head of wood duck-nesting boxes he'd put up nearby and which he meant to check in the morning, sat down to wait for dawn, and went to sleep.

Wood ducks wakened him, flying in from the river to feed. He watched them coast through the trees, wings cupped, and land on the water sixty yards away without a circle. He turned his head and saw a pair of blue herons close by, wading, waited till they waded away, not wanting to disturb them, and as he waited became aware that he was muddy, cold, and miserably thirsty.

Got up to his knees and a cloud of kildeer, feeding on the mud flat, went up trilling and scolding.

His mouth was dry, his throat full of choking sand, the joints on which his head turned rusty. Like an animal, he went on all fours to the edge of the slough and drank muddy water.

Huge drafts to slake himself, needing the stuff so bad he didn't taste it. Then he got up and moved along to a place where the water was a little clearer, scaring his herons, flushing the wood ducks, and cupped water in his hands and drank more slowly, storing moisture in his body for the walk back.

On the way back through the woods, he heard deer start twice but saw neither of them.

Saw a red fox on a deer trail. It was an old fox, with a thin coat.

Heard the crows wake, regular, forty-five minutes later than the ducks each day, as the sun came out and Brill stepped into an open place, let it warm him, stopped shivering, and watched the big birds wheel and fly out cawing toward their day of feeding and fighting.

The songbirds were up next, chickadees, titmouses, cardinals; then the resident woodpeckers—redhead, hairy, downy—why should flickers and sapsuckers and the big pileated woodpeckers be migratory and these others stay?

On a white oak stump he saw a goat's beard mushroom, an extraordinary branched mushroom the size of a cabbage head. He didn't pick it; it was way past its prime. There were some button mushrooms, late gold but in good shape, but he declined the offer of the woods; in five more months, or six, it would be spring, and morels would be out.

These woods had always been a place to find morels in.

He came to and paused at a particular red elm, around which he could always find, each spring, the earliest and scarcest of the three morel species, the little gray ones year after year since boyhood he had found them here, the first wild food.

The elm was his signpost tree, four feet through and rising like an enormous wineglass, visible above the other trees; sometimes he dreamed of it in the winter before he went to it in the spring.

It was dying now. The Dutch elm beetles had found it; Brill could tell, more or less, looking up, which branches in the crown had failed to leaf out. It was half gone. He put his hand against the trunk.

The Dutch in America weren't so bad. Sailed into the Hudson and found oysters in the clean sand of the estuary with their shells scrubbed white by the fresh to salt water changes, a foot and a half across. A single oyster had enough meat in it to feed a half a dozen men a magnificent meal. There were roe shad running in the river, Atlantic salmon and, a little farther out, lobsters so thickly populated they were harvested at low tide out of the seaweed.

No, the Dutchmen weren't so bad: built a city which would be a long time killing the river, and a century or two before that happened the Dutch were back in Europe, tulip-breeding, rolling good cigars with Indonesian tobacco; bided their time, owing the continent which had been more hospitable to rival colonizers, a little something, wooden shoes, silver skates, wham. They gave it to us good. Dutch elm disease; total, irreversible as the Asiatic fungus sent to curse our chestnuts earlier in the century.

Maybe there were trees that could resist the Dutch disease? Not Brill's particular old red elm, the mushroom elm, in the secluded woods. Caught now.

"That's all right, boy," said Brill, stupidly. Patting the trunk. "It's all right."

He reached the car, stiff and thick of tongue, and drove carefully back to the deserted farmstead he had stopped at three or four hours before. He stopped again, got the old pump in the yard working, drank clear water from his hands, and felt quite drunk again. That being so, it seemed logical to finish the inch or so of whiskey still left in his bottle before he started on the road for home.

Back on the highway, going rather slowly, for he really felt almost ill from whiskey, he saw a rabbit run in front of the car, jabbed the brake more violently than he intended to, skewed, one wheel locking, and felt the car careen off the edge of the pavement, cross the shoulder, and slide into an eight-foot ditch. Passed, or was knocked, out. Cold.

The state patrol car which stopped a few minutes later had been watching for him, Brill eventually learned, since a telephoned complaint much earlier in the morning from the college boy whose motorbike Brill had damaged.

But he really didn't know who it was at first, when the trooper slid down the bank, opened the door, and started to lift him out.

With which, it is recorded in the police court testimony of Trooper Spinner, Robert Brill said:

"Shit, Roy, I'm all right. Let's get the man out of the truck there, before it blows."

Laughed uproariously when told no other vehicle was involved, scrambled enthusiastically up the bank without assistance, stopped when he saw a rabbit carcass on the road. Threw up, on his own and Officer Spinner's shoes.

The rabbit had been struck and killed several days before, and the carcass was dry.

At the Rosetta police station, to which Brill was driven in the highway patrol car, Brill felt reasonably sober but conceded he was drunk, was processed accordingly, and posted bail. Since he was known, he was allowed to do this by check and told to be there for police court next day at ten o'clock, after which Trooper Spinner drove him home.

4.

Trinket Brill was in the kitchen when her father came in, starting on her breakfast, school books stacked beside her plate.

She said: "Daddy! Where have you been?"

"A couple of, couple of places, Trink. Uh, Captain's Slough was where I slept. Do you remember it?"

"You slept out there?"

"Sort of camping out." Brill found, gratefully, cold coffee in a pot and turned on heat under it.

"In your business suit. Daddy, really."

"Really what, Trinket? What are you eating?"

"Sugar-frosted cornflakes."

"Are they good?"

"Yes. You ought to have some, too."

"All right."

"Did you take the pup to Mr. Rebranch?"

"Yes. Tommy loved him."

"Harriet slept on my bed. But I got up twice and took her out."

"Good girl."

"That's how I knew you weren't home. Here." She set an enormous bowl of cornflakes in front of him, poured a pint of milk over them, and served him coffee. "Eat those, Daddy. I mean, your car wasn't here."

He had to tell her: "It still isn't, Trinket. It's in a ditch, about eight miles south of town."

"You had an accident."

"Yes. Not a very bad one, but I'd had too much to drink. And the police came, so I'll lose my driver's license for a while."

She was going to cry. He got up and put his arm around her. "I deserve it, Trink," he said. "Now don't cry for me."

The tears came, stopped, and she said: "How, how will you get to work?"

"The same way you'll get to school," Brill said. "Tough walking in the cold weather, and I'm sorry."

"I don't mind."

"I know. Trinket, I know what we'll do. Now listen." He sat her down and grinned at her. "Let's get Big Mac and Goldie in from the farm." Those were the horses; he could easily fence off enough lawn, around the fruit trees, to keep them on and there were stalls and mangers in the shed. "Trinket, I can ride to work. And afternoons, when you want, we'll school the horses if the weather's nice."

"Can we build a jump?"

"If I don't have to jump it."

"Will you really ride to your office? Would you be allowed?"

"Your grandfather did it," Brill said. "During the Depression, and later, in the war when gas was short. He rode all the way in from the farm."

Trinket wondered about traffic, but her father was always up early, in the office before the rush started.

He went to the phone, and called Kress Hartke. "Can you put a stockrack on your pickup, and bring my two horses in? Around noon, and I'll want some of that second cutting hay for them." He said. "No, I'll be right here, working on the fence."

Hung up. His daughter, relentless, brought the bowl of cornflakes. "Okay," Brill yelled, grinning. "You stay home from school and help your father."

He was impatient now for the lumberyard to open, so he could order posts and wire and a block-and-tackle stretcher. His arms ached to start wrestling the posthole auger which was out in the shed.

"Do you really need me?" Trinket asked. "I mean, we have play practice this morning."

"Damn right I do, miss," Brill said. "Need you to hold the stretch on while I staple wire."

Grinned and wagged his big head at his daughter, who couldn't see it was a hollow helmet-liner; moved cautiously forward, hand a bit unsteady, probing with his spoon for pockets of resistance in the cornflake field.

5.

One more thing about Dutchmen. And wood ducks. From an article in *Birds of America*, copyright 1917, okay?

By Herbert K. Job, okay?

> This bird was classed by our government as a vanishing species. This aroused widespread concern, and caused a number of states to prohibit shooting for terms of years; the same action was adopted also by federal regulations. There seems now (1917) to be a marked change for the better, in which result artificial propagation is playing an important part. It has been found that this duck, *through somewhat peculiar but perfectly practicable methods* (our italics), can be bred and reared in captivity, birds thus raised bringing high prices. Quite an industry arose *in breeding American Wood Ducks in Holland* and selling them in America.

You get a wood duck, and put on your wooden shoes, and go out behind a windmill?

7

Want to look at it from Tommy Rebranch's point of view? Start with the horse.

Anybody with average good sense loses his driver's license, he's not going to have too much to say about it—shrug, grimace, talk about something else. Not the big grandstander; he's going to let everybody in town know, first thing Wednesday morning, riding down in a fur-collared greatcoat we hadn't seen since his father died, with the back vented up to the coccyx so that a panel of fine wool covers each thumping thigh and drapes gracefully over each big nubbly knee. Stetson on his head, across the lawn, along the bluff, beside the river, on the park strip; east through the alley, two blocks brings him in behind his building, father's building, grandad's building.

Any of us didn't see Brill that first morning heard about it at lunch and watched for him going back at whiskey time.

There's a lean-to shed, half brick, shiplap and a sagging shingle roof, on the south side of the Brill law office; just behind po'r Tommy's window.

For years Tommy's been asking Brill to tear the shed down, build a small wing there with a supply room, file space, and a separate john for the secretaries.

Know what he says Brill told him? "Tommy, you couldn't reproduce the way that roof line sags for seven thousand dollars."

Wasn't as if Brill had to look at it: it was out Tommy's window.

Brill comes to work on his horse, gets a hacksaw out of the saddlebag, cuts the hasp on the old padlock, and what's inside? A big box stall, and a little floored-over room for grain and tack, and of course Brill's father used to keep his horse parked in there in the goddamn olden days.

Tommy'd be waiting for Charlene, Nadine, and Rosemary to get through in the john for the rest of his life.

Jokes: "See where you can put the rear license plate, Bob, but where do you hang the front one?"

"Comes to a red light, up goes the tail and the stoplight turns on, right?"

"How many horsepower, Mr. Brill?"

"Get a car."

Harf, harf the larf on heavy gait rises.

2.

Telephone: "You okay?"

"Yeah, Martin."

"Understand you drove to work this morning in a kind of . . . one-seater sports model?"

"Old buddy."

"You remember calling me about two yesterday morning?"

"Did I, Martin?"

"You said you wanted me to drive to Springfield with you. Seems there were these two nice girls . . ."

"Oh, God. Yeah, I remember now."

"Anything I can do?"

"I'll let you know."

"I got up and came looking for you. You didn't sound very good."

"I wish you'd found me."

"Family taking it okay?"

"Trinket's got me on a cornflake cure. Hey, Martin? Here's something. Pat drove the car today. First time in four years."

"No kidding?"

"I was damn proud of her. She just drove a little way, down the drive. And backed up to the garage again. Sweating and trembling but didn't hit a thing. Christ, maybe this'll be good for her."

"Good, Bob. That's nice." Martin said. "Has pretty Mrs. Light come back?"

Other phone.

"Want to hold, Martin? . . . Brill speaking."

"Robert," Tommy Rebranch said. "Old horseman. There's a highly attractive young lady sitting here talking to me. I think she saw you about a divorce the other evening?"

"Named Light."

"Yes. She's come back to the firm, but I think she might prefer I took the case instead of you."

"Go screw yourself, Tommy," Brill said. "Send her over."

"Well, sir, it seems . . ."

"Just tell her I do the divorce work," Brill said. "It'll be me stepping into your office while you're telling her that."

Hung up.

"Martin? She's here."

Hung up.

Two-phone Brill holstered his weapons, hitched up his pants, and moved down main street.

Tommy was actually saying, ". . . handle these things in conference . . ." when Brill entered the office.

"Gabby Light!" Brill said, and let his smile do the rest. It was pretty reliable, a wide-open smile full of big, even, very white teeth; if it worked it didn't matter what he said. If it failed, you could always try a run of words on a woman, and then let her have the smile again. And again. "I'm so glad you've come back."

It felt good, like twisting the posthole auger into hard ground yesterday, using sheer physical strength against resistance, to push the smile. The blood running, not entirely because she was pretty, but also because of the resistance to him set up by Tommy's smooth, fraternity-boy obduracy and reassurances.

"Will you forgive a country drunk his lousy manners?"

"I suppose Mr. Habib talked to you," she said.

"You bet he did." The smile. "Just now on the phone. I called to ask him how to reach you."

"That's right," the girl said. "You didn't know."

"You're not in the phonebook, you know."

"Not here. University City."

"I should have thought of that."

"Bob, maybe we ought to sit down with Mrs. Light and hear about it," Tommy said.

"Oh, I don't think we need to involve you, Tommy," Brill said. The smile. For Tommy now; now for her. "Unless Mrs. Light prefers it . . . ?"

"Oh, no." The girl stood, bobbed her head at Tommy, smiled at Brill, a disturbing little number of her own, acknowledging that he was good, suggesting she might not be altogether without strength herself. "No, I think since Mr. Habib advised me to come to Mr. Brill . . ."

3.

Tommy's point of view? The horse, the dolly—not that Tommy'd ever play around with a woman client—the whole insufferableness of the situation. And maybe Tommy honestly did misunderstand, and think they meant the alley. Anyway, when the city architect dropped by to talk about street widening, and pointed out that it would mean some alteration in the building, Tommy figured that would be a wider alley and the horse shed would damn well have to come down, and Brill was tied up with the Jew dolly so Tommy said, sure, he didn't see why there should be any difficulty, but why didn't the city architect have the city attorney go ahead with a *pro forma* condemnation, just have it ready in case there was some difficulty in negotiating, the city architect knew what a wild man Brill could be about things, and he, Tommy, would try to keep it all smooth, work through him, huh, Perk?

Doesn't take much to reconstruct that little scene. Anybody who knew Tommy could. Even, eventually, Brill.

4.

There is no passenger service between Rosetta and University City any more. There used to be a two-track shuttle, two round trips a day, but we all drive now, in wretched traffic, and the railroad tracks carry only occasional freight. They carry it just often enough to tie up a couple of miles of traffic at the grade crossings a couple of times a week.

The railroad doesn't like to run freight at night. When they have to, the engineer really leans fearfully on his whistle, coming to the crossings. When he hits a car with a half million pounds of train, he's quite sorry.

"I'm sorry," Brill said, "to have caused you a second trip here from U City."

"I don't mind. It's a pretty drive." Brill was being measured.

"I'm afraid I forget to notice that." Okay, try me.

"Where else would I ever see farms? You get drunk every night?" Hot lavender eyes gazing into his with disconcerting steadiness.

"No. But when I do, I do a pretty thorough job of it. Does that bother you much?" Give her the smile again.

"It's a cultural thing." Chin up, look away. Look back, lavenders.

"Excuse me?" Widen smile.

"Jews don't drink a lot. My mother used to say she'd rather I came home with an illegitimate baby than drunk." Sincere, suggestive.

"I'll take you to my farm sometime." Sincere, natural.

"I'd like that, Mr. Brill." Voice a little hushed.

"I haven't known many Jews. Your husband one?" Matching intimacy.

"Oh sure," she said. "Well. He's a history student, grad student. Very good at it."

"Well."

"Ever study history?" Lavenders caught him off-guard.

"What's the problem, Mrs. Light," Brill said, conceding the round.

"Sex."

"Pretty much the rule in divorce cases." He remembered, and decided not to tell her, a very big Chicago divorce lawyer talking to his law school class: ninety-eight percent of all divorces start with husband getting outside tail; wife catching him; husband feels so guilty he'll do anything; wife demands divorce; he cooperates reluctantly, and a year later she wishes she had him back. The other two percent, the lawyer said, are more interesting. "Are we talking about infidelity?"

"'Incapacity," she said.

"Your husband?"

"The man can't make it. He's on speed."

"I'm sorry," Brill had to say. "I don't know what that means."

"Amphetamines. He takes a dozen diet pills a day, when he can't get it to shoot."

"A dozen?"

"Sometimes more. You ever take them?"

"Once. Just one. I had a prescription, supposed to take three a day for a while. I took the first one and still have the rest of the bottle."

"You didn't like it?"

"I was even ruder to people than usual."

"They work on the central nervous system."

"What do they do to your husband?"

"I sing," she said. "He used to play behind me. Lovely guitar. Beautiful hands. A real musician. Better than me. The only thing he'll do now is screw up all the tuning pegs tight and make it squeak like a mouse."

"Not exactly grounds for divorce."

"He can't get it up."

Brill understood that.

"I said to Gene, why not go up to student health and get yourself castrated? Then I" she started laughing, "I shot it with a water pistol."

"You what?"

"The man was in his dressing gown with the apparatus hanging out, Mr. Brill. I guess I thought I could get him interested by being playful. So I filled a water pistol and started shooting at it, you know, saying 'Dead men tell no tales,' things like that. Dancing around silly, like being Annie Oakley."

"Was he offended?" Brill asked.

"He got the giggles. He was smoking pot on top of the speed. I was offended. No. Embarrassed I guess. You make a big play, cut loose like that . . . and it doesn't work. You feel silly and exposed."

"It sounds like a good try, Mrs. Light," Brill said. "May I ask how long . . . Gene's been on speed?"

"How long since we consummated?" She smiled naughtily at him. "We consummated up a storm about a year ago. I've been consummating around a little since, or was until I decided that I had to get divorced."

"Will Gene agree to the divorce?"

"No."

"Why not?"

"My family has a little money."

"I'll have to get some medical advice. Drug addiction would give you grounds, but I don't know if amphetamines are classed as addictive."

"Can't we stay away from that?"

"The drugs?"

"Yes, please. If we start on that in court, there are a lot of neat kids over in University City who might get dragged in."

"Yeah. There are some neat kids over here that might get dragged in, too," Brill said.

"Really?" She seemed a little startled. "You mean high school kids?"

"I was thinking of a neat kid we have named Train Pacek," Brill said. "Who's pretty sure to be on the wholesale end of whatever it is people are using."

"Would you like to try? To drag him in?"

"No," Brill said. "Someday maybe I'll have a chance at Train. Or if I don't, someone will. Or he'll die rich. I'm not sure it matters. He's part of the system; knock him down, something else would take his place. Nothing to do with your divorce, is it? Would your husband come see me?"

"No. I don't live there any more."

"One thing I have to ask, matter of ethics," Brill said. "If you and Gene could resolve your differences, would you consider a reconciliation?"

"Oh, boy," the girl said. "You are country, aren't you?"

5.

Martin was in that afternoon and they talked, by agonizing coincidence, about murder statistics.

Agonizing because Martin entered those statistics the following morning.

There had been a number of armed robberies in Rosetta that fall, and Train Pacek was on Brill's mind.

"Train's boys don't do those things," Brill said.

"They don't think of themselves as criminals," Martin said. "You give one of them sodium pentothal and ask him what he does for a living, he'd tell you, 'I'm a truck driver, a good teamster union man. A distributor.' When he steals it isn't because he's a thief, it's because it's a part of distribution. When he runs a package in from Chicago, he's no dope runner. He's doing a favor for a friend, maybe for pay, maybe not."

"He doesn't use a gun," Brill said. "He may or may not have guns, like anybody else might or might not, depending on whether he liked them. He's not going to get himself in a gun-using situation in the line of business, is he?"

"If he does," Martin said, "it will be accidental and passionate, and not because he's a criminal but because he's like other people."

"Scared or angry or out of his head," Brill said.

Suddenly Martin smiled and said softly: "Train's been avoiding me for months now."

"Why? You still have to get along, don't you? Vending machines in the theaters?"

"Yes, but that goes without much friction. Do you remember when Buster Wortman died?"

"The old St. Louis gang boss?"

"Yes. He lived in Collinsville. When I bought the first theater and Train came to see me about vending machines, he mentioned knowing Wortman and I was too dumb to be impressed. So I found out all about him—did you know old Buster was a member of the Shelton gang when he was a teen-ager? Whatever the hell that means. It meant a lot to Train. So after Train and I reached our understanding, I used to ride him about having tried to bulldoze me with knowing Buster Wortman. And when I read in the papers that Buster'd died, I couldn't resist sending Train a little bunch of cut flowers."

Martin's understanding with Train had been simple and regular: as long as Train made the best bid, his vending machines were in the theaters. But Martin had been to Memphis and St. Louis both for other bids, and had had the Memphis firm in for a year before Train met the competition.

Martin had arrived in Rosetta as a high school Spanish teacher, became a client of Brill's when he bought the first theater, became a friend when people were saying darkly that if Martin didn't play ball with Train Pacek, he'd wind up in the river. Now, fifteen years later, Brill and Habib just by keeping the thing public had cost Train some of the power of fear, though many thought Martin went along secretly. Brill had supported the operation, and crime was something they talked about. Today they were dicking around with some figures, relating type of establishment robbed to age of armed robber. They played statistics pretty often.

"Someone's got to keep track of the sex and violence around here," Martin said.

Fifteen-to nineteen-year-old group, seventy-one percent filling stations, eighteen percent Mom-and-Pop groceries, open at night, eleven, others; taverns, none.

"Law-abiding kids. They know they're too young to go into taverns."

"Why do the papers always report the bad things about youth and leave out the good?"

The *nineteen- to twenty-eight-year-old group* started hitting taverns, and *twenty-nine to thirty-five* damn near specialized in them, except for those who attained the poise and maturity to start doing small loan companies, working up toward banks. But if you had that combination of talent and ambition, a place like Rosetta was too small for you; you moved on to St. Louis and the odds on your coming back to do a job which might involve violence in your home town were pretty small.

Most violence was accidental; it occurred as part of a crime which had a different original direction. A kid on the age borderline between filling station and tavern work, making his first try at the latter, got rattled and killed the night bartender, just after closing—the bartender not going for a gun, but getting the cash as directed—that sort of thing.

If violence against a person were the prime, not the accidental, direction of the crime, then the matter was personal, not professional, and the origin was likely to be sex or race. The University kid, living off-campus in Rosetta, who kills his girl; the husband shooting up his wife, or her lover, whichever he comes upon first; or simple fear and hatred of some group of people, focussing in an aggravated moment on an individual member of that group.

"It's going to have sex or race in it." Brill would never forget Martin saying that on Thursday afternoon, about eighteen hours before Roswell Echiz shot him.

Roswell Echiz was a factory worker, who happened to come home Thursday afternoon from the penitentiary, where he'd been serving a term for aggravated assault after stomping a Negro sailor in a bar fight. The rest was easy to reconstruct:

While he was away, his wife had contracted with a local plumbing firm to install a shower, as a surprise for her husband when he came out. A surprise and an amenity, too, because, as the wife explained, Roswell never liked to take no tub bath.

Roswell Echiz was delighted with the new shower. He and his wife opened a fifth of Jim Beam, stripped off their clothes, and bathed several times that evening.

The next morning Roswell asked how much it cost. When she showed him the bill, his delight turned to outrage. Who was that goddamn plumber to take advantage of a man's wife while the man was away? He spoke, as he and Mrs. Echiz breakfasted together, of serving his time as if he'd been serving his country. The more he thought and talked about it, the madder he got, and Mrs. Echiz, to keep Roswell's wrath from turning against herself, supplied quite a few hints, some true, some false, as to what sort of scoundrel the plumber might have been.

Whether or not to deny the possibility of frequent adulterous opportunity, she did certainly want to deny that the plumber had spent as many hours in the house as his bill showed.

At about nine forty-five, having finished the Jim Beam for breakfast, Echiz took the itemized bill and went off to see the plumber, to see if he couldn't get the cost reduced. He had a notion, probably, that the simple fact of his being just out of the pen would be fairly frightening, but he took a pearl-handled, .25-caliber automatic with him too, something he'd given his wife as a going-away present in case she'd needed it in his absence to protect herself.

If it seemed to Echiz that he would be more intimidating carrying the little gun, it was also true that the plumber, whom he knew slightly, was a big, heavy, gray-faced, ill-tempered man, and that Echiz was no longer in the lean, hard physical condition of his peak sailor-stomping days.

Martin Habib was coming out of the door of the plumbing shop when Echiz drove up and parked. Martin had been calling on the plumber to ask for a Christmas Seal contribution. Because he'd been brought up Orthodox, Easter always seemed a more exciting holiday to Martin than Christmas, but he tried to get in the spirit of the latter; in addition, his was the most prosperous business in the area where the plumber had his shop and it was therefore easy for Martin to collect from business neighbors.

Martin looked nothing at all like the plumber.

Nevertheless, Echiz, who knew both men by sight sober, pointed the little gun at Martin, called him by the plumber's name, and said he was a sonofabitch.

Seeing the gun, Martin turned to run back into the store. As a dog will automatically attack that which runs, Roswell Echiz automatically pulled the trigger; he fired four times, hitting Martin only once. But the single bullet severed Martin's spine, between two vertebrae, and he fell like a tree.

Then Roswell Echiz was seen by a witness to fumble in his pocket, pull out and put on a pair of glasses, and heard to say by a man who ran up to the left-hand side of the car, unaware of what had happened,

"Shit, that ain't him. That one's got a suit on."

Echiz was probably a corruption of the Scotch name Eccles. Habib, in Arabic, means darling.

6.

The city architect was back, nervous, next day, asking to see Brill and Brill said whatever it was, for Christ's sake let Tommy handle it. Brill worked on nothing that week but Martin Habib's affairs.

Brill's wife, Pat, drove him next day to work, something we'd have certainly talked about pretty intensely if the Martin thing hadn't been so fresh and resonant.

Heartless? Our town? We make distinctions. For example, Donnie Rebranch, Tommy's brother, running for Congress, was forgiven for carrying on as if Martin had been his best friend in the world. Martin liked Donnie all right. But Pete Canaday was put down hard, and probably failed to make River Club that year, for saying maybe there'd been something not so accidental, maybe Martin and Mrs. Echiz . . . ? It was the aspersion on Martin's taste in women we resented.

7.

"He was such an appealing man," Gabby Light said.

"Fine," said Brill. "Yes."

"I'll bet everybody liked him."

"That's a hell of a thing to say about anybody."

"Am I being dumb and girlish?"

"Yeah."

"Shall I go, Mr. Brill? I really just came to say I'm so sorry . . ."

"Sit still," Brill said. "Thank you for coming." It was dusk. He had the horse out in the shed again. It was kind of nerve-racking to have Pat drive him, though at the rate of speed she went no one could get hurt, and he continued to be pleased that she was trying.

There was a bottle. Brill indicated it. Gabby shook her head. She hardly drank at all.

"Do you want to talk about something else?"

"There's people around." Brill fixed himself a light one. "Saying the justice was poetic. And a few who are just plain pleased to see him go."

"Who, Bob?"

"Crooks and cuckolds, Mrs. Light. Your friend Train Pacek would be one. Did you know a girl named Rose Meyers at the University?"

"Yes. A little hippie chick."

"Shut up. You're a little hippie chick."

She looked hurt.

"Stop looking hurt, and I'll tell you . . . Martin's obituary. No. A story with Martin in it. Then we'll talk about something else."

"All right. Is Rose Meyers in the story?"

"Rose is in it. I'm in it. It's got everybody in it but Dean Rusk and Spiro Agnew. They were busy messing up other stuff. It's about the time Train Pacek and a man named Robert E. Lee Trump tried to fix the Miss Rosetta contest."

Gabby smiled, and Brill talked on, needing to talk:

"Rose was our only, genuine home-grown Rosetta flower child," Brill said. "Father runs a stockyard, feeds cattle."

"Trump? She was Stoney Trump's girl, wasn't she?"

"That's Robert E. Lee's boy. Stonewall Jackson Trump."

"Real name?"

"Only son of his scummy father," Brill said. "Who didn't understand or sympathize at all when handsome Stonewall got to college and started playing politics and poetry."

"Didn't exactly cut the boy off without a cent," Gabby said. "I've been to some of Stoney's parties."

"No. Rob Lee was hurt when Stoney grew the beard," Brill said. "But all he wanted was not to lose his son. He's a weird old man, Gabby. I used to represent him.

"There's a table in one of the museums at Gettysburg. Pine table, I think; goes back to the Civil War, where it was in a farmhouse near Antietam. The original Stonewall lost his leg at Antietam, was brought back to that farmhouse, and the leg was amputated on that table. What got Rob Lee all excited when he saw it was a mark in the finish, a round mark about the size of a quarter, with a little rays going out from it. Something like what's left in a highly polished wood when you spill a drop of a drink on it.

"Only you don't drink.

"The mark is from a drop of Stonewall Jackson's blood. And damned if Rob Lee Trump didn't come back from a trip to Gettysburg and want me to start negotiating with the museum to buy that table. He was going to give it to Stoney for his twelfth birthday, price no object, but of course they wouldn't sell."

"Is Mr. Trump old South?"

"Not even new South," Brill said. "An immigrant miner's son. Changed his name from Cesar Trumpanek. The boy. I suppose he's turned out well, considering everything. My son Cal likes Stoney fairly well. You don't know Cal?"

Gabby shook her head.

"I guess he left the University before you got there. Montreal, Vietnam and all stops . . . what the hell are the other stops on that line, Gabby?"

She shook her head.

"Rich boys. Stoney Trump's all right for a rich boy, and his father was just a bit in awe of him. But pleased, I think, secretly tickled, when Stoney started sharing an apartment in University City with Rose Meyers. Rose was smart. She had ambition and imagination, and Trump got the idea everything would straighten out if Rose and Stoney got married.

"The only thing is, she wasn't the prettiest doll in all the world—not bad-looking, of course, but a little long in the face and somewhat . . . neutral in coloring."

"She was sallow," pink, white, and lavender Gabby said, with fine dark, floating hair. "As I remember her."

"Go to hell, Mrs. Light. Martin liked Rose. Any child that wanted to write poetry and make the world better. Well. Rob Lee Trump made his money buying low-grade oil leases cheap and making them look glamorous when he sold them. That's more or less what he figured on doing for Rose."

"I don't follow you, Mr. Brill." She gave him the secret smile and moved her shoulders back to raise an interesting, well-separated pair of possibly freckled questions. Brill found the smile easier to ignore than possible secret freckles.

"Okay, dammit. Now Stoney's an outstanding kid in many ways, and very competitive. He enjoys winning what other guys want. His father understood that perfectly. So getting Stoney to change from shack-up to legal housekeeping with Rose meant Trump would have to do two things: get Rose away from Stoney for a while, and fix things so that every other guy in town would want to be seen with Rose, take her out.

"The scheme was naïve and direct, which is the way Trump's schemes always have been and a lot of them have worked: he'd get Rose declared the official prettiest girl in town. Then Stoney'd want to lead her down the aisle, just to show the other guys who wins big prizes."

"I can't believe it," Gabby said. "A beauty contest?"

"The Miss Rosetta Contest went on in the spring, on the stage of the Riverside Theater, benefit of the Community Chest, sponsored by the Jaycees. With those auspices, the nicer girls in town get into it—high school seniors, college freshmen. There was a fashion division, and a bathing suit division, and a talent division. The fashion part is what the nicer girls talked about; they dared one another into the bathing suit part."

"One-piece suits, no bikinis?"

"Right. Talent meant playing an instrument or singing."

"No tap dancers?"

"Mrs. Light, this is not 1935, even in Rosetta."

"Sorry, sir. Ballet surely?"

"Now and then," Brill said. "Now and then. Piano or cello mostly, I'm afraid. Generally the Miss Rosetta contest leads nowhere. A local fund-raiser that engages mothers and clubwomen; a cut above girls' basketball . . . and every now and then some dolly we don't know, from one of the mining towns or a farm, will grow up gorgeous, win the Miss Rosetta, and go on into regional or state contests. We've never had a Miss Illinois, to go on to Atlantic City from Rosetta, but we had a runner-up one year, who went out to Hollywood afterward and married a TV producer."

"The big time," Gabby said.

"When you stop to think about it," Brill said, "the biggest contributor to the Miss Rosetta Contest was Martin, since he owned the theater. People didn't stop that much to think about it, but naturally the Jaycees wanted a good night—Thursday or even Friday.

"And they'd make Martin one of the judges, in compensation, which he used to grin about pretty insufferably. Another was the head of the drama department over at U City. You must know him. Curly Haynes?"

"Curly?" Gabby laughed.

"And the third would be some local lady. Well, Trump figured he needed two out of three judges to make Rose Myers Miss Rosetta, year before last. He started with Curly Haynes. Curly had a building fund going for renovating his theater, came over to talk it up at a Rotary meeting; Rob Lee took him down to the office afterward, and wrote him a check for a curtain. A curtain for a big stage costs six or seven thousand dollars, so we heard. Curly and Trump got pretty friendly, and Trump thought he might like to put up enough more of that tax deductible to equip a couple of dressing rooms, and Curly didn't see any reason not to go along with Trump's little joke he explained about—wanting his son's girl to win this little local beauty contest. Hell, somebody had to be a winner, and it wouldn't make any real difference who, would it?

"Now the lady judge: that year it was going to be one of the high school teachers, a zippy little doll named Sharon whose husband was in Vietnam. The Jaycees figured to have someone nice-looking to put the crown on the winner—the winner from the year before was out in Hollywood, remember, and not too eager to come home. And . . ." Brill hesitated, remembering that he'd lobbied just a little to have Beth Gibson asked to be the lady judge last year; wanted Beth around. Brill sighed. "You ever hear of a man named Pete Canaday?"

"I've met Pete," Gabby said. "He used to be at Stoney's parties sometimes. That clean, greyhound build."

"He works for Trump. God, what's the use of subtlety in the world when the obvious works so well? Trump has Pete start sending little Sharon presents. Going by to see her. She wouldn't have dates with him, not at first, because of the overseas husband and the schoolteacher's public-eye position; but of course those things started working for Pete pretty soon, Sharon found herself invited to parties, and couldn't be seen leaving with Pete, but they could make a private arrangement to meet at her place afterward couldn't they, if he left his car a couple of blocks away, and really had something to talk to her about, and pretty soon what they had on the lady contest judge was enough so she would have jumped through a flaming hoop naked, yelling 'Geronimo,' to start the show if Trump and Canaday said she had to.

"That left old Martin, and there Trump made his mistake.

"He overreached. Hell, he had two judges. Let them outvote the third; as I understand it, that was Canaday's advice. But the Trumps in this world—they'll always kill you two ways, once dead isn't dead enough. I'm sorry. That's an inappropriate goddamn thing to say."

She touched his hand. It was getting dark in the office. "Go ahead, Mr. Brill. May I fix your drink?"

"All right," Brill said. "Thanks. I'm telling a funny story, right? I mean not a joke, but comic. Light. Trump's stupidity: he just didn't know his man. Nobody knew Martin Habib. I didn't know him, his wife didn't know him; maybe what his wife and I and a few business associates and a girl or two knew together, if you put it together, would begin to explain the man. Would have begun. I don't know. I do know that Trump was stupid.

"Because of the business Martin was in, because it touches the rackets here and there, Rob Lee thought all you'd have to do with that kind of man was meet his cash price. Pete Canaday argued against it, we understood, but Trump was impatient. The contest was near. Rose Meyers was all duly entered in it. They gave Rose's mother a good bit of dough to spend on the girl in Chicago, on high-fashion clothes, and some very expensive sessions at a beauty salon and with a photographer. They ran a picture of Rose every day or so in the paper, which Trump controls, doing this or that. Starting the Girl Scouts off on their cookie-selling drive, breaking a bottle of Illinois champagne over a new police car that Paulie Siebert bought for the sheriff's office. And they took her into their confidence enough so she started dreaming of being that nice old man's daughter-in-law, and could see how it might work to stay away from Stoney Trump.

"Suddenly she was no flower child any longer. She was Princess Lee Radziwill.

"I have to say they did it well. They even had guys paid, you know, five bucks here, ten there, to start conversations in the barbershops and the pool hall—they had a couple of cabbies bought, and Jimmy who checks coats at the River Club. Canaday knows how to operate; he wouldn't say, 'Here's ten dollars to talk it up'—he'd say, 'Listen, I know you like Les Meyers and that pretty little girl of his. It'd be a kick to have her win, wouldn't it? Kind of bring that nice family back together, after Rose going off helling around with the hippies, now she's straightening out and starting to look so good, huh? But I tell you, there are people around this town so small-minded, so damn prejudiced, well, if you have a chance to buy a man a drink and just tell him how we feel about Rose, here's something for the bar bill.'

"Then there was another line, civic pride; you talked about how a girl needed some dough behind her, like a political candidate does, to win the big one and, well, as an insider you knew, maybe you'd better not say too much about it, that some pretty important Illinois money was ready to back Rose if she got through the first round on her own.

"Hell, it was snowballing pretty good. They should never have tried to talk to Martin. The way things were moving for them, Martin probably would have gone along with the other two judges, and the talk we were all hearing, without any other kind of persuasion anyway. Martin was human; Trump had to have him cooled.

"There's a bar waiter named Denny at the River Club swears he overheard most of this conversation; I don't know if he did or not.

"Denny's a good bar waiter, he's working his way through college doing it, always remembers what everybody usually drinks, talks with those that want to talk—he's going to practice law in Rosetta just like me, he tells me, and thinking about dental school, he'll tell a dentist. Denny tells you what he thinks you want to hear.

"Here's the conversation he reported, after it was all over, between Canaday and Trump:

"Pete says, 'Listen, Rob Lee. Sharon, the math teacher. It's much neater this way. I'll get Sharon and Martin Habib out together, like she's supposed to be my date and I've got a business proposition I want to talk to Martin about. We'll go to Cape Girardeau; I'll have a room hired, like I've been doing; see, we even leave our coats up there, so Martin knows where it is. We'll be in the dining room, the after-dinner cognac jug's up in the room, and I get called as we start up there. Rob Lee, Sharon. After her second drink, she starts fingering her ears, pulling on the lobes, playing with her skirt hem. Blushing. And Martin's not exactly a beginner . . .'

" 'That's immoral,' is what Rob Lee's supposed to have said.

" 'But she can handle Martin for us, and I don't mind telling you, sir, I'd be pleased to be off that particular hook.'

" 'You got yourself on, you get yourself off.'

" 'But what about Martin? How would it be to let nature take its course, Rob Lee?'

" 'Let nature take whatever it wants, what you're going to take is fifty-dollar bills,' Rob Lee told him. 'A nice handful fer a fella like that. You'll see how quick he'll take it, and I don't want to hear any more of your dirty talk.'

"So Canaday asked how much, and Rob Lee said, 'Go find out. What do you think you get paid for, anyway? Taking pretty girls across the river?'

"Rob Lee Trump was working himself up to where he might have tried to make Canaday pay back some of those Cape Girardeau romance expenses, just to show his power over Pete really, so Canaday agrees that Robert E. knows best. Three days before the contest, Pete goes to see Martin and find out what his price is to vote for Rose Meyers. But Canaday really knows it's the wrong move, and isn't his usual smooth, shrewd self. Martin catches that nervousness right away, before he even knows what it's all about.

"Martin had a way, when he was dealing, of being unusually polite, insinuatingly polite, I guess. His voice would get so quiet you could just barely hear him; his smile was kind and confidential. You could tell him anything, you felt, and his exquisite good manners would prevent it's ever being used against you. He took Pete. Suppose I go along, sir, it's a most attractive idea, but how can we be sure my vote will do it? Gradually it all came out, how the other judges were fixed, the reason for it, Canaday's stake in making Martin take the bribe, and all the rest. And of course Martin was terribly grateful to have had Pete consult him in this way; Pete would understand that Martin needed time to think things out, and as soon as Pete cleared the office, Martin called me.

"Martin's first impulse was just to pull the theater, and tell the whole town why. He didn't like Trump any better than I did, and something new had come up. Train Pacek was interested in the situation. Train had smelled what Trump was up to, and put some of his own troops to work on the talking campaign, talking up another dolly; the point was to get some local gambling money on the other dolly, which Train would cover at any odds they wanted, knowing the fix was in.

"So for a while, we tried to think if there was any way to rig it so the contest could go on and Rose would lose. We couldn't figure that one. And the more we talked, the less Martin wanted to just expose the whole thing. Rose Meyers would be hurt, and Sharon the schoolteacher'd be destroyed. We were still turning it over when I got called away, and when I got back to my desk there was a message to meet Martin at Doc Barragon's office.

"Barragon was public health officer that year. I went over and there are these two birds sitting there, waiting for me to play third bird.

" 'Sit down, Bob,' says Barragon. 'How's Trinket feeling?'

" 'Fine,' I say.

" 'Not complaining just a little, about sore glands in the neck? Hmmm?'

" 'Oh,' I said. 'Yeah. Now that you mention it, the neck has been pretty sore the last couple of days. I was going to bring her in.'

" 'Tell him about your kids, Martin.'

" 'Tight neck glands,' Martin said. 'Very tight. Thought of bringing them to see you.'

" 'No, I'm going to be all tied up with this suspected epidemic,' Doc Barragon says. 'I'm just going to have to accept your description, and diagnose from it.'

" 'Martin,' I said. 'I'm going to have to get a haircut tomorrow afternoon, sore neck and all.'

" 'Me too,' Martin said.

" 'That'll give me time,' said the doctor.

"Suddenly, there's no lab reports yet or anything, but everything starts coming up mumps. You take your kid into the office with a busted finger, Doc'll splint the finger. Then he'll casually jab a finger into the kid's neck, under the ear, hard enough to hurt, and say, 'Does that hurt?'

" 'Ow.'

"Barragon's got a fair-sized mean streak in him; I suspect him of liking that part of it.

" 'Better keep this one home from school tomorrow,' he'll say. 'Till we're sure about this mumps thing. Probably nothing to it, of course . . .' Probably thirty kids and a couple of dozen adults go through Dr. Barragon's assembly line that afternoon and the next morning, and by God every one of them was assured that in spite of the way that finger stung, he probably didn't have the mumps.

"I happened to be chairman of a public meeting next night on some zoning stuff; I canceled it and said I was going to bed. Martin made a statement. He felt that certain leaders of opinion in Rosetta were getting panicky. He mentioned one, not by name, who had actually gone to bed with suspected mumps who might simply be hypochondriac. Everyone knew adult males overreacted to mumps. He, Martin, was under some pressure to close the movie theaters but he hoped to avoid doing so, at least until there was more conclusive proof that we were faced with a genuine epidemic and not simply some virus that produced mumplike symptoms.

"Trump's paper put that on page one, in a box, and Martin sat back and waited for the phone to start ringing. Christ, I'll bet half the mothers in town called him up to scold. He gave in to popular pressure, of course, and the Miss Rosetta Contest was off. It couldn't be postponed. The name of the winner was due to be filed for the regional contest next day and, you see, Trump had been making a lot of use of the possibility of Rose going to the regional.

"He couldn't start saying now that it didn't matter. Trump knew, and he didn't know. Train knew damn well; he'd tried to deal with Martin before. But neither of them could do a damn thing, and next day Doc Barragon issued his statement demanding to know where all the irresponsible talk about epidemic was coming from."

"Poor Rose," Gabby said.

"Why? She went back to University City with all those slick, free clothes, gave up being a flower child, and married an associate professor of political science on the strength of all that publicity.

"Sharon?"

"That was the bad one," Brill said. "She was in love with Canaday by then. We figured she had to get out of town before she did something crazy, so Martin asked me to go with him to see Train Pacek. Martin told Train in that quiet, believable way that we'd saved him a pile of money. Martin said he and Sharon had it fixed up to cross Trump, and give the prize to Rose's competition. Martin said he didn't have much use for Train, but after all they were business associates, and he, Martin, believed in loyalty; so when he heard about the bets Train was covering, he called the contest off. Train wanted to know what he owed Martin, and Martin said nothing, really. But Train better help get Sharon out of town, because she was a silly thing and might talk. But she had a taste for nightlife and a good head for figures, and Martin didn't suppose Train's connections reached far enough so that he could get Sharon into one of those schools for card dealers at Las Vegas, could he? That's where the child is now. With her own blackjack table."

"Is that good or bad?" Gabby asked.

"I don't know. The best we could do," Brill said. "That's all."

8

Given the kind of choice of animal abilities we sometimes offer children —would you rather be able to run like a deer, dig like a mole, or fly like an eagle?—Robert Brill would have chosen hibernation.

He'd have gone for true hibernation, like a ground squirrel, whose pulse, normally about three hundred per minute, drops to less than ten beats while he curls up, sleeping, fed by the slow and blissful melting of the body fat. Ground squirrel wakes up in the spring eighty percent lighter than when he corked off for the winter. Each eleventh day he's had his eyes open, revved up his heat, and taken a little trip through the larder, and over to the drinking fountain and the pissing post. Then ahhh!, back to the snuggly.

Brill would not have settled for the brown bear's way, of long winter sleep in the den, with the body temperature staying high, the anus plugged with pine needles, so he needn't move his ponderous bowels till spring.

Because the best thing about true hibernating is that when the body temperature is down around forty degrees, there's no more electrical activity in the brain, which stops as soon as the thermoregulator drops into the fifties.

This suggests that brown bears dream—along with black bears, chipmunks, skunks, and possums; but ground squirrels, woodchucks, shrews, and hedgehogs avoid that stuff.

In winter, while nothing grew outside, Brill dreamed, endured, put on weight, walked sometimes in the snow, sometimes made trips to places farther south to hunt or fish, study or collect, swim, or just look around. But that was only passing time; he was a man tuned to the seasonal rhythm of his own turf, and in the winter his life and his profession interested him only intermittently. In early November, there were fits of attention for Martin's estate, for something Canaday and Tommy tried to pull, and for Gabby Light.

2.

There was a rosy rug in the living room at Habib's. It had, in addition to a great deal of complicated design, pictures in it of dogs, horses, riders, houses, and animals that might perhaps be stags. It was partly silk, a Princess Kashan.

"It is a scene of preparing to hunt," Martin had told Brill once. "But hunting was more sociable than you seem to make it."

"There are plenty of nice, agreeable, sociable hunters around," Brill remembered saying. "I just don't happen to like hunting with the sonsofbitches."

"I am willing to imagine a Persian knight," Martin had said, with his quiet smile, "who didn't like the ceremony and the other knights, and the eating and drinking. Who liked to send the page away, and saddle his own horses, and go out by himself with a spear; or with falcon and bow; to where the boars were, or the sand grouse, or the antelope . . ."

That would not have been in the country of Martin's fathers. Martin's father lived in a trading country, west of Arab chivalry, east of European, where feudal life ended early because the Crusades crossed back and forth through Lebanon. But those sea captains and caravan men had an eye for treasure, and especially rugs, like their New England counterparts for Chinese ivories.

The rug was still unrolled. Nearly everything else was packed. Beatrice Habib, Martin's wife, had said that she would go back to her home city now, Zahle, but the girls would stay in the U.S. for schooling, with an uncle in Detroit.

"When my girls marry, I come to Detroit or where they live, take care Martin grandson."

It wasn't until the second cup of Arabic coffee that they spoke of business.

"There is man to buy theaters?"

"Yes. One named Train Pacek, who'll be very angry if I don't sell to him. Another is a real estate man, who would operate the theaters until he found he could make more by tearing them down and selling the land. And I think a man named Trump would buy, just because he likes to own everything."

"Martin did not like Mr. Trump."

"No."

"Who gives most money?"

"I can get good money from any of them. What I'd like to do is set a price and terms, and offer it to one of them first. To avoid bidding. When you let people bid, you may get a little more money but you lose control of details."

"Yes." She seemed to understand, and they discussed the personalities of the prospective buyers more fully. Brill thought he'd talk with theater-chain operators as well. Beatrice, whose Arabic name she told him was Bahia, asked a number of searching questions; then to his surprise, asked him to draw up a power of attorney for her to sign.

"I not be here," she said. "You decide. Sell as Martin would. You Martin's brother." Then she gave him the rug.

He tried to refuse it. She insisted that it was one of two things Martin intended Brill to have. The other was a box of papers, sorted into file folders.

One of the folders said, *Brill, Robert,* on the tab. Brill assumed it had to do with business relations. He did not look into it for several days.

3.

You've got to understand what the ASCS is, and how it works.

No, that's right. You don't have to. It's one of those farm program things, isn't it? Agricultural and Soil Conservation Service. Who besides a farmer would need, want, or be able to understand it?

Do you understand $371,000?

How about that sum, coming into a single county, to be paid out partly as salaries and office expenses, but mostly to spread around among fourteen, fifteen hundred farmers—quite a bit for this one, none at all for that one, a little bit for the third. Well? The means for spreading the money around are going to be pretty diverse: payments for improving land, payments for growing this or not growing that, payments for support of prices. Lots of other things. Now:

The decisions on who gets how much are going to be made by a committee. Of farmers. Politically okay farmers, of course. And there'll be one paid, executive sort of man, to carry out their decisions, and perhaps advise just a little, and well, indicate things.

Like what the man who kind of got you on this farmers' committee might think ought to be done in such and such a case; that would be Train. Train Pacek.

Now let's realize that this ASCS office, operated by this paid man who advises the committee and carries out their instructions—he's called the secretary to the committee—is disbursing more money than the operating budget for the City of Rosetta and the county government put together. This then is both our main pipeline to federal funds, and main local source of federal jobs. Got it?

Here's the exam question: what is the main source of patronage in Delta County? Explain your answer, naming the man entrusted with the public exercise of all this slush.

Pete Canaday.

Brill couldn't believe it.

He walked into Tommy's office, not without knocking. He had with him a letter he wanted Tommy to sign—in the character of Brill's attorney—to the State Historical Society, offering to deed it a scenic easement on the Brill Law Office Building. This would enable the Society to interpose its power to protect monuments between the firm and the City of Rosetta, which had by now served notice that they meant to condemn the building.

Brill still thought only widening the alley was involved, and was pleased to let Tommy handle it: "You seem too sentimentally concerned," Tommy had said. "And after all, being here has meant a lot to me, Bob. Say hello to Secretary Pete."

"Excuse me?"

"New secretary to the ASCS committee."

"That's you, Canaday?"

"Get your applications in early for those farm practices, Counselor."

"You know something about farming?"

Pete said: "I'll learn. About the program anyway. I'm off to take a course."

"The important thing is working with people, isn't it, Bob?" Tommy asked.

"Yeah," Brill said. "Working on people." He sat down and looked at the two. They looked very pleased. Let's see: Train Pacek controlled the appointment, so Train and R. E. L. Trump had got together. What would Trump get? Bigger land-retirement payments on his dozen farms; government cost-sharing on projects to improve the hunting; leverage over his neighbors, if he needed it. What would he be doing for Pacek? A range of things; an understanding, surely, about how to treat the requests of the truck lobby in the state senate. Trump had his own state senator. Maybe further business arrangements.

But Canaday, to become the cement in the new bond, must have done some powerful making-up to Train Pacek.

"Canaday," Brill said. "It's a damn good thing you didn't play quarterback in single-wing days, before T-formation football."

"Bob, please," said Tommy Rebranch.

Canaday started to laugh.

"Because you'd never have been able to think of a way to get the ball passed to you if you were standing too far back to kiss the center's ass."

Oh my, Pete laughed hard at that, while Brill left the room.

Five minutes later, Tommy was in his office, angry.

"Damn it, what'd you do that for?"

"Do what?"

"Insult Pete."

"No one can insult Pete. I've been trying for years."

"This is a very important deal for me, Bob," Tommy said.

"Why?"

The door opened. "Don't mess it up," Tommy hissed, swung around and said: "Hi there, Rob Lee."

"Where's Canaday?" The short man in the doorway paid no attention to Brill. He had a day's growth of beard and a dirty shirt collar.

"Pete's gone on back to your place, Rob Lee," Tommy said.

"I told him to wait right here."

"He waited for you."

Trump stared at Tommy, shifted his eyes to Brill, and walked away.

After a moment Brill said: "I'd forgot how much I detest that little turd."

Tommy said: "Are you going to try to block it?"

Brill said: "Charlie Dean had to get sick. That meant Paulie Siebert could be treasurer. That meant Beans Getnik could be sheriff like he's always wanted. So Beans' job as the ASCS is open, and Train could always work pretty well through Beans; but now he's in a position to put a man in who'll owe it all to him. Because Martin's dead. And with Pete out of the way, you'll take over managing things for Trump. Now how could one man hope to block all that, Tommy?"

"Why should he want to ?"

"You ever hear about Cane County?"

"Oh, stop it."

"Six men up there got to split ninety thousand dollars a year six ways from just one agricultural program; there were a hundred applicants."

"Bob, I promise you. Pete's appointment will be perfectly acceptable. After all, Train controls the Democrats—with your advice, of course. And the Republicans go along with Trump because he pays their bills. The idea's not to change anything. It's just a new job for Pete, and a way of making the system work so everybody's happy. Who'd object?"

"Me."

"But why?"

"The Cane County secretary flies his own plane, and he didn't inherit the money to buy it."

"Are you going to try to block it?"

Brill shrugged. "You know what I'm like, Tommy."

Tommy started out of the room.

"If you don't rock her some," Brill said to his back, "how you going to know how good a boat you got?"

Tommy spun. "Will you think about it first?" he asked passionately, turned again and hurried out.

Brill did. He gave it about thirty seconds of thought, opened his shirt, scratched his stomach, buttoned the shirt, and reached for the telephone. Made an appointment for Friday afternoon with Train Pacek. He figured the rest of what he had to do would wait for morning; he wanted to see people, not call them up, and Gabby Light was due at five o'clock.

4.

Once again, they sat in Brill's office in the dusk, with a bottle between them on the desk.

"Divorce him?" she said. "I can't even find him."

Her husband had left town with a group that was going to New York to make some recordings, she said, but had never gotten there. Her guess was that they'd been picked up, somewhere along the turnpike. "Manning, the only one that's steady enough to drive, likes to turn on on the Interstate," she said. "He gets nice and high on pot and just drifts along, eighty-five or ninety miles an hour, with the others freaking out on this or that, their hair blowing in the wind, trailer full of instruments and amplifiers bouncing along behind. Wouldn't it be a pig's dream to bust something like that?"

"Gene wouldn't try to get in touch with you? For help?"

"I think I may finally have made it clear there isn't any help coming," Gabby said. "I took care of him long after it meant anything to me, Bob, just because no one else would. And he'd ask me, not his parents. But now, if something came from Gene, I'd forward it to his parents unopened. I'm done. They know that. He'll get used to it."

"I think you'd better open anything that comes, though," Brill said. "Because unless it's a request for reconciliation, we have a matter of desertion. You've got about three months accumulated—it takes a year in Illinois. It's about as clean and simple as divorce can be."

"Okay."

"Unless you're in a hurry? Other plans that hinge on it?"

She gave him a curious smile, and shook her head. "Oh, no, Mr. Brill," she said, and stood up. She walked to the desk, put her hands flat on it, leaned on them, and looked at him. Then she reached for the bottle, tilted it against her mouth, and Brill could hear the fluid gurgling out of it for a remarkably long moment; she drank steadily until she had to stop to catch her breath.

She put the bottle down. "God, that's nasty-tasting," she said, came on around the desk and sat down lightly in his lap.

Brill had a little trouble catching his own breath, but he got his arms partway up and around her just before her mouth came down, soft and open on his. He had a totally inexplicable impulse to fight her off before she smothered him; suppressed that, of course, but was having difficulty responding, as her shoulders, breasts, and diaphragm all came squirming in over his chest, her lips sucked at his face, one firm hand holding the back of his neck and the other worked under his arm and around his back.

She's got me papered like a damn wall, he thought, and began to heave for improved position. He rolled her, got her face under his, got her weight on his right arm, and felt a surge of comfort and control. He moved his free hand now up between her legs, found she was wearing pantyhose under the short skirt, and had to get the hand all the way up to the waistband and then back down underneath the silly thing, over her navel and across her belly, fingering through hair for the entry to her body, and found it, soft and open as the mouth.

They stayed that way, kissing, Gabby gradually working down into a state of impalement on Brill's blunt finger, responding to that with tidal movements of her hips, and Brill found himself full of surge and excitement as if he hadn't been with a girl for years, and goddamn, he'd better hang onto himself as well as her. This anxiety made things quite poundingly painful, as if his whole body were suddenly charged with extra blood—feet, hands, lungs, neck, and hair roots, all in a state of erection, just as all of her seemed ready to receive.

Then her mouth came over to his throbbing ear, and she whispered: "Will you take me to Chicago?"

"Chicago!"

The terrible, preejaculatory anxiety deflated.

"I'll take you anywhere you want," Brill said roughly, to conceal the collapse of tension, and hung onto her between the legs. "Including right here, right now. You like the desk or the floor, madam?"

"I'm not going to make love to you here," Gabby said. "I can't." She sat straight up on his lap, as close to prim as a girl could be with her skirt around her waist and herself surrounding a large and nubbly finger.

Brill withdrew it, considered briefly brutality, its chances of success and possible consequences, and had no feeling it would be to her taste. She was perfectly friendly, and either perfectly compliant within her rules or a tease. He thought she was probably not a tease.

She put cool hands on his neck, and said: "Love me in Chicago?"

"I don't think I get it. Look, I have a cabin on the river. Let's put a sign on the door saying Chicago."

She smiled and shook her head. "It would be haunted by all those desperate women struggling for what life ought to give so easily."

"Stop fortune-telling," Brill said, unwilling to laugh. "What makes you think there've been so many of them, anyway?"

"What about Louise Tonborg?" She slid off his lap.

"What?"

"The housemother?" She shook her clothes straight, two proud steps away from him now.

"That's a big university over there," Brill said. He felt the same hand which had just been engaged by her softest parts close for comfort around a cold, hard bottle. "How in hell would you know a sorority housemother?"

"Didn't Martin tell you?" she asked, turning back. "I've had a crush on you forever." A smile started, almost a wistful one for God's sake, and the voice rose a note or two and thinned into an odd, singing purity. "It started when I heard you speak once, Mr. Brill. I can't tell you what you spoke about, something about saving the wilderness? Canoe water. I don't know. I was so excited I was having trouble with my own water." A magic girl, she could turn herself from earth to ether and back again and catch him unprepared each time.

"And decided to avenge womankind?" Brill asked.

"Darling Mr. Brill," she said. "I just don't want to be one of them. I want to be something special, and I couldn't do that here, in your office, with your grandfather and your great-grandfather . . ."

This time Brill did laugh, and took a drink. For some reason he was feeling fairly good-natured about the turn she'd given things, though in part he was still calculating what the mechanics might be of using force. Tie her up with her own stockings? Tough with the damn pantyhose, and what do you do for a gag?

"I've known of women not wanting to go to bed with a man in his house," Brill said. "Even with the wife away and the coast clear—I suppose I get that. A house is an animate thing, almost; in a woman's mind. Like a damn bird's nest or something."

She came back and perched lightly on his knee. "Isn't there some kind of bird that lays eggs in other birds' nests?"

"Yeah. Cowbirds. You lay quite a few eggs, do you?"

"Please."

"Get off my knee," Brill said. "I haven't thought of what I'd use to gag you with yet."

She kissed him, swiftly. "Don't," she said. "I'm yours. I said I would. I want to, just as much as you do. Maybe more." She jumped up and scooted away.

"In Rosetta," Brill said, feeling a little tired, "there are several quite comfortable and thoroughly impersonal motels."

She came back and wrapped her arms around his head, standing to one side, pushing a breast into his ear, and crooned: "This town's your house, Robert Brill. Anywhere we might go here, I'd be a cowbird. And U City's not the place for me to feel free. Can't we just take your car and go now? I'll go now. To Chicago. I'm ready."

"We'd hardly make it tonight in time to get a room," Brill said. The lawyer in him suggested that the site must be negotiable; the negotiator suggested that the first alternative site be a throwaway, one he didn't much want agreed to.

"What about Memphis? We can be there in less than two hours."

"That's south," she said. "South scares me."

"We got Springfield." He'd keep giving the other side choices which excluded the original, too distant place. "We got St. Louis."

"Is St. Louis nice?" Gabby asked.

He'd begun telling her how nice it was, drawing her back against him, when the phone rang. It was Trinket, faithfully inquiring whether her father was coming home to supper.

The child sounded lonely, and he couldn't help saying yes, sure, he'd be there in a few minutes.

Told Gabby Light he was sorry to be such a square, and left her standing in the office.

5.

Things were changing at home. The responsibility Pat had reached out for, of driving the car, had changed her sherry-drinking schedule. Now she waited until she'd come back from getting Trinket, or doing the grocery shopping, in the afternoon—things Brill had done for years. She didn't begin on the sherry until after four; consequently, she didn't take the long nap after lunch.

Consequently, she went to bed immediately after a cup of soup or a slice of bread and butter that she ate in place of supper. She and Trinket were closer, Brill realized; but the girl ate alone evenings, if her father stayed away.

He was very attentive to her that evening, almost as if she were the wife he had nearly betrayed; he didn't know whether he had offended Gabby or challenged her. He supposed he'd know by whether she came after him.

He wasn't going after her.

When Trinket had, at length, finished her homework and gone up to bed, Brill got, from the back of his car, the box of file folders Beatrice Habib had given him, carried it into the house, and then, before he started on it, called Kress Hartke.

Arranged for Kress to come in with the farm pickup and meet him, first thing in the morning.

Then he sat down with Martin's papers, and was rudely shocked. The folder marked "Robert Brill" wasn't business papers at all.

It was a rather fat folder, consisting of perhaps forty pages in longhand, on different sorts of paper, so that the notes appeared to have been written at various times. What seemed to be involved were Martin's assessments of him:

Bob has affairs. I have women.

I do not have affairs, or understand why that is pleasant to him. They are like marriages, satisfying a woman's need for tender screwing, and are concealed only because a previous marriage requires it. So he becomes obligated to take care of this new woman in certain ways.

The world is full of flowers. A bee sucks any flower for its sweet, and doesn't even know if he goes back to it. Back at the hive, the queen bee and her drones speak of tender screwing: "Darling, I couldn't come if I didn't love you." But it is better to be out with the flowers, taking sweet sips and flying on.

Because the answer would be, "The hell you can't and the secret of how, madame, is what you are about to learn." Once I knew a college girl who liked to blow, and who she liked to blow were ROTC boys because they were stiff and didn't think it was nice, and she liked to melt the stiffness. Bob could have been a very important man perhaps, but cannot commit himself to anything.

What changed a good-natured young bear into a bear who broods? Brooding. Just goodwill, like hair, getting thin in middle age.

The world he belongs to is finished, and he has no relevance to the world he finds himself in. That is why he can be a great enthusiast for a while for almost anything, but cannot stay enthusiastic.

Bob . . .

Damn it, fifty pages of this? And in the other folders? He looked through them. They were other notes on other people in Rosetta, men and women they both knew.

There was a great deal, he supposed, of information and speculation. But he knew also that none of this had been intended for his reading or anyone else's. Beatrice, who couldn't read more than a few words of English, had seen and recognized his name, and given him by mistake what Martin surely intended to destroy.

Or if Martin had some use he'd meant to make of these papers, it was unknowable. There was a fire in the fireplace. Feeling a little melodramatic, but without hesitation, Brill dumped the whole box out onto a white oak log, and stood there with a poker, pushing pages into the flames as they built.

Little as he'd permitted himself to read of it, he was disturbed, not by specifics—he had hardly reached any specifics—but by the clear meaning of it, overall. That, in his best friend's view, Brill's life had seemed without meaning or direction. Brill snorted. Brill fed the fire, stared at the flames.

Come back from the dead, Martin boy. Come back. I'll. I'll . . . knock you on your Lebanese-Nicaraguan ass.

6.

"Beans Getnik's going to be moving to the courthouse, now. Going to be the sheriff. Who would you like to see be the ASCS secretary—not that you or I have a hell of a lot to say about it."

By Thursday evening, riding the county with Kress Hartke, Brill had asked perhaps thirty different men.

By Thursday night, seven or eight were doing as he'd asked—calling him to report having talked to a number of others. It took one day, if you knew who to go to, to open up the county like a can of peas.

Friday morning, Brill went back to his office and received: there were men in, the phone ringing, calls going out. By noon both phones were busy, continuously, and Brill ate no lunch. Too many farmers in at noon who wouldn't be there at other times.

Tommy stood in the doorway: "What are you trying to do? Get some kind of vote against Pete?"

"I haven't mentioned Canaday's name," said Brill, truthfully.

"You're getting a lot of people upset for nothing," Tommy said. "Pete's going away to take the course. He won't even be in that office for three months."

Brill shook his head. The phone rang. It was Train Pacek.

"You still coming over here?"

"Yeah," Brill said. "Be there at one thirty."

"Come now."

"I'm waiting for some calls."

He hung up and looked at Tommy. "I'm sorry it means so much to you," he said. "But even if I block it, things could still work out for you, couldn't they?"

Tommy turned and walked away without answering.

At one thirty the bowling alley, where Train had his office, was deserted except for a couple of drivers drinking coffee at the counter.

Train was reading the paper in a seat above the lanes.

"Get a cup of coffee and come over," he said, and when Brill did: "You ever bowl, Bob?"

"No. It's not my kind of game."

"Spot you twenty points and roll for the coffee."

"I've already paid for it," Brill said.

"You've been getting my farmers all stirred up."

"Just asking around."

"Asking what?"

"Heard there's going to be a vacancy at the ASCS."

"I got a man for that. Good man."

"Pete Canaday?"

"Yeah. I think Old Man Trump's going to let us hire Pete away from him."

Brill said: "I've been talking to some farmers. Haven't said anything except to ask them who'd be right for the job. Not a single man mentioned Pete Canaday."

"Don't matter, does it? If he's good?"

"Several of them mentioned Roy Ellender's boy, Mike."

"You mention him first?"

Brill shook his head. "No."

"Mike's a good boy," Train conceded.

"Well. He's been through agricultural school."

"Mike's with REA now, ain't he?" Train said. It wasn't really a question. Train kept track. "What makes you think he'd want the ASCS job?"

Brill shrugged.

"You talk with Mike?"

"I wouldn't do that to you, Train," Brill grinned. If this got done, Train would want full credit for doing it; Brill figured young Mike Ellender was smart and tough enough to live that down.

"Is he old enough?"

"Thirty-one. Had some pretty good experience in the Peace Corps. Met that funny-looking wife out there in India."

"She from some foreign country?"

"Vassar."

"I don't know," Train said. "It's sure worth thinking about."

"I've got your letter here," Brill said.

"On the theaters?"

"Yes."

"Am I still in?"

"Yes."

"Who's against me?"

"A Memphis group. They want the U-City territory bad. They'd take Rosetta to get it."

"That's Horst and Wendell, then."

"Maybe."

"They're crooks."

"They've got cash."

"So do I. Who else is against me?"

"A couple of others. Your new partner, Trump."

"Who says he's my partner?"

Brill smiled.

"I've talked to Rob Lee. That's all. He might buy into the truck line."

"Rosetta's own conglomerate. I couldn't let the theaters go that way."

"Why not?"

"Martin cared about this town. I'll make the deal I think he would have liked."

"If I drop Canaday, Trump will never speak to me again."

"Did he used to come around and speak to you a whole lot before?"

"When you going to decide? Who gets the theaters?"

"Couple days," Brill said. "When you going to decide who gets the ASCS appointment?"

Train nodded. "Couple days," he said.

7.

Brill saddled McAlester and rode home. He saw Tommy glowering out the window as he went, not quite hard enough to melt glass. Brill waved. That was enough of a work week, and if Martin Habib didn't think—hadn't thought—he Brill was committed, he ought to be here to see the reprisals.

The first came that evening, the rest much later. That evening Gary Pederson phoned, asked if he could pick up some of the books he'd loaned Brill.

Brill said: "I'd bring them over, Gary, but I'm not driving."

Pat, the bright-eyed car-driver, said she could take them tomorrow.

Gary said he'd be over shortly, and came, bringing a couple more volumes Brill had asked for of the Dibble and Anderson Sahagun translation.

Trinket was rather excited to meet Gary, a man she'd read about in the newspapers. Gary was attentive to her, and gave her a handsome flake of obsidian which he said was a blade.

Pat, who had seen little of Gary since school days, seemed to enjoy the visit. She had family news that she liked being able to tell again: there'd been a letter from their son Cal in Vietnam. He expected to be home for Christmas.

Gary said that was marvelous, talked with Trinket and Pat while Bob gathered and exchanged books, and didn't really say what was on his mind until Brill had walked him to his car in the cold night air.

"I saw Robert E. Lee Trump today."

"How'd you make out?"

"It was our third meeting actually," Gary said. "I'd have said things were going well. He invited me to bring in a proposal and I did, a modest one really. For five thousand dollars, just to extend this year's digging. He turned me down flat."

"I'm sorry," Brill said.

"Bob, I had the feeling. Please correct me if I'm wrong. But I said as we were chatting that I was an old friend of yours, and . . . well, it seemed to be the wrong thing to say."

"You think that's why he turned you down?"

"I'm confused, Bob. Things were very cordial before today."

"I'll get the money for you, Gary," Brill said.

"I didn't mean that . . ."

"I don't care if you meant it or not. I'll get the money for you. Thanks for the books," Brill said.

8.

She was sorry to call him at home, but it was Saturday morning and they needed a truck.

There was to be a protest rally tonight, outdoors; she was going to sing, and they needed a pickup truck for her to stand up on, with the microphone.

In the park, outside U City.

University policies.

The University wouldn't let them have it indoors.

They weren't asking for a permit. Parks were supposed to be free.

The sheriff's office, the ROTC, and some fraternity athletes.

Confrontation politics. Yes, she knew.

Someone would get the truck at the farm, then; leave his car; come in for Brill, if he was sure he wanted to be there.

Good-bye.

Brill was quite sure he didn't want to be there; he didn't want anybody else to be there, either.

Brill had been to a bunch of rallies, protests, and confrontations in the past three years. He was tired of rallies, protests, and confrontations. If there was any sight he found distressing in the world, it was the sight of a kid with a busted head.

Kids didn't know that the helmet of bone protecting their brains really would break if a man hit it hard enough with a stick. It was the loss of innocence showing in their faces that Brill hated: innocence, he thought, had nothing at all to do with sex. That was a big, smelly piece of Judaeo-Christian contrivance, that idea that innocence had some connection with maidenheads, masturbation, copulation, and, for that matter, as it was put so coyly, knowledge of good and evil.

Brill could imagine some Moses-like daddy, with a credulous young wife in the tent, making up that craven old man's lie. How could he have guessed that anyone beyond the sweet child of his lechery would believe so patent a fraud?

Innocence is a child's knowledge that he will never die.

Most of the energy in the world for getting things made, Brill thought, came from this true innocence; after you lost it, you might get things done, but you would never get things made again. Except out of the true opposite of true innocence, which was a man's accumulation of despair on the long downhill drift toward his death.

Brill thought that when a nation realized it could die, it, too, probably lost its energy for making things.

Nevermind. When a kid had his head busted, that was the end of innocence for him, and Brill had seen too many. Seen them freshly cracked like eggs; walked them to the courtroom in their bandaged heads and scared, sober faces, to plead them one way or the other. Guilty, usually, unless, beginning to accumulate despair now, they had learned to create defiance in themselves, which most kids didn't.

Draft protestors, protestors against war and repression, tentative affirmers of life, passionate yearners for freedom: the warlords' children.

Protestors against the makers of the rain that burns, the fire that drowns, the air that suffocates, and the medicine that brings disease, all the magic apparatus of the Americans, the great bloody shits of the world, khans whose children wept and sometimes hurled themselves against locked doors for their fathers' crimes. . . .

How did Cato's children feel about the salt plowed into Carthaginian fields?

How did Cato's children feel about Brill, for that matter? Trust him?

"You don't seem to find this protest relevant."

"This time? I think your position has about as much merit as the position of the boys over there with the hard hats." Brill pointed to about three dozen men, deputized by Beans Getnik in his first big night as sheriff; they wore construction-worker hats, carried sticks and cans of Mace. Some had sidearms as well.

"Then what do you want to help for?"

"What's up with Lawyer Brill?" It was the kid who was chairman for the evening.

"He says we're full of crap."

"Why don't you let me tell him what I said?"

The young chairman said: "What are you doing here, anyway?"

"Trying to finish a goddamn sentence . . ."

"You here to dig the young chicks, or what?"

They were drawing a circle of listeners. Brill said: "I might try to answer if you'll try not to interrupt."

"Want a little of that kookie nookie, do you?"

Brill said: "Why don't you restrain your youthful charm for about ten seconds, and Ill try . . ."

"Shit."

"Your protest is an imitation of someone else's protest. You read about one like it, didn't you?"

"Bugger off."

"There's no thought process in it. It doesn't come from your own analysis . . ."

"We need your truck. I guess we've got to listen to your crap."

"It's stupid on both sides this time."

"Maybe we don't need the old bastard's truck."

"But they're armed. You aren't. And I have the misfortune of knowing about it, so I'm compelled to be here."

"Gee, thanks. Has it got any gas in it?"

Then there was Joan of Arc, floating up to the back of the truck, with her long body and her long hair, managing to look both sexy and ethereal at the same time, turning her children on.

The chairman went away, striding toward the sheriff for a parley, and a thin-faced, slightly older boy said to Brill:

"Don't mind him, Mr. Brill. He's worried about what's going to happen."

"So am I."

"He's worried about Gabby. They went together up to a month ago."

"Is that why she's in this?"

The boy smiled. "It's an audience and she's a singer. Or maybe, how about, she's young and it's action?"

"You don't think she's serious about the politics?"

"It's like you were saying. No thought process, not for her. But she feels it, and she gets excited and she gets people excited." The thin-faced boy's voice was barely audible in the crowd noise. "Crazy, reckless chick. She'll do anything, and they know it."

Brill raised his own voice: "You seem to know her pretty well."

"I'm her husband," the boy said. "Or used to be. We don't communicate any more."

Nodded, and walked away, was lost in the muttering crowd, before Brill could get a real look at him.

Gabby held a microphone. She snapped her fingers in front of it, to test; it worked. The rest of the sound equipment was on the ground, behind the truck, and with it a boy with electric guitar.

The chairman crossed in front of Brill again, a heavy girl walking beside him, and Brill heard her say:

"Let's tell him it's a concert. You don't need a permit for a concert."

Then Beans Getnik's voice, amplified by a bullhorn:

"You have no permit for a rally. If there is any disorder, we are going to disperse this crowd."

People yelled back at him, drowning out the bullhorn, and Gabby raised her hand for silence, and the guitar began.

The air was cold, the sky clear, and Brill watched Getnik's deputies under the cool moon as she sang. He didn't think the new sheriff's men would start anything. They wouldn't have to. There were some antiprotest students, just as Gabby'd promised. Quite a few of them, if they were the ones who stood among the deputies, booing.

She sang a sad, tough poem by some girl poet, to her own setting, and the closer members of the crowd, a couple of hundred of them, were silent for it. The jeering stopped, momentarily.

She wasn't a good singer, or a bad singer; she was a young singer. That was the agent for combining delicacy and crudeness: youth. Brill felt a century old, and her song made him sad.

A speaker spoke. And another. The second, a radical, was scornful of the first who was merely liberal. The first got back up to reply, somewhat angrily. Jeers from the outer edge. The chairman, then. His meeting wasn't going very well. He tried some general, antiestablishment rhetoric, acceptable to liberals and radicals alike, and got them back together. Getnik was quiet on the bullhorn, smart enough apparently to let things fall apart rather than give them the unity of a sense of opposition. The chairman called Gabby to sing her antidraft song. There were cheers; hands passed her back up onto the truck bed.

It was quite obvious that she loved the crowd, the excitement she created in it; the song was the first Brill had heard her sing, about the dirty old man of war. The crowd knew it well. She had added a kind of cheer to it, which the audience knew too—she led them in it, in a mockery of athletic cheerleaders:

Catfish, ratfish, deepdish ratpack,
Old fag, old swish, climb into your Cadillac . . .

"Hey. You yelling about the President of the United States?" a voice called.

Take off, flake off,
Hurt your sacroiliac,

"The Commander-in-Chief?"

Proonface, goonface, doomface, bore.
Someone else can fight your war.

"Where's your respect?" the first voice hollered, and Gabby, going up in a cheerleader's leap and kick, yelled back:

"Kiss my flag!" Came down, swiveled, and bent. Up went the short skirt, to give them a cancan dancer's view of her bottom: stitched neatly to white panties, shining for a vulgar moment in the moonlight, the stars and stripes.

"Ho, Ho, Ho Chi Minh," yelled beards in the front row.

"Arrest that girl."

"Hell, no. We won't go."

"Come on. Break it up. That's enough . . ."

Brill moved. He threw a letterman one way, and a beard another. He put his head down, covered it with his hands because there were sticks out, and went through struggling bodies, big, low, intent, and powerful.

He slammed to the rear of the truck, where Gabby was still standing, proud and squealing with pleasure and excitement at the microphone, waving, laughing, wrapped his arms around her thighs and lifted her off of there.

"Mr. Brill. Bob. No, don't."

He carried her, plunging past more beards, to the left side of the vehicle, got the door open and pushed her in, onto the seat. There was a scared-looking boy already in there on the right. The key was in place. He pushed Gabby over against the boy, got up and under the wheel, slammed the door, started the motor, and began to move.

"The microphone," Gabby cried.

"It'll pull off," Brill said, and saw Beans Getnik himself, uniformed, gun drawn, blocking the way, his left hand up like a traffic cop signaling halt.

Cut the truck spotlight on and into the man's eyes.

Beans turned, blinded, jumped aside, and Brill, seeing an instant of clear path, roared out of there.

Down the streets of University City, pretty well deserted, until they had to stop for a light.

"All right, son," Brill said to the boy on the right. "Hop out."

The kid had some spark to him. "Where do you think you're taking her?"

"I'm a friend," Brill said. "Trying to save her stupid ass. Hop out."

Kid hopped. Brill grabbed Gabby's wrist and hung on to keep her from hopping, too, and as the light changed, drove off.

Went toward the east edge of town, thinking if he'd been recognized they'd expect him to turn west, toward Rosetta, hoping he hadn't been recognized since he wasn't a licensed driver, and after a moment Gabby pulled her wrist free, rubbed it, and said:

"My what kind of ass?"

"I don't think you'd have been killed out there," Brill said. "But they might have made it damned unpleasant, removing your little desecration."

"I thought of that," Gabby said. "It's only basted on. So I could rip it off in a hurry."

"Sure."

"Sure what?"

"Unless there were men holding your arms. So someone else could have the pleasure of ripping it off."

"Take me back there now, please," Gabby said.

He didn't reply.

"Bob, please? My friends are there."

"No they aren't. My friends have cleared the park and are putting yours in jail."

"Your friends?"

"I know half those idiots Getnik deputized," Brill said. "Known them all my life, and I've heard them lately. Spoiling for the kind of thing you did tonight to happen."

"What will they do?"

"Rough up the kids, and haul them off to jail. The more they fight back, the better the sheriff's boys are going to like it. That's why you can't go back."

"Isn't that my business?"

"No. If you were there, the inspiration of your presence would sure as hell get somebody hurt, Gabby."

"Oh." After a pause she said: "Couldn't you help?"

"I don't know. Maybe I should have stayed and tried . . . I wanted to get you out of there. I'll see what I can do tomorrow." He thought a moment. "If I could leave you off, and didn't get caught driving, maybe I should go back tonight . . ."

"You're not leaving me off." He was still trying to work it out when she added: "If my friends are in jail, I want to be in jail."

"Be a damn good place for you," Brill said. "Wearing a different pair of pants."

"You're offended with me."

"Yeah."

"And of course, you don't want the pleasure of ripping off my flag, do you?"

Who can answer a wise child? Brill snorted. Gabby pressed.

"Mr. Brill, the patriot. Save the flag. I know, if you took the pants and everything off intact, you could stuff them with a foam rubber ass, couldn't you? And put them on a walnut plaque and hang them on the wall at your cabin for a trophy. Couldn't you?"

"I'm offended because you wanted to provoke a bunch of hicks and squares instead of persuade them," Brill said. "I'm hick and square enough to feel we ought to be healing things up, not making new wounds. Here you are."

They had come to a small country motel: five wooden cabins, one with an old sedan parked near it. Brill turned in.

"I always used to think a radical was a man who loved his country so hard he couldn't stand its faults," he said. "Now I don't know."

"What are you doing?"

He stopped in front of a shabby house with a sign that said OFFICE on the door. He left her in the truck, biting her lips. He went in and registered.

"What name did you use, dear Mr. Brill?"

"Mr. and Mrs. Robert Brill," he said, feeling heavy and sullen, remembered he had talked with Mr. Light, shook that off, and drove to the designated cabin. "You can't stay in University City tonight."

He got out and opened the truck door for her. She hesitated, and then climbed down from the truck seat and stood waiting.

"Here's the key to the cabin," Brill said. "I'll get your autoharp. I'll be back for you in the morning."

She said, "Really?" Her tone meant to be scathing.

"How in hell could I go in there with you tonight?"

"Lord save us girls," Gabby said, "from small-town sheriffs and compulsive gentlemen."

He had to climb up into the back of the truck to reach the instrument, and when he got back with it was aware that her position had changed. To his surprise, she was smiling now.

She turned and let herself into the cabin, turned on a light. He handed her the cased autoharp.

"Such a stiff, compulsive gentleman," she told the instrument.

He said good night, but it was not until he had climbed sternly into the pickup and reached for the ignition that he understood her smile. The key was gone.

He had an instant of baffled anger. Then he looked over at the cabin door, and there she stood, dangling the key and grinning, and he started to laugh.

He left the truck, growling with a sort of animal delight at her, slammed into the cabin, grabbed her, kicked the door closed, and kissed her hard. Then he stepped back, grinned, and in a way that seemed no more than the next move in the contest, reached over the thumb and the tips of his index and middle finger, closed them on the tip of her right breast, through sweater and brassiere, feeling for a nipple, and tweaked. She smiled coolly, watching the hand, not moving.

"Beat me fair and square, didn't you?" He stepped back to her and folded his arms around her again. "By God, you beat me."

"Children always win children's games," she whispered, but was not through playing. For when he'd kissed her again, letting his lips register the extraordinary body heat hers held, pressing back against him, she suddenly wriggled free and threw herself face down on the bed.

He could see how the heat came: there were patches of red on her neck and cheeks, signaling a great throb and suffusion of blood beating through her.

"One of you men get her wrists," Gabby said, gasped, writhing, moving her hands violently now above her head and together, pounding with them as if she were trying to get them loose. "Grab those ankles." She kicked, thrashed; gradually her ankles were controlled, turned out, spread. "She's ready for you, Sheriff."

Damn right Brill would play. Too choked for speech, he landed on his knees, one between her legs, hauled the little skirt up and out of the way, and touched the flag. It was a little dime-store cotton flag, the sort kids carried to the park on Independence Day. It was a relic, a close-out, a forty-eight-star flag, but even in his passion he was careful of it. He wouldn't rip the thing, but hooked a finger into the loop of thread that held it in place, broke the thread, growling at her to be still, and tried to pull it all loose.

The edge of the flag bunched, the material of the pantyhose puckered, and Brill stopped playing. He pulled the pants down to her knees and took her from behind.

He was like a bull or a boy, meeting the slick, urgent inner moisture of the female, sliding through it till his pelvis met her buttocks and the thrust was stopped, forearms rigid around the girl's waist and belly, butt rigid at the end and intent of its stroke, locked around and within a softness which could now be apprehended to conceal another machine, equally rigid, locked open to receive.

They lay that way, Brill in a long, throbbing, inconsiderate orgasm, spewing and righteous, before it occurred to him to grin at the back of her sweater in insincere apology.

Then he turned loose, withdrew, and permitted her to turn, facing him. With which the surprising girl wrapped her arms around his head, and said into his ear: "Yes, mister. All right. Damn right." Kissed his neck. "Natural as a storm." Nuzzled him. "Shit, a girl gets tired of technique."

With which she extricated herself, began to wriggle out of her remaining clothes, punched him for undressing too slowly, put him on his back, and began to practice and elicit technique in a shameless and perfectly self-contradictory way, playing with him, fingers and mouth, skillful and unabashed, as Brill imagined a good professional might; Brill had never known a really good professional.

The only girlish thing she did, it seemed to him, before his objectivity began to weaken, was to ask if he liked it; a good professional would have known he did.

Objectivity be damned. He went down after her, using his own mouth, until she opened like a flower.

He mounted and he rode, proud and controlled now, amazed at her muscularity. For she accepted, pulled for, demanded all of his considerable weight on her body, abdominal muscles rippling easily under it, arms wrapping him tightly across the buttocks. A steel child she was, and all at once the steel melted and there was a general chaotic interchange—fluids, tissues, limbs, breath, and mortal souls, heaped in together, cooling in a disorderly pile like slag.

The boyish thing he did was to ask if she were okay.

She sunk her nails into the flesh of his shoulder to punish him for asking, and said: "I died."

9.

She slept.

He held her, her head incredibly light on his arm. In the dark part of the morning, hoping to finish wakefulness, he left the bed carefully, and walked out naked and barefoot to the truck in the cold night air, to get a pint of whiskey he knew was in the glove compartment. The one other car, the old blue sedan, was gone. They had the motel to themselves.

Going back in, he saw her sitting up. "Can't you sleep?" she asked.

"I will. Lie down."

"Making love is supposed to relax you."

"I get all clear-headed from the excitement of it." He sat down, took the cap off the bottle, offered it to her; when she refused, he drank.

"You're the most uncool man I ever met."

"I hope so. Anytime you prefer one of those walking dildoes with sunglasses on, you're no girl for me."

"I'll sing for you."

There was something nice, unself-conscious about that. She sat up, and put her sweater on. She got out the autoharp, made him put his head in her lap beside the instrument, and sang very quietly, barely chording, mostly poems she had set to odd little tunes for herself. Sylvia Plath? Brill hadn't heard of her but listened:

> ". . . I am inhabited by a cry.
> Nightly it flaps out
> Looking, with its hooks, for something to love . . ."

She sang Housman, in descending minors:

> "By brooks too broad for lee-ee-ee-ping,
> The lightfoot boys are lay-ayed . . ."

Oriental, and sang a Shakespeare song, and a Yiddish lullaby.

"That was lovely," Brill said. "Now lie down."

She put the harp aside, and her head came back light on his shoulder; she was asleep again, easy as a pup, and after a time, he slept too.

When he finally woke it was to stare at a girl, only gradually knowing who she was, a girl looking out the window of the shabby room, combing long hair, without clothes on. Sunlight came in and around her, making the separated strands of hair glow in a way he would remember, but he looked at the nakedness now feeling no more than friendly toward it. There was, curiously, no desire or lack of it; it was as if she were a boy, a roommate, or perhaps a girl in a photograph.

"Are you awake now?" The girl turned and looked at him, and from her voice was Gabby, toward whom, after all, he had many feelings—Gabby whom he had abducted in a way, who had bested him, submitted in mockery, submitted in fact, fused with him, slept on him, sung to him. "It's after ten o'clock," she said.

Brill nodded and thought about that, bemused, for he could not remember ever sleeping so late. His was the nervous, old man's complaint of waking early and abrupt. But this late morning he had waked slowly, lingering somewhere. "Long time going to sleep," Brill said. "Long trip, coming back."

Took a shower. Enjoyed it. Thinking with considerable wonder about the night, the passion and the games, and the strange, tender time when she had waked and sung for him.

Moved. He dried off, put on his pants, aware that he wasn't shaved. Didn't suppose it mattered. Went back into the room.

Dressed now, Gabby was sitting on the bed with the little flag, which she'd lifted free now, on her lap.

Brill was so generally relaxed and pleased that he hadn't thought of anything in particular to say; some spontaneous tenderness would form itself in a situation like this. He smiled.

"Nevertheless, you're a bastard," she said.

"Yeah?" Caught off-base.

"Just because I took the key and teased, you didn't have to come after me. You could have slept in your truck."

Brill stared at her, and shook his head. Kiddies had tried to climb this boy before. He was no goddamn jungle gym. "How the hell can you start an argument with *nevertheless*?" he said, and made her smile, whether she wanted to or not.

9

Friday morning after Thanksgiving, Robert Brill and a famous woman left University City, Illinois, for Tehuacan, Puebla, via Houston, Texas.

The famous woman was Gabriela Light, née Steiner, whose photograph, wearing the U.S. flag on her bottom, had been taken without Brill's realizing it, and distributed to the press, both

REGULAR	*and*	UNDERGROUND
The Limits of Disrespect		Gabby Waves It
A MATTER OF		Like It Is
STUDENT BAD TASTE		WHOLE-ASSED, HALF-MAST
WHEN IS A CHILD		THE STARS & STRIPES
TOO OLD TO SPANK?		4-EFFER

"I've been asked to appear lots of places," she said. "I want to go to Houston. You want to?"

"Yes, and on to Mexico," he said. "As long as I can be home for Christmas."

To Pat, his wife, he said: "I'm going to Mexico, with a friend from the University." Pat said it would be good for him to get away, but be careful about driving and drinking.

"There won't be anything come up that you can't handle," he said to Tommy Rebranch. "This dumb condemnation on the building, I suppose. Might develop. Keep a move ahead of them." Tommy wondered if he wouldn't need a power of attorney; Brill thought not, but gave it to him.

To Gary Pederson: "Any action down there, digging I could visit?"

"Young associate of mine named Stan Newman," Gary said "Working out of Tehuacan, on site survey. He could show you MacNeish's caves. One of the finest digs in recent years. They found the origins of corn."

The Houston appearance didn't amount to much. Gabby was restrained, ethereal, spoiled it, and was afterward exhausted.

Brill stood near her, facing the audience, and scowled at the first boy who yelled, "Wave your flag, Gabby!" He must have scowled pretty good, because the cry was not taken up.

Gabby made a pretty little speech, the beginning of which pleased and surprised him: "You know, that was a pretty silly thing I did? We want people swinging with us, not at us. People are okay. They better be. They're all we've got . . ." But then the vulgarity, irrepressible: "But if I ever do it again, I'll go all the way. I'll have the flag tattooed and wave it with my pants off."

Cheers, Brill scowled in the other direction. Gabby gave him an intolerably sweet and gracious smile.

2.

Brill was up early while Gabby slept, in a Mexican motel just south of the big steel and brewing city of Monterrey.

He read for a while, the first part of an article in *Science* on MacNeish's corn dig. The ancestor of corn was an extinct plant; it had taken archaeologists and botanists working together to find examples of it, preserved in dry caves, and reconstruct its history. Finishing, Brill was restless. He needed to move his body after two days of driving, and two nights of fornication. He left a note, and drove out along the highway. He turned onto a sandy side road, went a mile or so and stopped. Locked the car, as the guidebook suggested, feeling a little asinine about it, and started to walk out across the sparsely vegetated rocky ground.

In the distance, moving slowly toward him, were a man and an animal, a burro probably.

Brill left the wheel tracks, picked up a stick and ambled. There were white-winged doves active on the ground and in the cactus, and a small, bright-red bird.

He thought at first it must be some brilliant local creature, and wished for a bird book; then he realized, seeing another with the light obliquely on it, that what he was seeing were scarlet tanagers, here for the winter.

He poked around the base of a cactus with the stick, stirring nothing up, turned over a stone and saw a scorpion. It looked very much like a miniature lobster. It backed off, its tail lifted, ready to sting, but Brill thought only a barefoot man would be alarmed.

Looked up at the hills, and thought of Gary Pederson saying: "Arid land, made fertile a few months a year by a rainy season, supplied with hills in which there will be dry caves. Rain for cultivation, sand for preservation. That's what MacNeish needed to find the ancient cultivars preserved." That was the sort of region they were going to, farther south.

Brill heard shouts. He glanced back toward the road, couldn't believe the shouting was directed at him, but saw that the man with the burro was waving his arms.

He walked back, slightly annoyed, slightly curious. The man with the burro did not appear to be a brigand. He was a dark old man, barefoot, in a straw hat and a white, belted garment, and his burro was loaded with sticks. He wore a machete in the belt; Brill smiled and said good morning in Spanish.

The old man's reply was much to fast for Brill to understand.

"*Cascabel, señor. Cascabel.*"

Brill could hear the word now, and even repeat it; he didn't know what it meant.

The old man pantomimed. A finger streaking, zigzagged, stopped. Waved in the air. With his tongue against the roof of his mouth, the old man made a dry, buzzing sound.

"Rattlesnakes?"

"*Cascabel.*"

"*Muchos*?"

The old man waved his arms inclusively. "*Sì. Muchos.*" Took out the machete, pointed to a rather brushy plant Brill didn't recognize. Went to it cautiously, poked leaves, and almost immediately Brill heard the warning rattle as the old man leaped back.

A moment later, the snake appeared, leaving in a hurry.

"*Muchos, muchos.*" The inclusive gesture.

"Okay," Brill said. "*Gracias.*"

Gradually, Brill's ear for Spanish came back a little and they were able to converse. In certain seasons one could of course walk around. There were *codorniz* to hunt. (Brill noted the word, and later looked it up; it meant quail.) And interesting stones in some places. But just now one must stay on the road because of the snakes.

"In the hills," Brill wanted to know. "Are there pumas?" That word caused difficulty but they found one to settle on: *leónes*.

There were not as many *leónes* as formerly.

Brill could not have brought himself to offer the old man money for his friendliness. He offered cigars. The old man took two, and put them away.

"I was pretty pleased," he told Gabby, up when he got back and hungry for breakfast. She had a splendid appetite.

"My one-man peace corps," she said. "Pleased about what? Making a friend?"

"Because the land is still dangerous," Brill said. "Enough so that you overcome your reticence, if you live here, to warn a stranger."

"You're a stranger all right," Gabby said, pushing him out the door. "Strange, stranger, strangest."

They ate eggs on tortillas with hot sauce, and drove south through Ciudad Victoria.

Gabby's turn to drive, and she caught him dozing:

"Hey." Apropos of nothing. "I took Anthro One from your friend Sanctified Pederson. I'll bet I know something you never heard of."

"Who?" Brill said, classically stupid. "What?"

"Your big clean Indians. They ate deer shit."

He rallied. "You eat shrimp shit, girl. Every time you tell the man you'll have a shrimp cocktail before the Kansas City steak, medium rare."

She won: "Why would a nice Jewish girl order a nasty thing like that?"

"It ain't fair. It disconcerts me to hear a pretty girl say shit." Moodily. "Always will, I guess. What did you call him? *Sanctified* Pederson?"

"Does that disconcert you, too?"

"I think it's funny," Brill said. "What kind of teacher is he?"

"Poetic," Gabby said. "Which drives most of the class batty, or bores them. They need facts to pass exams—but there are always a few kids who really love him."

"Which were you?"

"Flunked it," Gabby said. "It wasn't my semester for going to classes. Who's the big archaeologist we're supposed to see in Tehuacan?"

"His name is Stan Newman."

"Wouldn't it be wild," Gabby said, "if it was a boy named Stan Newman I grew up with?"

Dipping down into Tamazunchale, late in the afternoon, they saw jungle for the first time, and Gabby could hardly keep Brill out of it. A woman they talked to showed them pineapples, growing on a bush, thirty feet behind her house.

"Look at this." They were drinking Cokes; Brill showed Gabby a road map. "Does this look like a road?"

"It's a line on the map, at least."

Over to the east of where they were, going down the coast from Tampico to Tuxpan. "It's a road I'd like to take," Brill said. "I wish we hadn't passed the turn to Tampico."

"We can go back. I don't mind."

It was sixty miles back to the Tampico turn, and eighty-eight from there to Tampico itself.

"If you're sure you don't mind? There should be water birds on that road."

"If you're silly enough to want to drive another hundred and fifty miles, I'm silly enough to ride with you."

He drove. Her night vision was poor and she didn't much like driving after dark. Shortly after they made the turn east, she went to sleep. Gabby's car was a Karmann Ghia, and Brill marveled that she could drop off so comfortably in so cramped a space.

Driving through the dark, he thought of the *Science* articles by MacNeish and his associates, not so much of the corn, for he hadn't really absorbed the botanical details yet, but on the prehistory of the particular valley toward which they were headed.

". . . about seventy miles long and twenty miles wide . . . ringed by high mountains."

The earliest evidence the archaeologist had found dated around 7000 B.C., and probably indicated a period of habitation that went back three or four thousand years before that. Ten thousand years ago, then.

". . . the inhabitants were grouped together into small, nomadic familes or microbands who changed their camps three or four times a year with the seasons (see Figure 2) . . ."

Figure 2 was a killer. It showed the valley, with its arid floor, where rain came only two months a year, when people lived on plants they hadn't learned yet how to store. Each year, as the plants died back or were used up, the people went to hunting, trapping, and starving for ten months. And in all that empty valley the population estimate was, ". . . three to four microbands of four to eight people."

The loneliness of prehistory.

Driving steadily while the girl slept, Brill found himself frowning over, but unable immediately to answer MacNeish's disparaging summary:

". . . although they hunted such animals as horses and antelopes of now extinct species . . ."

Glower away, Robert, but think of that: there were horses on the American continent which lived, and which became extinct, only a couple of thousand years before the Spaniards came and brought more in.

Which strange, by then supernatural animals, changed the course and shape of things on a continent to which they seemed perfectly well adapted and where they were soon able to live wild. Explain the gap; or conclude that evolution, like all the other cosmologies—theological or scientific—is a big giggle.

". . . even most of their meat came from smaller game, such as jackrabbits, turtles, birds, and other small mammals . . . these people in the so-called 'big-game hunting stage' (5) or 'mammoth-hunting period' (6) . . ." The put-downs announced by the quotes, if you looked up notes (5) and (6) were for a couple of writers named Willey and Arroyo de Anda.

". . . these people . . . were far from being the great hunters they are supposed to have been. As one of my colleagues said, 'They probably found one mammoth in a lifetime, and never got over talking about it.' "

Quite wrong, Brill scowled at the sleeping girl beside him in the car, moving toward Tampico. *We didn't talk about it afterward. Sometimes, afterward, sitting by the fire, we'd remember and wonder at it, and perhaps we prayed to it, not knowing we were praying, for in awe we remembered that it brought us here. . . .*

3.

The cave was decent and the valley safe. We'd moved a long way from our last valley, following the huge, crippled thing. I had four spear points in him, and Cal'd put one in, too.

The little girl followed her mother a short way behind as we tracked, waiting for the mammoth to die. We hoped he would before we began to die, one by one, of hunger. Women and children first.

Louise, the younger woman, was almost too weak to walk, but Pat helped her.

Sometimes, when the mammoth stopped, I'd drop back, leaving

Cal to watch, and carry Big Louise for a while until the group was all together again. She was a long woman, but light because she had lost much weight. We didn't dare to be spread out, and we had no cave then, in that season.

On the third day we had to fight. A man, the first we had seen in two fattenings of the moon, came out from behind some cactus and put a spear into our mammoth.

He didn't see us, but we had no spears left. Cal and I ran, each knowing what to do, as father and son must. We went behind the same cactus the man came out from and ran, keeping the ridge between us and the other hunter until we knew we were past him. We hid behind a rock and watched the mammoth go by at a limping trot.

Cal had a big stone, as heavy a one as he could lift, and when the hunter went by I jumped out onto his back and rode him to the ground; he was small, and before he could get his breath Cal dropped the rock on his head.

We do not usually eat a man when we kill one, but we were dying of hunger. The woman Louise was dying. I used my flint knife to cut off a forearm to chew on, and left Cal to guard the body while the rest caught up; and I followed the mammoth. The man had two spears, and I took them.

When the mammoth lay down to rest, he was too much in the open. I could not get close enough to throw a spear, so I went back and was just in time. Wolves had come and Cal had no spear. I gave him one. Pat was cooking the man. She is very fastidious.

The small girl couldn't wait, and was eating her portion raw. We gave Louise blood to drink, but she choked on it and died. We kicked sand over her and left her a flint knife to keep the wolves away.

Later we found the cave to sleep in, and the next day ate some more of the strange man. I looked at his face. Pat had washed it. I thought him nice-looking, younger than he had seemed when alive and on the trail. Pat took the face to cook it, and said it was nice-looking and young, so I knocked her down and kicked her and bred her. She roasted the head, and scraped the hair off with flint. When we had eaten that, the man was finished except for some meat on the shin bones that the dogs stole while we slept.

Where do dogs come from? These may have been with the man.

I kicked the dogs and threw rocks at them, but they wouldn't go away. They are like wolves, but they stay near us while the wolves go away. Sometimes we try to catch the dogs to eat them, but they are too fast except when they are puppies. When there are puppies, we can catch them to eat if the mothers do not have them hidden very well.

We left Pat and the girl in the cave, and followed the tracks of our mammoth, the dogs showing the way where the land was dry, and then the land became moist and we found that he was lying down in a watercourse, where there was a little mud from a spring. We were glad to see the water, and there was grass growing in the place, the kind that would have seeds on it later that we could eat.

We watched the mammoth for a long while, from behind a rock. Cal thought he might be stuck in the mud, and wanted to go in on him with rocks, but I said we should make spears. There was good flint in that valley. We went back to the cave.

Pat had killed some small, gray-plumed birds with her sling, and we ate them. But the next day, while we chipped flint for our spears, we were hungry again, and there were no more birds, and the next day, too.

Cal and I went to kill the mammoth at the watercourse. We went in on him, and he was stuck. We went in on him with our four new spears, and Cal's first one broke off. When he was trying to retrieve the point from the animal's shoulder, the mammoth tossed its head suddenly and a tusk went into Cal's side. I carried the boy back to the cave, bleeding.

The woman and the girl were hungry, and I had to stay now, to guard Cal. I could sleep because the dogs barked when the wolves came.

The woman cried and I told her to be still. The little girl found a few locusts to eat. They were in holes in wood, and about to hatch, but not very many. Night came and we were cold in the cave.

But it was warm in Tampico, and the lights of the hotel, as Brill pulled up to the door in front of it and Gabby woke, were bright.

4.

Follow Bob Brill's intuitive and greedy gut to a big, Mexican picnic: hard rolls from a bakery, open at six A.M., and Brill there with the first of the women in rebozos.

That track they were going to follow along the coast looked like a hundred slow miles between restaurants.

From a grocery store, in cans: Portuguese sardines, Spanish baby eels, Brazilian hearts of palm. In bottles, Mexican rum, one dark, one pale. Also, cheese, Spanish sausage, a jar of chili peppers, bottled water, British sweet biscuits, and American-licensed pop.

Walking back to the hotel, he saw a small market where he bought a big onion, lemons, and a pineapple like the one they'd seen growing in the jungle.

"Mire, señor . . ." The pineapple woman had a cardboard carton, with the flaps closed. Smiling, she opened it. *"Mire."* Inside were figurines and fragments of old clay.

He'd seen stuff something like it, at Gary Pederson's house. None of the figurines was quite complete; they were of a rather engaging kind, squat, grinning, flat-faced little women, five or six inches high. At first he thought the pineapple woman or someone must have put modern black paint on them in certain areas; looking closely, he saw the black was more like tar, and remembered there was oil on this coast.

"How much?" He held one up. The asking price was twenty cents. The other women in the market had them, too, were getting out clay pieces and holding them up, calling for his attention. No one, Brill thought, would bother to produce these things as fakes in such quantity for so low a price. He picked them over, bought one for Trinket, one for Cal, one for Pat; one for now, to take back to Gabby, and some flowers.

He left most of his purchases in the car, then went in and put Gabby's figurine and the flowers in front of her place at the breakfast table in the hotel dining room.

At a little after eight, they drove through the town to the ferry landing, to wait for the boat which would take them across the river mouth.

They stood on the bank, watching big, fast fish move in the brackish water. Tarpon, Brill guessed, and wouldn't one of those give you fits on a fly rod?

They crossed, and started driving south on the coastal strip. At first it followed high ground, but after an hour the road began descending. They found themselves on what seemed to be a coastal causeway, with Gulf water in the left side and salt marsh on the right.

Brill stopped the car and pulled off.

"Take a walk?"

"My very strange and lonely nature boy," Gabby said. "Should I get boots out?"

"I doubt there'll be snakes here," Brill said. "But it does look muddy in places."

There were hundreds of ducks on the water, on the marsh side, large groups and small, dotted over it as far as he could see. The closest group were blue-wing teal.

"This is where you guys come for the winter?" Brill said. "No wonder you leave home early."

They walked slowly up the edge of the marsh; the bird life, a lot of which Brill couldn't have named, was incredible. Mostly they were shore birds—stilts, avocets, curlews; there were herons and bitterns; coots, grebes, and what Brill guessed were gallinules; various members of the rail family. And the ducks, getting up, moving, settling down again.

"You like it?" he asked Gabby.

"It's not the kind of thing I ever thought much about liking or not liking," she said. "Sure. The birds are pretty. Some of them are funny."

Back at the car, in no hurry to leave, they drank warm pop and rested in the sun. There were no cars, no trucks. They hadn't seen a person since coming through a small town on the hill above the ferry area. Gabby took off her blouse and brassiere, and sunbathed, and rubbed her very firm, young upthrusts on his cheeks at one point and asked if he liked that.

Brill said sure, some of the teats were pretty and some were funny.

She poured Delaware Punch on his head. Then she put a drop or two on each nipple, and invited him to lick it off. He did. Then they thought they heard a car coming, and she quickly pulled a blouse on, but it wasn't a car; it was a tiny plane, very high up.

It was Gabby's turn to drive. "Sometime, I'd like to come back here," Brill said, as they drove slowly, looking at beach, marsh, strips of jungle. "To this road. I'd like to find a strip of beach and sleep here. I'd love to see early morning here. God damn, it must be beautiful."

She smiled. "You're beautiful."

He admired her patience. She would sense it each time he'd see something he wanted to look at closely, a plant or some bird on the water, and would stop the car. He climbed a tree, and for thanks picked her a rather scrawny orchid, recognizable though it wasn't quite in bloom.

About dusk, without his having asked her to, she pulled the car off the road to the left, and stopped.

"My turn to drive?"

"Not unless you're planning to drive away and maroon me."

"Maroon you?"

"We're sleeping right here. On the beach. If there's places you'd love to sleep, Mr. Brill, you're not going around doing it without me."

And the preposterous girl made a face like a tarpon, dropped her hand into his lap and squeezed.

"Hey!"

"Hey, yourself. I'll give you fits on your fly rod," she said.

There was a blanket in the car. They spread it on the beach. There were dark globs around, probably the same substance the old Totonacs had used to decorate their pottery figures.

"*My* pottery figure," Gabby said.

Brill gathered wood and built a fire in the long twilight. The evening sky was full of seabirds, wheeling.

"Why no sunset?" asked Nature Girl.

Because they were facing east. "I'll show you sunrise in the morning," Brill said.

Supper was rum. Hard, pungent sausage. Chilis. Hard rolls. Sardines. Onion. Lemon. Afterward, Brill peeled the pineapple and cut it into spears.

Gabby said: "That's the most delicious thing I ever ate in my life."

"Because it ripens on the bush," Brill said.

"Would you get stoned with me?"

"I'd love it. I'll get the rum."

"Not on rum."

"Pot, you mean?"

"Yes, please."

"You have some?"

"I got it from the maid at the hotel. Marijuana. My one word of Spanish. It's gold."

"Gold?"

"She said it's from Acapulco, so it must be what we call gold."

"I don't think it'll work on me, Gabby. I've tried once or twice . . ."

"It'll work," she said. "If I have to blow it into your lungs myself. I'll bet the Aztecs did it."

"They did . . . various things. Mushrooms, of course."

"Pot grows here. They must have used it."

"All right. That's a good argument."

"Let me wash the pineapple off your face," she said, spendthrift of bottled water.

She rolled a cigarette of marijuana; they smoked it together, taking turns. She rolled another. Time passed and became immaterial; birds roosted, and later night birds swooped and many bats. They sat close, and said little, and Brill for the first time enjoyed the stuff—or enjoyed something.

"But wouldn't I enjoy anything we did together tonight?" he asked. "Including the dishes?"

It took him a long time to say that and by the end of the sentence he'd forgotten it was a joke. He noticed, instead, that given the euphoria of the situation, it didn't much matter whether it was a joke or not, and found just having her to lean against him and the sea smell and sound to be everything he needed or might ever need.

After a time, speech became possible, a return of coherence, still, some feeling of elevation quite unlike that produced by alcohol. He began to know, or guess at least, what was fine about this, but regretfully, because it was nothing he felt he'd ever want to do by himself, or with anyone, really, but Gabby.

"Tell me more things you love to do," she said. "What do you love best of all? Your favorite thing."

Brill thought, and smiled to himself.

"I don't think I'd better tell you," he murmured.

"Why?"

"Because it sounds, would sound, very odd to you."

"Should I take that personally?"

"No, no," Brill said. "I wasn't thinking of something to do together. Anyway, you can't do it in the world any more, Gabby. Not in my world. Maybe you could down here."

"It must be very strange."

"Yes."

"You are going to tell me?"

"Yes."

"What?"

"Something I haven't done in thirty years, and may not ever do again. I like to plow, Gabby. On a warm, windy spring day, behind a team of mules. With the ground dried out just enough, after rain. I like to turn dirt with my own shoulders, open up the ground, spread it two ways, holding the plow straight as we go. Smell the dark, wet dirt as I lay it open, smell the spring smell. And the mules, the sweet mule smell, and feel the first real sweat of the year begin to soak my back and hair . . ."

"A plowboy," Gabby said. "That's so erotic. That's incest."

He held her close, and crooned, not doubting that the marijuana had him: "Opening old mother with your body's weight."

"Two round mules and a tall, straight boy leaning into his shafted steel," Gabby said. "The image turns me on."

He thought about that for a while and murmured:

"No. It's religious. There's a song we sang in high school glee club—you didn't know I was in high school glee club."

"I've never seen your yearbook," she said, and licked his neck, under the ear. "You're in my glee club."

He had to wait until she had the neck licked, and wiped it dry with her nose. "There. Tell about the song?"

"It used to make me shiver," he said. "Every time we sang it. A simple, masculine religious song, called The Blind Plowman. You have to see the singer as a strong old man, and blind now." And he sang:

" 'Set my hands upon the plow
My feet upon the sod.
Turn my face toward the West
And praise be to God!'

Those might have been the words."

"It makes me shiver, too," Gabby said. And after a moment: "I'll find your song. I know people with music libraries. But why can't you?"

"What?"

"If you really want to? Next spring, in just a few months now, on your own farm?"

"Well. Yes."

"Shall I buy you some mules?"

"I doubt if there's a team left in the state."

"I've seen them."

"Workhorses maybe, Gabby. The Amish still use them a little. Mules are different. I could get them in the South, I guess."

Yes, and some harness, and a moldboard plow. Make Kress leave him ten or fifteen good acres to work up, by himself. There was barn space; did he still have the strength, not for an hour or two but days of work like that? If he plowed with his mules, he'd harrow, and plant, cultivate, harvest. And what the hell would it all amount to but another of his futile acts of nostalgia?

"Ouch," she said.

"I'm sorry." He had squeezed too tight. He stroked her hair. "The Brills were always fit for plowing, girl," he whispered. "Maybe damn little else. My great-grandfather was hired to close his office for a month, once, and plow a furrow: from University City to River Crossing, sixty-seven miles through the forest. So travelers going west would have a line to follow. He got to the river, and never went back to that office again, but that's another story."

"Oh, we need Brills," Gabby whispered back, and began to press him backward onto the blanket. "We'd never get west without Brills. Blind Plowboy Brills," she pressed him down. "To make us shiver, damn you. Lie back there." She came squirming over him. "This time I'm going to plow you, buddy," she said. "You see how it feels to be mother earth one time."

Afterward, in spite of the night, and the beach, and his great contentment, Brill still didn't sleep.

He sat, sucking lightly on the dark rum bottle, staring into the fire, the girl's head on his lap while she slept, thinking of the names of the old races of corn. Where had he heard them first? Nal-tel and Chapalote.

They were an end product. Before them, long centuries of unintentional selection, until a plant was born that could survive only if men bred it, and cared for it, like a domestic animal. Corn would disappear if left to itself in the world. Contained in husks, with no ways of scattering its seed, helpless to compete against the weeds or survive the weather. Nor would it, if that happened, ever reappear, for the wild ancestor was gone now. If any of that race of grass had happened to survive antiquity, MacNeish said, in some inaccessible, spring-fed cranny in the hills, then the coming of the Spaniards with their goats, which climbed everywhere and ate everything, completed its extinction.

That was the reverie, and he was ready to lie back and take it with him into sleep when he heard, unbelievably, the sound of a heavy motor approaching at high speed on the road. A moment later there were lights coming, blinking on and off, and something swept by their parked car with a light smashing sound in the night, and zoomed on, leaving silence behind.

Brill put the girl's head on the blanket, and got up. The sonofabitch hadn't even dropped his speed; cut on that blinker and figured it would tell me to get out of the way, he was coming through.

Gabby said: "What?"

"It's all right. A truck. It's gone now."

She wriggled closer to the fire, smiling; settled back to sleep.

Brill went over to the car. Something projecting from the truck, which must have filled the road completely, had torn their outside mirror off. That was all.

God, if we'd been driving out there, he thought. There'd have been nothing I could do to protect her. He moved the car farther off the road. He went back to the girl. The bottle.

The fire:

After the third night in the cave, Cal was unconscious. Pat and I took turns hunting for small things nearby with the sling, but except for one mouse and some grasshoppers, there wasn't anything to eat.

The grasshoppers were thin in that season, and didn't have much flavor.

Twice a day I would go to see if the mammoth was dead yet, and to chase the wolves away. I needed to be there when he died, to get to him before they did. As long as he had any life, he could keep the wolves off by himself. I was afraid, too, of another man finding the mammoth. I was not strong enough to kill another man now.

When I went the third day, there was a human standing there, and I stopped and hid. I got downwind to smell, and it was a woman. It made me excited. From downwind, I could see she was pregnant, and guessed she must be the woman of the one we killed.

I knew it would be easy and right to kill her, but do not have a moral nature. Instead, I looked all around to be sure it was safe, went up and knocked her down and bred her. Then, because the mammoth was still alive, I led her back to the cave. I did not think Pat would care, because if the mammoth didn't die soon, or the wolves got him first, we could eat the woman.

The new woman's name was Gabby.

When we got to the cave I was right. Pat and Gabby only fought an hour or two, while I rested; sometimes I watched them, sometimes I didn't; to see which was strongest. As soon as Pat had knocked her down a few times, and been knocked down, she hit the new woman with a small rock, and then kicked her until she lay still, and then Gabby said all right, and got up and took her place in the cave.

Cal was moaning. I took two spears I had made and went back to the mammoth. I had decided I would have to try to kill it. Parts of it, injured days before, had begun to smell badly, and the huge creature was weak. Cal had to have some blood to drink to get well. If a man does not have a son to hunt with him, he might as well stop hunting, lie down with the women, and die.

The mammoth had turned on its side and was wheezing slowly. That meant it was nearly gone. Pat had followed from the cave, and I told her to go back, and get the new woman to help her carry Cal here, and bring the girl, while I chased the wolves away.

When they got back, I took the spears and went in on the mammoth. I walked up its side, and stood behind the head; then I leaned all my weight onto the first spear, between the ribs of the mammoth, and got finally, through all that tough hide, into the heart.

It gave a great, leaping shudder, which threw me to the ground, and then grew gradually still. I lay there laughing on the ground, in the mud, and later, when the women held Cal so he could drink the flowing blood, I walked off by myself, sat on a stone, and felt grateful to the earth. . . .

Brill felt rather noble. He'd resisted the temptation, back there when he was leaving the cave for the final sortie, to let the whole bunch die off tragically—Pat, Cal, Gabby, Trinket—let them all go and then himself be gored by the dying mammoth and eaten by the fangy, bastard wolves.

He put another driftwood log on the fire, and stretched out, fitting his body to the curve of Gabby's; he smelled her hair, and the burning wood and tar from the fire, seaweed, and sea wind, and he slept.

10

A guess can be made, one-quarter educated the other three wild, as to what, 452 years ago, the year before Cortes came, Tehuacan was like.

If Stan Newman will lend us his book.

We have stood, by now, briefly and in awe, among the huge pyramids of Teotihuacán near Mexico City, and learned that they were built not by Aztecs, or the people before the Aztecs (Chichimecs), or even the people before them (Toltecs): but by a people so little known they do not have a name. We can refer to them only by making a collective noun from the name of their great, dead city, calling them Teotihuacani. It was deserted a long time before Cortes came, all through the Aztec and Chichimec centuries. There used to be a neat theory that the Toltecs knocked it off between 900 and 1100, but the newest radiocarbon data say no. Say it fell around 650, the heavy isotopes of Carbon 14, holding the message for us: something happened here, longer ago than you think. Something happened.

We have walked in some wonder through the new museum in Mexico City, seeing the fine work in stone, clay, jade, crystal, mosaic, feathers, and just a little bit in gold, that the old American city builders from a whole throng of cultures could turn out; seen evidence (picture of an observatory at Monte Albán; calendar stones) that their astronomy and their mathematics were more advanced than were those branches of scholarship among the Europeans who came in, with cross and sword, to learn about turkey and potato raising.

We have seen the delicate fenestration of Tajín, the jewel in the jungle—"It doesn't look a damn thing like any of the other pyramids," Brill said.

"If we ever build one, I want one like that," said Gabby.

Papeles de Nueva España (1580–82)

"May I borrow it, Stan?"

"Sure."

"*Papers* of New Spain?" Gabby asked.

Newman smiled. "Documents, if you like." He was a good-looking, self-assured man of thirty, dark and trim as a Mexican though he came from Baltimore—was indeed the boy who had grown up in the same congregation there as Gabby, where his father was a cantor.

("*Stan* Newman?" She had said it again the evening before they arrived. "But I grew up necking with a boy named Stan Newman.")

They had recognized one another today with shouts, hugs, and a kiss of unseemly duration. But Baltimore was far behind Stan Newman now. His Spanish, he told Brill, was so practiced that even educated Mexicans tried to guess what part of their country he came from, by his accent. His boots and clothing were made for him in Mexico City, and his permanent address was Cuernavaca.

They had just finished eating ravioli. The best restaurant, in modern Tehuacan, was Italian.

"It's a collection of what are called *fuentes*," Newman said. "Fountains. Sources, rather. Springs? In any case, that's a general term for all the sixteenth-century documents relating to history or to Indian life . . ."

This particular group of *papeles*, he explained, were collected by a nineteenth-century scholar named Francisco Paso y Troncoso, who found them mostly in the archives of old agencies in Madrid.

"Can we have something Mexican for dessert at least?" Gabby asked. "Flan?"

Flan was custard.

"Makes you buxom, cousin," Newman said, just a little more proprietary than Brill quite liked.

2.

There'd been Phillip II, sitting back in Spain, writing checks to send out his captains and his monks to these wild new regions. Look at it his way:

He's a kid king at twenty-nine, a stiff kid who doesn't care much for travel; but who can avoid curiosity? And all the time, the captains and the monks are after him:

"You ought to look it over just one time, Your Majesty. I mean it's Treasureville. Am I kidding the king, Sebastiano?"

"You can't believe it, sir. I mean, it's so far-out, I can't tell you. Those cities, they gleam and twinkle like a woman's eye through a fan, and I mean you've just got to follow, follow as the fan goes back on down the hall. Toward dark or light, seeing more and more . . ."

"Little fight here and there. Maybe an Indian chick who digs you."

"Look, Your Majesty. A couple of galleons, huh? Just two this time, one for each of us? And maybe twenty horses?"

"We got Cortes conned into letting us go northwest this time, sir. With a hundred men, and we can pick up Indians to fill in. Some of them are pretty good boys, and that northwest: that's where the silver comes down the trail. Am I right, Sebastiano?"

"Silverino and golderino, King, sir. Yeah, I'll have another little goblet of the Jerez sweet, yessir. Hey, let me tell you about this pulque they drink, make it from cactus. Mean, it tastes like a glass of milk with a fart in it, sir, but it'll do the job. You've seen that, Federico?"

"They used to give it to the cats they sacrificed, 'fore we stopped all that pagan shit, sir."

"They felt no pain, 'bastiano, babes. No pain."

"There's this one pyramid, sir, with the little windows . . ."

"We would fain see it," young Philip must have said.

Listened to that, and wrote checks, for twenty-five years. And watched the stuff come back: gold and silver, jade and statues, puzzling books and strange slave girls, birds and fruits and animals, and the captains swaggering, knowing curious things, bragging picturesque diseases. And the monks, wild-eyed with mystery, hottonguing odd new languages, thin from stamping out old magic. Coming back to court, bringing more tales, taking more money.

Traveler by temperament or not, he must have wanted to go, dreamed of going, but the trip was like a trip to Mars—a whole year, there and back. Out of a king's life? What could Philip do, who had to fight the routine wars in Holland, dicker with Popes for treasure shares, keep the nobles and the priests in order, see that taxes came in and that his people got some service for them?

He grew older and, finally, tired of the tales. If he couldn't go he wanted facts, not yarns; wanted to know about people, not slaves with turquoise in their teeth, over whom these monks and captains had made him king. Wanted to undertsand his subjects over there; even wanted to protect them. Said, to the administrators, who helped carry his briefcase:

"Let's find out. Sebastiano's son is a worse liar even than his father.

He'll tell you anything he thinks you want to hear. Can't we find out?"

The administrators did what they were born knowing how to do: agreeing that it was difficult to make directives for gold cities and medicinal fountains, unless you knew how many gold paving stones to figure per block, and how much youth per mouthful from the average fountain. They devised questionnaires.

"I don't know how much good it did Philip II," Stan Newman said. "But it sure has helped the heck out of anthropologists. Every local mayor got a questionnaire to fill out; mostly they turned them over to a priest. Matter of who could read and write, and who was closely enough in touch with some elderly Indians to ask them questions."

"Griffins in triplicate," Gabby said, ordering another flan.

"Marvelous appetite, doesn't she?" Newman said. "Is she still a nibbler? No, thanks, I don't want a hamburger just now, and then eats half of yours when it comes?"

"I'd like to see the answers to the questionnaire on this place. Tehuacan," Brill said.

"Me too," Newman said. "I'm not sure there ever was one. When Paso y Troncoso started digging through them, they must have been in an extraordinary mess—suppose you waited four centuries, and then went to Washington to see what you could learn about the towns and cities of Korea in 1952, from stored reports by U.S. military government officers, huh? And let's imagine a tremendous decline meanwhile in American power, a couple of complete switches in form of government, and over there in Asia there hasn't been any official political connection for hundreds of years . . ."

"Yeah," Brill said. "Old Step and Trunk must have had himself quite a problem."

"Got a lot of stuff, but it's not often exactly what you're looking for. Closest thing I can offer you to here is this." He opened the book. "Petlaltzingo. It's not one of the places I'm surveying, but I have it in my card file because it's the only place in the sources that mentions another town. Called Tequistepec. That I surveyed a week or two ago. About ten miles from Petlaltzingo."

"How far from here?"

"Sixty miles."

That was when Brill asked to borrow the book, thinking a town just sixty miles away must have been pretty much like Tehuacan.

Newman shrugged, smiled, shook his handsome little head. He had close, curly hair. "It was Mixtec over there. This place was more likely run by Tlaxcalans. They were Nahuatl-speaking, rivals of the Aztecs."

"The guys that helped Cortes?"

"Yes. But before that, probably . . . I don't know. Petlaltzingo and Tehuacan may both have done things for the damn Aztecs. But . . . sixty miles. And over a mountain. That's a long way between two places that didn't have much reason to be connected by a road, in a country without horses . . ."

"Two good days' walking."

"Yeah. But was there any reason for walking it?"

"Promises to keep," Gabby said. "A gig to play."

"Your gig, darling," Newman said. "Of course. Up it."

3.

"No," Gabby said. "We were younger than goatshit, for God's sake."

"I wish you wouldn't say shit," Brill told her, but she was already asleep. Probably wouldn't have said it if she'd been awake, but it was still a word he'd never liked to hear girls use.

Papeles de Nueva España
(The Robert Brill translation)
Vol. 5. Geographical Account of
The Diocese of Tlaxcala

(Excerpts from the *Relación de Petlaltzingo*)
14. To the fourteenth question. Said town of Petlaltzingo was subject to the Mexican (that's Aztec) empire, but paid no tribute except that they had to give provisions to the Mexican army when they came through town, and to serve as soldiers with it. Nothing else. Petlaltzingo had its gentry and its native leaders to whom the common people gave proof of their vassalage and subjugation.

Common Gabby gave proof of her vassalage and subjugation by snoring lightly as he wrote it.

Much personal service was given by the Indians to the gentry, Indian girls did just about anything they asked. The gentry's corn was sowed for them, their chiles, beans, cotton, melons, salvia . . .

What the hell was *salvia*? The Spanish-English just repeated it. *salvia,* n.—salvia. Help you, sir? Got the English dictionary: the scarlet-flowered sage.

The Indians supplied many chickens every day, generally all the gentry wanted, along with shawls, cloaks, and petticoats. The Petlaltzingo boys, in the time of their gentility, worshipped an idol, called in Mixtec NUCHI, which in Spanish means "Six Wind," and this was the chief one, of whom there was a green stone image a span and a half high.

A jade statue, more than a foot tall.

They say that it was burned by Bachiler Malaver, who afterward became Bishop of Xalisco, and was then inspector of the Bishopric of Guaxaca.

Those would be present-day Jalisco, in the north, and, to the south, Oaxaca, where present-day Stan Newman and Gary Pederson would be pursuing knowledge with their spades next month. Brill had a question: how do you light a jade statue, Bachiler?

Maffachufettf. They also worshipped another idol called in Mixtec XACHA AHO, which means "Six-House" in Spanish. He was of green stone, too, and said Bachiler burned his ass.

To these idols they offered men, killed in their honor, putting the hearts in the idols' mouths and smearing them with blood; the people also offered incense; they had a hell of a bunch of priests; (but) they don't remember the ceremonies and rites of the days of their gentility.

He was hungry, but he didn't know if there was anywhere you could go in a Mexican town to get something to eat after ten o'clock at night. To hell with eating.

15. To the fifteenth question. Said town of Petlaltzingo was ruled by its native chieftains, who were absolute masters and had full and complete jurisdiction without any sort of higher authority over them, and these took counsel with the other leading men to decide what must be done: they made slaves out of thieves, killed adulterers . . ." (Bang, I'm dead) ". . . and for any act of disobedience to the chief, one would later die; they don't remember anything else of this. They were at war with those of Tequistepec . . ." (Newman's reference) ". . . and with those of the town of Acatlan; they fought in squadrons when battle was joined, on the plains or the hills, and the usual way was to go up in the high hills and fortify their billets with rock walls and ditches, and there to defend themselves with rolling stones and throwing weapons. They wore cotton armor and carried bows and arrows and reed bucklers . . . they ate bread made of corn, and beans and greens, and sometimes the bigger wheels had chicken or venison, and they maintain themselves now in the same way.

They say that formerly there were not so many sicknesses or such a high death rate as now, and that the town has diminished greatly. They don't know how to explain this.

How shall a people know how to explain a thing, when the days of their gentility are past?

4.

Gabby said, UNDERSTAND IT? Gee whillikens (for she wouldn't want to use a word Mr. Brill didn't like to hear girls say), after the number of times she'd heard Brill and Newman go over it and seen their grubby little hand-drawn maps, she could SING IT, with or without autoharp.

Encouraged not to, she did anyway:

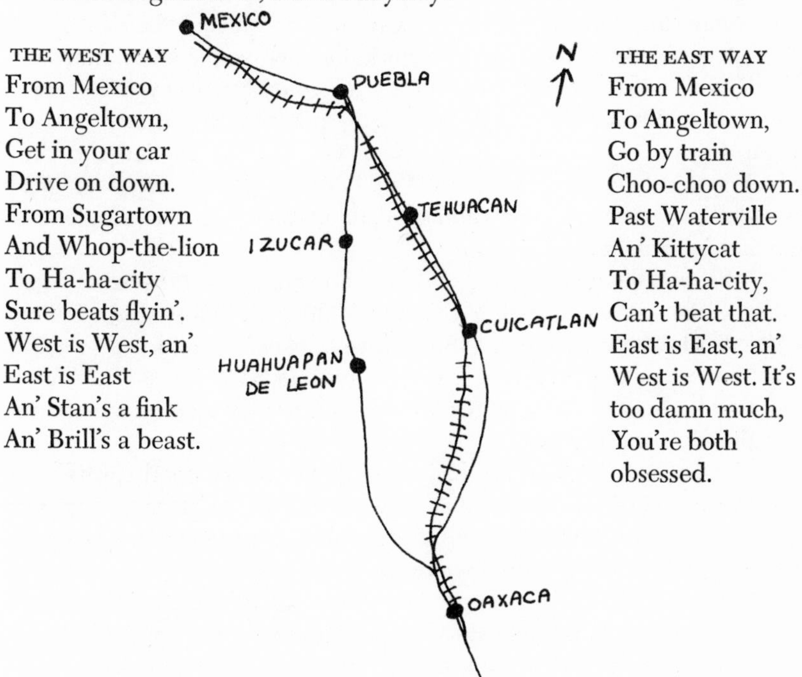

THE WEST WAY

From Mexico
To Angeltown,
Get in your car
Drive on down.
From Sugartown
And Whop-the-lion
To Ha-ha-city
Sure beats flyin'.
West is West, an'
East is East
An' Stan's a fink
An' Brill's a beast.

THE EAST WAY

From Mexico
To Angeltown,
Go by train
Choo-choo down.
Past Waterville
An' Kittycat
To Ha-ha-city,
Can't beat that.
East is East, an'
West is West. It's
too damn much,
You're both
obsessed.

Translation being an art in which Newman was skilled and Brill practicing, either might have been able to supply the following gloss of Gabby's lyrics: To leave the Mexican highlands, and go south one must first use the main pass to Puebla—Puebla de los Angeles. Then, if you were going by car, you'd swing west through Izucar de Matamoros, Huahuapan de Leon, and so to Oaxaca.

(Chorus: Gabby doesn't like site-surveying.)

Going by train, you'd again go from Mexico to Puebla but would, thereafter, bear east. Through Tehuacan (*Waterville*? Because there are springs there, dummies), Cuicatlan and down into a big Cañon de Tomelin—not mentioned in the song—to rejoin the automobile road just above Oaxaca.

(Chorus: Thanks a lot. You gentlemen go ahead and survey.)

What Newman had been trying to explain was that both routes through Mixtec country to Oaxaca were in use now and had been forever. They were the old Aztec and pre-Aztec trade routes, going down the middle of the landmass to the Isthmus of Tehuantepec, past which was Mayan country.

Because it was the more accessible, the west or automobile route through the Mixteca was at least cursorily known to archaeology. The east route through the Mixteca was not. However, the Valley of Tehuacan, thanks to the extensive work done by people associated with MacNeish's big corn dig, was pretty thoroughly surveyed by now. Newman had been working the edges, the passes, and was now moving south, beyond where MacNeish's men had charted, to find the sites which would begin to provide the link between present archaeological knowledge of the valleys of Tehuacan and Oaxaca, Oaxaca being one of the best-known areas of all.

"We're talking about a hundred kilometers, roughly, from Coxcatlan which is the cave where they found the corn to just above Huitzo where this eastern way rejoins the highway," Newman said.

"You're talking about a hundred blisters," Gabby said. "And a hundred backaches and a hundred sunburns, to pick up a bunch of stuff you already know is there."

She had joined them the first times out in pretty good spirits, and been disappointed to realize that Newman could sift through the pottery samples they'd laboriously brought back and put them in classifications with which he was already familiar.

Moreover, she had dysentery, which can be depressing. Brill would have been willing enough to stay behind with her at the hotel, but there was nothing he could do to ease things for her.

("Watch me run to the bathroom to gee whillikens?" she said. "What for? Christ, I've never seen a man so excited by anything as Brill about helping pick up little bits of broken jugs.")

Stan stopped the jeep in Cuicatlan, in front of the town hall.

"We'll use a guide today," he said. "Actually, I have a pretty good idea where to go, but it doesn't hurt to spread some expense money around."

Their guide, Mario, was the *alcalde*'s nephew.

It was an easy enough walk. They followed a trail out of town for half a mile or so, turned off onto a dry watercourse where the going was rougher. Each time they made a turn, Newman took and noted a compass bearing; between turns they did not talk, for each was counting steps.

It was one of the things Gabby had found most irritating—they not only counted steps without talking on the way in, they recounted them, to check, on the way out.

Went through a pasture with cattle and goats in it, crossed a crude fence, climbed a small bluff. There were a dozen large mounds on top of it, fifteen to twenty feet high, covered with dirt and vegetation, and perhaps averaging thirty feet in diameter. There were also any number of smaller ones.

"The little ones are house mounds," Newman said. "We've hit a complete village this time, by the look of things."

The day before had been a fortified hilltop, and the day before that some indecipherable ruins built over by a modern town.

"*El pueblo viejo*," Mario said. The old town. Often the Spaniards had caused a town to be relocated completely. The boy sat down in the shade of one of the larger mounds, accepting a Coca-Cola Stan offered him.

"He's not too interested?" Brill asked.

"He's probably been brought out here for family picnics all his life," Stan said. "Probably dug a little in a boyish way, looking for the crown jewels."

"Would you ever really excavate a place like this?" Brill asked, looking around. The hills nearby were high, and the sun fierce.

"No. Unless you had a reason to think you'd solve some particular problem by it."

"Like what?"

"Big or little? Little would be who lived here, how long. What relations with other groups. History and ethnology questions."

"What would be a big one?"

"Origin of ceramics," Newman said promptly. "In the New World. Because then you can answer large, general—even theoretical—things. There've been pre-ceramic sites dug, and early ceramic sites dug. But no one's found one where ceramics are evolving, starting—with crude little mudpie pots. Why not? Where were they? It's a gap of several thousand years, man, why can't we fill it?" He grinned and pointed at the ground between his feet. "Think it's right down there?"

"Yeah," Brill said. "What are we doing here?"

"Geography. How big a town, how far from the next. Can we tell from a surface collection without digging what people lived here—or rather confirm what we know from historical sources, that it was Mixtec. Let's go. I'll take pictures, you fill the sacks." He handed Brill a couple of white cotton bags and a check list.

Collections:

a. Surface, ceramic. Bags #____________.
b. Surface, nonceramic. Bags #____________.
c. By purchase. Bags #____________.
Notes?
d. Other.

Brill began kicking through the dust, picking up at random the larger pieces of broken pottery he saw. They'd work all day, Newman had said, at sites in Arizona where he'd done his graduate work, digging and sifting sand to find five pot sherds. Here you could pick up a bucket full in half an hour without digging at all.

When he'd filled the first sack, Brill started to play. He marked off with his toe in the dust what looked to him to be about a square meter. Then he squatted and carefully picked up all the bits he found inside the lines.

"Oh no," Newman's voice interrupted. "You're not?"

"What?" Brill was caught.

"Making a strat pit."

"Well," Brill said. "I was, I suppose I was just seeing. If I were to make a stratigraphic pit. I mean as the first stage of working this site, what would go into the first sack as the surface collection."

"Okay. Then you'd go down, staying inside your square. Keeping everything from the first layer in the next sack, till you got to a floor?"

"Stop grinning at me," Brill said. Newman made him cross as hell sometimes, preening his knowledge of the past of everything, from Mexico to Gabby Steiner Light. "Sure I would. And I'd find a series of floors, and keep everything separate between each pair of floors. Wouldn't I?"

He was repeating precisely what Newman had explained the day before; the pre-Columbian cities were paved with stucco, and each new floor, denoting a new building period, underlay the ceramic fragments peculiar to the period that followed it. Obviously. And a meter-square pit was something to start with, as a check. "All right, Newman, what's wrong? Why shouldn't I make a strat pit if we were going to be digging here?"

"You should. You should. Except, you make it right by the biggest building in the complex, you get your head bashed in by the man in charge. We gotta make trenches along this building."

Brill kicked his pile of sherds aside and started looking for nonceramic samples, now, whatever they might be.

He moved down the side of the bluff, away from the mounds, to what must be the head of the watercourse they'd turned at. It was a shallow cut, spread out, with lots of pebbles and occasional chunks of stone in it. He saw no nonceramic goddamn artifacts. Newman was not far away; Newman had come out away from the bluff and climbed a small hill to take a wide-angle photograph of the whole village. Newman finished, walked over to Brill, glanced around, and said, "Good eye."

"Huh?"

"This spot is loaded, isn't it?" Newman leaned down and picked up one of the chunks of gray stone. It looked like something you'd throw at an insulator.

"What the hell is it?" Brill asked.

"Flint core." Newman indicated a couple of irregular channels on one side of the rock. He struck here, and chipped off a piece. And here beside it."

"And said, Hey. Look at my little chip of stone?"

"No. He said, Look at my keen new scraper."
Newman bent, and picked up a flake. "That was a scraper."

"All right," Brill said. "But the Mohawks would have taken these guys in an arrowhead contest. What was it, Stan?"

"What?"

"The big double building where I was ruining the great dig by making my strat pit too close? Can you tell?"

Newman held out a chart he'd been sketching on a clipboard. "I've got it down for a ball court," he said.

"Take it easy on me. I mean well."

"No. Come on." He led Brill back up the bluff to the mound. Facing and connected to it was a second, the same size. "Shaped like a capital I, overall," Newman said. "What looks like a long connecting mound is actually two. There's room between them for a ball to travel down to the other end." They climbed to the top. There was, Brill could see, room in the stem of the I for several men abreast to run back and forth.

"Be a piece of cake to dig," Newman said.

"Kids played ball here?"

"Maybe. When the men weren't using it. Like your high school stadium in Rosetta, possibly. Want to help measure now?"

Even more tedious to Gabby than not talking so as to count steps was the measuring, with tape and eye-level, of the various mounds included in a site surveyed, so their dimensions could be entered on the chart.

Brill found it fascinating. Brill forgot to be irritated with Newman and liked the whole thing. Locating places, not unknown but uncharted; gathering whatever oral tradition there might be about this or that "*pueblo viejo*" locally. Seeing each place spotted in, later, on the big maps back at Stan's quarters.

(Q.: How many sites do you suppose there are?

A.: More than we'll ever find. So many in Mexico alone—let alone Central and South America—you can't even count them, let alone work them.

Gabby: Two big strong boys like you? I'll bet you could.

Q.: Suppose, out surveying, you found a really important one? Something big and startling, a lost city kind of thing. What would you do?

A.: Cry. There aren't even funds to *map* all the goddamn lost cities, let alone excavate, let alone consolidate what you dug up, let alone reconstruct. You've seen Teotihuacán. That's the most extensively dug and reconstructed thing around. It's 1,800 acres. How much of the area do you suppose they've even explored? Maybe twenty percent.

Q.: So if you found a lost city?

A.: The civilized thing to do would be not to mention it. Hell, Bob, there isn't even enough money around to hire guards.

G.: Guard, guard. Somebody stole my archaeology.)

"Got all your pictures taken?" Brill asked.

"Yep. Let's eat lunch. We could just about have done another one today."

"We could split some days," Brill said. "If there were two, and one didn't seem too imposing. I could probably get it mapped and sketched all right, and make the collection. I'm not much of a photographer, but I should be able to get snapshots."

"What about Gabby?"

"Why?"

"She isn't exactly eager to come along any more, is she?"

"We've only got a few more days," Brill said. "I like what I'm doing with them—and there isn't time to take her someplace else."

"Gabby hurts," Newman said. "Do you understand that? When women have dysentery, I suspect there's more pain to it than there is for us. The cramps are tougher, I think."

"What should I do? If I stay in with her, I'll be gruff."

"I think she might like to go on," Newman said. "She wants to see Monte Albán and Mitla."

"Ruins where the digging's all been done."

"What's wrong with that? You like process, she likes result."

"Know a lot about her, don't you?" Brill said.

"We were very close growing up."

"So I gather."

"Something eating your liver, sir?" Newman grinned. "Gabby taught me Zen love, sir."

"What the hell's that?"

"Sound of one organ copulating. Come on, Brill."

Liked Newman very well.

5.

"I'm sorry," Brill said, in the dark. "You've been hurting."

She snuggled against him. "I feel much better." She added: "Yes, tomorrow. I plan to feel that much better."

"I should have realized that you hurt."

"You don't even know you hurt yourself," Gabby said. Suddenly he felt her raise up, saw her face as a pale area hovering over him, as if she were trying to look into his eyes in the dark. "That's the trouble with you, Brill. You don't know you hurt."

"I don't even know what you're talking about, as a matter of fact," Brill admitted.

"Existential pain. You carry more of it around than anyone I ever knew, but you've always had it, so you don't feel it."

"You're full of gee whillikens, girl," Brill said. "You been talking me over with your friend Newman?"

"No."

"What'd he say?"

"He said your desperation is so quiet it's unconscious. That's existential pain." She kissed the socket of his eye. "I wonder what would happen to you if it ever stopped?" She said. "I know. You'd want it back again." She sounded almost angry. She turned her back and thrust her soft rear back against his pelvis, wiggling, making him sorry it wasn't tomorrow.

But the next day was Brill's turn for dysentery; he spent the morning in their room, while downstairs Gabby made some friends. They were a touring couple named Tony and Tacy, long-haired, guitar-toting, driving a nice white Pontiac. Gabby took them to shops and the market. At lunch Brill met and couldn't stand them, but didn't say so; he was having paregoric for lunch, and knew he seemed deceptively genial.

Newman was there, too. He'd decided to stay in that morning, because of Brill's indisposition, to do some laboratory work; he proposed taking all of them down to Quiotepec, an easy trip where he had photographs to take. Brill declined.

By evening Brill felt cured. The group came back from Quiotepec happy; with Stan's guidance, they'd bought quite a lot of stuff—crude jade beads, little clay heads, a pretty pot, and some fragments of small animal figures.

They played treasure, and Newman told a story:

That's how it starts (he said). When I first came to Mexico, I was a painter. I came for the light, but I fell in love with the clay stuff. Especially the things from the northwest. Tarascan and Colima stuff. I became a collector.

I didn't have much money, but it's amazing what you can do and buy, if you have time, speak Spanish, and can travel. My method was fairly standard.

For myself, I'd buy, bargaining hard for them, small and perfect things. But I always had a sum of money along that I withheld, for the one big, spectacular piece which could be resold at a big profit. Dollar for peso—that is, twelve times what you paid for something—was the way we operated.

I say we because there were hundreds of grubby little amateur dealers around like me, pushing pre-Columbian art to feed our own habits for it.

You tried to find a ruin where your colleagues and competitors hadn't worked recently. There's always a kid around, or an old woman, who wants to sell you fragments. Like what we bought today. You refuse. You say you might be interested in something larger. Maybe they take you, when they become convinced you're not a cop, to a man in a hut. Under the mat he sleeps on is a box, full of the stuff from the last tomb he opened by moonlight. You don't care about that; you don't give a damn that archaeologists will never know whatever it was that tomb could have told them. You want only the object, and you know that the man in the hut has other things hidden—not just what's in the cardboard carton, but one or two things hidden, perhaps, in the bush. They may have been hidden there for years, while he waited for the right buyer to come along, to pay enough—and the piece may well be worth it—to buy a little farm or give a big fiesta.

You get to know him; you get to see that piece. Maybe those pieces. You might see something for two hundred pesos, carry it to the States and sell it for two hundred dollars—and with that 2,300 peso profit buy the next seven pieces for your own collection.

There are stores in various cities. The storekeeper may have a dozen men out digging for him in the moonlight. Good pieces come through them, and of course they know you, what you're looking for, what you'll pay. Everybody, really, in the whole shady network—the diggers, the dealers, the collectors who deal on the side, the guys who haul loads up across the border in station wagons with false bottom floors.

Oh, we loved Mexico and Mexicans, us collectors. We were stealing them blind. We used to bitch about the Germans who took the big stelae and even buildings out on boxcars in the nineteenth century. But give one of us a boxcar, and an opportunity . . .

I made a trip to Los Angeles: I'd found something. It was a sacrificial knife, made of highly polished stone, with a figure on the handle. It wasn't as fine, say, as the famous mosaic one in the British Museum, but it was a museum piece; and best, it was small enough so I could carry it in my topcoat pocket without its showing very much. About ten inches long, and not too chunky. A lovely piece; I decided I'd go up there and sell it myself, and take all the profit, and that was how I learned why the interest was so intense—why movie stars and racketeers are big pre-Columbian art buyers.

I had the name of a dealer. He was reputable. He knew the really wealthy clients. I agreed to let him handle the selling, but insisted I be present whenever my knife was shown. I kept control of it. Twice he called me in. The first time he offered six hundred dollars. Instinct told me to refuse. He wanted me to leave it. I refused that, too. Finally he said all right, but would I bring the thing in the evening, after six? I agreed. There was a man there at the dealer's. He wasn't a movie star. He wasn't a racketeer. He was a museum man, an expert whose name I'd heard.

I got tremendously excited. They were talking four or five thousand dollars. Then the dealer, seeing how excited I was, laughed at me, but not unkindly: the four thousand was an appraisal, he explained. If the knife were to be given to the museum as a gift, the donor would get that much as a tax deduction. But I must realize that it would mean an actual tax saving of perhaps fifteen hundred dollars; so the donor would wish to pay much less than that—a thousand at the most, to save the fifteen hundred. And there must be something for the gallery as well as something for me. I sold the knife for seven hundred and twenty-five dollars, but it all made me a little sick. The movie star who bought it from me through the gallery not only didn't want it; he would probably never even see it.

I decided I'd become a real tough pro. I hadn't squeezed a tube of paint for six months, and didn't care. I'd have to admit that the intrigue, the illegality excited me, but at the same time, I'd grown even more acquisitive about owning a great collection myself. Jesus, the stuff that went through my hands. Sometimes I wish I had it back, but mostly I don't care.

What I'm trying to explain is why I don't care.

I was becoming an expert anyway, the hard way; as soon as you've been hit in the pocketbook by a certain fake once, you become an expert on fakes of that kind. You get to know the names and addresses of the important fakers. But what counts more is having information. Being able to supply the data, with the piece you sell, on where it came from, what people made it and how old it is. If you can give the dealer in the States that information correctly, and he hears it corroborated by the museum appraiser he calls in, it naturally sets up a situation of trust; it means, finally, that if you locate an important piece and find you can negotiate successfully for it, you don't need the big capital yourself. You can call the dealer and get him to advance it on a piece he hasn't seen, that you guarantee to him verbally.

Knowledge is money. I signed up for a course. I figured I'd outbid, outbuy, outstudy and outdeal the other guys; I was going to be the king of this art-smuggling business, and get rich. I was already living, and living pretty well, on money from pieces I sold, but my own collection was starting to go too; I'd sell anything. I began studying the whole range of stuff, anthropology, archaeology, history, ethnology. I wanted to know and make money out of everything there was to learn about Mexico.

Then my archaeology class went into the field for a practice dig. We needed to work someplace close to Mexico City. Somewhere where our practice work could be filled right back in, where we wouldn't make any discoveries that would compel that further work be done.

But it happened: I found something. A hole.

A goddamn hole, about five inches in diameter, and by no means perfectly round, in a stucco floor.

We were at Teotihuacán, the most dug-over site in Mexico. We were in the courtyard in front of the Pyramid of the Moon, where hundreds of people have worked in the last fifty years, ever since Batres went in and tried to clean the sides of the pyramids off with dynamite.

We were all but forbidden to find anything, there along the southwest platform that flanks the pyramid, but I found this hole.

I started a trench down to the stucco floor, about two feet down, about twelve feet out from the side of the platform. I was planning to extend the trench over till I reached the front wall of the platform, when I found this hole.

I called the man in charge. We agreed it looked like a hole someone had made, not an accidental break in the floor. The man said, "Take a compass reading along the damn wall, Newman," and I did.

No, it wasn't Gary Pederson. Pederson would have insisted the hole was accidental.

So we made a trench west, parallel to the wall, starting from the hole, at floor level, and I hadn't gone two meters before I came to a second hole, pretty much like it and right in line.

I can't tell you how excited I was. I didn't call the man back. Instead, I measured the distance between the two holes; then I measured off east on the same compass bearing, made an X in the dirt, and told my digger to go down carefully, right there. I watched the shovels full of dirt come up and right at the end I couldn't stand it. I told the digger to stop, and did what we do when we're taking out something very delicate: got down on my belly with a screwdriver to loosen dirt, a paintbrush to move it away, and a tablespoon to lift it out.

The millionaire expert and art collector, down on his belly in the dirt, looking for a five-inch hole in a stucco floor.

It was there. Exactly where it ought to be, to indicate a line of holes, evenly spaced, running in front of the platform on the west flank of the Pyramid of the Moon. It was knowledge; it was new; it was evidence of something previously unknown, and I'd found it.

I've found lovely stuff since—it all goes to museums now; we keep nothing—but never anything that excited me as much as the third hole.

That line of holes was a fact. Interpretation is something else, but what we decided still seems reasonable: that the holes must have been for poles. And such a line of poles would have been to hold up something like an awning, or a temporary roof. That would indicate people standing or sitting along there, in the shade. Doing what? The most reasonable theory was that they were buying and selling, that there was a market. If you can get other evidence to fit that supposition you begin to know something, don't you? About the relationship between religion and commerce among the Teotihuacani.

No headline. Not even footnotes in the technical journals. But a genuine piece of data, previously unknown, and I'd found it.

I haven't bought or sold a pre-Columbian piece since, except when we buy in the field, in connection with a dig, for a museum or for study. Or peso stuff to amuse friends, like today.

"What about your collection?" Tony asked.

"Gave my Mixtec polychrome pot to a girl and sold the rest to pay tuition for my next course." Newman smiled, an unburdened man.

6.

"Tony and Tacy want to go on to Oaxaca tomorrow," Gabby said. "Can we?"

"If I'm well enough," Brill said, "I want to spend one more day out with Stan. There's a place he's going to let me survey by myself." Seeing her pout: "You can come, of course. It may be a pretty steep climb . . ."

"I can't wait," Gabby said. "Let's start right now instead of going to bed."

"Just one more day surveying," Brill said. "Then Newman goes down to the other end, to work up the canyon from Oaxaca. We'll both be ready for Oaxaca."

"And Tacy and Tony might go on without us," Gabby said. "They want to see Tehuantepec and San Cristobal."

"We don't have time, Gabby," Brill said.

"I know. Home by Christmas. Jesus Christ, the first time I've been to Mexico, and I have to go with Santa Claus."

"I'm going to bed," Brill said. "I'm tired as hell."

"Go ahead," Gabby said; she opened her makeup case and got out a brown manilla envelope. It was her marijuana supply.

"Where are you going?"

"Out with my friends to look at moonlight, Good Saint Nick," she said.

When he woke in the morning, feeling strong, she was still asleep. He left a note:

We should finish the survey in time to go south this evening—tomorrow at the latest. Love, Plowboy.

At the town hall Mario and another boy were waiting, and Newman checked the tope map with them.

"Far as I can tell, it's about four miles each way for yours," Stan said. "I'll have to drive back as far as I can go on this trail, and walk a little farther—but not as steep. You want to trade?"

"I don't see why, unless you do."

"Let's leave it this way, and thanks. It'll be good to be done on this end. Don't worry about technical stuff. All we need to know is that there's something there, yes or no, big or little."

Brill and Mario picked up the gear. It didn't amount to much. Why the hell had Newman suggested a burro to carry it? Four bottled soft drinks, sandwiches, compass, notebook, clipboard, collecting bags, eye-level, rangefinder; and Newman's spare camera.

Mario had said it was too steep for a burro, anyway.

"Go through the camera operation again?"

"No. I've got it."

"*Mavistic.*"

"*Mavistic*, buddy," Brill said. Newman liked the word. So did Brill. It was Nahuatl—Aztec—for *wonderful.* Mario started; Brill followed.

They walked across level fields, southeast for about fifteen minutes, came to the edge of the fairly steep descent where Mario stopped. Brill decided not to count steps since it showed on the tope map, and listened. It was too far down for him to hear, but he was sure from the appearance of things that there must be a river or a stream down below.

The slope was rocky, and heavily covered with tough brush. Across what he assumed must be the river was an area of flood plain, rocky but with more vegetation than up here. Beyond the flood plain was a good-sized hill, bald on the side Brill faced, and it seemed that Mario was pointing to it and saying that there was the fortress—"*fortaleza.*" On both sides of the hill were canyon walls, and beyond it mountains.

Okay. It would be a good hike on the plain, and a tough climb in the sun up the big, bald hill. So move it, Mario babes, let's go.

Down the side to the river was a half-hour scramble, steep enough so that Brill wore the camera around his neck, needing sometimes one hand, sometimes both, to grab small trees to keep from sliding.

He was glad to be going down, not up it, though by the time they were at the bottom, farther down than he'd thought possible, his legs were already aching from the effort of so much bracing back.

It was hot. He grinned at Mario, and suggested a swim. They stripped down, internationally modest, to their shorts, carried the rest of their clothing and the gear across the forty-foot stream, then turned back and dropped into pools among the rocks, where shallow water was held back.

The water was clear and cool, and the current brisk; stream like that could have trout in it.

They dried, almost instantly, in the sun, got dressed and went on, easy walking except for having to pick their way through brush and cactus. It was another half hour (Brill lost count of the steps, but figured two miles) to the base of the big, bald hill.

Mario searched for, and found, a trail. He grinned. Apparently he hadn't been completely sure. Brill followed Mario.

When they had gone another fifteen minutes he realized that, though the trail climbed, they were not going up the hill but around it. He stopped his guide.

"*La fortaleza?*" He pointed up toward the top of the bald hill, lying now mostly to their left.

"No, Don Roberto." Mario pointed straight ahead, and up. "*La fortaleza, por alli.*"

Mavistic. If Mario was pointing where he seemed to be pointing, they hadn't even gone halfway yet, and the mountain in front of them was far taller and far steeper than bald hill.

In the third half hour they went beyond bald hill altogether; the mild rate of climb dropped, and the well-marked trail became more faint.

Brill had begun to save his breath, but Mario, nineteen years old, to whom walking was the only natural means of transportation, began to be talkative.

In season, he said, he came here with his father and his sisters to gather prickly pears. He capered. He dashed off to show Don Roberto the kind of cactus on which pears grew. He dashed back. It was like being out for a walk with a lively dog.

Soon they would come to a fine place, Mario said. A most agreeable place. Señor would see.

The fine place was indeed one. They had been climbing, ever more steeply for the fourth half hour, when they reached it: around a corner went the trail, and the land leveled. The trees opened. The grass was short. There it was and it made no sense: a ball court. It was precisely like the one Stan had showed him the other day, if that other had been excavated enough to show a defined structural outline. At the north end quite a bit of well-made stone wall was exposed.

"Is it modern?" Brill was puzzled. Mario didn't understand the question. "Is it old?"

"*Sì, sì. Hecho por los de antes.*" The boy was amused at Brill's question. How could anyone imagine that people would make such a thing today?

Goats were grazing nearby, accounting for the short grass.

One goat was tethered to a stone which had fallen from the wall. A small, brown man appeared in sombrero, and exchanged with Mario words in a language Brill could not identify.

He'd been resting. Now he got up, asked Mario to take one end of the fifty-meter tape, and began taking measurements of the isolated ball court.

When he had them all, he stood back and photographed it, trying to use the between-the-lens-exposure-meter in the way Newman had showed him, getting goats in the pictures for scale when he could.

Four shots; twenty-six left to go. He even climbed a tree to get the fourth from a higher angle. Got some insect bites on his forearm from it, too.

He picked up a few pot sherds and put them in a small bag, numbering it, to put in a larger collecting bag. After the bag number, on his site survey sheet, he wrote: "From a ball court near the foot of the mountain. In excellent preservation. Why aren't there any other mounds around it?"

"*Listo?*" Mario, wanting to know if he was ready.

Sure, but weren't there other mounds nearby? Mario shrugged and shook his head. Ask the old man? Mario did. The old man shrugged and shook his head.

Mario now pointed confidently uphill. Apparently he'd got some directions from the goat man.

Brill shouldered his junk, and allowed himself amusement at the notion of writing on his report: "Beyond this well-preserved but isolated ball court, according to local Mixtec(?)-speaking informants, is a 'fortress.' Information seems unlikely." With which our bold site-surveyor turned briskly toward home, leaving the goat man a coke and a cigar . . . ?

Leg-weary, but having no supervisor back at the hotel to dazzle with such annotations, over beers, Brill followed Mario on up the hill.

It was what you might call trudging.

His neck was weary, too. Each time you took a picture, you added the weight of the object photographed to what had previously been nice, weightless, unexposed film.

For a time he carried the camera over his right shoulder. Then he got a marvelous idea (*mavistic*) and hung it on his left. Then he carried it in his hands, by the strap. There was no trail, now. The vegetation was getting thinner, and the way much rockier. There were patches of loose shale in the way, which one had to skirt.

There was a remarkably heavy instrument on his left wrist, called a watch, which read 11:15, and the sun was talking to particular spots on his head and neck. It said, burnya, burnya.

Brill had a bandana. He tied it over his head, as an old woman might, and turned up his shirt collar.

The way got steep. Even Mario paused for a moment, though Brill's moment of hope—that the boy had to rest—was false. The boy picked up a pot sherd and gave it to him.

It was a monstrously heavy pot sherd, perhaps two inches square by one eighth inch thick, weighing seventeen pounds. Brill put it in his pocket.

"I was there once, as a boy," Mario said, smiling and pointing. Apparently the kid's index finger only worked in an upward direction. "Nobody goes up there."

Why be an exception?

"There is nothing there to take, only to see."

Informed that "there was nothing there," the investigator concluded that proper use of time suggested a return to . . .

"Let's climb," Brill said.

The camera went back around his neck. He needed both hands again for the climb, but to grab rocks, now, rather than trees, testing each to be sure it wasn't loose before he pulled himself up by means of it.

"See?" Mario pointed, in his usual direction, and Brill climbed the next boulder, on which the boy perched, to stand beside him and look up.

Somewhere between a hundred yards and five thousand, structures shimmered.

. . . *and the usual way was to go up in the high hills and fortify their billets with rock walls and ditches, and there to defend themselves with rolling stones and throwing weapons.*

It wouldn't take very damn many rolling stones.

"Let's go," said the Aztec captain to his scout, Mario. "Watch the stones."

Brill could not have said how much longer it took to gain the fortress—somewhere between four hundred and a million steps, he'd have estimated. His legs were so tired they seemed useless, as if he were going uphill hand over hand; but weren't his arms more tired than his legs? The sun smashed. The camera swung from his neck like a giant on the end of a bell-rope, pulling him to and fro, and Brill without his clapper.

At the lip, where the hill flattened and a wall began, he almost fell. A projecting flange of rock, worn on top from constant standing on—a sentry's rock perhaps?—gave him something to catch onto. Mario was standing on it, there above him, but looking over the wall; Brill felt the guide didn't notice he had nearly lost his client.

Brill regained his balance, rested for an instant, and at length got up onto his feet, on the flat. For a moment he thought, looking over the wall, that effort and sun might have addled him, what he saw seemed so unlikely.

There were rock buildings there, three main ones, roofless of course, and with walls fallen at places, but all their standing surfaces were exposed—not covered up by dirt—and inside of one of the buildings even pillars were standing.

It was as if, in Newman's jargon, someone had already excavated, consolidated, and mostly reconstructed. But it was even better, of course: there was simply no sand up here, no flying dirt, no people living to dump refuse; nothing but the wind and rain, and only the rooves had given in.

Brill wiped his forehead, and noticed then that Mario was looking at him with concern. Seeing that kept him, perhaps, from falling into the ruin over the low wall.

He forced a smile, climbed the wall, and removed the solid lead camera strap from the groove it had worn in his neck.

"It is fine to find the place so complete," he said, as briskly as his over-careful Spanish would permit. "Has no archaeologist been here before?"

Mario laughed. "No one has been here," he said. "Except the old man. For myself, I have never been farther than the place where the goats were."

"Open us some of that . . . champagne," Brill said, and each sat on a rock with a warm bottle of Orange Crush.

When he felt cool and steady again, Brill began the measuring, sketching, note-taking, and photography. He paced himself, doing it slowly, especially careful to go through the procedures Newman had outlined with the camera. He shot all twenty-six remaining shots; he had to. He wasn't sure anyone would believe this was up here in such perfect condition. Some of the stone in the wall was worked, and the pillar stones rounded. He looked exhaustively for any sign that the stones had been stuccoed over and painted, and decided it was not so up here, whatever might be true of other ancient Mexican structures.

Men had built this thing carefully, but had spent no unnecessary effort climbing up with materials for ornamentation.

There was very little to collect in the way of pottery fragments, nor would one do much excavating at this site. The buildings stood on bedrock, and the wind had kept the floors swept clean. Only in a few places, windtraps, was there any accumulation, and Brill thought, suddenly excited: One could dig this site completely in a couple of days, explore the whole area around it. You would have? A fortified billet, he guessed, in near perfect condition. And then? Then you would go to the ball court below, and try to figure out the relationship, and if you could establish one, then perhaps you'd know which people made the billet and at what time. And then?

Brill thought of Stan Newman's third hole; you'd have data. He had data, right here. He felt the surge of pleasure in it; he sat in the shade enjoying it, and lazily let Mario make the surface collection.

There was little enough: a few glazed fragments, which meant they were post-Hispanic. The usual chips of red and gray, cream and orange. And one fairly large fragment, quite a pretty one in fact, with a reddish slip over it and paint on the slip.

"Yes, my boy," Brill told Mario loftily in English. "If you'd just get your nose out of that stuffy little law practice in Illinois and learn a few things, you'd know this is what we Mixtecs call polychrome . . ."

Mario laughed. Brill wrapped the piece in foil and dropped it into the collecting bag.

There must be nonceramic stuff, of course, but Brill hardly knew what to pick up. There was a large piece of a metate, too heavy really to ask Mario to carry down. The boy'd have his hands full with the collecting bag and the empty bottles—Brill was damned if they were going to leave pop bottles up here, even if they had to throw everything else away.

Then he thought of the walk back.

Then he groaned.

"Eat now," he told Mario. It was nearly one o'clock, and he himself was much too hot to think of eating. "We must get started back."

At a quarter past one, Babushka Brill tied his bandana back around his head, fitted the camera strap into the neck groove, and clambered over the wall.

He'd have said later that he slid all the way down, but if so, how could the slide have taken over an hour? When they reached the bottom, his legs were a column of pain from the soles through the ankles, shins through knees, knees through thighs, stabbing right on up into the hips.

But as they started out along the trail past the ball court, it seemed to him that Mario, not tired at all, was practically bouncing with the ease of the walk. Suddenly Brill remembered the burro which Newman had decided not to hire because the going would be too steep to make the animal useful.

My God, if they could have a burro now, and tie Bob Brill across it like a sack, it would be worth all the money Brill would ever earn. If the damn burro could carry no more than the camera, it would be worth at least five thousand dollars.

Bone weariness. Like metal fatigue. Look at that Mario bounce. Curious that it should be Mario calling halts to rest now, when it seemed as if the boy was going strong. Poor little guy. He must really be dragging, to want to sit again so soon.

Don't let him have the camera, Christ, he must be out of his Mexican head with the heat, trying to take the thing.

Endlessly they walked, stumped, rumbled through the heat, and Brill wondered later if his life might actually have been saved by coming to the river. It seemed to him he went the last few steps into it on his knees, only barely remembering to throw the camera behind him before he went out straight, flat on his stomach into the cool water. Pigs did that. Pigs, which couldn't sweat, saved their lives in summer heat by stretching into water.

Ol' pig Brill lay there grunting for a long, long time. First it was the cooling out. Then, crawling in, the way the water took the weight and held it off his limbs.

It was some time before Mario's voice, urging that they get on up the final hill, was anything more than an insect sound in his ear.

But at length his brain, too, cooled, and he sat up in the stream water, clothes pressing damp against him, and considered the hill. It made him laugh. Five hundred yards, practically vertical; a quarter mile. Well, sir, if someone up there would just turn on the escalator.

"Now, senor? Don Roberto?"

Brill said to himself; Mario can make it. Mario wants to go. If Mario can make it, I can make it. If there was a fallacy there, he didn't know what it was.

"Okay." He stood. "Mario, you give me that damn camera."

The boy was wearing it around his neck. "I have it, Don Roberto."

"No."

"With your premission . . ."

"No," Brill roared. "Come on." Even in his hand the thing was more than he could carry; transferred to his neck it was going to bear him forward, face down into the water. He wasn't sure how he got across to the other side.

Up the hill, every step was an engineering problem—how to pull this enormous, sagging sack; with what combination of sore muscles and sorry rigging do we make the scrunch?

Up they went, Mario lightly, Brill like a great, self-propelled stone, until finally the underbrush thinned; the slope gentled; they were out of it. Heaving up past the last, gray-leaved, twisted shrub, he stood, wobbling, and saw, fifty yards away, the jeep with Stan and Nacio in it. He attempted the next level step forward, and it didn't work. The knee would not support. He went down on the right knee, then, trying to move the next foot forward, on the left. Then he tried to crawl toward the jeep like a dog, on hands and knees, and collapsed all the way. But was half up again, panting, when Stan brought the jeep alongside him.

7.

The recovery was quick. They stopped for a beer at Teotitlan del Camino, sitting at an iron table in a courtyard to drink it. It was Victoria beer. Brill, who had said hardly anything as Newman chattered on, thought it might make him sick. Not at all; cured him.

Restored him.

"Existential pain, my ass," he said. "I oughta clean your plow, Newman. One more beer and I think I might."

Newman laughed. "*Mavistic.*"

"Tell me again. How was your place?"

"You haven't heard a thing I said. We covered two. One had some good irrigation stuff, fossilized, on a side hill. Yours?"

"I can't tell you," Brill said. "It was. Well, it was damn striking. Maybe you've got a dozen like it, but I can't believe it. A mountaintop fort, but perfect. Here." He handed Newman the camera. "Big buildings. Complete. Except for roofs, Stan. Listen, we should go back."

"Brill, Brill."

"All right. In decent weather. Not try to do it all in one day. There's—I don't know. Some beauty and some mystery there. A ball court with no town around it. A perfect fort, with hardly any tools or pots. I think there must be . . . more. Something different, Stan. Unexpected."

"It's happened to you." Newman sounded quite sympathetic. "It does, Bob. To all of us. You start finding places. Where the resonance gets you. You know there's something you could find; it couldn't happen without you, could it? It'll stay in your mind always, Bob. That sounds romantic. But then, if you come back, there'll be another place. Just as unexpected. You'll see it, experience it, by some kind of accident maybe. And something will block your working there right then. But it will have the resonance . . ." He smiled. He ordered a beer. He took the camera, and started turning back the film to unload it.

He frowned, and looked at a dial. "Oh God damn," he said.

"What'd I do?"

"Nothing. It's what I did. Didn't do. I expect you used the meter didn't you?"

"Checked it every shot."

"Bob, I'll go back up and photograph your place myself."

"What's wrong?"

"The roll before this was Kodachrome," Newman said. "Slow color film. And when I changed it, I put you in a roll of Tri-X black and white. I thought for some reason you'd be shooting in the shade, so it's very fast film. But I didn't change the film speed on this knob here, Bob, so I've had you overexposing monstrously on every shot. I'll underdevelop, but I'm afraid the whole roll's going to come out black."

Brill was silent for a moment. Then he pursed his lips. "I think I'll have another beer," he said.

"I'm sorry."

"It's okay. I got the pictures, Newman. Right here." And pointed to his salty head.

Nevermind. He didn't really care. He didn't really care when he got back to the hotel, and found Gabby's note:

We've gone to Oaxaca. You bring the car
and come when you finish.

He would like hell.

He would get a bottle of El Presidente brandy and go to bed with it. And in the morning take the first-class bus to Mexico City. And walk through the new museum one more time, real slow. And fly back home.

11

Ungrateful Brill liked hardly any of his Christmas presents.

Like: call him up and congratulate him Christmas morning. Donny Rebranch (Tommy's brother, running for Congress) did—Brill's son was home, whole and sound from Vietnam for Christmas.

"Yeah, okay, Donnie. Okay. That's all right. Thanks for calling." You'd have thought the boy politician was calling up to say something was too bad, he was sorry, not *Great news about Cal being home.*

Cal looked slim and hard in his uniform. He had most of his father's height, but not the bulk; he was sandy-haired like Brill, blue rather than brown-eyed, and of the two he might have seemed the more generally composed.

"The sergeant's stripes," Brill said. "You didn't get them as a medic, I suppose?"

"No, sir." Cal had come in on the bus, late Christmas eve, and home by cab. Now packages were open, breakfast done, Trink already sewing something on her new portable sewing machine—fixing one of her new dresses; she learned to do that stuff in school—Pat starting to work on dinner in the kitchen. It was Brill's first chance to talk with his boy.

"Jesus Christ, Cal," he said. "You never called me sir before in your life."

Cal looked amused. "Habit I guess, Dad. No. I made buck sergeant as a squad leader, after I kicked playing doctor."

"What was wrong with that?"

"I don't know. I had a Schweitzer complex, I guess. Wanted to heal everybody—troops, natives, Saigon whores. Me and my tetracycline love for humanity."

"It sounds all right to me, Cal."

"I know. I'm sorry."

"And you're staying in?"

"I started out feeling like someone special," Cal said. "A special case in the world. But why should I be? Why not be willing to take everything everybody else has had to take in the world, and try to be good at it? Do you see?"

"I don't think so," Brill said.

"Nevermind, Dad."

"Are you talking about being in, well, some sort of competition for manliness? Seeing if you measured up? That kind of thing?"

Cal shook his head. "No. Six months ago I'd have said, it was being resigned and seeing what I could make of it. But then it all got positive. You've been a hunter all your life; can you see it that way?"

"You mean . . . killing people like killing birds?"

"No. Not exactly. But being in tough situations, being armed, knowing what to do and being good at it. Once, let me tell the *kind* of thing I mean. There were a couple of Cong one day, Dad. We were in the hills, and they were going up the side of a hill across from us. About four hundred yards away. And all the guys in my squad were shooting at them, automatic weapons, rapid fire, missing wildly. A couple of mortars even, were trying to stop these two poor little guys. Hell, I think the platoon leader was getting ready to call for an air strike to get them. I shot them both; I had a scoped rifle, and made the adjustments properly, and took them, one by one. Head shots. I didn't even feel as if I'd killed them. They were dead men anyway. But no one else was cool and trained enough, and . . . do you see what I mean?"

Brill said, after a moment: "All right. You're committed to a . . . a job like that. Yes. I suppose I'd have tried to do just as you did, Cal. But. Well." He shook his big head, reluctant to say it: "I don't think I'd have felt so good about it I'd decide to make it my career."

"I didn't feel good about it, Dad, or bad or anything like that. I just felt that I had some ability. And no real conviction about whether it was being put to good use or bad use any more. I just want to put it to use."

"How, Cal? Do you want me to get you into West Point, for example, if I can?"

"Maybe later. If I stay in I want to be an officer. Right now I want to go to helicopter school, that's all. And go back to Vietnam."

"That particular war, Cal. You were so sure a year ago that you opposed it. You were ready to go to jail."

"I don't feel one way or another about it now," Cal said. "I don't mind if people protest it. I don't think the war is right. I don't think it's wrong. If we didn't have that one, we'd have another one. I want to be a decent professional at what I do with my life, that's all. And running a helicopter gunship—it's a dueling situation, Dad—it fascinates me. I've flown a number of times now, as a gunner. I want to be really good at it."

"And spend the rest of your life that way, Cal? Being good at things like that?"

"You're offended," Cal said. "I'm sorry."

Cal looked well in the uniform—as Brill never had in his—keen, proud of it, bright-eyed and dapper. Had always had some style to him, even in his long-haired, Montreal days. Jeans and a ski sweater he washed himself. Beautiful.

As a little boy, Cal had been inventive. Brill's square dream had been that his son would want to make something; manufacture. Brill had thought of finding capital, and the idea still engaged him in a way he was reluctant to give up. Because nobody wanted to make things any more, or back that kind of enterprise, not when they could put their money out at twenty-five or thirty percent, just lending it. The most fantastically successful business or invention you could establish wouldn't give the kind of return money-lending gave. "All right, Cal. I'm for that," he'd have liked to have said, and gone up against the goddamn banks and investors.

When usury becomes the only sensible thing for a reasonable man to do with his money, then a country stops, and lives on its fat, and boys like Cal are lured or forced into defending it as the usurers eat one another till it's all gone. Autodigestion. The whole sad, sagging works. 'Bye.

"S'all right, Cal." They talked about Pat. Cal was pleased his mother seemed comparatively well, and engaged; Cal seemed mature enough to be amused that it had been his father's recklessness that brought Pat back a little way.

All Brill could think was: Be patient. Cal's changed so completely about the war. Maybe he hasn't stopped changing.

There was goose for Christmas dinner, but Brill hadn't shot it. The day before he'd traded Billy Boykin, whose place adjoined his on the river, four frozen mallards for a frozen Canada goose too large for Billy himself to use.

Billy had something else for Brill, too. Brill had a strong suspicion it was coming when he stopped his car in Billy's drive and heard, from the window of a car parked in front of his, an oddly familiar and objectionable voice say,

"Merry Christmas, Mr. Brill."

It was the young engineer he'd tried to fight with.

"Merry Christmas," Brill said, feeling reasonably genial this time. "What are you pipeline assholes up to now?"

"Oh, I'm not with the pipeline company any more, Mr. Brill. I think you'll get a notice from the sheriff's office pretty soon about that, though."

"That's a nice friendly prospect," Brill said. "What's your job now?"

"Laying out subdivisions," said the fine young man; started his motor and roared off waving.

Billy's place started at the river next to Brill's and reached back almost a mile. It included both sides of a narrow, timbered ridge which Billy'd grazed and lumbered half to death; at the east end it adjoined a fairly good, flat forty acres on which Brill held an option to buy, and this, in turn, adjoined the Brill family farm where Kress Hartke lived.

Billy's was a place Brill had always wanted to own; even the old Boykin house, a smaller and more graceful version of the limestone house on the family farm, appealed to him as one in which he might one day live, when the kids were grown. He'd have said it was understood between him and Billy Boykin, a man not really much older than himself, that if ever Billy wanted to sell, Brill would meet his price. More as a neighbor than a lawyer, he'd taken care of things—dealing with the ASCS, the tax assessor, the people who repaired wells and septic tanks—for Billy for years.

Once every year or two Billy'd say, "What I owe you for your lawyer work, Bob?"

And Brill, straightfaced, would say: "Comes to ten dollars, Billy." People didn't think of Billy as mentally defective; they thought of him as slow. The year before Billy'd needed an operation, and Brill had loaned his neighbor three hundred dollars for it.

The day before Christmas, as Brill'd walked in, having arranged to trade ducks for goose over the phone, Billy had a check for him.

"Got the farm sold. Goin' to California," Billy said.

"I didn't know you wanted to sell, Billy," Brill said.

"Never thought about it, till this fella came along with a deal."

"What deal?"

"Don't worry, I didn't sign nothing but a option, so's I could get the money to move and pay you back. Then you can handle the rest for me."

He'd been hustled. When Billy'd refused to sell at $250 an acre, they'd gone up to $300. When he hesitated, they explained that that was a flat price, and that every time a half acre lot was sold, on the timbered ridge, Billy'd get $200 more. It sounded like $700 an acre to Billy and hell, nobody ever got a price like that for land before. Not around here.

What the half-acre lot would be priced at, and what guarantees might be made about the land surrounding it, did not seem to have entered into the discussion. Young fellow named Canaday had made the deal, Billy said.

Brill had figured there'd be reprisals; and of course Tommy had known how much he wanted the Boykin place.

He said he'd see Canaday, and have a look at this option; there wasn't much sense upsetting things for Billy yet. That hassle would come, he supposed, and only thanked him for the goose, and the check.

"Going to call 'er Hickory Ridge Homes, I guess," Billy said. "Leave a few big old shagbarks there. Said if I wanted to stay on, they might get me a job with the contractor, supervising building. Said us farmers knew a lot of things . . ."

All right. In a way Brill was not displeased. He'd anticipated that Pete and Tommy would hack him back. What he'd have to find out next was whether Trump's money was in the deal with Billy Boykin; if it wasn't, there was a good chance Brill could find some money, make a good cash offer, and break the option. They might be figuring on selling lots first, then paying Billy off from the proceeds, and Brill thought he could stop that.

What he hadn't anticipated was that Tommy too would have money ready—not for Billy Boykin but for Bob Brill—when he got to the office, Monday morning after Christmas.

It was the third gift Brill was ungrateful for.

"Good trip?"

"Damned interesting."

"Leave your friend down there?"

"What friend, Tommy?"

"Pete knows her, you know."

"Knows who, Tommy?"

"Look, I handled the condemnation thing. I think you'll be pleased."

"Condemnation?" He supposed Tommy must mean the pipeline matter. "What do they want to do?"

"Wanted to tear down the building, pay eleven thousand, and leave you the land."

"The building? Eleven thousand for the duck shack, Tommy?"

"No, no. This building. I'm talking about this building here, for the street widening."

"Tommy. Now wait a minute. You said it was the alley."

"Oh, that was a little confusing at first, I know. No, it turned out it's the whole street they're widening. All out in front here. Everything but us sets back far enough, so they just wanted to condemn us."

"For eleven thousand dollars? The whole building?"

"Of course I appealed."

"You what?"

"Not formally; I mean, I threatened appeal if they went through with the condemnation."

"It went that far? A sheriff's jury . . ."

"That's what I'm trying to tell you," Tommy said. "They were ready to draw it up that way when I said no to eleven. So we dealt. We spent a solid week of afternoons on it, Bob, and I got you thirty-eight thousand dollars."

Brill rose. "You did what?"

"Thirty-eight thousand, and you keep the land." Tommy was backing away.

"Are you telling me," Brill couldn't keep his voice down, "that you used that power of attorney to sign away my building for thirty-eight thousand?"

"That's way over value," Tommy said. "You'll have the money to build something modern in the space. You'll be able . . ."

"*I* will," Brill roared. "Not *we* will, but *I* will. Is that right, Tommy?"

Tommy had backed as far as the door. "Do you think I could stay here, the way you've been acting?"

"And what's the little man going to do?" Brill asked. "Open up a nice big shop, all by himself, right? Maybe with Petey-boy Canaday, little real estate shit on the side, little insurance shit, and let's see? Well, what a surprise. Nice old Mr. Trump just happened to offer to pay the rent, right? Here's what we'll do, Tommy. We'll cut that slob Brill off at the pockets. Take his building away, so he can't operate; cut his farm off. Tie him up fighting all that stuff, and we'll just open up a big sweet suite, sweetheart . . ."

"No," Tommy yelled back. "It's not like that."

"Where? In the bank building."

"You think you can do anything you want around here."

"Get out of my office," Brill said.

Tommy stood his ground.

"You think I can't repudiate your stinking little signature in that agreement?"

"I have a power of attorney," Tommy said. "You told me to use my best judgment . . ."

"You better back down the hall," Brill said, going toward him. "If I see anything to kick I'm sure as hell going to swing my foot. You send somebody else in for the stuff from your office, Tommy. If I ever see your face in this building again, I'll smash it."

"Bob, wait now . . ." Tommy started, and Brill moved. He grabbed his partner by the belt and by the shoulder, swung him once, and threw him sliding down the hallway.

Tommy screamed. Brill went after him, and the man screamed again in actual terror. Brill stopped.

The scream stuck him like a pin. "Hell, I'm sorry," he said.

Tommy was getting up, over his fright now that he'd learned how to protect himself; unhurt. "Try to sound a little bit sincere when you say that."

Brill was astonished at how effeminate he sounded; perhaps a man must, who has just saved himself from injury by screaming. "I'm sincere," he said, wishing he hadn't heard that.

"The time to be sorry was weeks ago, wasn't it? When you started sticking the little Jew-girl, and found you couldn't let it alone? That's when you should have been sorry . . ."

"You're unbelievable," Brill said, turned, and moved heavily back toward his office.

He thought a while; then he called Nadine, the senior of the three secretaries in length of service, and told her that Mr. Rebranch was leaving, that they might help him get his stuff out if they were asked to; otherwise, she and the other two could think of the office as closed until after New Year's.

"You mean, Mr. Brill . . . take all the rest of the week off?"

"No," Brill said. "Come down at nine in the morning and sit in front of the locked door all day."

In about half an hour the sounds the secretaries made had stopped, Tommy was gone, and he had the building to himself. He walked all through it: his room, Tommy's office, the secretaries' room, the meeting room. Just four. And the graceful little hallway, off which they opened. The john. The closet.

When he pulled his head out of it, there was someone in the hall. Gary Pederson. Yeah, Gary, he said; he'd found Mexico damned interesting.

"Bob. Can we go in your office and sit down?"

"Maybe another time, Gary?"

"There's something I want to say."

"Not really open for business, Gary."

"This is personal."

"All right. Come in and sit."

Gary said: "I've been regretting something, and I wanted to apologize for it. My mentioning that I thought Trump might give some money, and then saying he withdrew the offer when I said I was a friend of yours. I ought not to have told you that, of course."

"It's all right," Brill said. "What was the sum?"

"I didn't come to talk about it. I came to say I wished I hadn't."

"Five grand," Brill said. "All right. You got it."

"Bob, really . . ."

"You can run it through a foundation or something, can't you? So it's tax deductible."

"Of course. But . . ."

"I'll give you the check January second," Brill said. "So I can put it on next year, okay?"

"That's terribly generous of you," Gary said.

"I saw the kind of thing you're trying to do. Your boy Newman showed me some of it. It's good stuff," Brill said. He began, as they talked along, and had a drink together, to like Pederson quite well, better than he'd thought he did. Effect of doing something for the man, perhaps.

Gary was talking about being lonely. "I mean in the, uh, specific way. My position here, you understand, Bob."

"Yeah," Brill said. "You're supposed to be raising funds, not nighties."

"After the divorce," Gary said, "there was a lady, one of my colleagues actually. In University City . . ."

What the hell? Old Pederson, what was he up to? Pushing. Pushing on, crudely, letting nothing stop him, toward a degree of male friendship he and Brill had never reached, the sign of which is comparing sexual experience. Exchanging wisdom, reminiscence; telling those stories about this time, and how I, and whether she . . . boys together. How he did run on.

". . . . where she'd done her field work, the universal position was squatting face to face. Malinowski mentions something like that, as a matter of fact, and her report was more extraordinary. So of course we had to try it, but my word, just to keep your balance that way, Bob."

Brill laughed. It was a funny idea, particularly when you put thin

Gary and a scholarly lady down there in imagination, duck-walking nude toward one another. But why should he be doing what he found himself agreeing to—couple of dates—not for New Year's eve but for the night before it if he could—and going out to the shack?

What made him say yes to a thing like that? When Gary left, and before he could allow himself to change his mind and start the tempting process of reversal and apology, he made himself pick up the phone and call the Funny girls.

2.

They were Darlene Heneschel and Betty Martin. They worked in an insurance office up the street, and shared an apartment. Darlene was Funny Ha-ha and Betty was Funny Peculiar.

It required care to keep his voice buoyant while he talked to Darlene, Funny Ha-ha, making the arrangement, because it had been Martin, curiously tender toward them both when he first suggested it, who had named them.

The cabin was cold, of course, when they arrived. Damp, too. Betty (Funny Peculiar), who had clung to Brill all the way out, hampering his driving and saying tearful things, now remembered Martin's pride in fire-building.

Darlene, Funny Ha-ha, cried a little.

Brill lit the pilot on the wall heater, turned the thermostat up, listened for the nice roar as the burners caught and the fan went on.

Then he picked up a light stick of firewood, and cracked Funny Ha-ha in the rear end with it. She stopped crying, chased him, caught him in a corner, and demanded the stick.

"Put it on the fire?"

"I'm going to slug you with it."

"How about slugging me with a drink of bourbon?"

Gary, who'd been standing around awkward, sprang to open the bottle, and the other three laid the fire on cold ashes with a maximum of squeals and pushes.

"They always have to beat hell out of me," Brill said to Gary. "I go home black and blue."

That made Funny Peculiar, who was a little bit aggressive in bed, rather impelled to express herself with tooth and claw, whoop and look for another piece of firewood to brain the man with.

"Go look in the grocery box," Brill said. "Go on, girl. Get the steaks out. I want you to tell me how pretty they are before I cook them."

Funny Ha-ha still seemed tearful, so he raised his voice, higher and merrier: "Gary, old pr'fessor, get us an armload of wood. Darlene, you bring me my drink and some kitchen matches, let's make this fire roar."

"Can't you . . ." The girl was trying to rally. The associations here with Martin were terribly strong for her, of course. "Is it ready to light?"

She brought the matches, sitting on her heels beside him to watch him light the fire, and he remembered Gary and his lady colleague. He grinned at Darlene, Funny Ha-ha, pert, short, round-shouldered and round-bottomed in her miniskirt, and said: "Uncle Gary here is what we call an anthropologist. He studies all the strange ways people make love, Betty, and I want you to stay just exactly the way you are now . . ."

She moved to rise, but he restrained her, hands on her shoulders. ". . . get him to tell us how the natives of the Trobriand Islands . . ." Even Gary started laughing, then, and Betty, Funny Peculiar, tried to push Gary down on his haunches by Darlene, to show them; Darlene, snorting and squealing, struggled away from Brill and flounced about, the cabin warmed up, they all had second drinks and Brill put music on.

Darlene settled chuckling in Brill's lap; he watched the situation and became concerned that angular Betty wasn't really taking much to Gary—Gary continued tentative which made it hard for her; Darlene was the more forward of the two, Brill decided, so he rose up, picking her up with him, and delivered her to Gary instructing his old school buddy that the time had come to dance with the lady. Gary could manage that; Darlene, still chuckling, could manage Gary.

Brill danced with Funny Peculiar for a bit, simulating more physical interest then he felt, hoping the whiskey would touch him amorously in places the girl couldn't reach. Betty was tall enough to dance with, had a nice jut to her bosom, enormous dark eyes and short-cropped, very black hair. She had been an athlete, a tournament caliber girl's basketball player, and could do trick roller-skating.

"Once I tried out for the roller derby," she'd told him. "Do you remember that on television?"

"Yes. What happened?"

"God, they're so rough," Betty'd said. "The short girls have such an advantage, you know? What they can do with their shoulders to you? I just bowl now."

Funny Peculiar was a phenomenal bowler, so Brill heard, best woman bowler in town, captain of the undefeated Insurance Premiums.

She was dancing moodily now, forehead against his chin, and he looked to see how Darlene was doing with Gary. Darlene was clinging pretty good, and her chuckle had risen to a happy gurgle which meant she was getting physically turned on. Funny Ha-ha turned on easy as a worn faucet, turned herself on really without help, and Brill thought: The natives of Rosetta generally wait till after supper, but let's see what we can do.

It was pretty simple. "We want you two out of the way," he said. "Clear out of the way, so we can have this room to cook in. Now git."

Darlene led Gary, simpering and surprised, away to the bedroom, and shortly there came, through the thin door, the gasps and giggles he and Betty had pretended not to hear before. A number of times. How many? Brill could not have said. The Funny girls were his dependables, for hell-raising evenings. Or had been Martin's, rather. Martin had found as well as named them. When there was a man around from out of town, Darlene and Betty could be called, tractable—a little wistful perhaps—cooperative as long as their own quirks could be expressed.

There was a sound, a three-note rising chortle and a fourth descending note, continuous, involuntary, unamused, which started now in the bedroom. Brill put the steaks on; once it started, it wouldn't take Funny Ha-ha much longer.

When the chortle rose to a series of little laughing screeches, he turned the meat.

They ate, drinking all through the meal, not touching their salad, and Gary was quite relaxed and gay now for which small favor Brill was grateful. Let the archaeologist grab the bone.

"I want you girls to come to Mexico next week, and bring your shovels, hear?" he said. "You too, Bob."

"You better not say that again," Betty said.

"You've got yourself three field hands."

"I mean it," Gary Pederson said expansively. "It's going to be a great dig. You come, Bob."

"When are we leaving?" Brill asked, knowing he was a little drunk, and in his little drunkenness accepting seriously what in sobriety he would have to decline. He hoped Gary was worldly enough to assume this, for he heard himself carrying on: "What do I need? Sleeping bag, tent, mosquito bar . . . ?"

"No, it's not a jungle dig," Gary said. "We'll be staying in Oaxaca, and working about ten miles from it. It's a fair-sized city, a state capital."

"The Springfield of Mexico," Brill said. "I hope they have better hotels." He was already disappointed in the lack of hardship on the trip he wasn't going to take, so he goosed Funny Ha-ha, with whom he had once been asked to leave a Springfield hotel, by a detective who objected to the noise she made. "Right, Darlene?"

"Whoop," she said. "Damn yew-ew."

After supper while the girls were crowded into the cabin john together, whispering, Gary said: "My God. I can see why you call her Funny Ha-ha. She laughs all the way up the hill, doesn't she?"

"She can get damn near hysterical with it at the climax, when she's having a good one," Brill said, a bit morose. "One night we had to put her out the door in the snow, bare-ass, to stop her."

"Why did you call the other one . . . Betty . . . Funny Peculiar?"

Brill, who had some time since realized that tonight he had no taste for the sport, whether because of Martin or of Gabby or for reasons unbefuckingknownst, said: "I think we'll arrange for you to find out, old chum."

Gary said: "What about you?"

"I'm out tonight. You'll have to make both our girls happy."

Boyish delight. "I can't say I ever, that is. Well. Two different girls."

"They're different all right," Brill said. "Just one little thing you're going to have to sit still for."

"What's that?"

Brill laughed. The girls came out, drinks were poured, and Gary kept looking at him, inquiringly. Mean Brill just waited, and finally Betty Martin went for her purse.

"May I?" she asked Brill. Not Gary. "Would it be all right?"

"Sure," Brill said. "Darlene, fix the lamp. I'll get another glass and the basin."

Gary said, "What is this? What's happening? Come on, please."

Funny Ha-ha, laughing at him, got two sofa cushions, and told him to get up. All right now. Put them under him. Adjusted the lamp so it shined on his face.

And now over came Funny Peculiar, with her equipment: dental mirror, scaler, tooth powder, and a rubber suction-cup brush.

"Open wide, please, Mr. Pederson."

Going along with the joke, Gary opened wide. Quickly and seriously, Betty set to work, and Darlene said:

"Thank heavens she's got him to do. She was threatening to clean mine again for New Year's and I'm still recovering from the job she gave me for Christmas."

"Ouch," Gary said.

"I'm sorry. So much tartar, Mr. Pederson. Now, we'll try not to hurt."

It made Brill's own teeth ache a little, watching. "It's what she really likes, Gary," he said. "Betty was going to be a dental hygienist, but she couldn't pass anatomy."

"It's like, I don't know." Betty was chipping happily away between the lower front teeth. "Just spit out. Would you like to rinse?"

"Here." Darlene offered Gary straight whiskey. "Rinse with this."

"It's like, oh, cleaning some old pans with steel wool, you know? How satisfying? To work and scrub and get them clean?"

"Come on, Darlene," Brill said. "Let's dance."

Eventually Funny Peculiar led Gary off, a bit bloody around the chops, to his reward. Brill sat on a big leather hassock in front of the fire, one arm around Funny Ha-ha who said pensively:

"I always liked you, Bob. I really did."

"I know. I like you, girl," Brill said. "Sorry about tonight. Call it middle age and alcohol."

"There'll be other times?"

"Of course."

She whispered: "Will you call me sometime to go out . . . by ourselves? Without her or your friend?"

"Okay."

"You're not really going to Mexico with him?"

"No. Don't you like him?"

"He's all right," she said. Then she giggled: "I had to hold onto him. He wanted to roll off."

"Betty will take care of that tendency." Brill smiled. Funny Peculiar had a great variety of whims, mostly concerned with being in charge or playing at it. She liked to be on top, and suck your nipples, nails dug into your rear end, squirming. Martin had enjoyed her fantasies; Brill had never quite been able to relax with them, tended to compete with her, two wrestlers in a contest with very odd rules; winner takes the nipple.

"Kiss me, Bob," Darlene said, and he did. Stopped before she could start chuckling, firmed his arm around her, and stared into the fire.

There was something poignant he was going to have to recognize here in a moment, something that had been stabbing at him, stabbing for a soft spot, trying to make him notice it: all right. It wasn't about Betty Martin or Darlene, was it? No. Or about himself? Gary and Mexico? No. But Gary, yes. And went back to boyhood, yes. And Felix; and of course, Martin, and as soon as Brill admitted that it was clear enough: the purpose of this evening for old Gary wasn't girls at all, but friendship. In Gary's mind, the void in Brill's life, resulting from Martin's death, must be filled now by Gary.

As once before Gary had been the friend on hand when Felix was killed.

So there was no question of his going down to Mexico, of course, to play in Gary's sandbox. Couldn't be.

3.

New Year's eve: Cal out with friends. Pat asleep in front of the tee-vee in the bedroom, in her bed, wine glass empty by her side. Trinket at her first such party, in a blue dress. Brill waiting for her, prowling. A new year begins.

Twelve forty: Are we late, Mr. Brill? No, of course not, Jimmy. It's okay. Good night, Patricia, Happy New Year. Thank you, Jimmy, thank you. Good night.

Oh, Daddy, yes, it was beautiful.

Gawky, leggy, thrilled child in blue. Beautiful? Go on, go to bed before you break my wheezing heart. Watched her go up.

Two o'clock: Brill sleeping.

Pat woke him, turning on the light.

"Wake up, Bob. Please wake up," she said. Slow and lugubrious, he woke.

Reached out his arms for his wife and held onto her.

"What's the matter, Bob?"

"Huh? Nothing."

"You were crying. You were crying out loud, in your sleep."

"Me?" He sat up and scowled. She sat up on his bed, looking at him, patted his hand, drew hers away; nodded.

"Crying so loud it woke me. I thought you were awake. Did something happen?"

He shook his head.

"Is it . . . because of poor Mr. Habib?"

"It's enough to make a goddamn goat cry," Brill muttered, evasive and profane, for it did not seem to him that he could tell Pat.

Or anyone.

What, through the sounding corridors that led back to but did not quite obscure his dream, it seemed to him the tears had been about:

How do you comfort a dying elm?

PART TWO

1

What ever became of Old Bob Brill?

He went down to Mexico, and turned into a coelacanth.

He didn't stay a coelacanth for long. About fifteen minutes all together. The transformation started while he was taking quite a hot shower on a pretty hot day. By the time Big Bob had finished drying off from the shower, he was all evolved up to human form again. Or down, or crossways, however it is that direction goes. A coelacanth is an old fish.

It is a tough-looking, carborundum-scaled, primitive fish which turned up living off the Comores Islands, between Mozambique and Madagascar a dozen years ago, half a million centuries after it could be proved from fossil records that the thing was absolutely extinct. It was pretty much as if a live dinosaur had been found, but this fish went even further back.

If fifteen minutes seems long for a shower, consider how luxuriously dirty Lawyer Brill was. His hair, which he was considering shaving off completely, was loaded with Mexican dust. There was a dark gray film of the stuff marking off parts of the body not generally covered by hot-weather clothing—the hands, arms, face, and neck. The rest of him was only a slightly lighter shade of gray, for dust sifts through clothes, mixes with sweat, and, if you're out there long enough, the wash gets to be fairly uniform. Only Brill's feet, which had been protected by socks and calf-high boots all day, looked pale and white. A little detached down there.

Somebody else's feet perhaps?

Archaeology, which is what engaged him, is a dusty science.

Each afternoon he came back to his hotel room in the City of Oaxaca just so dirty and, though he was a man who had always previously enjoyed being clean, quite pleased with himself. On coelacanth day he was experimenting with scrubbing the top of his head, through the very short hair, with a stiff hand brush. Felt damn good.

He started to work over the left forearm with a certain kind of coarse, fiber sponge you could buy in the Indian market in the city. He began to sing a primitive song:

> "It was from Aunt Dinah's quilting party,
> I was seeing Nellie home . . ."

As he sang and scrubbed he kept an eye on those pale, disconnected feet, where they stood in four inches of warm water, backed up by the slow, Mexican drain. And perhaps because even his mind was grayed-over, full of dissolving sweat and dust, he thought only dimly of the hour's reading he might do next, while sipping a scholarly Victoria beer, from among the stacks of books Gary Pederson continued to press upon him.

One of them was *Old Fourlegs, the Story of the Coelacanth,* by J. L. B. Smith, thinking of which suggested an agreeable interpretation for the peculiar things he was looking at:

undeveloped feet. (Pronounce: *see-la-canth*) The wavery things down there in the water must be the hind pair of fins. Anal fins.

Take some pretty strong evolving to get the old anus moved along between them, out of the belly and up the backside. Have to do it, though, if we're going to start walking, I suppose. Or you'd crap on your toes.

And I seem to be. Holding. A sponge, here in the pectoral fins. *Lobate* fins.

Meaning what? Well, Counselor Dumb-ass, how about *fins with membrane flaps hanging down*—like the fleshy little buggers here at the bottoms of today's ridiculous ears. Women know what to do with silly appendages like these.

Pierce the bastards. Decorate them. Stick in something shiny.

As did the Aztecs, Zapotecs, Mixtecs, and the Mayans. All those boys. Why hell, not to mention Africans, pirates, and now and then one of the guttier hippies.

Is it, then, gentlemen, the most perfect distinguishing characteristic of the Western male, that he lacks the humanity to decorate his earlobes?

Us coelacanths wouldn't decorate our lobed fins if we could. Need 'em for swimming; always will. Two hundred and fifty million years from now our cousins can turn the fins into feet, and crawl up on land. We'll just stay here, underwater, and continue extending our fins downward, thanks, when we're not swimming.

Use them for points of balance, yeah, as we CROUCH! Yeah, here in the deep reefs! Waiting for food and female coelacanths!

There was some kind of sound, possibly a knocking on the door of his hotel room, and Brill yelled happily:

"In the shower. Try me later."

Whoever it was, Stan Newman most likely, ought to know better than to interrupt a coelacanth crouching on his lobate fins, waiting for a female.

2.

Chock full of eggs she swam my way, looking more like Gabriela Steiner Light than most of the nutty Devonian fishes around here. A great-looking set of lobes on her, lords and ladies: couple of thousand more millennia, there'd sure be something suitable for walking on down there.

Five feet two, steely blue, she swam around flirting. Wonderful the size our species had on it already: human dimensions, five to six feet long, between one hundred and two hundred pounds.

We were pretty special in other ways, too, in this age of fishes. The rest were sharks and rays and succulent little guys with gills (Go ahead and eat him, Gabby; I just had one). But we were crossopterygians, we were. With important extras, all adding up to quality. Internal nostrils! Functional lungs! Skulls with dermal bones! Cosmoid scales . . .

"Cosmoid, Plowboy? Really?"

"World-shaped, ma'am; hey, swim a little closer."

"It's nice right here."

"Then I'll swim your way."

Hesitated to drool over it on such brief acquaintance, but she had the cutest, most symmetrical little *diphycercal* tail.

"What's it mean?"

"Diphycercal? Probably means it's got flags on it. I don't know. It's not even in the big Random House Dictionary over in Newman's room."

"Newman! That lantern-jawed lungfish."

Wowee, buddies, swam to the surface, rocketing, water slick on my scales, enjoying the compaction of power in a streamlined body, propulsion that a hawk would envy, took a fine leap into the pure, warm, Devonian air.

"Oh my," said Gabby as we drifted back toward the rock bottom. "I feel like laying some eggs. I don't suppose you'd care to fertilize them for me?"

Covered 'em like a quilt with guiltless milt. *Mavistic.*

And the particular and peculiar characteristic we will pass on most importantly through those eggs is not the lobes so much as this thing about our teeth: "labyrinthine infoldings of enamel," pass it on. Till it gets to a class of primitive amphibians called, you guessed it, labyrinthodonts, boy adventurers who will sometimes leave the sea for a little stroll upon the beach . . .

Carboniferous bastards. Probably looked like scaly, snake-tailed catfish with legs. From which would come the next pretty little things: lizards. Insects. Mammals. Me.

Grinning, Brill moved his human form out of the shower to dry it off.

3.

Scientists, exhaustively logical with their fossils, closed the book on coelacanths, did they? Noted that they flourished like crazy in the Devonian, died out for sure in the Carboniferous. And then one day a South African chick, out collecting specimens for her local museum, is given a queer-looking fish by a trawler captain. Chick calls up a chemist named Smith, who dabbles in icthyology and paleoick, and old Smith, old James Leonard Brierly Smith, says: "Hey!"

Says, "Believe it or not!"

Says, "Listen here, we got one!"

And the world replies in a sort of bored, Harvard accent, "Hog, Professor Smith. Wash."

It's down in South Africa, quite a way from the Comores, this first coelacanth. Ocean current, playing tricks.

Smith gets a little support, puts up a reward, a hundred pounds for an extant coelacanth in good condition.

("Oh, really, Mr. Smith? And what would you pay for a brontosaurus?")

Way up the coast a man named Hunt, one of those nice-looking, moustached, free-lance Englishmen, a sailor of fortune who trades by schooner off the French part of East Africa, carries the reward notice with him.

Two years go by.

One day some natives appear at Hunt's boat, dragging a new coelacanth with them. In Smith's *Old Fourlegs,* where Brill looked:

> Hunt realized the full importance of this find, and wisely questioned the natives. Was the fish known to them? Oh yes, they knew it well, they were rare but caught regularly. They called them *Kombessa,* and they were not much valued as food when fresh, but were good salted. When cooked fresh the flesh became soggy and jelly-like, and was not very good to eat, but they were eaten . . .

Sensation in the scientific world. A fish so unexpected and important that journalists, not quite understanding but coming close enough for their hit-or-miss trade, would call it "the missing link."

Brill, drying as he read, feeling still somehow the exhilaration on his scales of that fast swim to the sparkling surface, couldn't stop himself from reading:

> . . . They were nearly always caught with the Oilfish in the deeper water, and on flesh bait, using squid or any kind of fish. Hunt found out afterwards that a good many people there knew those curiously rough scales, for they were used to roughen bicycle tubes in mending punctures . . .

Momentarily sad, Brill turned to a photograph of Hunt's coelacanth.

"Joke's on you, huh," he said. "Not going extinct when your time came."

4.

There'd been a knock on the door all right, because now there was a note under it:

Turd Seminar today

It was written in peculiar, slanted, left-handed printing, and thus both form and content made the signature "Stan" unnecessary.

It was also enough to make Brill, in clean undershorts now, pick up old Bernal's *Conquest of Mexico,* just as if the message hadn't come.

He stretched out on the bed to finish Book Two, Chapter One. Let Newman describe archaeological excretions to the young, Bob Brill would read.

Bernal had been a soldier with Cortes. His memoirs were real and absorbing, the unornamented recollections of a blind, proud, straight-backed old man, a man who was there in the time of hardship and glory, a man with no complaints if the rest of his life had been disappointing, because complaint was not his style, reliving the campaigns of 1523, sixty years earlier: which companion was wounded, the name of the horse he rode, how the fight began well and ended badly . . .

"I am an old man now," said Bernal, in 1586. He must have been dictating. "Over eighty-four years of age, and have lost my sight and hearing, and, as luck would have it, I have gained nothing of value to leave my children and descendants but this my true story; and they will presently find out what a wonderful story it is."

Lawyer Brill responded to that with the same straightforward love of fact and a clear record the old soldier himself had felt so keenly.

But look at Brill, big, sandy-haired, freckled, sagging bull of a Midwesterner, lying there dehydrated, physically tired from a day of putting out energy, volt for volt with the young. They had mapped their site today, walking, climbing, clearing away stones and obstructions in the lines of sight.

Those big bare feet, recent subject of such delicate fantasizing, are size 13. He isn't going to be able to lie there with the weight off them for very long without going to sleep, especially if he orders a beer, and if he corks off now, he'll sleep poorly tonight.

Acknowledged. Heaved up, closing the book, snorting at his frailty. He would go hear Stan Newman after all, drink cold beer there, and endure coeducational scatology.

5.

One block from Brill's hotel on the main square of Oaxaca were the *portales*. These were a series of open arches, supporting a roof over the sidewalk. They ran in part along the front of the principal hotel, the Monte Albán, named for the great Zapotec ruins on the hill above the city.

Under the *portales* tables were set up; meals and drinks could be had.

Going there after his shower, during the week of orientation now concluding, was a good habit Brill hoped to avoid. This was a teaching expedition Pederson was running, and the sessions when they returned to town were classes. The difficulty was that Brill, saturated with recent reading and tired, felt he set a poor example of paying attention for the kids.

Either Gary or Stan Newman would talk, conduct a discussion into which Brill didn't feel he ought to intrude, since it was the students, not himself, who would be graded and examined at midsemester time.

The alternative, and he'd have had to admit he needed it but didn't consider going, was a Spanish class, conducted by a man named Sandoval for about half the students.

Stan's turn to conduct the seminar meant Gary Pederson would—or might—be free, but Brill hesitated to look for him. When Gary had a beer with you, he managed to make you feel he was doing you a favor—or perhaps repaying a kindness? No calculated graciousness today, thank you, Professor. If anything, Brill thought, the night before New Year's eve defined the distance between us rather than reduced it. If I hadn't had a check to take him January 2, we might have managed not to see one another again for a year. The invitation to come down cordially renewed. Is it tough for Gary, too, that he caught me with it at a time when I had no zest for hometown crap, so that for the first time since school he sees me every day? No. It seems to please him, and the distance is in me.

He saw Stan, sitting at a round table, his group gathering. There was Colonel Mazzard, whom the kids called Colonel Mustard, a retired army man trying to learn a new field. There was the little undergraduate girl, Nancy something-or-other, and the two best graduate students, Berkowitz and Minnegerode.

They saw Brill.

Berkowitz, a comedian, yelled for the waiter in mock alarm and terrible Spanish. He had a gift for being able to mispronounce the language so that the Mexicans both understood and found it funny, and was popular with them. Help, he called to the waiter in this outlandish tongue; here came a man so thirsty and so cruel that no one's beer was safe unless the waiter could beat Brill to the table, bringing a fresh bottle.

"Don't try to hold me back this time," said Berkowitz. "If he tries to get my beer, I'll sacrifice him."

Brill, who had picked up Berkowitz' beer last time he'd come to class, was rather pleased to be kidded. "Hone up your stone knife, boy," he said, and to Newman: "Your message moved me."

"The beer moved you."

The water arrived with a Carta Blanca, sweating cold. "No. There's boys at the hotel will carry me up one of these, if I ask real nice."

Newman was waiting to see if his final student would show up, a boy named Peter Franchot.

"You weren't here yesterday," Nancy said.

"Reading Bernal Diaz," Brill told her.

"That's a fast nap," said Minnegerode. "When you've been out in the field."

"I was soaking in the shower, thinking about earrings," Brill said.

"Earrings?" said the colonel.

"I always think about earrings in the shower," Berkowitz said. "Don't you, Jack?"

"I think about Nancy's earrings," said Jack Minnegerode, put his arm around the girl and sighed.

"Quit," Nancy said. "It's too hot. What about earrings, Bob?"

"Remember Bernal telling about the landing at Cozumel? They hear about a couple of shipwrecked Spaniards, who'd been made slaves a few years before?"

"Aguilar and Guerrero," Newman said. He had just taken PhD comps, and his memory was spectacular. "Aguilar was glad to be ransomed, but Guerrero had a native wife and three sons by then. He'd been made war captain, and liked it fine where he was."

"There's a speech he made to Aguilar I just looked up," Brill said. "Guerrero said he wanted to stay where he was. He had a new life; maybe he hadn't done so well back in Cuba. His Indian wife cursed Aguilar for disturbing them . . ."

"Did she really?" Nancy asked.

"That's what wives do, little honey," Minnegerode said, going with the arm again. He was after Nancy's pretties like a lunging animal.

"And then Guerrero said: 'What would the Spaniards think of me with my face tattooed and my ears pierced?' You see, he didn't think of himself as a Spaniard any more, with those marks on him, and I was thinking how unnatural, really, for a man not to have his ears pierced."

"I know an old lady in the market who'll do it for you, Bob," Nancy said. She shook her short, blond hair so that it moved away from and showed first one ear and then the other. "It doesn't hurt."

"But what would the Spaniards think of me?" Brill said. "Hello, Willa."

He pushed back his chair to rise, then recalled that none of the younger men would do that—and were, perhaps, right: camaraderie, equality, all that. He noticed that Colonel Mazzard checked the same impulse, and exchanged a small smile with him.

Willa was a plain, shy, severe girl whom he rather liked for her directness.

"Aren't you supposed to be doing Spanish?" Stan asked her.

"I wanted to hear about the coprolites." Squeezed into a chair, between Minnegerode and Nancy.

Willa, Brill thought, a little sadly, might be in the same fierce soup as Minnegerode—seriously after Nancy's pretties, too.

"Coprolites?" said Colonel Mazzard.

"Here in this box." Newman held up a box which had once held large kitchen matches. "Borrowed back, ladies and gentlemen, for your education from the Regional Museum. To which I presented it a month ago. Aged thirty-five hundred years by radiocarbon dating of associated material. I have one: well, let's be accurate. Not a coprolite, which would be fossilized. Something better, actually. A genuine, immaculate, thoroughly dried-out human turd." He smiled. "Bummed it from a man in Tehuacan, who stole some for what might be called religious reasons, and had more than he needed."

"Who did the dating?" Willa asked.

"A lab in Chicago . . ."

"Tell about religious reasons," said Minnegerode.

"A Mexican schoolteacher," Newman said. "Who observed MacNeish's corn dig in Tehuacan, and felt a certain ativistic awe for these relics. He figured they were what his ancestors left him, so he swiped some."

"From Coxcatlan Cave, Stan?" Brill asked. They had stopped off one day to see the cave, carefully dug out in squares.

"Yeah. I think we'd better have a lecture on that, too." Newman made a note. "And one on radiocarbon. Anyone seen Franchot, by the way?"

No one had.

"You're just going to be full of little lectures, aren't you, buddy?" Berkowitz said.

"Enough to bulge your tiny brain," Newman promised. "Anyway, there's a story about an archaeologist going through customs with a number of specimens like the one enclosed . . ."

"May we see it?" Willa asked.

"Don't spoil his story," said Berkowitz.

"The man had all sorts of material he was taking back, in match boxes, big and little, wrapped in foil. Including several like this one, and all of them in a larger cardboard carton.

" 'Whoa, there, professor,' says the inspector. 'What's in the carton?'

" 'Specimens, sir,' says the archaeologist.

" 'Open up,' says the inspector. He knows about academic types, and this man is coming right out of prime pot country.

"The archaeologist opens his carton, and inside are thirty or forty smaller boxes, neatly arranged. Mighty suspicious. The other people in the customs line are craning their heads forward to see what's going on between the bearded man and the brave customs guard.

" 'Those are your specimens?'

" 'Yes, sir.'

"Tap, tap." Newman tapped the box in his hand. "'Open this one. Right here.'

"'But . . .'

"'Open it, please,' so . . ." Newman demonstrated. "He slides the box open, and there it was."

It was, all right: an unmistakable formed segment of human stool. From where Brill sat, it didn't even seem all that dry.

"'But it looks like a piece of . . .' cried the inspector, and clapped his hand to his mouth. 'Exactly,' said the archaeologist, and apparently the whole line of people burst out laughing behind him."

Newman put the tray from the open box down on the table. "Examine it, if you like," he said. "It's been dry for quite a while now."

No one quite wanted to.

"Was there a lot of it left in the cave?"

"A family, maybe several, spent seasons of their lives there. These are good evidence of diet, when you get them analyzed."

"They pull it apart and look at fragments under the microscope?"

"No," Newman said. "Who wants to read some reports and discuss it with us next week?" He looked around. "No, Willa, you're supposed to be doing Spanish, not coming here. All right, Colonel. I have the publications. But to give you a general answer, they reconstitute this material with various laboratory oils, before they examine it. And do you know what happens?" He paused and looked around. "After three thousand years, when the oil soaks in, some of it starts to smell again. Just as it did when the cave dweller left it. The bacteria get right back to work."

That was his introduction. The real topic, it now turned out, was how to handle organic material if they came on any during excavation —they were more likely to find carbonized wood and, of course, bones, than anything else.

The rich kid, Peter Franchot, whom the others had decided not to like, came to the table then and said, "What's the topic, Newman?"

Since no one else made room for him, Brill pushed back his chair and said, "Move a seat in here, if you like."

"You sure you can spare the time, Franchot?" Newman said.

Franchot stared at him, but replied sarcastically to Brill:

"Don't put yourself out for me, Mr. Brill."

"Here now," said Colonel Mazzard.

Franchot turned to the waiter now and ordered: "Whiskey-soda," white hunter to African camp boy. Then his eye was caught by the object in the box.

"Hey, what the hell?" He had almost sat down. Now he rose up again.

"What's the matter, Franchot?" Newman said.

"What are you doing with that?"

"The waiter brought it to us," Berkowitz said. "You want to order one?"

Franchot backed off a step.

"It's the season for them," Minnegerode said. "They're nice and fresh."

"It's archaeological, son," said Colonel Mazzard.

Franchot took his chair, and demanded to know where Newman'd got it.

"I just finished describing that," Newman said. "Maybe you can borrow someone's notes. Shall we go on?"

And he did, but Bob Brill, sitting there, nursing his beer, seemed to hear two voices: one was Newman's, sharp, sure, talking about interdisciplinary procedures, illustrating by the case at hand. And the other, which had been with him quietly since he'd left his hotel room, the voice of the old soldier, Bernal Diaz del Castillo, about the first expedition, under Grijalva. A skirmish near the river Chompoton, with Mayan townsmen:

> . . . I remember that this fight took place in some fields where there were many locusts, and while we were fighting they jumped up and came flying in our faces, and as the Indian archers were pouring a hail storm of arrows on us we sometimes mistook the arrows for locusts and did not shield ourselves from them and got wounded; at other times we thought they were arrows coming toward us, when they were only flying locusts, and it greatly hampered our fighting . . .

6.

There was a delay next morning. The crew of diggers was not complete yet. The head man in the village of Huitzo, from which the diggers were to come, was away, attending a wedding.

Gary Pederson, improvising nicely, took his group to a village to watch an old lady make pottery. She was called Dona Rosa.

"It's not only the same technique," Gary said. "We've broken a couple of her pots, and compared the fragments with one of the common Monte Albán Period Five wares. The gray wares; you've all looked at them. Her paste and temper are exactly the same . . ."

In an enclosure over to the right, a goat was giving birth. It was distracting the girl students, Nancy, Willa, and the third whose name was Rosalie.

Newman, who had watched Dona Rosa work a number of times before, was photographing the goat, which didn't help Gary.

Gary was snappish with him on the way back, and rather pointedly asked Brill and the Mexican archaeologist, Sandoval, to join him for supper, omitting Newman. Gary had an apartment in Oaxaca, and a cook who did very well by him.

Sandoval declined; his sons were coming for the weekend, he said, and he had to meet the bus.

Brill, it turned out, in spite of misgivings, had a decent time with Gary. They looked at maps and aerial photos of the Oaxaca Valley—"Do you see how it lies?" asked Pederson. That was a little annoying, the phrase a real estate man would use to a farmer.

But later Brill repeated the passage he'd found in Bernal, about the locusts, and Pederson said, quite nicely excited:

"Of course. Look, this must be the same locust." Got out Volume 11 of Dibble and Anderson's Sahagun, and first among the six kinds of locust described by Aztec naturalists was the *Acachapoli*:

> It is large, a little tall, rough; the upper leg is long, smooth; its lower leg is jagged. It is a flyer, a buzzer, a hummer. It is pale. Its name comes from *acatl* [reed], that is, arrow, because when it flies, it is as if one shot an arrow . . .

Brill was quite charmed by Pederson's enthusiasm for the small adventure of making a connection like that.

"I'd like to make poetry out of anthropology, really," Gary said. "That's my weakness, Bob. Don't tell."

"What do you mean?"

"To organize and teach a course entirely out of the *relaciónes*—the sources. Directly. The works of the great witnesses, the firsthand men, the interrogators."

Brill agreed that it could be exciting. Brill wondered if that wouldn't mean learning Nahuatl, and Gary agreed. He knew some; he knew some Zapotec, but no Mixtec. Brill, drinking brandy, felt as if he himself could learn Nahuatl, when Gary explained the structure of the language to him.

Brill walked home to his hotel, impatient for Monday, when the digging would start, like a boy waiting for spring.

2

Saturday morning Brill woke up, feeling country and western, bought himself a machete, missed his dog, and rented a car.

"Let's us git the feel of this here By-hecky Valley," he said to the car, getting into the driver's seat and shooting it back from the position in which the last short-legged Mexican renter had left it. Sang:

> "In the Mixtec mountains of Oaxaca,
> On the trail of the fourteen toads."

Song based on a Gary Pederson, professorial, orientation lecture joke: "Remember, these people believe you're digging for treasure. There's a local legend every place you work, about *'los de antes'* burying fourteen golden toads to hide them from enemies."

That was all right. He didn't even mind having been patronized in a more personal way, Gary saying last night like a man trying to sell a farm:

"Do you see how it lies?"

"Sure, Gary," he'd said. "It lies like a rug with its hand in the goddamn cookie jar," but he had to admit the geography was interesting; he wanted a quiet look at it. Maybe he'd buy the farm. The Oaxaca Valley was three small valleys—Etla, Zimatlan, and Tlacolula—with their hub at the city of Oaxaca; or at Monte Albán, rising behind the city, if you preferred.

He spread out a map on the Mexican plastic seat cover, which looked exactly like a U.S. plastic seat cover, but had a tag that said, *Hecho en Mexico.*

Here along the valley floors had lived the gentle, sensual, and eventually decadent Zapotecs—husbanding and smiling and crafting up a storm of big stone buildings and grim, ugly, clay funeral urns.

And all around them in the hills were the Mixtecs, peering down. Prickly mountainmen, crafters too, but of more lyric and sometimes even playful stuff in material less yielding than clay, mostly: jade, crystal, obsidian, and metal. Ready anytime, the Mixtecs, perhaps through nothing more than irritability, to steal into the valley by night and awake the Zapotecs out of their dream of peaceful nookie with clubs and spears and maquauhuitls.

"Maquauhuitl," said Robert Brill the linguist, aloud, prospective student of the Nahuatl tongue, and rubbed the soybean steering wheel. Take you a good strong club, and run nice, razor-edged pieces of obsidian up and down the sides. Good maquauhuitl man could probably have stood up against a knight with a mace. If they were both bare-chested.

He started the motor. The knight would have worn metal armor, the warrior quilted cotton. Not much of a contest that way, and no contest at all when the Spaniards came spilling over from the Caribbean with horses, cannon, beards, and crucifixes.

Brill considered critically his inclination to spend the day driving alone, starting at Huitzo at the head of the north valley, near where their dig was taking shape, and exploring southward along the highway. Undecided whether or not he wanted company, he drove over to the *portales,* parked, and sat down with Newman and Minnegerode who were having breakfast. They seemed in no mood or physical condition for a day of driving.

"Ah, sir," Newman said. "Why did you go off carousing with Gary Pederson last night when we had a field trip scheduled?"

"A field night," said Minnegerode. "Many events. Berkowitz won."

Brill smiled and ordered Mexican coffee. You had to specify, to avoid Instant and get the real thing, the dark black roast, presweetened, from Veracruz.

"The cribs," Newman said, "are just down from the market. Berko'd never seen such things before."

"Can't say we have anything much like that in Tennessee, either," Minnegerode said. "But old Berkowitz. It was love at first sight, wasn't it?"

"Yes," Newman said. "With all of them simultaneously. Every girl in the district."

"He was drunk as God making the world," Minnegerode said. "Scattering peso notes around. Telling them collectively in that miserable Spanish what beauties they were. It was a parade, Bob. Berkowitz singing at the head and thirty whores following."

"He was going to rent a bus and take them all up to Monte Albán to marry him this morning."

"At sunrise. A Zapotec high wedding mass."

"Let's go wake him up and get him dressed for it," Minnegerode said. "The girls are probably waiting."

Brill watched them leave, saw Colonel Mazzard come in, and had an impulse to invite the colonel. Might be interesting to hear how a military man would comment on the terrain.

But the colonel sat down to breakfast with Willa and Nancy, as Brill was rising. Nancy called over to ask what he was going to do today, and Brill smiled and waved. The old eagle wearer would perhaps have accepted an invitation; but the girls would, almost certainly.

Brill did not like the image of himself, middle-aged and affluent enough to rent a neat, little car, on some kind of damn double-date excursion with a retired officer, a lesbian, and a college chick. Why hell, they'd probably send up for fat little Rosalie, and want to take Gary Pederson along too. And have a picnic. Oh boy.

He drove alone, after all, up the InterAmerican twenty miles to Huitzo. Today's road didn't fork there but as he'd learned last month, the old road had forked like a mink, one branch going as today's did north and west, the other due north up the Cañon de Tomelin. He wondered what it would take—jeep, horse, or foot—to cover the fifty miles up the canyon between here and where he'd gone with Newman in December.

With Newman, and that, shall we say, tempting Totonaca teacup from Tajín . . . which teacup, so Stan tells me poker-faced, is still in Mexico, or back in Mexico again, or some such piece of information . . . gittin' her a liddle Ti'wannee dee-vorce, mebbe?

"Which fork," said Brill to the car, or the unsharpened machete on the seat beside him, "would the Mixtecs have used for an invasion route?"

Depend on which Mixtecs, he guessed, and where they started from. Simple as that? But the one down the canyon would have been more secret. Brill got out. He could see car tracks going up the hill to where their site was hidden behind it. The hills were brown. Only cactus offered cover, but there were dry watercourses deep enough to hide in.

"We moved by night," Brill guessed. "And hid in the twisting ditches during daylight."

2.

Their dig near Huitzo, at the northwest end of the Etla Valley, was (so Gary Pederson assumed) a traditional frontier town between Mixtec and Zapotec country. Gary was guessing it had been Mixtec sometimes, Zapotec at others, and frequently jointly populated.

What you hoped to confirm by digging such a place depended on what books you read and who you listened to.

1. The Mixtecs might have been the original people in the valley, got driven out around 200 or 300 A.D. by Zapotecs, fighting their way back in finally in what was called the Fifth Period, just before the Conquest.

2. Or the Mixtecs might always have lived in the mountains, till they started yearning for some of that good Zapotec television and Coca-Cola in the Fifth Period.

3. Or the Mixtecs could have been semicircular boys (a lot of people liked to see them this way), northwest to southeast, to start with, Valley of Puebla and around through Guerrero; then they themselves might have been driven gradually *south* into the mountains, leaving great art and great cities behind—some even wanted to give them Teotihuacán. Then (so it went) after generations up where the nights were chilly they decided to move south again.

"Archaeologists are like sports fans," Brill had said to Newman and his boys. "Rooting for one or another of the big-league pre-Columbian cultures."

"Yeah," said Berkowitz. "Newman's for the Mixtec Goldsmiths. I'll take the Totonac Tarbabies."

"How about the Zapotec Weavers?" Newman suggested.

"The Teotihuacáni Classicals."

"No one much likes the Aztec Butchers, do they?" Brill said.

"Like the Yankees and Notre Dame," Newman said. "But the real spoilsports were the Spanish Horsemen. They came in and the game was over."

"And there's a team everyone likes," Minnegerode had pointed out. "The Olmec Mothers."

In a place where everything was legend, the Olmecs were more legendary than anybody else. It was a name, Newman said, given to a whole, precursing culture—running from the archaic (B.C.) to First

Period—that might have been one or many, from which the sentimental liked to think all the rest derived.

3.

Brill drove slowly back through Huitzo, wondering if there had been an ancient town here where the modern one was. Newman was pretty certain that there had been. "Look," he said, "at the hill the church stands on. That isn't natural. I'll bet it was a pyramid they covered over, and I'll bet there's reused stone from it in the church walls.") Pederson thought their site, though rather far removed, might have been old Huitzo, and pointed out that people referred to it as El Pueblo Viejo.

Brill wished he knew. Where the town was located rather affected which watercourse his war party was going to spend the day hiding in.

Then he saw his men standing beside the road, hitchhiking, and decided he'd better move them out of there.

It was a Mexican family, waiting for the bus. When Brill stopped, they all climbed into the car, two women and five children crowding into the back seat, only the man getting in front with Brill.

Driving south toward Oaxaca, he asked in Spanish how his passenger felt. Perhaps the man regarded it as a prying question; he smiled but didn't answer. Brill tried saying forthrightly that it was a fine day. That didn't seem to go over too well either.

Either Brill's Spanish was unintelligible, the man spoke no Spanish, or, what seemed most likely, the man was convinced a priori that he would be unable to understand the driver.

"Okay," Brill said, in English. "I'm just trying to tell you there's thirty Mixtecs armed with atl-atls out behind your corncrib, right now."

"Thank you," said his friend in Spanish. "Turn left here, please."

They had just gone through Etla, and the turn was onto a dirt road. Brill took it.

They went off past rough farmland with irrigation ditches, jounced finally onto the cobblestone street of a little town the name of which Brill didn't catch.

A dozen reasonably ragged children, and a young man who seemed pretty drunk for this early in the morning, watched him stop the car. The passengers in back got out; the man in front, assuming perhaps that their journey together had taught Brill his language, sat where he was, talking faster and faster about something. A funeral. Uh-huh. A niece who had worked in Oaxaca for Don Somebody-or-other—the man seemed confident Brill would know the name.

The niece had got pregnant in the City of Oaxaca; that much became clear. It was agreed that this sometimes happened to girls from the country who went to the city to work, even in Brill's fatherland.

In the street a large woman had appeared, heaving something toward them which appeared to be a boulder.

The niece had come home here for the weekend, last weekend, and tried to abort herself with the last supper.

La Ultima Cena?

The woman with the boulder stopped now and smiled; from the car Brill could see that the stone was crudely worked; there were features on it.

He and his rider shook hands. The woman came to the window and suggested that he ought to buy her boulder. The young drunk gave wild directions, calculated to help Brill turn his car around.

He had intended to ask if someone here could sharpen his new machete, but a second lady had appeared and was stalking him, this one with serapes to sell; it was getting to be too much for him. He turned the car.

The meaning of his rider's tale came to him in a delayed take, for the rider was back now, at the righthand window, with a box which said: *La Ultima Cena,* and showed a dead rat lying on its back.

Rat poison. The kid whose funeral the family had come here to attend had tried to abort herself with rat poison.

Brill finished making his turn, and drove quickly away.

Outside of the town he slowed down. He was getting an idea of distance and terrain now, and he realized for the first time that from Huitzo, where he'd started, to Zaachila—the last of the Zapotec capitals and west of Oaxaca—would have been a pretty rough one-night walk. Or armed trot.

He reached the highway, and continued his invasion southward. There'd been an Aztec garrison, remember, where Oaxaca itself now stood. So if you were coming this way, along the Etla Valley, wanting to make it into the Zimatlan Valley where Zaachila was, without the Aztecs knowing, maybe you should go up over the sacred mountain, Monte Albán. This would have been in the Fifth Period, and Monte Albán a deserted city, a place of ghosts, but certainly the shortest route for bypassing Aztecs.

Even so, you'd have to know some pretty damn good *arroyos* out there on the valley floor or foothills, among the cactuses and other xerophytic plants.

4.

Question here of etymology: *xeros* was Greek for dry.

Xerophytic, a word he and the other students had become readily addicted to, meant *adapted to dry conditions.*

That would include cactus, of course, but also, for example, a horned toad, which so well conserved its moisture it could urinate in crystalline form.

Ouch.

Brill stopped the car, and took a little walk, out behind some organ cactuses. Thus we have *Xerox,* for a dry copier, but we also have all the words in the family of serene.

Dry, bright, cloudless, free of storms. Here (he sat on a stone) the land was what? Xerene? Back there in the mountains?

5.

My mother was a Mixtec, my father Zapotec. A slim, dark, intense, nervy little bugger with fast hands, I speak both languages.

That doesn't reassure anyone.

Here in the valley, the Zapotecs call me Mixer, a piece of cheap irony because the popular myth is that all Mixtecs are antisocial.

Joke: a Mixtec traveler is staying in a Zapotec's house. The host says, "Time for dinner." Mixtec gets up with the other guests, says thank you, and walks seventeen miles home to eat and seventeen miles back again.

Up in the mountains the Mixtecs call me Zap. They say it in the tone of a man calling his litter-bearer Boy. They call me Zap even when they want something from me, some interpreting or spying. But on the whole, I am more comfortable with their contempt than with the patronizing down in the valley.

There are quite a few half and halves like me around. It comes from this crap of chiefs giving enemy chiefs daughters to marry whenever some damn little peace treaty is signed.

Maybe this is okay on the big-deal level, where the kids are going to be brought up in palaces, and fixed up with cozy jobs in the bureaucracy when they grow up. That would be the Zapotec bureaucracy; better still because bigger, the Aztec one—there barely is one among the Mixtecs; all chiefs up there, no Indians.

If you really care what happens to your grandchildren, fortify hell out of the hill above your city, train up some good tough boys with the atl-atl, and annoy the Aztecs into throwing a siege on you. It helps if your village is near the trade route, but not too near—if it's too near, the Aztecs aren't going to make a deal and lift the siege, they're going to have to say clobber. So just far enough off not to be worth a major campaign, and if you've got a teen-age girl around the place that isn't going to be doing anything else, you should be able to work things out so that your grandson will be slipping you all the Nal-tel and Chapalote you need in your old age out of some federal granary in the Valley of Mexico.

It's on the small-town level these peace-treaty marriages aren't so hot. What's involved isn't much of a king on either side—not enough corn land in it or water rights or feather-weaving to interest an Aztec—just a rug-loving Zapotec in one town, a Johnny-come-Mixtec in the next one over. Comes the thorny part of the cactus, and it's hide-with-your-uncle-kids; and up the old pyramid for one king or the other, peace-treaty wife or not, with some saintly bastard of a priest up there with the obsidian knife ready.

I know the priest that cut Dad's heart out: 5-Tiger sacrificed him, a fat, sanctimonious, slippery-handed old boy from Etla, who could never make it in the city.

The Zapotecs gave him tryouts in Zaachila any number of times—he has family connections there at the capital—and he'd do all right for a while. Then a big sacrifice would come along, and he'd choke up; no style. He gets worse as he gets older. They claim he hasn't gotten a heart out whole on the first stroke in five years. What kind of a priest do you call that?

I'd like to slip 5-Tiger a little obsidian one of these days, and one of these days I will.

6.

Reaching the outskirts of Oaxaca, Brill considered going right, down the road to Zaachila, to see what the modern town looked like and decided instead to sneak past the Aztec garrison (finished their breakfast at the *portales* by now) and up to the ruins of Monte Albán again. He made the right turn, and then another, threaded through town and started up the serpentine.

At the entrance he bought the two-peso ticket and a six-peso guidebook from the attendant, who looked like a rundown ex-soldier.

"English?"

Brill, just a touch sour with pride about the way his Spanish was being received today, said, "*no, Castellano, por favorcitatito.*"

Then, to sweeten the pride or punish it, sat in the car in the parking area before going in, sending away guides—it seemed a slow Saturday for tourists—and read the preface through:

> . . . *so conocen mas de doscientos ciuddades or pueblos, hoy desparecidos, pero los que han quedado vestigios.*

There were more than two hundred cities and towns, gone today, but of which vestiges were left . . . and only a few had been explored partially . . . (a list of nine; make it ten. Add Huitzo. Or a town near Huitzo, depending on whether you were a rooter of the Newman Newbuddies or the Pederson Peterpals, or Christ Almighty, let's geddoudt of this car.)

He goddoudt.

He had Monte Albán to himself. It was, of course, still early. He went directly into the Great Plaza, climbed the worn, shallow steps of the building called "G," and sat, looking across at the complex called "North Platform."

All right. Sit there. At the dead center of a dead city which did, by 500 or 600 A.D., cover sixteen square miles of leveled mountaintop and terraced slopes.

Where he sits has no less past importance, *pinchés cabrónes del mundo,* than the Forum in Rome, or the Capitol in Washington.

The Gran Plaza is three hundred meters long and two hundred wide, and Brill, transposing that into the U.S. system of measurement, figured you could get twelve football fields into it, with enough space left over for modest sideline areas for each and, if you were strict about the end zones, a five-furlong racetrack surrounding them.

Look (he addressed, of all creeps, the young engineer who made pipeline surveys and laid out subdivisions): the yellow-gray masses of rock rise on each side of that staircase of shallow steps 250 feet. And there are column bases at the top six feet in diameter. How are you going to cut stone columns that size without metal tools? You can't. Any more than you can move them up here, without even the help of oxen and horses which the Egyptians had to raise the pyramids.

You know the engineering factor, Whipcord Hank, boy engineer? Religion. That's what got them up here. That's the big generator of horsepower in early history, and who's in charge of theological engineering at the engineering school in University City, Illinois, these days? Ronald Reagan?

Religion was the engineering principle here, and at the great pyramids of Teotihuacán, and the beauty of El Tajín (bugger off,

Gabby), the anthropomorpholithicolumns at Tula, and one wouldn't doubt Chichén Itzá—great, indecipherably related theocratic civilizations that ruled down here.

Raised these cities, not necessarily benignly; created this art, evolved this knowledge. Faded. Faded, Hank; faded Ronald. Like you. Fell very easily, their great-great-grandsons did, in the twelfth and thirteenth centuries, to the barbarians from the north. The Chichimecs, who were the general tribe, from whom came the real sweethearts, the Aztecs.

The bloody, doomed, sweetheart Aztecs. Who met, in turn, a different dynamo—also religious, also greedy; that's how you run reciprocating motors, Hank.

Brill rose, went down the stairs of Building G, turned right, and walked around the Plaza. Past the ball court, beautifully restored. Past the Palace, with its many adjacent flights of steps. And the connected buildings, paused: to look up at the huge South Platform. Looked like that was where you got sacrificed; or married thirty whores at sunrise.

Monte Albán was not, of course, completely restored, because: *this had been a colored city.*

THIS HAD BEEN A COLORED CITY.

Colored red.

The whole floor he walked, and every building, had been covered with stucco, painted red. He tried to imagine that, the great solid blocks here of unadorned color, with sun shifting over them, and was staggered.

He started moving toward the observatory and heard tourists' voices. He decided to keep moving. Crossed, quite a ways, to the building on the other side where the mystery was: carved stones, each with a single figure on it. Strange, line-drawn figures in relief, called, for some reason, dancers. The *Danzantes.* They did not seem to Robert Brill to be dancing, but he had no alternative word to suggest.

Nobody has ever had an alternative word to suggest, so far as Brill knew, and he figured John Keats even would have looked at those grotesque go-go boys, six feet high, on the Zapotecan stylae and been as stuck for the right word as John Keats was looking at the Elgin marbles. What Brill meant was that Keats could handle urn figures all right, and Keats' poem on the Elgin marbles was at least a good try, but nobody, not even Hank the boy engineer and his friend Ronnie Reagan, would have the rhetoric to know what to say about the *Danzantes* of Monte Albán.

The tourists were coming. There were two groups. The first was Mexican school kids, about sixty of them with three teachers trying to keep control. Then, after them, a North American pair, male and female, and seeing them was enough to make Brill really dig in and take off: the young man was Peter Franchot, his objectionable fellow student. With, presumably, his wife, but Brill didn't wait to look her over.

The school-kid vanguard was streaming around Mound J, the observatory, when Brill took evasive action. He ducked around the side of the System IV pyramid, another huge one, crossed packed dirt toward the North Platform, went up the steps three at a time, disappeared behind a column, checked back and scurried down the back steps toward Building A. Then went up and over Building A, and back around toward his car—but stopped off at the small building under which Alfonso Caso had found Tomb 7, and treasure.

He inspected Tomb 7 soberly, thinking that IF one had come over Monte Albán in the Fifth Period, to avoid the Aztec garrison at the foot of it, on the way to Zaachila, a tomb like this would have been a damn good place to hide. Assuming it was open. And there'd be no more ghosts in it than in the rest of the deserted city.

He made it to his car, bracketed now by a Mexican school bus on one side and an air-conditioned Chrysler with Pennsylvania plates on the other, which must be Franchot's.

The Aztecs had left their litters to follow him on foot.

Only an old man was there, looking at the big Chrysler from some feet away, and it seemed to Brill that the jolly old fellow had concealed a piece of wire, just as Brill came up, perhaps a little something to be inserted into the wing-window crack of a car, playfully, if a chap wanted, playfully, to get its locked door open. Brill could see a purse, binoculars, and a small woman's suitcase in the Chrysler.

The old man waved to Brill in friendly fashion; Brill waved back, and settled moodily into the front seat of his car. He had meant to end his visit by going way over to the other side, to Tomb 105, to see the murals there again and pay his respects to 2-Tiger and his wife, 1-Deer.

But he supposed he'd better sit until the old wire man went off, or until he saw people returning in the rear-view mirror, at which sight he'd be able to drive away fast, avoiding greetings.

7.

How did I get into a damn tomb at Monte Albán, anyway, with a naked priestess rubbing magic balm all over me, singing a golden Olmec song?

8.

Started, like most everything, with drinking too much. Midmorning in the mountains, not so long ago, I met 6-Rain and her brother in the street.

Why do I always want to boast about how drunk I get?

"Hey, Zap," 4-Wind said. Windy's a pretty good joe, even of he does call me Zap. "You were about forty rabbits last night, weren't you?"

"That was early," I said. "I was two hundred and eighty rabbits by the time I got to bed. I was falling down rabbits. I couldn't even find the bed, I woke up this morning on the floor."

I couldn't stop myself. I looked at 6-Rain when I said this stupid thing; she kept her big eyes on the red stucco street, but just looking at the top of her head, at the magic pallor of the scalp where she parts her heavy black hair, is enough to make my heart spin and my mouth run off. I'm glad Mixtec girls don't cover their heads like the silly little Zapotec cunts down in the valley.

"Listen," Windy said. "We're looking for you. Grandad wants to see you. Feel up to it?"

4-Wind knows damn well that if his grandfather wants to see me during business hours, I'm going to shag on up to the south side of Number Two Pyramid fast, no matter how I'm feeling. But Windy's nice enough to make it sound like an option. I mean, I'm not a slave around here, and not about to be sacrificed tomorrow or anything but —well, much as I prefer the hill people to my Zapotec relatives, I'm still here on sufferance. And always will be.

"I'm off," I said. "Ball practice this afternoon?"

Windy said sure, and I tried to sneak another look at Rain. But she had turned away completely by then; 6-Rain isn't promised to anybody yet, as far as I know, and maybe if I could do a couple of hot-shot things . . . get in a battle, and bring back some decent prisoners to go under the knife, something like that. Hell, the only prisoners I've ever got were two poor little Mazotecs . . . I'd better do something around here, she wouldn't look at me at all. Why the *hell* do I boast about drinking?

Grandad, if you stop to think about it, but no one does, is actually my great-grandfather.

But he's that to half the town, and great-uncle to the rest, not counting slaves and peasants.

His first son was my mother's father; when this oldest son, my real grandad, got drowned in the river, trying to swim across after some Zapotecs with his quilted armor on, a campaign was lost. My mother was moved to the Zapotec village (it isn't there any more; we burned it) down the canyon as the young chief's girl-wife. I was born there, the first and only child. There's lots of girl-wives don't make it through childbirth.

Meanwhile, my great-grandfather's eighth or tenth son had got married to some cousin or other—the family traces a line of direct descent from 7-Deer, the great conqueror, and is very jealous of bloodlines because of it. 4-Wind and 6-Rain came along, among others, and I suppose in a weird way they're all my uncles and aunts, though I'm older than any of them. And never knew them as a kid—never came up here at all, as a matter of fact, until after Dad got sacrificed, down in the canyon. That was when that village got burned, and I was brought up here; so as for Auntie 6-Rain, I cannot think in terms of consanguinity, not when there are eyes that big and ankles so mocking slim.

Grandad was waiting for me all right, and half a dozen other big boys. I knew they were big from their clothing, but there was only one I recognized: King 9-Reed from up the canyon at Teotitlan, a boy with half the Mixteca Alta sending corn and robes to him (but not Grandad, whose town is small but tough enough so that he doesn't pay tribute anywhere).

I didn't, as I say, know who the others were until we started in on the ceremonial presentations, and they answered in Nahuatl. Aztecs, for God's sake! Arrogant bastards won't even learn the language of the places they're in. My Nahuatl's fair; I got what they were saying.

Grandad was going through the standard stuff about me being a great warrior, capturing eight prisoners for sacrifice last year (it was two as noted, and they were only Mazotecs), and one of the Aztecs said:

"Yes, yes. All the Mixtecs are great warriors, of course."

At least Grandad didn't go into my cluttered background. These guys were merchants, he told me, though they managed to make their merchant suits so ornate you'd have taken them for kings from some oddball place or other. I've heard they dress shabby at home so that people won't envy them, but it's sure different when they're on the road. They wanted a guide to take them into Mitla. They said things were safe enough for them at the north end of the valley, but Mitla itself, where there were Zapotec high priests living on top of a Mixtec town, might be tough. It's one of those open-city, co-religion places.

Of course I said I'd be honored to take them down. I haven't been to Mitla since I was a boy, and I remember it as being beautiful. One of the Aztec merchants was fat and chocolatey—the other severely pockmarked. I thought of them as Fudge and Hole-in-the-Nose.

"How many days will you need to get ready?" Fudge asked me.
"None," I said. "We'll leave three dots before sundown."

9.

Brill drove slowly through the Oaxaca slums, able to imagine what was behind the painted doors and high stone walls only from having read yet another book, an overwhelming one by a man named Oscar Lewis called *The Children of Sanchez.* Would he be in the bloodline of Pederson's great witnesses?

Behind the painted doors, that book had taught him, were not small houses as it might appear, but little neighborhoods: courtyards, lined with other doors, each opening into a one-roomed, dirt-floored dwelling where a family of four or five might sleep. Might keep a pig, or chickens, on the roof. Would send out children, washed in a single community washroom, to get on school busses like the one he'd just left up at the ruin.

The fathers would go out to city jobs as laborers and dishwashers, streetcleaners, tire repairmen, factory hands. The mothers would work as maids and laundresses. The livelier children? Brill did not know, whether the Mexican situation permitted upward mobility for some of them; he suspected that in most cases liveliness could best be expressed in lawlessness.

In amplitude their lives would be not very different from the lives of the rural poor—the families whose men, for example, they were hiring as diggers—but there would be the usual country–city differences: a certain worldliness, an illusion of possibility, a protective indifference as against the more limited horizons which permitted mutually compassionate behavior.

Town poor or country poor, there'd be hunger, brutality, and exploitation—and could it have been much different for them in pre-Hispanic times?

Hadn't solace and focus for their lives always come in the same intermittent ways—from churches, festivals, sports, and parades? And could archaeology tell you any more than that? The living patterns of the poor didn't survive as monuments; cruelty might be more open at one time than another, protection under law incorporated more or less strongly in theory; but it seemed likely to Brill, braking violently to avoid hitting a burro led out of an unexpected alley by a small boy, that when you spoke of a civilization perishing or declining, you were speaking only of the rulers and a few beneficiaries. You meant the priests, soldiers, artists, teachers, entertainers, professionals, and businessmen perished; or attached themselves to another culture with stronger weapons.

Life on the animal level went on pretty evenly, most likely, as Greece rose and fell, Persia, Italy, India. Harlem and Appalachia.

He was going south and east as he cleared the outskirts of town, down the InterAmerican instead of up it. He gave due thought to whether or not he might like something cold to drink: *una Coca, o Naranja, o Delaware ponche?*

Sure. Pulled the car off the road at the square of El Tule, where an enormous tree gave the town its name. Something historical about that tree, but Brill couldn't remember just what.

There were a number of old men on benches under the tree. Brill stepped toward them and inquired where he could buy something to drink. Several answered; one got up, and Brill followed him to a grocery store, a place whose shelves were stacked with dusty cans and bottles; there were dried red chiles in a box on the counter, and pickled green ones in a jar; bins held rice and macaroni and beans.

"Mescal, senor?" his guide asked hopefully.

Misunderstood but tempted, Brill said: "Will you take some with me."

"Without doubt."

Brill bought mescal. He hadn't tasted it before, but as he understood the matter, it, like tequila, was made from the maguey cactus. Mescal was, in fact, the general name, and tequila the word for a particular quality of mescal, made in the Jalisco region. *Appellation côntrolée, messieurs.*

This mescal had, and fortunately Brill had heard of the usage, a caterpillar or two floating in the bottom of it.

"Okay. Good." Cool Brill.

He followed his friend out.

"Will senor not want a grapefruit?"

"Clearly," said instantly acclimated Brill; off they went to an outdoor stall, where his man picked out two strange, warty-looking grapefruit, peeling one back to show skin half an inch thick.

"Now this?" Pointed to a paper cone of crude salt.

Brill paid in coins too valueless to comprehend and back they went to the bench, his friend explaining something about the salt. He kept pointing to the bottle, then to the paper cone, but it took dense Brill four times through to understand what anyone should know—that the salt in the cone was made from drying the bodies of the same kind of caterpillars he could see in his bottle. The Agave worm, a resident of the cactus head when roasted up for mash to be fermented.

To know the process was to love it.

They sat, opened ceremoniously the bottle, and on Brill's making his invitation general, one more old man came to join them.

"My *compadre,*" said Brill's first friend, and there came in that moment, for Brill, a little series of connections which turned on a small floodlight of illumination: Mexico, *compadrazgo,* a whole particular system of male friendship. Sanchez, in the Oscar Lewis book, speaking of the seriousness with which he had chosen his *compadre.* Illuminated: Pederson, choosing Brill.

"I don't know if it's worth the price of a bottle of mescal," Brill said in English, turning his biggest smile on his two companions to atone for the rudeness. "But thank you anyway."

A grapefruit was peeled. A section torn off and handed to Brill. He indicated that the others were to drink first, and watched.

Sections distributed to the others. Sections peeled down. Dipped in salt. Then a drink taken from the bottle. Salted grapefruit, fast, for a chaser.

Brill's turn: it had the turpentiney taste of moonshine, raw. The grapefruit was bitter beyond belief. The wormbody salt was delicious.

Shy, courteous, observing many arcane formalities, other men joined them. Another bottle was sent for. Discussion was hardly general, until Brill remembered the machete. How, Zapotec gentlemen of El Tule, shall such a tool, made in Hartford, Connecticut, where all the best machetes come from, be sharpened?

It gave unity to the mescal interlude. Boys were dispatched to houses for files. One particular file, judged suitable, was pressed on Brill as a gift, and the technique of using it properly demonstrated by several different hands.

None of them, they told him, owned land. All worked for men who did, when they worked. One had been to the United States as a *bracero.* All the younger ones hoped to go, some day.

Several of the older ones said it was too late for them. Brill asked the age of one of these, a worn-out, wrinkled man. It turned out he was Brill's age, forty-eight.

Brill left the second bottle with them, and went on.

Soberly intoxicated, he got in the car, drove back to the highway, and there, beside it, saw Aztecs from the garrison, Willa and Nancy gaily hitchhiking. They recognized him; he could hardly fail to stop for them.

"Where are you going?" they asked, getting in.

"Where are you two going?"

"We wanted to have lunch in the museum at Mitla."

"I'll run you down there," Brill said.

"Won't you have lunch with us?" Willa asked, and Brill probably would have accepted if Nancy, looking past him out the window at the countryside, hadn't remarked that there certainly were a lot of xerophytic plants out there. In spite of the push of her hard little blue-jeaned thigh against his, Brill withdrew everything but his grunt-producing mechanism from the conversation.

10.

"Be back for corn-planting?" Windy asked me. He was sitting there on the floor, clay jug of pulque between his legs, watching me pack. We'd canceled ball-practice.

"Hate to miss it," I said. Windy and I had a tremendous time at corn-planting last year. "Maybe I can pick you up a new tortoiseshell to play for the dance."

"That'd be great. Get me a baritone if you can," Windy said. "My little shell's pitched too high."

"I haven't been in Mitla for a long time," I said. "But as I remember it you can get anything you want in the market."

"Man, I wish I were going too," Windy said. "Eat a little armadillo with you, and drink some palm wine for a change. Hey, Zap?"

"Yeah?"

"How are the girls in the valley?"

"Same problem as anywhere," I said. "Only if you've got some dough, there's more down there to spend it on."

Windy sipped on his pulque. "Sure you won't have a shot?"

"No thanks," I said. "I'm going to walk a few pounds off those Aztec bastards before moonrise."

Windy laughed. "You are like hell. They've got litters." We had a great talk. I said everything in the world to Windy that might be said, except the only thing I really wanted to say, which was: *Tell Rain good-bye for me.*

Windy was right. Fudge and Hole-in-the-Nose were having themselves carried through the hills on litters. I walked between them, where the road was wide and level, and went ahead in tougher places.

"It's shorter this way, through the eastern pass?" Hole-in-the-Nose asked.

"Yes," I said. "But steep and slow. The easy way's to go over west. That's where most of the traffic is."

"We don't have to walk." Nose lay back in the litter. "Might as well take the short way."

It was a little more elaborate an explanation for why we were going down the canyon than he needed to make. I began to get the idea they wanted to get to Mitla without Zaachila knowing, but I was too busy trying to figure out something else to think very hard about their motives: I was working on the problem of why Grandad was willing to supply me, or any other guide. Grandad has never been an Aztec ally. No taste for it, for one thing; fairly small, as kings go for another.

But 9-Reed having been there; he was a good-sized king. Grandad might not pay tribute, but favors were a different matter.

"So you're not planning to go through Zaachila?" I said to Hole-in-the-Nose.

He didn't answer.

"You'd better tell me," I said. "There are Zapotec villages on the east side of the valley, when we get down there. If you want to stay clear of them, it'll affect how we come out of the canyon. And what time of day or night."

We were going down a sandy road now, between rows of cultivated maguey cactus.

"We won't be going into any villages when we get down there," Fudge said.

"9-Reed planning a little push?" I asked.

"This is a mighty warrior we got here," Fudge said to Hole-in-the-Nose. "A mighty inquisitive warrior."

"Oh, he can ask those good old questions, can't he?" said Nose.

"On and on. I wonder if he ever stops?"

"Maybe he'll stop if you tell him."

"I'll try," said Fudge. "Hey, mighty warrior. Stop asking questions."

"I don't really have to," I said. "Things are getting real clear. You boys are getting ready for another go at the Valley of Oaxaca, aren't you? Didn't you get licked bad enough last time?"

"This time we're using mighty warriors like you," Fudge said. "This time the Mixtecs are on our side."

"Shut up," said Hole-in-the-Nose. "Let the guide guide."

He closed his eyes and we went on without any more conversation for a while. They had four men each to carry the litters, and some sort of body servant in addition. He didn't seem to have much to say either.

We spent the first night in Chila, which is a little village two hours away that pays tribute to Grandad—an hour and a quarter if you're armed and running. I picked up some disturbing information.

We were in the guest patio at the house of 1-Smoke, the head guy, stretched out on our mats. Fudge was snoring to beat hell. Nose seemed used to it and was sleeping anyway, but the noise kept me awake. I decided I'd go out and talk to Smoke for a while; maybe he'd offer me a drink to go to sleep on, and if not I could get directions to a wine-seller.

I knew 1-Smoke from the campaign last year against Datzingo, and by God if he wasn't talking about Datzingo with somebody, laughing about it as a matter of fact:

"Zap ought to be getting there with his two Aztecs about noon," 1-Smoke was saying.

"I'll let them know."

"The Aztecs look like ransom bait to me."

"What do I tell the Datzers to do with Zap?"

"Whatever they want. He'd make a decent slave, maybe, if they'd castrate him. Or they can just . . . you know. Save him for the next festival."

My good old campaign friend 1-Smoke.

"Grandad wouldn't like it much," said the other guy. I got a look around the corner at him. He was wearing a yellow feather cloak, beautiful thing.

"That's the nice part," said 1-Smoke. "Our hands are clean. It's Datzingo's baby. If Grandad's mad enough to want to run another campaign against them, hell, we'll go with him. It'll get us off some of the damn tribute we're paying the old bastard."

"All I do is tell them who's coming, then?"

"No. It's gotta be better than that. They might be a little leery of Grandad. No. Tell 'em you hear Zap's been run out of town—drinking and fornicating, huh? And he's signed on with these Aztec merchants. That'll sound right to them, because they won't know anything about the new alliance. We wouldn't have known ourselves, if Zap hadn't spilled it at supper."

That was true, or half-true. I'd only said enough to get us put up overnight and fed—that Grandad and 9-Reed, the big shot, wanted us to get down to the valley safe. But 1-Smoke was smart enough to see that that meant a new Aztec-Mixtec alliance in the planning stage, to invade Zapotec territory. The only thing I didn't understand was why 1-Smoke would be so eager to spike our little mission. He's as good a Mixtec as any, and would stand to pick up more from a well-financed valley campaign than he'd get by stirring up trouble between Grandad and Datzingo.

Then I found out, from the guy in the yellow feather cloak:

"Trying for a clear track, are you, Smoky?"

"What do you mean?"

"I've seen 6-Rain, boy. If I had any chance there, I'd want to clear out the competition, too."

"Shut up," Smoky said. "Zap's not competition."

"Sure."

"I've got a town. What's he got?"

"Then why do you want him out? I thought he was your buddy."

"Take off, will you?" 1-Smoke said. "You want to get there in time to start talking tonight."

"I'll be on the road in two bars," said the guy in the yellow feather cloak.

I turned around in the little dark passageway, took a step back toward the guest patio, and bumped smack into someone who'd been standing behind me, listening too.

There was stark silence for a moment. Then I felt a hand close on my wrist and start to pull me along the passageway. I had a knife in my hand, five inches of nice sharp obsidian, but I didn't want to use it till I had to, so I let myself be pulled.

Whoever it was was leading me back to the guest patio, and not making any noise about it, either. Just before we got there I realized who it had to be. I was right—Hole-in-the-Nose.

"That was damn close for you," I said, as we came into the starlight, showing him the knife.

"God, put that thing away," said Hole.

I grinned.

"What are we going to do?"

"How much did you hear?"

"Not much. I don't speak much Mixtec. But enough to know it's trouble."

"There's a guy in a yellow feather cloak," I said. "He's supposed to get down to Datzingo, where we stop tomorrow for food and water. He's to tell them that I'm out on my own—not an official guide."

"Wait a minute," Nose said. We were still whispering. "What's that mean?"

"If you're seen anywhere with me in the Mixteca," I said, "they figure Grandad's behind you, and you go through. That's why I'm your guide. But if they think I'm on the run, trying to make it down to the valley where I'll be safe, they'll take all three of us, your litter-bearers and your other man, too."

"We'd better go back," Hole-in-the-Nose said. "We'll go back in the morning, and get your grandfather to send a big enough escort with us . . ."

"It's all right with me," I said. "You're the guys that want to get to Mitla quietly. Get that much escort and they'll know about it all the way down to the Isthmus."

"The three of us, and the man," Nose said. "Shall we seize 1-Smoke?"

"Right in the middle of his own town? I thought Aztecs were supposed to be smart?"

"What else can we do?"

I looked him over. He looked soft and noisy, and I didn't need him. "You can go to sleep," I said. "And forget you heard anything."

I took off my cloak, a shabby old blue one. I poured a little water in the fire pot, mixed some nice gooey black, and daubed it on my face and chest to cut the shine. Nose watched without saying anything, and I didn't have anything special to say to him. I stuck the obsidian knife in my girdle, took a run at the patio wall, went up over it and dropped into the street beside the building.

The guy in the yellow feather cloak was standing in the doorway, about forty yards up, saying good night to 1-Smoke. I watched until he started off down the street, and then went south through town by a different alley, and out onto the Datzingo road running. I went down it a couple of miles until I was well past the last farmhouse, and then settled down to wait in the shadow of a big clump of moonlit cactus.

11.

Brill left Willa and Nancy identifying themselves as student archaeologists to the man in charge at the pleasant restaurant of the Frissell Museum in Mitla.

He bought a straw hat at a street stall to keep the noon sun off his head, and walked up to the ruin. In Mitla it was right in town, partly built-over, and had been part of a thriving and beautiful little city when the Spaniards arrived.

Even sixteenth-century European sensibilities had been struck by the beauty and uniqueness of Mitla. There was nothing else like it in the world.

Only twenty miles from the Sacred Mountain and you could see immediately why it had teased art critics so thoroughly, for Mitla was an architectural complex as gay and graceful as Monte Albán was monumental and austere.

It was as hard to believe that the same people, even people acquainted with one another, had built both places as to try to understand why the Spaniards in their holy zeal had failed to destroy it.

"The Heart of the People." Brill couldn't recall for a moment what the phrase meant to him, or why it should mutter itself now.

It was a name: the Heart of the People, given to a great Mixtec jade, in the shrine city of Achiutla, in the mountains. Alfonso Caso had written of it.

When the Dominican friars arrived in Achiutla, one Fray Benito Fernandez, who'd left a trail of burned codices and smashed art through the Mixteca, was moved to tears by the beauty of that stone. He therefore pulverized the Heart of the People, and scattered the powder.

"*Sin nada de mezcla, señor Brill,*" said a severe voice, and Brill turned to see, standing just behind his shoulder, Tomás Sandoval M., the Mexican archaeologist who was accompanying and perhaps policing their dig, and moonlighting, in Pederson's pay, as a Spanish teacher.

Gary Pederson was not comfortable with Sandoval M. Newman liked him and said he was bright, one of the young comers.

There were two younger comers with Sandoval, standing respectfully behind their father and looking to be about six and four.

"No mortar," Brill agreed. He had learned on their group visit to Mitla, earlier in the week, that this was the standard observation to make about the stone decorations which were the great wonder of Mitla: put together with hundreds of small stones called *mosaicos,* so perfectly cut and fitted they required no mortar to hold them forever in place.

"This design," Sandoval said, indicating one of the less elaborate geometric patterns into which the *mosaicos* were arranged in the various rectangular spaces into which the wall was divided. "You will find this one at Yagul. You have been there?"

"No," Brill said, realizing that Sandoval was announcing his choice of sides. Young comers held the final and most striking period of building at Mitla to have been the work of Mixtec conquerors. Old goers still worried the idea that this, in spite of the great difference in spirit and technique from Monte Albán, nevertheless represented a final evolution of Zapotec architecture.

Yagul, back up the road, where Paddock had found similar designs in a formative stage in association with Mixtec wares and offerings, gave the young comers something to overbear about.

"You must go to Yagul." It was an order. "Here. This design is another. You must go to Tomb Thirteen at Yagul and see."

Sandoval was young but unsmiling, an intense man.

Brill said: "Senor Sandoval: the Heart of the People. Does anyone have any idea what it may have looked like?"

"I'm sorry?"

"A great jade carving that the Mixtecs worshipped. At Achiutla."

"Yes. Caso tells of that."

"Is there any information about it—what was carved on it? What it looked like? Could it have looked something like these walls, these designs?"

"But it was destroyed," Sandoval said, and shrugged.

The little boys were growing restless. "You have handsome sons," Brill said. They were diminutive, brown, strong-looking kids, the same sort physically as the boys who had gone to fetch the files at El Tule, but already showing in general sturdiness the improvement in diet of a middle class family.

"Thank you. Wigberto. Ernesto. Senor Brill."

They snapped to. Little rascals bowed.

"I'm surprised," Brill said, noticing that each boy wore a gold chain around his neck—of the sort crucifixes are worn on—disappearing under his shirt. Sandoval had one, too. "Newman told us that few Mexican scholars are Catholic."

"Not any of consequence."

"But yourself?"

"No, senor." With furious courtesy.

Brill, confused, wishing he could withdraw the conversation. "The chains on your necks?"

"They do not refer themselves to the Church. No, Ernesto . . ."

But the little boy, proud to have something to show, had pulled his out. Pendant from it were the hammer and sickle.

"Yes." Sandoval's manner became suddenly charming. He smiled. "You are shocked, my good friend, offended."

"No," Brill said.

"You will report to Congress, the President, the CIA."

"I think they're rather attractive."

"You share my politics?"

"No. Is Ernesto named for Ché Guevara?"

"There you are." It was Willa.

"And Mr. Sandoval." It was Nancy. "Oh, what darling boys. Hello."

"We're going to spend the night here," Willa said. "At the museum. Will you tell Mr. Pederson?"

"No we're not," Nancy said. "I have to work." She had a working scholarship, as expedition secretary.

"Tell him, in case we don't get back."

Wrapping his shabby blue cloak around his shoulders, Brill fled.

Understanding, he felt quite sure, something neither young comers nor old goers would have figured out. It took a middle stander to see what Mitla was, those delicate, perfectly made small buildings, and why. Some really high priest had put that doll house together, Brill could tell you, for the cuddliest little high priestess ever seen in that valley.

12.

It was a very big deal (Newman had said in a seminar) a few years back. The bones of Cortes were rediscovered at the Hospital de Jésus in Mexico City, where they had lain forgotten for generations. Well, buddies, that was great for the right wing and the Church. So the left-wing and the anticlerics had to counter it. That meant most Mexican scholars and journalists, and a bunch of exiled professors from the Spanish Civil War. I mean pure science is fine as long as the purity works your way, but us truth-seekers were up against the wall.

You were probably up against your crib rails (Berkowitz had said, and Minnegerode): clutching the bones of your teddy bear.

Shut up, dear students. The intellectual community struck back. What they did was delegate a lady who had a degree in anthropology from some years back to go find the bones of Cuahtemoc.

How do you spell it? (Nancy had asked). That was the last leader of the Aztec resistance, his statue's in Mexico City.

Every magazine and newspaper in Mexico said the bones of Cuahtemoc were authentic.

Anything to it?

Not a shred. But the bones of Cortes were real and comforted with veneration. Bones like that sort of stuff.

13.

I stayed behind my cactus in the moon shadow for half an hour. It started to get cold and I wished I'd brought my cloak. I tried to keep warm thinking about 6-Rain, and it partly worked. When she was a kid, eight or nine; I was fourteen, Windy was twelve. The summer after Dad was sacrificed.

6-Rain was a prodigy of prettiness, and a tremendous child on the loom, weaving stuff that amazed older women. Happy, grave-eyed, but bubbling behind the gravity . . . the guy with the yellow feather cloak almost got by me on the road.

I hadn't heard a sound. He was a quiet runner, and the moon sent his shadow back the other way. He was clear past the cactus and out in the open in front of me before I reacted, and by then I had to sprint after him. He was only trotting, of course, and I caught him about sixty yards down the way. The first thing he knew, I had an arm around his throat and had grabbed the maquauhuitl out of his hand. I threw it behind me, and pushed him away hard, so that he fell forward onto his knees.

He yelled.

"Get up," I said. "And turn around."

He did. "You're . . . are you Zap?"

"That's right," I said. "I hope you've got a knife, baby."

At that he turned and started to run again, but I was on him before he could get ten steps. I hauled him down like a deer. He was a wiry little guy, but his throat cut easy.

I rolled the body off the road, into some mesquite, but there was something I wanted. I'd always wanted a really nice feather cloak. I took the yellow one, put it on to keep the night air out, and trotted back to Chila. I climbed back over the patio wall, lay down with my cloak around me for warmth, and slept real fine.

Fudge woke me in the morning. Nose was still sleeping.

"Where'd you get the feathers, Zap?" Fudge asked.

I woke up grinning. "Smoke gave them to me," I said. "My old buddy-system buddy 1-Smoke put me in the way of this cloak." I took it off, shook it out, and put it on again.

Our talking woke old Nose up.

"Feathers?" He looked at me reproachfully. "Yellow feathers? . . . Zap, you can't wear that."

"That so?" I said. "What's the authorized uniform for today, an empty rib cage?"

Nose winced. "I just meant, it's like coming out and telling 1-Smoke, isn't it, when we go into breakfast?"

"It's just like that," I said happily.

"Look, Zap." Nose bent down to his bundle. The stuff he was carrying was in a sack of polished alligator skin, with gold clasps. "Is it a feather cloak you want? Here. I'll trade you this for the yellow one." And he got out the most beautiful garment I ever saw: troupial feathers, blue and green and iridescent. The thing was worth half a province.

"Sure you can spare it?" I said. It had the look of something that was being carried along specially, as a gift for someone of the greatest importance.

"It's yours," Nose said. "For the yellow one."

"I'm glad to see it," I said. "And I'm glad you can spare it. I'll trade . . ." He started to hand it to me. "When we get to Mitla."

He started to protest, and I told him to shut up. I even suggested that I knew what I was doing, which is a curious claim for a man to make. But I did know that breakfast was going to be a delicious meal, and it was: corn cakes, fried turkey, chiles and green tomatoes, flavored with a little cold sweat from 1-Smoke's brow. I wouldn't have missed it for all the cloaks in Tenochtitlan.

I let Nose and Fudge go in first, and listened to the way Smoky greeted them, all unctuous hospitality.

"There's a very interesting jaguar shrine," he was saying. "A few minutes off the road, about an hour and a half out from here. A huge stone figure of the beast, captured from the Zapotecs. Zap can take you to see it . . ."

"Sure," I said. "But we were planning to be in Datzingo by noon."

Whatever word of good morning Smoky had for me stuck in his throat like a bone.

"We'd better eat and get on the way," I said.

"Yes," said Smoke. "You had."

"Too bad they're not expecting us at Datzingo," I said. "They won't have food like this ready."

"No," said Smoke. My Aztecs were uncommonly quiet. "That's a good-looking cloak, Zap."

"Thanks. I hoped you'd notice."

Smoky gave me a long, bitter look. He wasn't eating. "My brother has one exactly like it," he said.

"Your brother?" I said. "Must be a *well*-dressed fellow, Smoky."

14.

Yagul was white.

Brill stood across from it, a thousand yards away and reluctant to go closer, on a Period Two hill site called Caballito Blanco, where a dig in progress was closed between seasons.

From there Brill found it easier to imagine Yagul alive and inhabited than he had either Monte Albán or Mitla. You couldn't get distance on either one without wings.

Flightless Brill stood at the summit of Caballito Blanco like a reprieved dodo, enjoying the vision of the rising temple, the streets, the walls of small palaces, able to project people there, grave and gay. It was white not because that was its true past color, which must mostly have been red; it was white by a trick of the sun, like an Arab city.

Relocation. Here the Spaniards had moved a population quite completely to a new town site on the valley floor, now called Tlacolula, a mile away, behind him and out of sight. Yagul had been thriving one year, empty the next. Such a place was unadministrable, with its concentric, circular city plan, grown outward from the ceremonial buildings, ringed first by the houses of the wealthy and important, then each ring of houses poorer than the last till you reached the peasant homes of the farthest ring, closest to the field, made of the same eternal mud and reeds as today's, houses scooped out of the ground wherever a man found himself.

Only the fortress at Yagul avoided the concentricity; it was at the highest, most easily defendable point above the city, to which the whole population could go in time of attack, in idea exactly like the feudal remains in European towns.

But apart from its fortifications, a city evolved in such a shape belonged to a society which conducted business and defense on foot. When the Spaniards came, they had to be able to move horses, carts, and cannon, and to be able to look at a flat map, on which a rectilinear town could be divided with a straight edge into neat, symmetrical barrios, each accommodating a more or less even number of subjects and parishioners. Brill wondered, and thought he might ask Colonel Mazzard, if we followed the same principals of design in relocating people from villages in Vietnam.

The nitty-gritty of cultural genocide probably didn't change much from Joshua at Jericho, to Cato at Carthage, to Columbus in the Caribbean, Pizarro in Peru to Vestmoreland in Vietnam. The inventor of defoliation was whatever happy conqueror first cried. "All right. Hitch up those horses, and let's get the salt plowed into these fields." The advantage of relocation over extermination was obvious: you couldn't get much labor out of corpses.

Was that all history had to teach, that we are the same murderous shits we've always been?

Now Yagul looked empty to him.

15.

Sunday evening Brill returned the car. He had spent the day driving north, out of the valley and into the Mixteca. He'd taken Newman, who had doubts he wanted to discuss about Pederson's plans and motives for the dig, now ready to begin. Brill had had a little trouble solving some of Newman's own plans and motives—he wasn't certain whether Stan hoped he, Brill, would now review things with Pederson, or whether he, Brill, was simply being invited to join in Stan's emotional disloyalty.

Perverse Brill was beginning to understand Pederson, as a man who really did half-live, half-lie, push his appearance and his personality back home, because of a genuine love for the work he did down here. Brill hadn't known about the love before.

Newman had also mentioned that Gabby was now staying at a certain pension in Acapulco, and Brill thought of calling there and thought he'd better not.

The weekend had produced, more than anything else, a kind of low-key intellectual confusion as to what was going on, and what he, Brill, was doing in the midst of it; he decided to muddle his head still further with a couple of margaritas.

Newman had gone off to have supper with Sandoval. Hopeful someone would come along to drink with him at the *portales*—Berkowitz and Minnegerode, for example—Brill went there, sat down alone, and ordered. It was quiet, and he was hungry.

He ordered the drink, and *tamales de yucatan;* by the time he was through the second margarita, the *tamales* came, curiously dark-tasting and wrapped in a banana leaf. He was thinking that he wouldn't even try to read tonight, might do something as genuinely wild as try to find a movie to see or call home and talk to Trinket, when a girl came tentatively onto the scene and sat down, several tables away.

A tourist girl, by the look of her, in a white piqué tennis dress with piping and, for all her elegance, a somewhat helpless look about her. Brill stared at his remaining *tamale* and found to his surprise that he was weighing his chances.

He had lost some weight already, he knew, and begun to pick up a tan. On the other hand, there was a lot of good-looking, shirt-open-to-the-waist, tight-crotch boy stuff around for a chick like this. He glanced.

She was looking at him, neither frowning nor smiling. What? Pleading? She looked away and Brill found in his *tamale* things to consider.

Such as: why not Nancy? Because Nancy, if she was coming on, did not happen to be coming on at *tamale* time?

Pleading, for Christ's sake? The tourist girl must be looking for a waiter.

All right, Crusader, go ask her, dost need help, appealing tourist maid with slim waist, taffy head, and tiny teats, need help ordering in my impeccable, unless you happen to know some yourself, Spanish?

Had that amount of weight on the ball of the right foot needed to push back the chair, and that amount of tension on minute muscles at the corners of the mouth necessary to push back the lips in an entrancing, Illinois smile, when he felt something sullen push along behind him. The girl's eyes left his and rose.

Peter Franchot flung past muttering and sat down brusquely with the girl without speaking. Her face turned toward Franchot and Brill recalled that, though he had seen her only at a distance (one football field plus the width of a five-furlong track), Franchot had a wife.

Franchot began talking to her now, low-voiced, looking rather urgent, and finally they got up without ordering and went past Brill's table, the girl dropping a step behind her husband.

Looked at Don Roberto de los Tamales Yucatecos again, and he could have sworn that her lips formed words: "Help me."

3

Monday morning the diggers were at the site when Pederson and his group arrived, riding there together on a retired school bus Newman had arranged to rent.

Huitzo was three miles away, but apparently the men had walked. There were sixteen of them, a foreman and a one-eyed man who got his instructions and left: he was to return to guard the tools and the dig at night.

Pederson put them to work, rolling away rocks and cutting cactus to make a roadway so that the bus, on top of which the picks and shovels and wheelbarrows were tied, could be driven closer.

Then he had Newman gather the students, with Brill and Sandoval, and laid out his dig.

Tall, slightly stooped, with wispy hair that blew around while he talked and a somewhat tentative smile, Pederson was clearly beginning to enjoy himself:

"Mr Newman and I are in some disagreement to start with," he said. "I think the site we're about to begin work on was the town from which present-day Huitzo was relocated. Mr. Newman feels that Huitzo is right where it always was.

"Perhaps we'll turn up some evidence, one way or the other, but I'm not sure that it matters. I do agree that there must have been some pre-Columbian building where Huitzo is now, but this site seems considerably more extensive.

"Mr. Sandoval and his group—that's Colonel Mazzard and Willa—will be working on completing our map. When they do we'll know more precisely what's here, but for now we can all see that there are three pretty good-sized mounds in this central group . . ."

The largest they had called Mound 1, but were already referring to as "the Temple." Near it, quite clearly, was a ball court, and beside that another large mound they referred to as "the Palace."

"Newman's group will work on Mound One. That's . . ." He consulted a sheet of paper. "Mr. Franchot and Rosalie. Mr. Sandoval's group, in addition to mapping, will be making stratigraphic pits, trying to find natural stratigraphy. Do you all understand what we mean by that?"

It wasn't very difficult. Anywhere they dug where there were buildings, the stratigraphy would be artificial because a building in any period would probably have reused materials in it from the building it was superimposed on. What they needed, essentially, was the town dump, where the layers of stuff from each period would have accumulated undisturbed.

Brill was a little disappointed. He'd have liked to work on the stratigraphic pit, under Sandoval himself.

"When they've done the mapping and stratigraphy, Mr. Sandoval has asked to work on Mound Two, which I believe you've started calling the Palace.

"Mr. Brill, Mr. Minnegerode, and Mr. Berkowitz may have the least thrilling but most important mound. I want them to take the smaller mound west of the Temple, in the hope that it will be a house.

"I'll take Nancy and Mr. Gonzalez with me even farther west, and higher, to the round mound there with rather straight sides . . ."

Newman punched Brill lightly in the back and when Brill looked at him, whispered, "Sonofabitch."

"Now we have experienced people in each crew who will know how to start. Bob, you're in charge of yours, but you'll find your colleagues both know how to go about things, and of course if there are any questions, I shan't be that far away. There'll be two pairs of diggers with each crew to start with, anyway."

He smiled. "Are there any questions?"

Pudgy Rosalie said, "Mr. Pederson, you've talked in class about having a sense of problem. I mean, not just digging to see what we find, but a . . ."

"Yes. I'm sorry. I thought we'd covered that last week. Well, because this site is on the border between the valley and the Mixteca—in the last foothill, really—I hope we'll find evidence of continuous use by both Zapotecs and Mixtecs. That might help answer several questions, wouldn't it?"

"Horseshit," Newman whispered.

"What questions?" Rosalie wanted to know.

Pederson said: "We can talk about that this evening."

"But I was sick last week."

"Where was Moses when the lights went on?" Pederson said impatiently. "That's the question. All right? We know he was down in the cellar eating sauerkraut when they went out, don't we?"

Rosalie was in her thirties and not particularly bright; she didn't really qualify to be on the field trip, Newman said. But there was a minimum enrollment to make, so that the University would underwrite it. She looked, for a moment, as if Gary'd slapped her.

"All right." He softened his tone. "According to some of my colleagues, the Mixtec people had a Moses-like role here—law-givers, teachers. We do know where they were when the lights went out, that is, when the Spaniards came, don't we?

"They were behaving very much like Aztecs. Fighting and up to their knees in sauerkraut. Way back between the Olmec and the Classic periods—there's evidence that the Mixtecs had this Moses-like role. There are people who think they may have been the first builders, for instance, at Teotihuacán, and Cholula.

"But what happened to them in the Classic itself?"

Rosalie nodded. "When the lights went on," she said, radiant with comprehension.

Brill picked up his machete and followed Berkowitz and Minnegerode toward Mound 3, passing Newman.

"Stan."

"Hey."

"What was all that expression of deep loyalty about, anyway?"

"He's not looking for proof that both people lived here at all," Newman said, in a low, disgusted voice. "We were talking about it last night. There are two or three more big mounds, east and halfway over the hill. That's what ought to be the center of another part of town if there was one. Do you know why he isn't going over there?"

Brill shook his head.

" 'A round mound, with rather straight sides'—" Pederson spoke with a trace of a lisp, Newman mimicked it bitterly. "That's what I asked for last night, but I should have known better than to tell him why."

"Okay," Brill sighed. "Tell me."

"Because I made some measurements, and some of it's exposed, and I think it might just be another observatory. Like Mound J at Monte Albán. And if it is, it's going to mean some damn nice publication for the man who digs it."

2.

Two of their diggers were named José. They were called Chico and Burro, to distinguish them.

Like Brill they had machetes with them. The other two men didn't.

"Lot of cactus to cut, and stones to move before we start anything," Minnegerode said. "Shall I start 'em going?"

"What do we do with the loose stones?"

"Stack them till we see where they go. They probably came out of the walls."

"Okay." The two Josés began cutting. The other two men, under Berkowitz' direction, to stack stones.

"Can I get into this?" Brill asked, picking up his own machete.

Minnegerode smiled and shook his head. "Pederson'd come running down the hill and stop you," he said.

"Why?"

"They do the manual work. We supervise."

"Cheer up," Berkowitz said. "It'll loosen up in a few days. We might even let you roll a wheelbarrow."

Brill shrugged, and climbed to the top of their mound, a matter of fifteen feet or so, to look around. The same things—cutting and clearing—were going on elsewhere around the site.

Minnegerode and Berkowitz called that they were going up to higher ground to take photographs of what the mound looked like before work started. Brill waved, and watched the workers. That seemed to be what he was supposed to do.

3.

"You have incurred that man's undying enmity." Fudge seemed a little sententious as we started off away from Chila.

"Yeah?" I said. "We'll see who's going to do the undying around here."

"Were you really required to let him know in that way?" Nose asked. It was the tone of an ethnographer, sort of a request that I explain our fascinating Mixtec customs to him.

It sounded a little better than sententiousness first thing in the morning, so I tried to be informative: "It didn't seem to me it made much difference," I said. "Smoky was trying to arrange to get me killed or castrated, anyway."

"But what about us?" Fudge asked.

"Oh, I'll keep you alive," I told him. "Grandad expects me to. Anyway, I wouldn't want to take a chance on losing that troupial cloak Nose promised me."

"We go along as if this hadn't happened?" Nose asked.

"Pretty much. We ought to be ready to improvise, if the situation changes though," I said. "How would you feel about getting rid of your litters?"

Fudge didn't like the idea of walking at all, but Nose could see that we'd have more mobility and present less of a spectacle. He paid off the litter-bearers with cacao beans—they'd come from 9-Reed's town—and they seemed happy enough to go back. They kept the other man, the one who never seemed to say anything; Silent Sam.

It was a good morning for walking, not too hot, and after a while my Aztecs cheered up. About midmorning we came to a little town where they were having market day, and Fudge suggested we stop off and shop around to see if there wasn't something pretty for sale in the way of a slave girl.

"It's always fun to browse these small-town stores," he said. "When you're on the road."

"Me, I'm not far enough on the road," I said. "Anyway, what would you do with her?"

"Oh, it really works out to be a rental arrangement," Fudge said. "We buy a couple one place, and sell them off a few days later when we hit another market."

"Fact is, if you dress 'em up a little and give them some city makeup, you can sometimes make a small profit," Nose said.

"A nice little piece," said Fudge, "of business. Hell, Zap, there's no sense getting lonely on the road. Remember," he said to Nose, "the twins we bought near Cuicuilco last year?"

"You know that nutty little ruin?" Nose asked me, forgetting my having said I'd never been up in the Valley of Mexico. "Fuckin' savages must have built it thousands of years ago, and then a volcano got it. Wham. Know a guy that's done some digging there, but he says no jade or gold, just funny faces."

"Anyway, we bought these twins." Both my buddies were being real buddies this morning. "Used 'em pretty good and the next day sold one to a guy in Xochimilco. He hustled her off home and we went on down the road. An hour later, we were selling the second twin when that first buyer comes along, spots us and gets furious. He was damn sure it was the old Go Home, Dog trick—you know, that his twin had made it out a window and come back to us. He started yelling cop from fifty yards away."

"That was a hairy episode," Nose agreed. "Luckily the second twin had had her nipples cut off somewhere. We stripped her down and showed him, and the guy knew it was a different girl—it was only half an hour after the sale but our buyer'd already had her home and checked her out."

"It sure messed up the sale on the second one," Fudge said. "We hardly made expenses."

"Your second buyer didn't want to strip her down and look her over?" I asked.

"We were running a little con because of the nipples," Fudge said. "We'd been telling him these Cuicuilco girls were famous for their modesty."

"Look, Zap," Nose said. "We won't buy one here if you think we shouldn't." My yellow feathers made him kind of respectful.

"I'm your guide," I said. "Not your chaperon. Do whatever you want."

We went on into the market then. It was just like any small-town market—food and herbs in one place, a section of clothing. Some cage birds and monkeys that a peddler'd brought up; dogs and turkeys for livestock, but the dogs looked too thin to eat.

The slaves were over in a corner, near the local pyramid, and they didn't look very fat either. There were a couple of old guys with their hair dyed much too bright, and one kid, maybe fourteen. The way Fudge looked him over I wondered if he was considering making do with a boy for company on the road if there weren't any girls available. Turned out there was one, though. She was sweeping out the stall, a grimy young country girl with pudgy cheeks. I figured she was the guy's daughter; I figured wrong.

"See what we have here," he said, taking the broom out of her hand, and then pulling her arms back from behind so the girl arched toward us. "A very fine slave for gentlemen. An excellent cook, this girl, and as you have just seen a housecleaner of fantastic devotion."

"Tell him to turn her around, will you, Zap?" Nose said.

As I did, Fudge was moving closer and started to reach for the girl's rear end.

"Please don't pinch the fruit, gentlemen," the dealer said, and I translated. "You can tell all you need to know by looking."

"Tell him we can't see anything in the wretched sack she's wearing," Nose said.

"Ah yes," said the dealer, switching to Nahuatl. He opened the girl's robe at the throat, and spread it back so we could see her shoulders. "Firm-fleshed, without a scratch."

"We need to see a little more," Fudge said.

"First let us arrange about the price," the dealer said. "Should you decide you're interested."

"One previous owner," Nose said sarcastically. "An old priest who only used her for festivals."

"No, no," the dealer said. "Brand-new. Zero mileage, gentlemen. Zero."

They got to bargaining, and I enjoyed the slick way this country boy got my Aztecs going. He sat his merchandise on a stool, and he'd show now a knee, now a shoulder. Finally they reached some kind of agreement, and Fudge said:

"Okay. Now let's have a look and see if we want to buy."

The dealer told the girl to take her garment off. She looked at him dull-eyed, and stood up. I wondered if she was all there mentally. Later I decided that the dealer kept her drugged.

"Take it off," he said, and she did, rather gracelessly. Just undid the robe at the throat and let it fall down around her feet. She wasn't wearing anything under it.

She had a firm enough body under that vacuous face, after all, though her teats were kind of banana-shaped.

I could see Nose, clearing his throat, getting ready to see if he couldn't knock a little more off the price, but old Fudge liked what he saw: "Sold!" he said. "She looks strong enough to cook and carry for us."

Nose looked a little disgusted with his partner, but he paid up—six of those new-issue copper blades all the coin collectors are nuts about, and a half sack of good, old-fashioned cacao beans.

We left town, but we hadn't been on the road five minutes before Fudge said, "Excuse me," grabbed the banana girl by the arm and started to pull her off toward a clump of brush.

Banana Girl moaned and I said, "Stop," at about the same instant.

"I thought you weren't going to chaperon," Fudge said. "Anyway, what's she moaning about?"

"You don't understand," I said. "This is rocky country through here."

"What's it going to do? Hurt her tender backside? Come on, Zap. Tell her I'll kick the rocks out of the way."

"Sure," I said. "Like this." There was a flat stone just beside the path. I lifted it with my toe and flipped it over, jumping back away from it. I'd counted on there being at least one there; actually, there were two—big, fat, brown scorpions waving their tails at us. "Things like that could give the girl's backside quite a thrill," I said. I killed the scorpions with the butt of my maquauhuitl. Banana Girl was looking at me with big, round eyes, quite lively now, but I couldn't say whether with fear or adoration. "We'll be at the river in half an hour," I said. "You can take her off in the sand, under some willows or something."

4.

In the final hour of the morning's work, Brill couldn't sit by any longer. He took his machete and joined the two Josés, and by lunchtime there was no cactus left around their mound to be cut.

There was no reprimand from Gary, either; in fact not long before lunch Gary and Sandoval left the site together in the bus to go to Huitzo. Gary called: "Like it, Bob?" as they left.

Newman said they were going to file papers at the town hall, because they were digging, in part, on agricultural land.

They sat, eating sandwiches, by a patch of *mala mujer* cactus, and Brill felt he had to say:

"Stan, when you've got some bitching to do about Gary, don't pick me for an audience, huh? Pederson and I are very old friends."

"Are you?" Newman said. "It didn't sound much that way last month."

"All right," Brill said. "I've told you. Don't tell me anything you wouldn't want repeated to Gary."

Newman laughed. "This one he'll tell you himself," he said. "About your irresponsible behavior? Or has he?"

Brill shook his head. "All right. What'd I do, besides cut a little cactus?"

"Saturday. You abandoned poor little Nancy to evil Willa, didn't you? For a delicious overnight in Mitla."

"I did?"

"Yessir, Mr. Brill. Heard Nancy's report of it myself last night after supper. All shy and reluctant to say such a thing about anybody, but it seems you took them up there and they couldn't find you when they were ready to come back."

"My goodness."

"You see, Nancy is only twenty."

"You know, I don't think I could have stood the suspense of not knowing that for another minute?"

"But did you know that either Gary or I is supposed to sign her in at night?"

"Why, for God's sake?"

"Orders from the dean of women."

"Yeah?"

"Any girl child on a field trip's got to be signed in and out."

"Naturally," Brill said. "Why of course."

"If she's going to get herself knocked up, she's got to do it before eleven at night, midnight on Saturdays."

"That gave Willa a whole extra hour to do the job at Mitla," Brill said. "Even if they'd had a way back."

"Actually, I guess Willa's another reason Gary let Rosalie come along. That way he has three girls in a room—hey, how come you didn't bring them back? They do something to piss you off?"

"My, my," Brill said. "The legend of the Brill temper. I hardly considered myself their primary means of transportation, your honor. They were hitchhiking."

Still he supposed when Gary got back with Sandoval he ought to offer the same explanation, and tried.

Gary seemed barely to understand what Brill was talking about. "Oh, really? Now about the machete, Bob."

"I know," Brill said.

"Yes, then," said Gary, and raised his voice. "All right, children. Back to work, Dig, dig, dig," he cried. "You know, Bob, I'm very pleased with the way things are starting." Raised his voice: "If anybody finds the fourteen golden toads, hide two and call me over."

The man was beaming with excitement.

"Jesus Christ," said Stanley Newman.

"How can you be such a prick" Brill asked, "when the man's beaming with excitement?"

5.

Berkowitz and Minnegerode asked: "Want to start here?"

Here was a low spot, twenty feet west of their pile of dirt and rubble. Already it seemed a somewhat more shapely pile.

"Start what?"

"A hole," said Minnegerode.

"In the ground, sir, in the ground," said Berkowitz.

"Over here, Jośe," said Brill.

José Chico began with the pick. Galdencio, who was José's uncle, shoveled away what was loosened. Brill picked up pot sherds.

"We saving these?"

"They'd only duplicate the surface collection," Minnegerode said. "Got some thin orange already, haven't you?"

The diggers were going down in a half-meter square Berkowitz had drawn for them in the dirt with a stick.

"Why so far out from the mound?" Brill asked.

"We don't want to come down on top of anything," Berkowitz said. "Especially not a wall. You come down on top of a wall, it looks very much like a stone."

"*Piso*," said Galdencio, who had dug for archaeologists before. *Floor.*

"*Con cuidado, pues*," said Minnegerode.

"Con cui, Daddio," said Berkowitz. Galdencio finished clearing the half meter, got out of the hole, and Berkowitz into it with a paintbrush. He swept the floor clean; Brill and Minnegerode knelt and looked at it. Gray stucco, fairly level. Brill remembered Newman saying, up in the Mixteca, that all these cities were paved; it was pretty damn convenient for archaeology.

"Here we go, then," Minnegerode said.

Maintaining the half-meter width, they directed the diggers to start trenching toward the mound. The extra pair of men went off to get another shovel and a wheelbarrow. They were going to be moving quite a pile of dirt.

It took an hour for the trench to reach a point a foot from the side of the mound. There was a rock in the way the size of a cinder block.

"Is that the wall?" Brill asked. He was a little nervous about the possibility of digging through something that ought to be left in place. How did it go? *An archaeological site is a historical document which can only be read once, because in order to read it we must destroy it.*

"Not yet," Berkowitz said. "We can pull that one out."

"How can you be sure?"

"You'll see in a minute."

The rock was lifted out of the trench. Brill did it. He realized that part of his faintly foolish anxiety came from the frustration of watching other men do physical work.

"All right, comrade," Berkowitz said. "Stop with the muscles. There's your wall."

Brill reached for the paintbrush, and a screwdriver with which to loosen what little dirt was left. He could see immediately why the boys were so confident: the stucco of the street floor was continuous: when it reached wall, it simply turned up.

"Hey," Brill said. "Look at that."

"It's going to be a good wall," Minnegerode said. "There are about four courses of rock in place."

Along the edge of their mound, now that the piled dirt was cleared away from this much, the wall was waist high.

"We go right or left along it?" Brill asked.

"Doesn't matter. Let's try left. What we need next is a corner."

"Or some steps," said Minnegerode.

But they'd found neither when the afternoon ended. They'd exposed about eight linear feet of wall, waist high or better; piled some stones, some of which could be replaced where they'd fallen out. Brill hated to quit, though the thought of his shower in Oaxaca was powerfully attractive, after the heat and dust of the afternoon.

6.

When we got to the river, Fudge suddenly recovered from the limp he'd been developing and cried:

"Now, gentlemen. By your leave."

Nose sat in the sand and said quietly: "No."

Fudge said: "Come on, You went first on the one at Toluca last week."

Banana Girl turned her eyes away, and looked at me. She might not know Nahuatl, but I had a strong feeling she knew what they were saying.

Nose got up. "We drew then. We'll draw now."

"But it's my turn."

Nose got out a couple cacao beans and said: "Come on. Get your beans out, we'll go odds or evens."

"No." They were getting pretty hostile over it. It wasn't exactly what we needed at that point, so I said:

"What difference does it make?"

"He's queer for virgins," Fudge said. "He likes to make them squeal."

"And you just want to protect her from it, of course?"

"For God's sake," I said. "The dealer must have broken the seal."

"He sold her for new."

"I thought Aztecs were supposed to be smart." It was getting to be my big line.

"She's tight," Fudge said. "Tight as a turkey. I tried with my finger."

"Maybe you'd better stick to turkeys," I said. "All the boys up here pack a little tlaxocotl around the bearings."

Nose was indignant at the dishonesty. As a matter of fact, I'd checked the matter out with girl herself, just out of curiosity, and she'd said the dealer hadn't used her. He was a fag, and she was just as represented, so she said.

But I didn't see any reason why Nose had to know that; if Nose liked to use a new one hard, I decided to root for Fudge, and it seemed to work. Nose turned indifferent, and told Fudge to go the hell ahead, but save him first on the other side, okay?

Fudge took Banana Girl by the arm; she was docile about it. Accepting anyway. She gave me a big brown-eyed look, one that acknowledged there was nothing I could do to help.

"Mind walking down the bank to the sandbar?" I asked Fudge. "This road isn't much traveled, but someone could come along."

So we all walked down a hundred yards or so—Nose, Fudge, Banana Girl, Silent Sam, and me—to a sandbar where some willows were growing.

Fudge was pretty excited. He got out some soap, which he'd probably paid more for than he had for the girl, and showed it to her. She seemed pleased, and even smiled a little when he stripped her, led her into the water, and started to wash her down. He was pretty lascivious about where and how carefully he washed, too. Had her sit and kept sloshing soap and water and fingers into her, front and rear, till his panting got so loud you could hear it above the noise the river made. Nose had sat down, and was ready to enjoy watching.

"Come on, Zap," he said, as Fudge led the girl up onto the sand and dropped his girdle. "This is going to be good."

Old Fudge had quite a whang on him for a short, fat man. I don't know whether Banana Girl had ever seen anything like that before, but she didn't seem to like the look of it especially.

"Tell her it's a plumed serpent," Nose said, chuckling.

"I'm here to guide," I said, "not to watch every little thing you sports do with yourselves along the way," and started back toward the road.

It was a damn good thing I did.

7.

Gary's seminar this time. Brill was curious to hear him teach:

"More about excrement," he said. "I won't apologize. A different aspect than Mr. Newman dealt with. Sanitation. Vaillant tells us how the Aztecs managed it, doesn't he?

"Remember their city, Mexico City, then called Tenochtitlan, must have been like Venice. Built on a lake, canals instead of streets.

"Why not?

"They had no horses, after all. A canoe was obviously the elegant way to travel in Tenochtitlan. For excrement, they had barges.

"Barges tied up along the footpaths. When you needed to relieve yourself, you nipped into one. The proprietors of those barges may even have competed for your morning business, because Vaillant tells us that the contents were sold for fertilizer, when the ships got fully loaded.

"By your bed you kept a pot for urine. It was valued, too. It was saved, and combined with colors to make what is called a mordant, for dying cloth.

"Fast colors."

"Vaillant also points out that when this system for dispersal—no, no, for *use*—of human waste was broken up by the Spaniards—too fastidious, I suppose—the plagues started.

"In the same way, but we do not know as precisely, these hill towns and cities had systems of drainage. Perhaps we'll find remains of one in our dig.

"They must have worked, though, like any sewer, by the flushing power of water, the dispersing power of gravity, and the drying and cleansing power of sun.

"It seems reasonable to suppose that the excrement from the hill towns was collected, too, for agriculture—and when the Spaniards moved the towns down onto flat places, then people had to live in their own waste, especially in dry times, rather than up above it, where they could look down and see it growing plants in the fields.

"And the plagues came.

"Take a small jump now to Woods Hole, Massachusetts. What are the ecologists up to with their famous balanced aquaria? They want to learn to seal a world and keep it healthy, keep it recreating its life continuously, by maintaining a perfect balance between the excretions of the right number of animal forms and the use of them by plants which in turn become the food which feeds the animal forms . . .

"Another jump: into space. How do you suppose it is planned that men will travel several years in a capsule? By making that capsule into the equivalent of a balanced aquarium, you see. Excretion becomes not a waste at all, but a product, to be reused to maintain life.

"Maybe it's our finest product.

"At least it's clear that many civilizations, high ones unlike our curiously uneven culture, regarded excretion as something to venerate because of its richness and utility.

"Peruvian civilization may have risen because of the guano islands off the coast, rich in seabird dung for fertilizing crops.

"If you know gardeners—like our friend Mr. Brill here—you know how excited they can get over particular sorts of dung—sheep dung for roses, for example. Why should we hold in distaste human dung, with the incredible, complex chemical richness of the omnivore?

"Do you know how the Aztecs thought of gold?

"Let me read you a passage from Sahagun."

Pederson read: "Volume eleven, of the Dibble and Anderson. 'Gold occurs in the earth. It appears, it is seen in this manner: where it is, there is its mother. When its mother appears, when she rains her water (as they say) her urine stains deeply.'

"Listen to this, now. Talking about gold from river sand, and silver too:

" 'The name of this gold, the yellow, the white—its name comes from *teotl* [God] and *cuitlatl* [excrement], because it is wonderful, yellow, good, fine, precious.'

"Gold, then, urine of mother earth, excrement of the gods.

"And this: '. . . sometimes, in some places, there appears in the dawn something like a little bit of diarrhea. They named it "the excrement of the sun"; it was very yellow, very wonderful, resting like an ember, like molten gold. The advised took this excrement of the sun,' ah yes, listen. Listen. 'for they said it was pustule medicine. They said it was pustule medicine.'

"Let's close the circle, with the words of the Marqués . . ."

"Of whom?" asked Nancy, who was taking shorthand notes.

"The Marqués del Valle. Cortes. Remember what I just read? Gold was called precious excrement, and considered medicine. Cortes said: 'There is a Spanish sickness of the heart which only gold can cure.' "

Pederson paused, and whispered: "Dismissed."

8.

They still didn't have a damn corner on the west wall.

José Chico and Galdencio kept moving along the west wall, the other pair of workmen hauling away dirt and stacking the rocks. But the trench already extended north, past the edge of the mound.

"Maybe we'd better hold it here?" Brill asked.

Minnegerode said, "Let's get this sketched, and photographed, and then decide." They told the workers to take a break. He and Berkowitz measured out from the wall, drove stakes at two points, and ran a string between them. They photographed what had been exposed, and made a note of the compass reading along their string.

"Our building's going to be more or less right with the world," Minnegerode said.

"Suppose it's got steps," Brill said. "Which wall would you expect them to be on?"

Berkowitz looked at Minnegerode, back at Brill, and said: "South."

"That way at Mitla and Yagul," Minnegerode agreed.

"We want a corner before we find steps though, don't we?" Brill meant it as a statement. "Let's try a new trench from the north."

This time, knowing how far down the floor would be, the diggers could move more quickly. By the time they broke for lunch the new trench had reached a new wall, turned along it, and they were within four feet of intersecting with their first trench.

"Okay, okay," Brill said, as the workers went off. "We're coming to it."

"Lucky for us those boys took their shovels," Berkowitz said.

"I agree," said Minnegerode. "It'd be no lunch for us. Comrade Brill would have us in there."

"We could go with bare hands," Berkowitz said.

"Tear the dirt out."

"We could eat it, instead of lunch."

"What are you guys, hungry?" Brill said.

By midafternoon, they had made their intersection, and still had no corner. It didn't make sense.

9.

Little Gonzalez was a Mexican-American from Rock Island, Illinois, who spoke no Spanish. He was in his junior year at the University, spoke often of the importance to him of being in Mexico because he would learn pride in his origins, and adored Gary Pederson.

Little Gonzalez and Nancy were Pederson's crew because they were the only undergraduate students along. Going to look for Gary to consult him about the nonappearing corner, Brill found the two youngsters sulking.

They were more or less the same height—five foot three or so—and even much the same build. Nancy had boy's shoulders, Little Gonzalez, who wore his black hair long, had girl's hands and feet. They were an interesting-looking pair standing together, male and female, dark and light, both in jeans, short-sleeved shirts, and bareheaded.

Fussing. Nancy spoke Spanish; Little Gonzalez wanted her to tell the workers to start in again. Nancy wouldn't till Gary got back. They were clearing a wall, too.

Brill resolved it: "You've got dirt to get out of the way," he said. "You can have your other boys stack rocks. That way you keep them busy without exposing any new stuff, don't you?"

"Okay," said Little Gonzalez. "Okay, Nancy?"

"Where's Gary now?" Brill asked.

They thought he was looking for Brill, as a matter of fact, and when Brill got back to Mound 3, there was Pederson, sketching something for Berkowitz and Minnegerode.

"You got two very dumb guys to work with," Berko said, offering Gary's sketch to Brill. "Here's why we can't find the corner."

"I think it's probably inset," Gary said, smiling his tentative smile. "Like that."

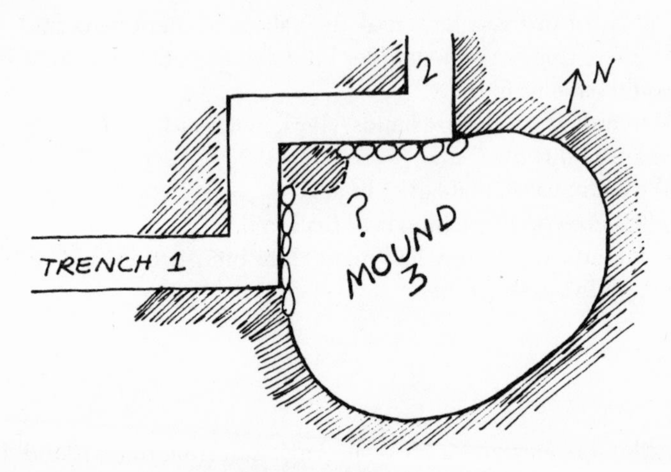

"What are we waiting for?" said Brill.

"You," said Berkowitz.

"What are you inclined to do when you finish exposing the corner?" Gary asked.

"Finish cleaning up the first wall, so we get the other corner."

"That would take the rest of today and all day tomorrow. Why don't you go to the other side?"

"Excuse me?"

"You'll have the northwest corner. Clear the southeast one. Then you'll be pretty sure of the outside dimensions and shape of your building, assuming it's symmetrical."

"Okay. But we still want at least one complete wall exposed, don't we?"

"Do the south one."

"Why, Gary?"

"That's where you'll most likely find an entrance. Then you'll know where you are when you work inside the building."

"Are we going to have to fill all this up again?" Brill asked.

"We'll see what you get. And what else we have on the dig. Then I'd like you to help me decide." It was a delicate reference to Brill's having contributed money. "We can spend a little for consolidation, and we'll have masons on the payroll. We may even have something we'll want to reconstruct."

You can do three things when you dig out a building: reconstruct it as you think it must have been; consolidate what's showing without adding to it; or take your pictures, make your measurements and sketches, and put the protective dirt right back where it was to begin with.

Brill took pleasure in Pederson's competence. You don't know a man until you've seen him work.

By the end of the afternoon, when the corner was cleared, nearly everyone had been around to see their corner except Peter Franchot.

"Your boy's not too interested in what's going on?" Brill asked Newman, who had come up with Rosalie.

"Cabeza de Zorillo? No. He keeps both eyes on his imported chronometer, with the alligator strap."

"Eager to get back to his wife," Brill said. "I can't blame him for that."

"Think she's nice?"

"Don't you?"

Brill'd been staying away from the *portales* at margarita time. On consideration, he didn't think a cocktail consisting of tequila, lime juice, tripel sec, salt, and "Help me" was the stimulant he needed. He'd given the girl a chance to speak with him if she wanted to, at breakfast Sunday, a less dangerous time of day than Oaxaca dusk, perfumed, murmurous, and alcoholic. But though she'd come in alone, and Brill had paused at her table to say good morning, she had only returned the salutation and not asked that he sit down.

He though he might well have misunderstood on the evening before, the movement of her lips, and hoped quite genuinely that it was so.

10.

They were ready to work inside. Two inset corners suggested that the building had consisted of four rooms, one on each side of a square patio, facing and opening onto the patio. There were no steps; in fact, the door to the outside of the building might prove to be quite inconspicuous when they found it, tucked away perhaps in one of the inset corners.

Elsewhere on the dig, things were in fairly similar shape: outlines known, interesting details ready for excavation. Newman had found a fine wide staircase on the temple and was ready to clear it: Pederson's hoped-for observatory was about to prove to be a round building, which, of course, he wanted. Only Sandoval, working with Colonel Mazzard and Willa, was failing to make progress. They were trying for the fourth time to locate a stratigraphic pit where they wouldn't come to floors—and even buildings—half a meter down.

"The first place we came right down on something we thought must have been an irrigation ditch," Willa said. Brill had stopped off for a minute to visit with them while Minnegerode and Berkowitz did photography.

"We went over there a quarter of a mile," said the colonel. "We found ourselves in some kind of building. Senor Sandoval recognized mud bricks, so we filled that up."

"The house of a peasant. Later we go back to it," said Sandoval. "In one more place, we find the floor of the city, just as you did. But here, I think it will be all right."

Their fourth pit was down about five feet in a measured meter, stepped back as they went down to give the diggers room to work in while keeping one wall perfectly straight.

In the straight wall, Brill could see, if not altogether clearly, changes from layer to layer in soil color.

"It is most clear first thing in the morning," Sandoval said. "When the ground is damp."

"Hard to photograph?" Brill said.

"Yes. There is a new technique I have read of. You spray the wall of the pit with plastic, a thin sheet. It becomes like rubber, and you peel it off to take away all the features of the stratigraphy. But we do not have this yet."

Willa and the colonel were sifting the dirt that came out of the measured meter, collecting the sherds of pottery that came from each stratum, and bagging them separately.

"We're only allowed to sort them roughly out here," the colonel said. Spread out on newspapers was the collection of fragments from Layer Three—a couple of hundred of them.

"All from one meter of dirt, thirty centimeters deep."

"No," Willa said. She had acquired a small woolly dog, and was speaking to it now, pushing it off the newspaper. Brill caught the dog, picked it up, and rubbed its head. "In the museum we'll wash these off and sort them again, won't we?" she asked.

"Yes, Senorita Willa," said Sandoval.

"Then why are we sorting them out here?"

"Senorita has something she prefers to do?"

"Oh no," poor Willa said. "No, of course not. I just mean—well, we separate them into kinds and colors, and make a list. And then put them all back together again in the bag, because we don't really know if we've been accurate out here where we can't wash them and test them."

"Yes," said Sandoval. "This way we will have notes of the rough division?"

"Yes."

"Then we will have notes of something, you see. Now: always on an excavation, the digging goes ahead of the laboratory. The digging is exciting, interesting. The laboratory is work, detail, counting. So all over Mexico, there are bags and bags like that: of pottery and bones and stones. In storerooms. Which have never been washed or counted or studied. This will not happen here? Fine. Very good. But in case it does, we will have at least a field count. All right?"

"All right," said Willa.

Brill put the dog down and went along to his own mound.

They began that morning to clear along the inner wall of the north room as it faced on the patio; the layer of dirt covering the patio itself was not deep, and the room wall in good shape. It went quickly. By lunchtime the doorway from room to patio was defined, quite a nice wide entrance with two square columns in it. There was a shallow step down, from room to patio floor; the line of this step, it appeared, would continue all around the edge of the patio, and be found to be faced with small cut stones.

"A banquette," Stan Newman called it.

"Find the other corners," said Gary.

That was pretty easy. The four inside corners of the banquette were only about twenty centimeters down; then you came to patio floor.

"Clear it?" Brill asked.

"Yeah," said Berkowitz and Minnegerode.

"Why don't you check the center first?" said Gary, with a smile and moved off, beckoning to Nancy and Little Gonzalez who had followed him over.

"Brill, buddy," said Newman, who'd been invited over to consult. "You rate, You rate indeed."

"As usual, Newman buddy," said Brill, "I don't understand you. I sometimes wonder if I'm even meant to."

"He wants you to make a find," Newman said. "He's betting you will."

"Why?"

"There could be an offering in the center of your patio, sir. You can be pretty sure your building is a superimposition, even if you haven't gone through the first floor yet to see. And when the boys built a new building on top of an old one, they were pretty likely to make some kind of offering with it."

"Like putting a half dollar and the mayor's picture in a cornerstone," Minnegerode said.

"I can't wait to see what the mayor of this ugly joint looked like," said Berkowitz.

Brill got four stakes, and set one at each corner of the patio. He tied string to each diagonally opposed pair, making an X.

"You want to start from the edge," Minnegerode asked. "Or are you going to make the spectacular play here?"

"Let's do it for the grandstand," Brill said, and fetched himself a trowel. "You want to, Jack?"

"Go ahead."

"Ten pesos there's nothing there," said Berkowitz, and Newman took the bet.

Brill marked his center, took the string out of the way and began to dig cautiously with the trowel. At eight inches he began to find stucco fragments.

Newman came over, watched, and said: "Do they match?"

"Match what?"

"The rest of the floor. What you've uncovered on the edge."

They didn't quite. "I'm about to win ten pesos," Newman said. "That floor was broken and patched; they put in an offering, patched, and the patch was weak so it broke."

"My, you're objectionable," said Berkowitz.

Brill increased the radius of his hole till he stopped getting stucco fragments, and at Berkowitz' suggestion put the trowel aside and commenced loosening the dirt with a screwdriver.

Minnegerode stopped him, and took a picture.

Brill loosened some more, swept up the dirt with a paintbrush, and sifted it between his fingers into a paper bag from which he'd removed his lunch. The limit seemed to be about a thirty-centimeter circle. Almost down to where the floor would be, Brill found something:

"Look." A jade bead. It was only slightly polished, nothing of great value, and Brill would have picked it up to examine but Newman, kneeling, said, "Better leave it in place, Bob."

Brill brushed some more but had to move five centimeters—hell, a couple of inches, okay, Newman?—of dirt before he found the next bead. When he found the next, he found a lot.

They were lying together in the dirt, just below floor level, for apparently Newman was right. The offering had been put in after the floor was laid, put in, patched, and the patching stucco had broken out.

The beads were a series of little round humps, covered at first with dirt but discernibly enough there to be photographed if you kicked the light past them with your flash to throw an exaggerated shadow. They were close together, about the size of a fingernail each, and quite orderly—a set of crude beads, reminding him, with a little stab he knew where to shove by now, of some Gabby had bought, how many years before, at Quiotepec, how many miles away, walking?

The beads lay buried as they'd been placed, except that the string which had held them together was rotted away.

There were more photographs, measurements, sketches; loosening of dirt around the beads until they were almost totally cleared, and then, off to the right of them, the first bone. A hand bone, Minnegerode said; he'd done physical anthropology and anatomy, and they deferred to him, Brill turning over the paintbrush.

Minnegerode brushed around the first bone. There were more, some really tiny, mixed in with the others like the first.

"Fingers out here," said Minnegerode. "A left hand, wasn't it? But I don't know about the tiny bones."

He shifted the paintbrush to the right, and worked some more. Something flat and whitish began to show, next to the hand bones.

"Top of a skull?" Newman asked, and Minnegerode nodded. Newman was taking the pictures now.

"Child's skull," Minnegerode said. "And look." Beside it, on the other side, a second set of hand bones began to appear. "Here." It was exacting work. He handed the paintbrush and screwdriver to Berkowitz.

Brill said: "The little bones in the left hand, Jack?"

"I can't read them. You suppose a mouse got in there or something?"

"I've seen them by the hundreds," Brill said. "They're bird bones. The left hand held a bird."

Berkowitz looked up. "A tomb in the center, you think? A little shallow tomb, for a child, with its necklace in one hand and its pet bird in the other . . ."

"No," Newman said. "There's no neck. There aren't any arms to go with those hands. There aren't any shoulders."

"A child's skull, and two hands; a necklace and a bird," said Minnegerode. "They finished the house. Then they made a hole the right size. Then they cut off . . ."

"An offering," Newman said.

"A sacrifice."

"A child."

4

Brill was never quite sure how much blame to allow himself for what happened the Friday afternoon and evening after they found the sacrifice.

He and Newman were sitting together on the bus. Usually he sat with Pederson, but tonight Nancy had taken that place, triumphing over Little Gonzalez who was sitting silent and dour in his shoulder-length hair by Sandoval.

It was just after four o'clock when they got to the outskirts of the city, and perhaps a quarter past when they turned into the street that led past the Regional Museum, beside which the bus unloaded. The museum was four blocks down, but even at that distance you could see someone in white waiting there.

As the bus got closer, Brill recognized Peter Franchot's wife, and Newman said, loudly enough for everyone on the bus to hear:

"She's up early this morning."

Franchot as usual was sitting by himself, in the front seat behind the driver, the side away from the museum. Obviously, he didn't expect to be met, nor had his wife ever been out there waiting before. Newman's remark was probably lost on him.

Nancy, though, sitting in the opposite front seat, leaned across Pederson to say: "Look, Peter. There's Libby," but Franchot didn't look up from the magazine. He always had a news or picture magazine to read on the bus, buying them as soon as they arrived from the States at the hotel newsstand.

As far as Brill could tell, he read every word in every one.

The bus stopped. They were as filthy as they always were when they came in from digging. They were also boisterous, hungry, and thirsty.

Pederson and Nancy were off the bus first. Then Berkowitz, Minnegerode, Little Gonzalez and Sandoval, all the males responding to Libby Franchot's clean clothes, her sweatless prettiness, with grins and bobbing heads. They barely knew her, Brill supposed, but the sight of her seemed to make them happy.

He thought of walking into the dining room of the limestone farmhouse of his boyhood, in work clothes from the field, coming out of the summer heat, and seeing flowers fresh-cut from the garden by his father, perhaps, dewy in the center of the polished walnut table. Willa and Rosalie got off. Franchot with his magazine got up, and was next off, with Newman and then Brill behind him.

Franchot kept reading the magazine as he went down the steps, got onto the street, made the turn past the front of the bus—Brill could see what was so absorbing. It was a story about what happened when the committee met to choose a queen for the festival. Finally, Franchot came face to face with his wife. He was down a small step on the street, she was up on the curb.

Brill couldn't have said, seeing only the back of his head, that Franchot didn't smile, but he could hear the greeting: "What are you doing here?"

At which Stan Newman pushed Franchot out of the way, stepped up off the street, took Libby in his arms and hugged her hard. Then he kissed the top of her head, pressing his dusty lips into the silky, clean, taffycolored hair, and said:

"Hi, darling. Thanks for meeting me."

There was a general permissiveness about the girl, and it certainly didn't exclude any of that.

Franchot said, in his sullen, unemphatic way: "You've got my wife's dress dirty, Newman." And he had.

Newman was printed on the white dress like the outlines in the cartoon, when Popeye knocks some guy through a wall. Well, no. Not that complete. There were smudges on the waffled white fabric at the high points, if you thought of her body as a kind of relief map. It was the same gold-piped tennis dress Brill had seen her in the previous weekend, and extremely becoming. The smudges began with a line in the fabric behind the right collarbone. Then, of course, heavy ones where Newman had flattened her breasts. There was a bell-shaped smudge spreading lightly down from her diaphragm, swelling to a dark curve across the top of her stomach ending almost in a bold dot at each hip-bone. And finally, there was a light brush of Oaxaca dirt halfway around the left thigh.

"You got my wife's dress dirty, Newman." Yes, Mr. Franchot. Yes, he had.

2.

That was one thing for Brill to get out of his mind, the broken stucco of a young marriage. Right under it were the child's hands and skull. Try this, Counselor:

Nose had. Um, hmm. Yeah. Finished. Washing off Banana Girl, sure, and was standing over her, his Xipe skinned for action; I'd decided I didn't care to watch.

I walked partway back to the road, and knelt down in a willow clump with a good field of vision. Yeah. I was just kneeling there, idly, wondering if there'd be any traffic on the road at all, when I saw something that made me drop to my belly and wriggle off like a damn snake.

As soon as I was sure they couldn't see me from the road, I jumped up and tore back to my party. Fudge was tickling the girl between the legs, using some sort of pomade to lubricate her, and she didn't seem as disinclined as when I'd left.

"Get him away," I whispered to Nose. "Quick. We've got to move."

"What's the matter?" Nose jumped up.

"Our boy 1-Smoke," I said. "He's just now trotting up to the ford."

"Hadn't you better take care of him like you did his brother?"

"Sure," I said. "And the six armed guys with him would stand around in a circle to make sure we'd fight fair."

Nose didn't waste any more time in conversation. He jumped up, ran over, and grabbed poor drooling Fudge by the shoulder. Another ten seconds and he'd have had to lift his fat friend up, off, and out.

There was some low-voiced but vehement complaining. Even Banana Girl, all greased up and tickled, seemed miffed at the interruption. She couldn't understand the reason for it, I suppose, since we were whispering back and forth in Nahuatl, and the look she gave me this time wasn't at all adoring.

But of course, she came along after us. I took off at a trot down along the riverbank, with all four following. I trotted them in the water for a while, in case 1-Smoke wised up and started tracking. If that happened, I figured he'd conclude we'd entered the river to go across it, so as to keep going in the right direction.

So after a couple of hundred yards, we left the river and turned back north, up over a steep, hard volcanic bank that wouldn't take tracks of any kind, and then onto a hardpan flat area of giant organ cactus and rocks the size of houses. It made you feel small, but above it, in the hills, were loads of caves. I figured we'd be okay up there for the night, if we didn't happen to strike a cave that was already being used by lions, snakes, or outlaws.

I passed up a couple, with my charming foursome panting along behind—Fudge was limping as he had been all day long, and Nose had skinned up a shin and was limping too by now. Unlike Fudge, he didn't whine.

I saw a nice little cave then with its entrance pretty well concealed, and told them to hold up. I went in and checked for prior occupants, animal, reptile, or human, and found it empty with a good dirt floor.

It had been used. There were remains of a fire. But they were old remains, and I thought we'd be well-off there. If there were road agents around, they'd be in a big enough group to need a larger cave. This one had probably served other travelers like ourselves, forced off the road for the night by bad weather or bad luck.

The boys came in, leading Banana Girl, and made themselves comfortable.

"This where we spend the night, Zap?" Nose asked.

"Yes."

"We eat?"

"Sam's carrying tortillas and jerky, isn't he? I'll go out and try to find some tunas." Those are prickly pears, the fruit of the nopal cactus. I went out to look for some, glad to get by myself to try to think things out, but it didn't take much thinking. First, it was clear that 1-Smoke couldn't be after me publicly unless he had Grandad's permission. I had to assume that he and his six chums were authorized to take me and take over the guiding chores. Grandad had cut me off.

Nose was smart—smarter than Fudge certainly, and with other things than poonie on his mind. I had to hope it would take him a while to figure out what was so plain to me, that I no longer represented safe conduct for them. In fact I wondered if they mightn't say nothing, wait till we came to a town, turn me over to whoever was in charge and demand new guides, all on their own?

It was going to be tight tomorrow.

I found the tunas and got back to the cave. I rather hoped they'd have their defloration job out of the way by then, but they didn't. Fudge was nursing a swollen ankle, and just generally looking beat and hungry as a little fat man will at the end of a tough day.

Nose was talkative. He'd had a drink of something Silent Sam was carrying that they didn't offer me, and was telling Fudge about a summer place his brother-in-law had built. Nose said he wished he could build one like it.

"Real, no-expense-spared class," he said. "It's got a golden toad in every room. Made in the Mixteca. Maybe Zap can tell us where you get those?"

"No," I said, noticing the change of tone toward me. "No, I don't know that."

"Old Zap could show us how to make one of those neat Mixtec offerings in the middle of the patio, though." Nose said. "We've really learned a lot of stuff from the Mixtecs, haven't we?"

"Tell you what," I said. "Suppose you tell Silent Sam to offer me a drink of whatever he's toting, and maybe I'll share these tunas with you."

Nose laughed. "Silent Sam," he said. "That's good. Hey, Silent, give the young man some of that double x."

I don't know what it was—pulque, basically, but there was other potent stuff in it, too. I figured this was no night for me to go on a high rabbit count, but Nose was going after it and I encouraged him to. The fuzzier his thinking, the better it was by me.

I gave their servant some tunas; he divided up the jerky and tortillas, and then went out to stand guard. I told Nose it wouldn't help, but Nose thought he'd sleep better, and I was all for whatever was going to make Nose sleep better.

I put some of the tortillas and jerky away for tomorrow—and made five shares out of the rest. I put Sam's away to give him whenever he came off guard. I didn't want to risk a fire, even in the cave; we'd have to eat what there was cold.

"Is that all there is?" Fudge wanted to know. He'd taken his share down in a couple of bites, while I was still handing the rest around. I didn't bother to answer. Nose had another pull off the jug, and offered it to Fudge, but Fudge had something else on his mind.

He'd got up and was limping over to Banana Girl, who'd taken her food and gone off across the cave by herself. At first I thought the idea was to urge her to hurry eating so they could get back to their other game, but I misjudged. Fudge was holding out his hand. He wanted her food.

A tear came rolling out of Banana Girl's big, brown left eye, but dumbly she was handing over what he demanded. I went over.

"No," I said. "Absolutely not," and let him have a short, straight one, right to the point of the chin. I didn't mean to hit him hard at all, but he fell the way an ocelot does from a tree, when you hit it in the head with a stone from your sling, and the claws relax. His legs gave way, and he said topple. He lay there looking at me, and I said:

"Whatever else you have in mind, friend, the girl eats."

She was looking at me with a kind of frightened gratitude. Fudge said not to hit him again. Nose, who was about half-bagged, was laughing. Fudge picked himself up and went back to sit by Nose, defiantly taking the jug of liquor out of Nose's hand.

"You're not going to be in charge forever, Zap," he said.

"You hungry, fat man?" I said. "Eat mine." I wondered if he'd be contemptible enough to do it.

He was. Then he was overfed, sore, slightly liquored up, and absolutely exhausted. He said he wanted to lie down a while. I spread some cloaks, and he went promptly off to sleep.

Nose said, sly and drunk: "Isn't 1-Smoke going to get in trouble with your grandad, hunting us openly, Zap?"

"Nobody has to know what he's hunting," I said, not at all sure I was going to make it convincing. "If he can catch us and put us away, it'll look like outlaw work."

"What would be in it for him?" Nose asked.

I shrugged. Nose chuckled meaninglessly, lay down, and quite abruptly went to sleep.

It was possible, from his questions, that he'd already figured out that 1-Smoke had the all-clear to knock me off and take over guiding.

That meant that all my good men had to do was leave trail enough for us to be found, even if I took them around towns the rest of the way. I sat by the entrance of the cave, and thought about Silent Sam out there in the dark somewhere. He was young and strong enough to jump me, and I wondered if I ought to get the obsidian knife and go look for Sam right now. Or I could just leave for the valley on my own? But I couldn't; I'd said I'd guide.

Then I felt two warm arms go around me from behind, and a little hand went sneaking into my loincloth. I turned and felt as much as saw Banana Girl, and I thought, what the hell? I didn't say I wouldn't deflower, did I?

Serve the bastards right. And as for 6-Rain, her grandfather had let me know today that she was for Smoky, not for Zap, however Rain might feel about it.

So I took Banana Girl away down the path a little, found some sand, laid her on it, spread her, and went for the middle. Fudge was right. She was tight as a turkey, but that turkey was ready to gobble, had been all day, all it needed, seemed to me, was some stuffing. So there on the sand under the high stars, I stuffed.

Made fairly quick work of it, and got her back. After which, instinct told me not to go to sleep, but I did anyway.

When I woke, it was a long way from morning, but the shadows of men showed in the fading moonlight on the back wall of the cave.

3.

He turned off the shower.

There was no seminar. It was Friday. Newman came while Brill was still dressing, with a jug of mescal and some need to justify himself.

"I don't give a damn about the dress," Newman said. "Franchot had it coming."

"Where's the salt and grapefruit for the mescal?"

"He *did* have it coming."

"How much more like it does he have coming?" Brill asked, the mescal getting to him, and when Newman looked annoyed: "Your attitude reminds me just a little of a man I see from time to time named Fudge."

"Make sense," Newman said. "I'm sorry about the dress. I'll apologize to her."

"Why not apologize to Franchot? He has to pay the cleaning bill."

"Come on, Bob."

Brill poured another shot, and said judiciously: "Maybe she isn't looking for an apology. Maybe she's going to put the dress in her scrapbook, with the old dance programs and the dried gardenias from her first corsage."

"Get off me," Newman said. "I wonder if she did have—some kind of feeling about it? What do you think I ought to do?"

"You're asking the dumbest man in the world," Brill said, but he was flattered. It made his forty-eight-year-old tonsils open to have smitten youth coming by for advice. Bringing the old wisdom right up from the diaphragm, he commenced: "Did she slap you? Back away and brush herself off looking scornful. Or maybe say, 'Thank you, sir,' with a cool smile, take her husband's arm, and walk off smiling at him? True, she didn't put her lovely, mad little lips up for a kiss, but that wouldn't be her style, would it? My guess is she hasn't any particular ideas, but might not put up much of an argument against whatever ideas you've got. That appeal to you?"

"He's such a *sorry* bastard," Newman said.

"And you're such a *white* knight," said Brill.

Newman left, taking his mescal with him. Brill took a copy of

Willey and Phillip's *Method and Theory in American Archaeology* and went down to supper.

He had finished eating rice, and was reading, waiting for the next course, when a voice said:

"Mr. Brill?"

Damned if it was old Skunk Head Franchot himself. Brill said, "Hello, Peter. Sit down."

He did, and let Brill order him a beer, which he didn't drink. He played with silverware instead, and then said all in a rush:

"I can't talk to Newman, Mr. Brill, but you can. About Libby. She's a disturbed girl. She's been in and out of institutions."

"I'm sorry," Brill said.

"I've been trying. Well. She's my wife, and I'm responsible. Look, let me tell you why we came down here. I thought I ought to get her away from University City. I was studying art history, and one of my friends—well, I was a teaching assistant, and I worked with him. A young instructor. We were very close. That's my field, you see; I don't really care very much about this down here, you know."

Brill said he knew.

"Well, he and Libby. It was my fault. I was painting a copy of a Gauguin painting. I had slides, and I was working frantically on it, night after night, in one room. And she'd be sitting in another, and sometimes my friend with her. They'd ask me if I wanted a drink, or some pot or something, and I wouldn't even answer. I was, well, I don't know if I was really so absorbed in making my copy. But I told myself I was."

The rest of Brill's meal came. Franchot said no thanks he just wasn't hungry. Franchot said: "You see, I could hear them in the next room. I kept painting, pretending I couldn't. And . . . when I heard him leave, I went in, and she was just lying there, with her clothes off. Looking at me in a crazy way. She's sick. Maybe I am too."

"Aren't there doctors?" Brill asked.

"We've tried. Different ones. I thought maybe coming here . . ."

Brill said, "I'll speak to Newman, Peter. Of course." He didn't want Franchot to realize there might be any hurry about his doing it, but he pushed the plate away, refused coffee, and got out as quick as he gracefully could; at the Monte Albán, Franchot went to his room, Brill to the *portales.*

Minnegerode and Berkowitz were there, and said Newman had been, briefly.

"Just long enough," Minnegerode said, and he and Berko laughed.

"Long enough for what?"

"To sweep Mrs. Franchot off to hear the marimba band or something," Minnegerode said. "She was sitting here alone. He arrived with half a bottle of mescal sticking out of his shirt front."

"She's crazy for marimba music, Bob," said Berkowitz, in a deep, lugubrious voice.

Perhaps Brill should have sat down, had a beer, and laughed sadly with them, but he did not feel yet he could be too late. He even thought he might catch them at Newman's hotel, actually listening to marimba music, though when he got there he realized it wasn't Friday but Saturday night the band played there.

The lobby was empty. So was the bar. Brill thought: I can't be more than fifteen minutes behind them. Permissive or not, it's got to take longer than that. They've barely met.

At the same time he had an image of the hunger and beauty of a face that wanted help, just help, offer whatever kind you have and we'll see if it's any good. He imagined her following Newman across the big lobby, with broken tiles in the floor, of what had once been a most elegant, was now a most dilapidated, hotel; up the long first flight of stairs with broken marble balustrade swinging around and around a central patio; going up floor after floor to the cheapest rooms; holding Newman's hand as they climbed? Mouse-quiet, puppy-trusting, cat-hungry.

Brill didn't want to go busting in like a private detective, but he'd been touched by Franchot, a young man he couldn't stand. Brill started up the stairs, and met her in the third flight coming down.

She was like a damn wraith, pale in a pale dress. She stopped, and Brill did, too, six or eight steps apart and they looked at one another. One of her hands came out toward Brill, and he had an absurd feeling that if he opened his arms she'd have jumped down the stairs into them, like a child. But Brill couldn't open his arms; Brill didn't know his motives; later he thought, I think I'd have soothed her and led her back across the square to Franchot, who really wants, I guess, to protect her.

But at the moment he did not feel that sure about himself; he stood like a clay urn, staring at her, not realizing in the dim light until she moved her hand to cover it, that the front of her dress was open to the waist and the brassiere was gone. Whatever it was Brill was getting ready to say went back into the chaos of intention, and it was then she cleared her throat. A soft, moaning little clearing of the throat and she turned and ran back up the steps.

Where Brill stood, halfway up, his eyes were just above the level of the balcony floor. He saw Newman starting along the balcony, with the bra in his hand. Gallant.

She hurried to him and Brill heard her say, "I'm sorry, Stan," and run back into his room. Newman turned quickly after her without seeing Brill, and closed the door. Brill heard it lock.

Brill did not see now how he could knock on it, what he could call out to them that might not terrify her, to interrupt what must for sure be going on.

Libby Franchot didn't spend the night with Newman. In fact, their roll didn't take long at all. Brill saw her half an hour later come in with Newman to the *portales,* where Brill waited the thing out himself, and sit down. Newman stayed for about sixty uneasy seconds. He was clearly dying to leave, and Libby was utterly pathetic, in gesture and expression, about how badly she wanted him to stay and sit with her. Brill supposed those sixty seconds were a minute of hysterical high courage on Newman's part: at that point, all drained and feeling it must show, after a roll, it doesn't occur to you that people who see you may make the least complex assumptions, like: they took a walk, maybe held hands.

Newman jumped up and got away as soon as he'd ordered for her; she sat there looking helpless and miserable, and about the time her drink came she looked directly at Brill. She made herself get up and come over; Brill would, in a moment, as soon as he was sure she wanted him to, have got up and gone to her.

Now he stood and indicated a chair, saying: "Hello, Libby. It's all right."

"Mr. Brill."

"It's all right," he said, pushed her chair in, and patted her shoulder. The shoulder felt very young. Brill thought of home, sat down opposite, inordinately sad.

After a mostly silent time, during which he smiled at her, nodded to her, occasionally repeated his big reassurance ("It's okay, you see?"), Franchot found them, and seemed very relieved that his wife was with Brill.

4.

On Saturday morning, hoping to put it out of his mind, for Brill found it difficult to think reasonably about a situation he'd only been a margarita away from getting into himself, he rented the car again.

He saw Sandoval on the street, stopped, and proposed going to

Zaachila, the last Zapotec capital, where there were some stunning tombs.

Tomb 1, in particular, was what he found he needed to see to redirect his imagination to what, after all, he was trying to learn and do in Mexico.

Tomb 1 had plaster sculptures on the walls, brilliantly colored, so imaginatively conceived that his feeling for the people here, especially in the last period (when they were said to have been pretty sloppy), improved in a most cheerful way. There were owls, a god inhabiting a turtle; and what were those? Tusks?

"No, of course," said Sandoval. "Those are speech glyphs. Okay. Do you know? The treasure of polychrome pottery from this tomb is finer than anything of gold ever found?"

"Was it a king's tomb?"

"Say a cacique, Senor Brill. Not a king. Caso thinks it was for a man named 8-Deer 'Fire Serpent.' "

Brill grinned, slightly abashed. He'd been ready for Sandoval to tell him this fine tomb had been for Cosijoesa, a Zapotec king known to history–Cosijoesa could have had some Mixtec funeral directors in to work on his tomb, couldn't he?

Cosijoesa had been a wily king, cacique if Sandoval liked, who had made an alliance with the Mixtecs to fight the Aztec invaders, garrisoned by then at the foot of Monte Albán.

Cosijoesa's alliance had worked so well that the Aztecs finally gave him a princess named Cotton Ball to marry, in order to make peace.

When the peace was broken (just before the coming of the Spaniards, over on the east coast), Cosijoesa, his princess, and his allies had withdrawn to the fortified mountain Giengola, near Tehuantepec to the south, and withstood an Aztec siege.

Back in Oaxaca, the *cuitlatl* had hit the *acatl*. They could tell because there was nobody there when they parked opposite the *portales* but Gary Pederson, who was never to be seen there alone, looking bereft.

5.

While he was dressing that morning, Pederson said, the student Peter Franchot had knocked on his door. Franchot's car was on the street outside of the place Pederson was renting; its back seat was piled with suitcases, there were clothes on hangers, Mrs. Franchot sat in front, and the engine was running.

Franchot was extremely pale. He explained that he had been up all night, finishing a paper which he wished to hand in. He insisted that this paper was his semester's work for the course, that Pederson give him credit for it, and that he be permitted to leave Oaxaca immediately.

They were still discussing this, Pederson trying to explain why it was quite impossible, when Peter Franchot, who kept watching out the window, apparently saw his wife start to get out of the car.

Franchot had then screamed an obscene accusation against Pederson for his conduct with Nancy and Little Gonzalez, Robert Brill and Stan Newman for their conduct with Franchot's wife, said he'd let the University authorities know about it, and run into the street. He had thrown his wife back into the automobile, slammed the door, run around, got in on his side, and driven off.

Hearing all this, Sandoval grew stiffer and stiffer, more and more withdrawn.

Brill said: "What did you do, Gary?"

"You know I . . . I couldn't think what to do. I sat down and read the boy's paper."

"I must go," said Sandoval. "With your permission." And he did.

"Sit down, Gary," Brill said. "Let's have some coffee. How was the boy's paper?"

"Quite good, as a matter of fact," Gary said, and smiled. "Quite good."

"What else happened then?"

Gary had sent for Nancy, as his secretary and a student to whom he was close—though not of course in the way Franchot had suggested—and asked her whether she knew anything about the accusations. She had said she could find out, and gone to see the student Jack Minnegerode.

(Brill could see that scene: "Oh, Jack. Come out a minute."

"You come in here."

"I can't. Well, just for a minute while I ask you something . . .")

Nancy brought back information damaging to Newman, though certainly not conclusive, but apparently after giving it Minnegerode had felt exploited. Therefore Minnegerode had gone to report Nancy's visit to Newman, and before Gary could even begin to think what he ought to do about the situation, Newman had arrived.

"He was in a fit about things," Gary said. "I think, to be honest, he was feeling terribly guilty. Yes, Nancy?"

For Nancy and Little Gonzalez now came buzzing up to say that they had been to Newman's hotel and Newman had checked out.

"Stan objected violently to what he called Nancy's spying on him," Gary said.

Nancy looked noble and injured.

"And said he wouldn't stay. That his presence was damaging, and I apparently didn't trust him. He seems now to have gone off on the bus."

"You don't suppose he's trying to . . . follow the Franchots?" Brill asked.

"No." It was Little Gonzalez' turn to triumph over Nancy. Brill was once more irrelevantly struck by their similarity of stature and dress, dark boy, bright girl, rivals and siblings. "Stan left a forwarding address for his mail, sir. Care of Francis Ledyard, in Tehuantepec."

"For heaven's sake," said Gary.

"You know Ledyard?"

"An old British amateur," Gary said. "Yes. Not exactly a mountebank. A dilettante? Yes."

Brill sighed. "It was a very nice morning in Zaachila," he said.

"Bob?"

"Yes, of course I will," Brill said. "I've got the car. I want to see Tehuantepec, anyway."

"May I go?" said Nancy.

"No," said Brill. And then, to soften it, because she was after all not that much older than Trinket: "It wouldn't help persuade Stan to come back, would it?"

Down the InterAmerican without any lunch, past Yagul and the Mitla turn-off, and into the mountains, heading for the Isthmus.

6.

A torch came flying into the cave, and then another. They weren't taking any chances.

I got up with my back to the wall, near the entrance, tried to look around the corner to see how many were out there, and damn near got an arrow through the throat.

"Come on out, Zap," said a voice I'd never heard before, and when I complied I saw why I hadn't: it was Silent Sam.

Only Sam was standing straight and tall now, and wearing the uniform of an eagle knight—not the dress uniform, of course. The fatigues.

Behind me came Nose and Fudge, chuckling, and pushing Banana Girl in front of them.

Behind Sam must have been forty Aztecs, but they weren't all soldiers. They had a couple of litters with them, and plenty of men to carry them.

Sam saluted Nose and said: "It's a little farther than I thought, sir. I'm glad to find that you're safe."

"You must have run like hell, boy," Nose said. "I'll see they hear about it in Tenochtitlan."

So my boys weren't merchants after all. Nose was a good-sized Aztec general, and Fudge somebody who counted in Intelligence. Apparently the drinking and grousing about food had been put on for me, to cover Sam's move. Probably they even figured on letting me pass time with the girl. They must have realized almost as soon as I did that Grandad had cut me off, and that therefore there wasn't any way of getting through to Mitla without attracting some attention. So they'd sent Sam for help from the big Aztec garrison at Oaxaca.

"What about Zap?" Sam asked.

"He's no use," Nose said.

"Kill him," said Fudge.

"No." Nose was clearly in command. "Let's give him to Mitla for a present. Or give him to the Zapotecs at the garrison."

It was time to run. Back up over the hill with the cave in it was steep and slow; I'd have been a fine target for those Aztec bowmen to practice on in the moonlight.

I went low, and right between Sam's legs, spilling him, twisted off right, and really whistled going downhill.

They didn't have more than twenty trained runners in the bunch fast enough to catch me before I was halfway to the river, and that was about seventeen more than they needed.

I'd always been curious to see what the Aztec garrison at Oaxaca looked like, but I hadn't planned to arrive with my hands tied, my feet hobbled, and Silent Sam's spear halfway up my butt.

7.

Brill had Francis Ledyard's address, but didn't need it. He saw Newman as he drove into the central square of Tehuantepec, sitting on a concrete bench with a couple of suitcases by his feet.

He stopped the car almost in front of where Stan was sitting, and said: "Hello."

Newman got up and came over to the car. "Hello. Catching my breath. I just got off the bus."

"Put your stuff in the car. I'll drive you where you're going."

"Thanks." Newman opened the back door, put the two suitcases inside, and then got in front with Brill. "The man I'm going to see takes a siesta. It isn't time to go there yet."

"I'm hungry," Brill said, easing the car out of the parking place and around the block. "What's that stand selling?"

"Iguana tacos," Newman said.

"Iguana?"

Newman made claws of his hands, and darted his tongue in and out.

"Let's do," Brill said, stopping the car.

"Oh damn it," said Newman. They got out of the car and locked it. "What'd you have to come to Mexico for? I've been coming here for years and always managed to avoid iguana tacos up to now."

They each took two, and crossed to a corner café. They ordered Dos Equis beer, cold, dark, and sour-sweet, swished their throats, and bit into the tacos.

"Good," Brill said. "It's like pork, isn't it?"

"Rubbery," said Newman. "I'm sure it's against my religion."

Brill said: "Coelacanth. Maybe it tastes like coelacanth."

"They smoke that, don't they?" Newman said. "Well?"

"Gary's pretty upset. Know what I think?"

"No."

"I think you ought to go back with me tonight."

"Why?"

"You know the Franchots have left?"

"Of course."

"Gary isn't being highly moral about this, Stan. Naturally he's concerned at losing a student, especially when his enrollment for the trip is so damn low. Did you know Franchot threatened to make trouble at the University?"

"You think he will?"

Brill shook his head. "Doubt he'll ever go near it again. But a little show of solidarity on your part right now would . . . help us all. It's the dig that matters, isn't it?"

"I'll think about it," Newman said. "Yeah, I suppose it is."

They strolled the market until time to go to Ledyard's house, debating the appearance of Tehuantepec women, often said to be the most beautiful in Mexico. They were big and round-armed, like walking statues.

Francis Ledyard was pretty picturesque too.

"I was here for the revolution, you know," he said, as they sat in his patio. He was tall, florid, silver-haired, and white-suited. "Graham Greene stayed with me, and Huxley came to tea. But I never met the Lawrence chap."

His house was a disorderly museum of unattributed antiquities and lovingly cared-for wild orchids.

"Had to sell some of the best pieces," he said. "Met Stan here that way. Meant to give the rest to Mexico, and so I shall. Love Mexico. Came after the First War to try to do myself a bit of good in mahogany, but I couldn't stand the way they ran the camps. Prisoners, you know. Still more or less slaves, really. Beat the poor sods. That was fifty years ago."

"You've been here fifty years?" Brill was slightly awed. He also had a feeling this was meaningful to him in a way he couldn't quite see yet.

"Except for the Second War and all that. Joined up, and they put me in some hellhole in Africa. You say Mexico to British Intelligence, you know, and they think you're married to the cannibal queen. Jungle expert. Couldn't explain to them about Tehuantepec and the way, well, civilization here goes back to when Englishmen still painted themselves blue, you know?"

Brill wondered if they still made white suits like that anywhere in the world, and old Mr. Ledyard said Hong Kong. Sent away for them.

"One for each day. Have a woman washes them for me; it took her three years to learn how properly. Remittance man's life. Not bad. See about some tea for us, shall I?"

He went out and Newman said: "That old man has seen every dig in Mexico for half a century. Ran them himself for years, but he gave it up, some time or other. And he's never published."

"Saw the great stone heads at La Venta, years before Stirling made them known," Ledyard said, coming back. "Like seeing God in the jungle. Would have told someone, but damned if I knew where we'd been when we came out. Didn't keep it a secret, you know, but I never found an archaeologist who'd believe me. Might know some other things, you know."

Newman said: "I want to do the rain forest. Mr. Ledyard has some recollections and perhaps some notes if we can find them."

"Like to get back in once more," Ledyard agreed. "Know a man who wants to go, do small mammals, too. Bugs. Birds. May be a fair number of new species."

"Interdisciplinary," Stan said. It was a somewhat magic word.

"Exploration, too," said Ledyard. "Cartography, even. A good deal of it's quite unmapped."

"Good God," said Robert Brill. Then, because he guessed that

Newman had some confidential things to talk with Mr. Ledyard about: "Speaking of maps, do you have one of Giengola?"

He left them talking, took the map, and went off to climb Cosijoesa's fortified mountain, which was just northeast of the city of Tehuantepec, the last high ground really before you got into the Isthmus.

The trail was easy to find. At the foot of the mountain it crossed a shallow stream, where Brill sat for a while. The air was full of butterflies, the day not too hot, and he thought that, in spite of the absurd things which had been going on, he was quite happy.

He picked up a stick and dabbled it in the water. To his left in the water, fifty small eyes turned toward him.

Huh? Frogs? With their bodies just below the surface. With eyes that saw above the surface?

When he rose, the eyes disappeared and fish swam away. They were like something you might keep in an aquarium at home. This wasn't even rain forest, Brill thought, but immediately, as soon as someone called it to his slow attention, he could see there was zoology around.

Walked up the stream, and saw the eyes up again, above the surface. Stopped, and crouched so he could watch without disturbing them. But he couldn't decide whether their eyes were fixed to work out in the air because they fed on something outside the water, or because they needed to be able to get a better view than most fish get of terrestrial enemies.

The portly field scientist in his Hong Kong suit (took Brill three years to train a woman to wash them right, and what a fine, big round-armed statue of a woman she was to train), switched back to archaeology, and started up the hill. It was fairly steep but the trail was a switchback, and the going quite easy.

And almost as he started, Brill began seeing fortifications: stone-walled angles at corners, within which defenders could stand above the trail, and by which retreat to a higher position would be protected.

Big clay jars were set in the ground up to their necks, and Brill assumed they had been buried that way intentionally, five hundred years ago, for steady storage of food and water. There were stones piled around in these alcoves sometimes, but he saw no other evidence of weapons.

The higher he got, the larger and more elaborate were the outpost points; he began coming to buildings. He found himself amazed as he moved among them that the site had never been developed. It would be, he supposed, of small value scientifically, since what this battlefield had to tell was, if very roughly, known historically. But then, what a place for tourists, he thought, and for students learning. For them it really should be dug, he thought—as a place to visit, like Gettysburg or Yorktown.

Because it had to do with a particular war, a certain battle, issues and people that were clearly known; he sat on a stone, and thought about money:

His net worth was somewhere around $300,000, but a good deal of that was in house, farm, and condemned office building.

Suppose he gave Pat, in effect, the house and farm. She'd live there, rent-free, with about $11,000 a year in income.

The river property would bring $30,000 he guessed, and if he let his office building go and sold the property it stood on, that should give him something like $56,000 more. He had $1,200 a year from a foundation directorship, which only required a couple of days a year, to attend meetings, and there was income from old settlements and from investments which would bring about another $4,000. There was insurance, which of course he'd keep for the kids—since in this way of figuring Pat was all set; and he had an inherited interest in the Ford place, from his Uncle Ed, which could be sold. That, with savings, would give him comfortably over $100,000 in capital; the interest on that plus the fixed earnings he'd already computed meant he, like Pat, would have about $11,000 in income. It he had to go into capital for Trinket's college bills, he felt he could do it, and simply live on less.

It had been a long time since Brill had met a man he could envy. Who'd have thought that when it happened, it would be an old remittance man who'd once had Huxley to tea?

When he got back to Ledyard's, Newman was photographing pieces from the old man's collection. There were maps spread out around the room, and Brill had a very clear and pleasant sense of how decent it might be to grow old knowing things.

"Giengola's beautiful," Brill said.

"A sort of pre-Columbian Camelot, Mr. Brill?" Ledyard asked.

"I'm not quite that soft-headed, but I could feel people there."

"It hasn't been so very long since they were there, has it?"

"Listen," Newman said, putting down his camera. "No, stay away from the map. That's rain forest, you can look at it. But tell me something first."

"Okay."

"Where do you go when Gary and his students finish the half-semester and head back?"

"No plans. I thought if Gary wanted me to, and there's some money left for it, I might stay on and supervise consolidation. Possibly even some restoration, if there's something worth restoring—the round building you got so irritated about, for instance."

"Forget it."

"No, you really were. And you know, it's going to do just what you thought it might, too. Take Gary right back into the pre-Classic."

"I meant forget Pueblo Viejo, or Huitzo, or whatever it is."

"I'm not going to be in a hurry to get home, any way," Brill said. "I think Sandoval might stay on, too."

"Shut up, will you, Brill? And listen, please, sir? There's an old mahogany camp Mr. Ledyard knows."

"Yes, I think I could find it," Ledyard pointed to a place on the map. "In here you see. It isn't all in Yucatan."

"We've been planning a trip," Newman said.

"I would like to do the rain forest once again," said Ledyard. "An old man's memory you know, but I do have some recollections. Well, that is, I don't want to say too much but, um, things you might find striking. And there's my zoologist friend; I could write to him."

"We could do it for a few hundred dollars," Newman said. "I think Gary'd give me a department grant."

"It sounds as if you're going back to Oaxaca with me," Brill said. It wasn't until they were almost to Oaxaca that smitten youth said to forty-eight: "Bob. Was she, is she . . . out of her head? Crazy?"

"I guess so," Brill said. "I realize you didn't know, Newman."

"How can you tell when a girl's crazy?" asked the Doctor of Philosophy in Anthropology.

8.

Sahagun's informants knew about the forests:

> It is a place of verdure, of fresh green; of wind—windy places, in wind, windy; a place of cold . . .

No, not that kind.

> It is a place of gorges, gorge places; a place of crags, craggy places . . .

No, not that kind.

> It is a place among moist and fertile lands, a place of moist and fertile soil, in yellow soil . . . a place of jungle, or dry tree stumps, of underbrush, of dense forest . . .

Yes, that kind.

It is a disturbing place, fearful, frightful; home of the savage beast, dwelling place of the serpent, the rabbit, the deer; a place whence nothing departs, nothing leaves, nothing emerges . . . the ocelot, the cuitlachtli, the bobcat; the serpent, the spider . . .

Yes, that kind.

There is fright, there is constant fright. One is devoured; one is slain by stealth; one is abused; one is brutally put to death, one is tormented. Misery abounds. There is calm, constant calm, continuing calm . . .

That kind we've still got, Sahagun.

5

In the following week, everybody turned up stuff on the dig though it was again Brill's crew which hit it big. Berkowitz put up a sign: "Lucky Bob #3 Artifact Mine."

The first find of the week, though, was at the temple—a crude representation of a dog. Or a toad. Or a jaguar.

Or, as Sandoval, who had studied a good deal of carved stone, told the group: "An inner structure. Today we make a frame of wire for a stuffed animal. But they shaped a stone. They covered it with stucco and painted the stucco."

"Can't we ever know more than that?" Willa demanded.

"Perhaps by comparing it to many other stone shapes from the locality. Now we know what it is not: it is not a human figure. It is not a serpent."

"It is not very pretty," Nancy said, and Little Gonzalez gave her a push.

Sandoval, now that stratigraphy was complete, had started clearing and consolidating the ball court, supervising Colonel Mazzard.

"We will learn nothing new here," Sandoval explained. "But it will be a handsome ball court, one without rings, I think." Some courts, in other areas, had doughnut-like stone rings, one centered on each lengthwise wall between the two broader areas where the players presumably grouped to face one another. "It is always nice for tourists to see a ball court."

His exploration had not produced what Newman and Pederson originally had hoped for—a second area of ceremonial buildings, elsewhere in the site, which would have indicated the cultural center of a second, coexisting group in the same town.

Pederson's mound—they kept calling it the observatory—was proving to be round as hoped. Pederson had begun to fret about it; he wanted to go through the wall, and down through the floor, to try to find evidence of prior building at the location, but this was not authorized by his digging permit.

At Lucky Bob #3, with all four outside walls exposed, and the south room cleared, and the patio completely cleaned and swept, they found broken floor on the patio in front of the south room.

Patching stucco once again. Brill called Sandoval, Newman, and Pederson all over to see it.

"Berk and Minnegerode think we got one," he said. "And so do I."

"You probably do," said Newman. Sandoval grinned and agreed.

Pederson sighed. "Thank heavens for one thing, anyway," he said. "If you were going to find a tomb, thank heavens you found it in the morning."

"Why's that?" Brill asked.

"You've got the whole day to get it dug and cleared," Pederson said. "You'd need a troop of cavalry to guard it tonight if word got back to town that it was open but still had things left inside."

Huitzo Viejo (?) Tomb 1.

Tomb, apparently built after building. Floor patched with weak plaster (Photos #23, 24, 25), broken by weight of dirt.

Entry from Jack Minnegerode's field notes. They requisitioned José, Chico and Galdencio back from Colonel Mazzard, to have a double crew.

They went fast through the broken plaster, rather ruthlessly tearing up the patio floor surrounding the break to make room to dig in. By noon there was a trench, waist deep and two meters wide, stopping just in front of the doorway to the south room, directly under which there now appeared the lintel over the tomb entrance (Photos #26, 27).

Tomb confirmed.

"Aren't we going through superimpositions as we dig down?" Brill asked.

"No, the guys who built the tomb did," Berkowitz explained.

"Can we give our crew different lunchtimes, so we can keep one pair going?"

"They wouldn't go for that," Newman said.

"Any volunteers?" Brill asked, picking up a pick. "If not, at least borrow One-Eye's shotgun, and keep Gary off me."

"I'll sit here holding a shovel and watch you," Berkowitz said.

"Promised my mother back in Tennessee I'd never dig ditches," Minnegerode said. "Oh, Ma. Bad companions are leading me astray."

They had a hard time keeping the work to themselves. Newman and Little Gonzalez wanted turns. Colonel Mazzard had a bad back, and wasn't allowed the pick but insisted on a turn with the shovel. Pederson and Sandoval watched benignly, but did not actually participate, and it seemed perfectly correct.

Brill loved the rhythm of it, the urgency and the heat. Berkowitz claimed to have to hold his arms to give Newman a turn with the pick, and in fact, the whole hour passed in boisterousness, excitement, and sweat, and they were working shoulder deep by the time the Mexican crews returned.

The long lintel stone was now exposed. It was set across and on top of two upright rectangular stones, and there was a huge, flat slab against the three-stone doorway.

The Mexicans, excited too, returned early and claimed their tools. Brill sat with Sandoval and Berkowitz.

"When I was in school," Sandoval said, "there was a mammoth skeleton dug in the Valley of Mexico, and very nicely. I would go every day to watch. The man in charge sat in a folding canvas chair, like a movie director, under a beach umbrella. He gave directions through a megaphone, drinking lemonade."

"Yes," said Berkowitz. "Ah, yes."

Rinso, Willa's dog, was brought to the dig white every day and went home brown; now he was tan. He sat with his head against Brill's thigh, watching the men dig.

The slab was clear. There were two wheelbarrows working now to get the dirt away, as Colonel Mazzard had mobilized yet another pair of diggers. An hour after lunch there was room for the big slab to be moved away.

Berkowitz slid into the pit. "I have a back of formidable strongness," he announced, bowing, first in English and then in Spanish, as the Mexicans climbed out.

Brill slid in beside him, laying hold of a pick. "And I a brain to match his back," said Brill, and set the point of the tool behind the lower right-hand corner of the slab. Berko steadied, Brill pried. Slowly, they worked it out, inch by inch, from the bottom. Minnegerode photographing almost as quickly as he could wind film.

A rope was handed down, and the end passed around behind the slab. Darkness could be seen on each side; Berkowitz said:

"Smells pretty dank in there."

And Willa cried: "Rinso."

Into the pit leapt the little dog, went past Berkowitz. Brill made a grab and missed, and Rinso, squeezing fast, disappeared inside.

"Rinso," Willa cried again, and out came the dog from the other side of the slab, eluded Berkowitz again and ran out of the pit, carrying what was quite clearly a human armbone. Willa ran after him; Rinso capered. Not only was the game fun, apparently the ancient bone was good. It was soft and dry, and Rinso ate it like a cracker.

The colonel yelled, furiously, "Collar that damn dog."

Willa wept.

Pederson was calm. "Never mind," he said. "I don't think we're going to find a primary burial. We so seldom do."

The colonel subsided, Rinso finished his cracker, the stone was moved, and Pederson proved right.

Inside the tomb was a mess of bones, dirt, and pottery fragments. By a skull count, there were remains in there of twenty-six or twenty-seven people, and there'd have been no way of telling which bones were those of the people for whom the tomb originally was made.

Nevertheless, sifting the contents produced a good deal in the way of jade beads, teeth inset with turquoise, and such curiosities. And there were fragments of some lovely pots, though the only whole ones were small and very crude.

They talked about it, going back on the bus, chiefly Newman and the colonel:

"You see, someone beat us to it."

"These natives here?"

"No. Beat us to it by a thousand years. What period is that tomb by its shape, Colonel?"

"Third," said the colonel promptly.

"I think so too. That means perhaps three hundred A.D. But we went through only one floor, of a Fourth or Fifth Period building, to get to it. That means that when they rebuilt, they probably rifled the tomb. And then they reused it for a mass burial. Perhaps there was an epidemic, or a siege or famine. And then they sealed it up again."

2.

The Aztecs, using a bunch of untalented slaves, had thrown up a hasty little pyramid at their Oaxaca garrison.

They led me to a shed on the east flank of it.

"That's a lousy-looking pile of stone," I said to Nose. "Why don't you get some decent Mixtec builders down to make you something?"

"Politics, Zap," Nose said. "You know the Zapotec contractors."

He was affable now that he didn't have to pretend to be a merchant any more. He had a lot of authority in his manner and, at the same time, setting aside a little evidence of sexual aberration, the kind of human softness toward individuals old generals often have.

Fudge said: "Since you're such a big architectural critic, maybe we'll let you try the steps in the morning. Nice and slow."

Fudge was half-merchant, I guess, half-spy, a pretty sleazy character, and now that they weren't traveling together Nose seemed to hold him in distaste. Me too.

"I'm sorry about the troupial cloak, Zap," Nose said. "I'd really rather we'd got to Mitla where I'd have given it to you."

"I gather I wouldn't have very long to wear it here, anyway," I said. "Would I, if we'd got to Mitla?"

"I honestly don't know how that would have gone," Nose said. "But we'll see about here." But it was two days of solitary on tortillas and water before I had a chance to find out what he meant.

The morning of the third day I heard bustling outside the door. The guard opened it and there, of all unexpected people, stood my friend, uncle—well, Rain's brother—from the hills. Windy. Grandad's boy.

"Hi, Zap," he said.

"Well, I'll be hummingbird-on-the-left damned," I said, cussing in Aztec just to goad him a little.

"I brought you a few things from home." He had a sack of woven maguey fibers with him.

"Who's here?"

"Everybody from town."

"Grandad?"

"Of course. Once you blew the trip, we couldn't keep it a secret any more."

"1-Smoke blew it," I said. "Not that it matters, but that's where things started to go."

"I know that," said Windy. "But Grandad likes Smoky's story. He's getting old, Zap, and well, Smoke's going to marry Rain. That's part of the deal now."

"Yeah," I said. Grandad's town, Smoke's town—all of them now, going with the Aztecs? Disloyal Zap, keeping quiet about what hurt; I wondered if Cosijoesa knew all this, over in Zaachila.

"I brought your hip leathers," Windy said, and took them out of the sack. I couldn't help smiling. I'd got those leathers over on the coast long ago; real peccary, Mayan-made. I'd played a couple of hundred games of ball in them; Windy and I and a couple of others had won some damn big ones, up in the hills.

"We going to play ball?"

"Didn't they tell you? The Aztecs want you to play for them."

"Screw the Aztecs."

"It's a chance, Zap. You're up for sacrifice right now, but if you do well, things could get better."

"What's the matter with the Aztec ballplayers?"

"They haven't got too much of a team down here, I guess. Just a bunch of soldiers."

"Some of those army recreation program boys are okay," I said. But Windy and I, if I do say so, were pretty close to pros. "I play against you?"

"I don't like it either."

"Well," I said. "I'll take pleasure in shoving a hard rubber ball down the throat of Grandad's boy, Windy, with the old prick watching."

"Stop it. Play a good game and I imagine you'll save your ass," Windy said. "You keep driving it at me, and it won't be a good game."

"Go to hell," I said.

He dropped the sack. "If that's the way you want it," he said, and walked out.

After a while I calmed down, and looked to see what else he'd brought me. It was a jade I'd been working up, and my carving tools.

Windy was a pretty good guy. The jade was what I needed to pass the time. I was doing Bobala and some rabbits on a flat piece, two hands wide, in high relief.

When ball-game time came, two days later, I was stiff as hell, but I'd finished my main rabbit and, I don't know why, started cutting 1-Smoke's brother in it—the glyph for Smoke's town, the date, and my yellow-feathered prince dead on the road. Maybe I was a little sorry about it; it wasn't much of a historical event, but it sure had changed things for me.

The guards were waiting and I put on my leathers and did some knee bends, glad I was going to get some damn exercise.

I was marched out to the court, and let into the players' area. We lined up four on a side: Windy, two other guys who used to be on our team at home, and 1-Smoke, playing my right forward position for them.

On our Aztec team there were a big Tarascan mercenary from the northwest who could hardly speak Nahuatl, but could really drive the ball; a little eagle knight called Chipmunk who grew up tough in the streets of Tenochtitlan and had made it in the army on sheer ability; me; and our team captain, Silent Sam.

"Where do you want to play, Zap?" he asked.

"Right forward," I said.

"Okay. The Chipmunk will play left. Me and the big boy will play right and left back and defend. You guys just worry about scoring."

"We'll score," I said, and bounced the ball off the side walls a couple of times to test them. We'd score by sending the ball off hips, or shoulders, heads—anything but hands—all the way downcourt and bouncing it off their rear wall before they intercepted, and they'd try to make points against us the same way. The walls were okay, but up high on them was a new wrinkle.

"You play with rings, do you?"

"Yeah. You ever use them?"

"Never in a game," I said. "I've practiced on courts that had them."

"They're kind of silly," Sam said. "Nobody ever gets the ball through one, but I guess it makes for a good show if you shoot for it once in a while, trying to wrap the whole game up in one play."

"With the new jackrabbit ball," I said. "You may see more of it."

"It'll ruin the game," Sam said.

"Well," I said. "Let's cream these guys," and looked up above the rings to the tops of the side walls where the spectators were standing. There were Nose and Fudge, and there with them was Grandad; and there beside him was 6-Rain, and my intention of playing a hard, cool game flew off like a bird.

Windy served, a lovely long looper which the big Tarascan returned hard to 1-Smoke. Smoke blocked and it came back to Chipmunk. Chipmunk blocked but didn't get much lift on the hard little ball, and 1-Smoke had an easy chance to score. He got the ball pretty good with his right hip and sent it screaming across behind me into the rear corner where Sam leaped up to try a chest block and couldn't handle it. One for them.

They served again. This time the ball came my way, and I went up for it, bounced it high off my head, and as it came down turned the hip and sent it. Really hard. But I didn't try to score, I admit. I let Smoke have it in the neck, and damn near knocked him down.

It's the kind of play the spectators like these days, rough stuff, no finesse. I could hear excitement up above, especially among the Aztecs. Anyway, since they failed to get it back, it was our serve. Mine.

I did try to score on the serve, tried to ace them, but their left back had played with me too often and knew my tricks. He returned it and we had quite a long volley before the Chipmunk managed a liner that scored for us.

After that it seesawed back and forth, but every chance I got to do it, I whammed the ball at either Smoke or Windy. I could see bruises on both of them, and at the quarter they were ahead by four, 16–12.

"What are you trying to do, Zap?" Sam asked, while we rested, but since the Aztec spectators were cheering me by name, he wasn't complaining.

"It's a long game," I said. "And basically, they're the better team. I figure our best chance is to get their two front guys really spooked by the ball; then they'll stop scoring and we'll start."

"I didn't think Mixtecs played that strategy," Sam said.

"I'm an Aztec today," I said.

So that became our game plan in the second quarter. Sam, the Tarascan, and Chipmunk all joined in creaming Smoke and Windy every chance they got, and those were two sore boys as we went along. Pretty soon, as a matter of fact, they got mad and started hitting the ball at us instead of the wall, mostly at me. The spectators loved it.

Just before the half, 1-Smoke faked a chest shot, dropped the ball to his hip, caught me off-guard, and really cracked it into my cheek. I could hear some damn little bone break.

At the half the forwards on both sides were all bruised up and sore, but the score was low: 41–27.

Their favor.

"Now we start scoring?" Sam asked. He was worried. "They're ball-shy all right, but they've got a hell of a lead."

"Right. We score," I said.

"Come on, Zapper," said the Chipmunk. He was a bright-eyed little guy, and not a bad ballplayer.

They crossed us up. That left-corner back, a kid who grew up imitating the way I walked down the street, and whom I'd trained myself as a ballplayer, took Windy's place in the front line and was phenomenal. He could go high in the air like a deer, and his scoring shots were all hard and high, real stingers, like mine should have been.

I was trying too, of course, and not doing bad, but they'd started well ahead and we weren't closing the gap. In the fourth quarter, it began to look like we were going to lose. Sam was sullen and rattled, missing easy defensive plays. The Tarascan got wild, and was trying to boom them all the way down to the back wall from his defensive position for scores—doing it just often enough so you couldn't tell him to stop. As for the Chipmunk, he wasn't a bad ballplayer, as I've said, but he just wasn't the same class of player as the guys on my old team. They were playing together; we were four wild individuals.

I was scoring pretty hot by then, accurate as I'd ever been, threading it between the four to the wall when I couldn't get it high, but there were only a couple of dots to go in the game and we were still nine points down. We needed more time, and I could see by the sun we wouldn't have it.

They called time-out.

"Quetza H. Coatl, Zap," Sam said.

"Don't worry," I said. "Next serve, drop back and let me have your corner if it comes your way."

"What for?"

"We gotta win this bastard," I said.

Smoke served, his usual lob over my head, but as the ball left his hip I started back for it. I got it just where I thought I would, along the right wall, and went up. I fired it, not with my hip off the leather but with a bare thigh, straight on, stinging, right along the wall and rising, so hard I crashed against the wall and fell. But I knew from the cheer that I'd done it: the ball had traveled fast along the wall, rising, into an arc, right through the center of the stone ring without touching.

Pandemonium. Spectators running away so that the supporters of our team wouldn't grab their cloaks. Laughing and screaming, collecting of bets up there by the Aztecs, and as I lay there, something floated down and partly covered me on the ground.

It was the troupial cloak. Nose was an honest old general. I lay under it, with 6-Rain smiling sadly down to see.

I figured I was a free man, now. Sam came over, helped me up, and hugged me. Chipmunk and the Tarascan banged my back and yelled.

Then the three fell in, and marched me back to my cell.

"What the hell?" I asked.

"Orders, Zap," Sam said. "That's all I know. Orders."

I was a unique guy all right. There weren't too many prisoners around the country keeping warm with troupial cloaks.

3.

When Brill got down to the lobby there was an Operator number in Rosetta to call, an unfamiliar calling number with it. That meant it wasn't from home, and he didn't have much enthusiasm for returning it.

He supposed he'd better. Gave the details to the desk clerk, and sat down with a beer to wait. After a time the bellboy came to get him. Brill, carrying the beer, lit a cigar and went to see what the hell.

The voice that answered when he said, "Bob Brill speaking" was only half-familiar.

"Bob," it said. "I need help. I really do."

"Is that Tommy?"

"They didn't tell you? Yes, it is."

"Oh."

"Bob, can you hear me?"

"Sure."

"We've got tax trouble," Tommy said. "I need an affidavit from you."

"You talking about something formal?"

"Oh God, yes," Tommy said. "They're right on our neck."

"Who do you mean by *our* neck?"

"Yours and mine."

"Tell me about it."

"It's about the boat, Bob."

"The Big Stinkpot?" Brill asked. For six years, much to Brill's annoyance, Tommy had maintained one of the larger Chris Craft cruisers in the area. He'd bought it secondhand, for the price of a small house; used it weekends to take his family aimlessly (in Brill's view) up and down the river, contributing a good deal in the way of noise and engine fumes. It was something of a party boat, furthering Tommy and Martha's local social ambitions, and had more recently been at the service of Donnie Rebranch's political career. There'd been talk of Donnie going up and down the river in the spring to make campaign stops, taking politicians with him in the manner of a campaign train.

With a sort of chill, Brill knew what was coming, so he said it:

"Tommy, you been writing off your boat expenses as business entertaining?"

"Well, part of them," Tommy said. "Yes."

"Like how much a year?"

"Bob, you know how it is. I spend about four grand a year, on upkeep and operating and depreciation. And, well, the first year I put eight hundred dollars down as business entertaining. And then when that was okay, I kind of increased it. The last three years I've been going ninety percent on it."

Brill made a calculation, and said: "You're talking about fifteen, sixteen thousand dollars, Tommy, over five years?"

"Yes."

"Christ almighty," said Brill.

"Bob, what I'd like. If you can do it. Is an affidavit, saying that I did entertain clients. You know? Yours too, sometimes. Well, when I first got it and Trump was your client, remember? We spent a Sunday on the boat and you and Trump were fishing for . . . walleyed pickerel?"

"Walleyed pike," Brill said. "Tommy, that's the only time I was ever on your boat."

"But I asked you. I mean, if you could say that . . . well, you see, the books show we were splitting everything fifty-fifty. But since you had the building, and the name, and were established, it would make sense, wouldn't it? That I contributed something more than you did, somewhere. I'd have been willing to, since you were being so fair. So it would have been in business entertainment. I thought you could say in the affidavit—I mean it would be understood that it's from Mexico and you don't have exact records. That sometimes clients came in the boat for weekends at your duck shooting place on the river? Like Martin? I don't want you to swear to a lot of lies . . ."

"Just one or two, Tommy?"

"Bob, however you'd put it—look, I'm willing to pay this thing. It isn't that. I'll borrow and pay it, if I have to. But if you could say enough to make it a matter of law, a matter of judgment. So there's no intent to defraud, just bad judgment on my part? I can get the money to pay it, Bob."

"Yeah. I know you can."

"Bob, listen to this. I found a house mover, and some masons. And I bought the lot behind your building. Now listen. Nothing's happened there yet. I've got that lot. I can have your building moved back far enough so they can widen the street, without tearing the Brill law office down."

"Just one or two lies, huh, Tommy?"

"Things were so tough when I started doing it, and . . . if you'd liked the boat better. I thought you'd like it. We could have used it for entertaining a whole lot more than we did."

"It's my fault," Brill said.

"I'm not saying that. Martha loved the boat, and the kids."

"Do you know what I'd have to do to make an affidavit?" Brill said. "I'd have to be away from what I'm doing three days. To go to Mexico City, to the consular office at the embassy to get it acknowledged properly."

"Bob, I could go to jail on this. I could get disbarred."

"That's right," Brill said. "I don't much like you, Tommy, but I wouldn't want to see that. Who's the tax examiner?"

"Kristopoulos."

"I see."

"Will you do it?"

"I doubt if what I could do without really lying would be enough," Brill said.

"I knew you'd be that way," Tommy said.

"If I can think of any way to help, I will," Brill said.

"Please, Bob."

"Let me think," Brill said. "Good-bye, Tommy."

But he could, of course, and knew it. What he would have to do was make the affidavit, make it general enough to hold them off. And he'd have to go back, and what would happen then was perfectly simple: he would use up his reputation with Kristi, a man with whom he had dealt back and forth, hard on both sides and honorably on both sides, for years, to tell whatever minimum of lies were necessary to keep Tommy out of jail and in practice.

Whatever happened, and whatever he did, he didn't want the Brill law office saved as a gift from Tommy Rebranch, and that told him something: he didn't really want to go back to Rosetta, Illinois, and resume the practice of law there. Not really.

4.

Why the hell Willa's finding him in the basement at Photomex should have had any bearing on what he eventually did about Tommy and other matters, Brill could not have said, but there was some nutty relationship there he never really figured out. Being Brill he probably didn't try very hard, willing enough to accept the conclusion of causality, leaving nits to the pickers thereof.

They used to ask Jim Thorpe, "What's the best day you ever had, Jim?" and Thorpe would say, "Don't know that. I was in a lot of games in a lot of places." Remember what you can use; analyze what helps; the past is a blueprint for more past like it.

Brill was pulling prints in the darkroom for Minnegerode, who'd been too tired to stay up any longer doing it. Pulling them, washing them, putting them on the drier—something any jerk could do—when there was a knock on the darkroom door. Brill said he'd be out in a minute, and a female voice said please, it was important.

It was Willa. She was waiting in the basement of Photomex, a shop which let the archaeologists use its facilities sometimes after hours. Brill was done. He turned out the lights, and said:

"Come upstairs."

They stood in the shop at street level, with light coming in through the steel grill and the plate glass from the streetlights. There was a big, full-size cutout, a Kodak display ad of a girl in a white swimsuit, cutting through some cutout water on water skis. Waving. Willa stood in front of it, and the waving hand kept appearing over her head when she bobbed it talking.

"Bob," she said. "I'm petrified. The little fool waited till after sign-in, and she's gone riding off on a motor scooter she rented, with a blanket."

"Nancy?"

"She's been saying she wanted to sleep out there. At the site."

"More likely has a date," Brill said.

"She's gone. She's gone to do it. That one-eyed Indian. She'll be raped."

"You don't want to tell Mr. Pederson?"

"Oh no. He came. He made bed check. I told him she was in the bathroom."

"I don't have a car," Brill said. "I only rent one weekends."

"The bus?"

"I'll have to get the key from Newman. I'll have to tell him why."

At this she started to cry, this tall, severe girl, in love and unloved probably. And Miss Kodak kept smiling and waving, over her head.

"All right," Brill said, "I won't tell Newman," and became a bus thief. He'd defended enough kids who jacked ignitions on cars to know how to do it on a rather simple old bus.

Goddamn Tennessee Jack Minnegerode. Says he's tired. Leaves me to pull his prints while he's off pulling pants.

Brill'd better go and get them back. They should have had time by now to cure their itch, and Gary, fretful as he was about these things, was quite capable of torturing himself by going back to check the girls' room again. Wanted to spare Gary; was jealous of the dig, an enemy of its disruptions; finally, Willa could be right. It seemed unlikely Nancy'd go out there by herself, but on the other hand, Minnegerode hadn't seemed to be doing all that well. Maybe she *was* alone.

He drove out to the highway, thinking about Jacinto, the one-eyed Indian, and decided he might need a little help with Jacinto. He stopped at a shack-cantina on the edge of town and bought a fifth of mescal to help.

The hillside east of Huitzo looked eerie and deserted in the moonlight, and by the time he got there he'd persuaded himself that there might be some sort of chance, after all, that Jacinto was capable of raping Nancy or at least giving her a nasty time. He kind of wished he'd stopped off for his machete.

He stopped the bus by the watchman's shack, got out, and almost immediately Jacinto materialized out of the moonlight on the path in front of him.

"Don Roberto," he said. "*Buscale la señorita*?"

"*Por supuesto*," said Brill.

"*Que bueno. Ja estan juntos, por alli.*"

Estan? That was plural. And yes, there by the watchman's shack were two little motorbikes, side by side.

Jacinto seemed very glad indeed to see him, to be relieved of whatever the responsibility was, and Brill offered him a shot of mescal.

Jacinto declined, explaining that he took no alcohol. He said he was a Jehovah's Witness convert. There'd been a team through town two years ago, and Jacinto was the leader of the dozen converts they'd made.

It explained his being watchman, all the crew having been selected by the alcalde. One from the Jehovah's Witness group, apparently, deserved an appointment; matter of representation, but it was the outsider's appointment he deserved.

Every week (Jacinto wanted very much to talk) he got literature in the mail. He was unable to read, though the tracts were in Spanish, but replied occasionally anyway, using the public letter-writer in Oaxaca to dictate to. And every night he sat out here alone, with a single barreled, hammer-action shotgun across his knees, witnessing Jehovah with one eye.

So Brill took a long, lonely pull off the jug, stuck it in his jacket pocket, and went on up the hill.

He went first to Mound 3, his own patio, but there was no one there. He climbed the next big mound, overlooking the temple platform, and saw them, but it wasn't Minnegerode; it was Nancy and Little Gonzalez, leaning against facing column pedestals in the moonlight, the small-limbed, almost beardless boy, the girl, both quite nude. A baby Adam and Eve, stoned on pot, so new in the world the difference between them in gender seemed hardly to have grown distinct yet.

There were blankets spread together, and since they'd been here for an hour, according to Jacinto, they might be ready to leave the garden.

Brill climbed quietly down again, went partway back along the path, and turned again toward the temple, making plenty of noise. In fact, singing.

On the way back to Oaxaca, Little Gonzalez spoke of marriage, and of going to California afterward to join Cesar Chavez in the grape strike. Pervert Brill. His sympathy was with the poor and hungry. Willa.

5.

The next morning he told Pederson he'd learned he had to go to Mexico. He'd decided to go ahead and make the affidavit Tommy wanted; he doubted whether it would be enough to save Tommy's neck, but he could mention the time he and Trump went fishing on the boat and perhaps remember enough more that was fact about Tommy's use of the boat to cast some doubt.

If he didn't do that much, Brill thought, then he'd suspect his own motives for being unwilling.

Pederson was delighted, somewhat to Brill's dismay. Sandoval had to go to Mexico too, where he would try to get their digging permit altered to allow proper excavation of the round mound on which work was now almost stopped. Consequently, the dig would pay for car rental and for Sandoval's expenses.

"That may sound silly when it's your own money, Bob," Gary said. "But otherwise I'd have to send him up by plane, I suppose."

They were away by nine. Brill drove as far as Yanhuitlan, where they stopped for coffee. He was enjoying the Mexican's company; ever since Brill had been unflapped by the hammer and sickle, Sandoval had been personally friendly, and this morning had been actually loquacious, pointing out mounds and roads to sites almost constantly as they drove north on the InterAmerican Highway.

He had even managed to sound boyish as they went through Huitzo and could see the track up the hill which led to their own site, where already Gary and Newman, Willa, the colonel, Berko and Minnegerode, Adam, Eve, and the rest would be covered with dust in that curious state of suspended excitement and workless work in which most hours of the days were spent.

"It's like a holiday from school," Sandoval said, and then, in Spanish, began deploring his countrymen's general ignorance of their proud prehistory, Mexico's need to know and take pride.

Brill's comprehension of Spanish spoken at a normal conversational rate was pretty good in the morning. It was only toward the end of the day, when he was physically tired, that he began failing to understand. Even so, he realized, as they finished their coffee and Sandoval offered to drive for a while, that he had missed something:

"From here to Huahuapan will put us in the middle of the second day." Sandoval said it with a grin. He was a trim, serious man with a black moustache, in his thirties, and grinning wasn't one of his usual expressions.

"The second day?"

"What I was telling on the way up." In English now. "The greatest race."

Of course. The legendary Mexican road race, held during the fifties, when Sandoval was growing up.

"When I am a boy, I will tell you the name of every winner, second place and third, for every class of car, and what they drove." With a slight scuffle, Brill managed to pay for the coffee and they stepped onto the street. Sandoval gestured.

"Past here, they came. All across Mexico, from south to north. My friends and I would go to watch them pass, then take the bus at night while the drivers are resting to find a watching place farther up, on the next leg."

As they got in the car, Brill had a sudden, premonitory wish for a seat belt.

"The first day," Sandoval adjusted the seat, "they drove in the south, from San Cristobal to Tehuantepec, over the mountain." Sandoval's hand went over a mountain. "Into Oaxaca, fast on the final flat from Mitla turn." The mountain-climbing hand became a fist, and hit the other hand, crossing the finish at Oaxaca. "Ha, ha." Sandoval laughed, grinned, started the motor, shifted, and crouched over the wheel, gripping it strongly. "Now. We are in the second day."

Vrooom. They were out onto the street and out through Huahuapan, going around a bus in first, a truck in second, and a heavy older car in third. "My driving does not molest you, Mr. Bob?"

As they came to the first big mountain curve, he shifted down expertly and took it at high speed, turning the wheel in little bites, each causing a tiny squeal from the tires.

"I trained, but when I was ready, no more road race," Sandoval said. "This car," he recovered from the curve, and Brill felt he could do with quite a lot less conversation if they were going to race to Mexico, "is not for racing, but will perhaps surprise you. Cars go around curves, only drivers sometimes stop turning them from fear."

Help, I'm a prisoner in a road race that hasn't been held for fifteen years.

"I will not drive so fast," said Sandoval, driving fast. "But when I trained, they would nail a tin can to the accelerator, no? You put your foot inside it, and you cannot go to the brake." Wham, he went to the brake as they came up behind another truck, swung out and around it. "My teacher was co-driver for a Porsche in the road race, a German. My father hires him to give lessons. His job: they would drive the whole five-day course before the race. Once frontwards, once back. And he will mark the map, how fast the curve, how steep the hill, what is on the other side. Then he must follow the map, hardly look at the road, and tell the driver in the race what speeds and gears have been determined; and the driver is not to judge for himself by looking far forward, only at the immediate road."

"Be a little risky for stray burros up there, wouldn't it?" Brill asked.

Immediately, hurt, Sandoval dropped the speed by twenty miles an hour. "You would like to resume driving?" He asked stiffly.

"No, of course not," Brill said.

The other man was silent, deliberately slow.

"I rather enjoy your driving," Brill lied. "You're very good."

"So?"

(To hell with it, Brill thought. Go ahead and drive the sonofabitch if you like to, Tomás.)

He said, "I think I'll take a nap."

He closed his eyes, but sleep was entirely out of the question.

6.

I was awakened, the morning after the game, by considerable shuffling and thumping outside the door of the cell.

My cheek hurt like fire and my sense of hospitality wasn't particularly keen: that's probably why I was just a little short in greeting the old acquaintance who stood in the doorway with Fudge, the pride of the Aztec merchant-spy fleet.

The old acquaintance, even fatter than Fudge and a head taller, was 5-Tiger, the Zapotec priest who cut my father's heart out when I was a kid. He had a round head and a big, round, drooping nose. I remember hearing that when 5-Tiger was still a kid in calmecac they called him the Mayan Idiot.

"Well, my boy," he said. "Fancy meeting you in a place like this. Not very comfortable quarters for a king's son."

Behind them were a whole bunch of assistant-priest-looking guys, carrying clothes and food and stuff, but I didn't register what that meant right away.

"The quarters suited me all right up to a minute ago," I said. "The smell's just gotten bad in here."

"Tut-tut," Fudge said. "5-Tiger tells me he's a family friend."

"That's a nasty-looking cheek, boy," 5-Tiger said. "We'll have to put a little çacacili on it for you right away."

"You got a license to practice medicine?" I asked.

"Zap," Fudge said. "5-Tiger is a very accomplished priest. He's been assigned to us to help get our religious practices set up here at the garrison. Rude soldiers, far from home, you know. We appreciate his serving as our chaplain."

"I've been given the honorary name of Quetzalcoatl," Tiger said. "Perhaps you'd better use that name."

"5-Tiger, baby," I said. "You're a damn wonder."

"I'd show a little respect, Zap, if I were you," Fudge said. "We had you down for the Xipe festival, and you know what that means."

Sure I did. The bastards would have flayed me alive, and old 5-Tiger would have got to walk around wearing my skin. I could remember seeing him in Xipe parades, too, when I was little, and he never once found anybody with a skin big enough to fit over his fat belly.

"Why don't you flay somebody your own size?" we used to yell at him.

"So you're an Aztec now, 5-Tige-Quetza-Baby," I said. "Have they taught you any neat new ways of skin-stretching?"

He chose to answer seriously. "We can learn more from the Aztecs than you realize, my boy," he said. "We and the Mixtecs may still be the teachers in arts and crafts but Aztec technology is doing things you never dreamed of."

"Tell him about the dedication," Fudge said.

"When they dedicated the new temple to the war god in Tenochtitlan last year," Fudge said, "they made a real breakthrough, and I was privileged to see it. They sacrificed twenty thousand captives between sunrise and sundown, on a single pyramid."

I admit I was impressed. I mean, our best boys can't go more than nine sacrifices an hour (5-Tiger would have to hump to beat four)—you get a priest who can average a hundred a day on a three-day festival, and you've got yourself some priest.

So in a one-day burst, for any collection of priests to hit twenty thousand in a one-day burst—well, they'd have had to have it organized so that two hundred priests could all hit a hundred on the same day, in the same restricted work area. Man, that's sacrificing.

But I didn't want to show I was impressed so I said, "What a pair of sweethearts. Going to skin me out, were you?"

"Your grandstand play in the ball game saved you, Zap. You're getting a break. It was his honor 5-Tiger Quetzalcoatl's idea, too."

"Your family line's too good for you to end up as a rug," 5-Tiger said. "This is going to be a most civilized garrison here. We're introducing the Tecatzlipoca ritual." He paused a moment for me to show delight. "Here's your flute, my son. I understand you're rather good on it."

"I play a little."

"There are your eight priests out there." So that's who they were. "They'll see that you have everything you want, starting tomorrow. Today they've got to work on getting suitable quarters ready for you, and we have a call out for some virgins. It may take a little time. I think today we'll just have you warm up, though—they'll help you dress, and you can take your first stroll around the city, playing the flute."

"I know the rest," I said. "I'm a regular little jadite god for a year. I get four great chicks, after a while, don't I? to keep me company, night and day. And at the end of the year, it's good-bye, girls. Out and lead the last parade, everybody cheering, as I go off with those eight jokers to this dumpy little pyramid back here, and up the steps, breaking a flute on each step, right? Up at the top my eight true friends grab me, spread me, pluck out the ticker. And oh boy, they have to carry me back downstairs, instead of the old rolleroo. Big mark of respect."

"Zap!" Fudge said. "How many people ever get to be a god for a year?"

"He isn't worth it," 5-Tiger said. "Sacrilegious young pup. Let's go back before the council on this. They might reconsider the Xipe . . . such a moving ceremony."

"No use," Fudge said, sorry about it. "Nose and Grandad worked out the Tecatzlipoca for him."

"My skin wouldn't fit you anyway, Fatty," I told the Tiger. "If you put it on, I think the arms would still have strength enough left to strangle you."

5-Tiger looked at me. "I'll eat those arms," he said. "They'll be nice and plump after a year of feasting. And with them I'll drink pulque out of your skull, my young friend." He touched my temple. "A bit of turquoise would look nice here, don't you think?"

He was so close I couldn't stop myself. I smashed him in the nose. "Don't touch your god, you old fool," I yelled, in a stern, terrible voice. "That finger will wither by evening."

Had the satisfaction of scaring them, anyway. I figured if I was a god, I might as well start exercising prerogatives. I let the assistant priests dress me up, and took a stroll, playing some mountain music on the flute. The assistants might have been there to serve me, but it was clear they were there to guard me, too, so that the people who stopped and bowed their heads as I walked by didn't cheer me up all that much.

Brill opened his eyes. Sandoval was still glowering at the steering wheel. Brill closed his eyes.

Night came. I'd had a decent supper, but my cheek was keeping me awake. They'd spread the çacacili on it—not 5-Tiger who didn't come back but someone he sent—and you know the way it hardens. Like glue. Acted as a cast, I suppose, but it still hurt.

I was lying there in the dark, thinking of nineteen hideous ways of killing 5-Tiger, when I heard a scratching at the door. Then the latch moved, and it opened very quietly.

There in the moonlight stood Banana Girl, with a dripping knife in her hand, and lying dead on his back on the ground, just as she'd rolled him off herself, with his loincloth down around his ankles, was my guard. It was the little eagle knight I'd been calling Chipmunk, who played beside me in the ball game.

"Go, Zap," she whispered. "Here." Pressed the bloody knife in my hand and a wet, desperate kiss on my mouth.

"You're coming," I said.

"No. They gave me tochtepeton in maguey wine. For what? A joke? My hands don't move right. Soon I'll start breaking up inside . . ." And she ran, not too steadily. I was starting after her when she went around the corner and I heard a man's voice in Nahuatl yell, "Here. I've got her. Come here."

I grabbed my troupial cloak, my jade, and, holding onto Banana Girl's knife, with her gift of blood on it, I ran the other way, toward the City of the Dead. Monte Albán.

7.

Once at a party Pete Canaday had said to Brill: "That's a pretty suit, Counselor. Is that a Hong Kong suit?"

And Brill, scowling: "No, it's a King Kong suit."

A recitation of that exchange could hardly be expected to divert Tomás Sandoval M., now going flat-out on a short, uncrowded straight, fighting for seconds of corrected time.

Once Gary Pederson claimed to have swatted the state record housefly . . .

"Mrs. Light," Martin said. "Judging by the ring finger."

Brill found the water in that stream of consciousness unsuitable for raising native small-mouth bass, and sighed.

8.

I was almost up the mountain, and exhausted, when an arrow hit me in the shoulder from behind.

It was a heavy blunt, made to stop and bruise, not to penetrate. You use arrows like that on big birds, geese and herons. It knocked me down.

In extraordinary silence men appeared in the night from behind deserted buildings and surrounded me. Without a word they got me up and led me east a quarter mile, then into a small building, then into a hole inside and down a flight of steps, cut in dirt. I noticed there was a cover lying in the room to conceal the hole.

A stone door moved, and the man behind gave me a shove. I was in a torchlit tomb, at the end of which sat a woman on a throne made of skulls.

"*Schnell, schnell,*" said a hoarse German voice, and those short, sharp noises of protesting tires pulled Brill from a rather happy doze.

Tomás Sandoval M. was totally absorbed in his driving. "*Ja,*" and he shifted. "*Was? Ja.*" His co-driver, sitting in Brill's lap with the intricately marked chart, must have given him the speed and decision on technique for the coming curve. The champ waited, hand on the stick shift. Grunted. Hit the brake, threw the rear end into a brief, controlled four-wheel drift, recovered with a real squawk from the tires this time, as they skidded the curve and speeded up again.

Fascinated, oddly detached, and a little horrified, Brill watched the driver through half-closed eyes. A steep up-grade. With a curled lip for the floundering Maserati, the champ burst past it and swung into lane again.

Brill couldn't watch . . . the woman, yes. On the throne of skulls, was? Ummm, totally nude . . .

Totally nude except that her body was set with stones, like a statue. In her navel, an extraordinary green jewel, such as traders, making a year's journey south to the wide land beyond the narrow land, sometimes bring. There was a pound of worked silver hanging from each ear; her nipples had been removed and replaced by two huge garnets, each tooth was inset with a spot of perfect jade, in her cheeks and on her bosom sparkled obsidian moles, and she had a turquoise mosaic nose.

"You may kiss me," she said, extending her foot, and on the delicate silver instep I kissed her.

"You may rise," she said, and called me by the full name I hadn't heard in years: "9-Serpent 'Feather Serpent.' "

She came down off the handsome skull chair and touched my cheek: "Is it broken?"

I nodded.

"Some quack put çacacili on it," she said. "Don't tell me. 5-Tiger?"

"Yes, ma'am," I said.

"He thinks traction's the answer to everything," she said. "We'll have to peel it off, and fix you up with some cozcaquauhxiutl. You know what it is?"

I felt pretty stupid having to admit I didn't.

"It grows in Chiconauhtla and Tepepulco," she explained, clarifying things. "But we have seeds here to sow in the low Mixteca." In the eye-sockets of a life-size clay head without a body, tilted back, she showed me very fine seeds, drying.

"Is that your home? The low Mixteca?" I asked.

She shrugged. "I was born here in the City of the Dead," she said. "I am Sorrow's sister, and my dead brother was Joy." She was pretty weird. "This has always been my home. Outlaws and outcasts come to me from many tribes, to be their queen."

"But you speak Zapotec?"

"And Mixtec, too, 9-Serpent 'Feather Serpent,' " she said, in that tongue, but with an accent I had never heard before. I knew by some kind of intuition that the accent was removed from me, not in place but in time.

And I knew by glancing back over my shoulder that we were alone now in the tomb, with the door sealed.

She began to sing.

Mockingly, sadly, softly, some ancient song I couldn't translate in that old, old Mixtec, but when she changed from singing to chanting, her chant was something like this:

> We are the true Mixtec, the lowland, warmland
> Sons and daughters of Olmeca, gone a thousand years.
> Our fathers hewed great heads of stone
> And carried them, such was their strength, to deep jungles.
> And met Gods there. Our slaves and our weak nephews,
> Fleeing to the mountains from the fate of the Rubber People
> Became the Mist People, became the Cloud People, became Ñusabi,
> Became your people.

Only a few of us are left,
Only I am left, living in my tomb.
Here in the tomb I live, here I shall die,
But not while brave young men still come to nourish me
With their love.

Her meaning was clear enough, even before she gestured slowly with her hand and arm that I was to climb up and lie down on a trestle made of oak boards, already polished to a deep shine by the movement of young male shoulders and buttocks across it.

I figured if all the other trestle polishers could work things out with her, turquoise nose or not, so could I. So I went out flat on my back, just as she indicated.

With something or other she dissolved the cast on my cheek, and the stuff she put on to replace it was wonderfully cool. Then she came floating, or at least I had a strong psychological impression of levitation, up, saying, "Be still. Be very still," and moved through the air a slow and golden leg to meet rigidity and find surcease.

Then she let me sit up, sat beside me on the trestle and said: "Tell me about the new alliance."

I told her, and she didn't like it.

"That would mean more Aztecs in the valley. What we need is fewer."

"How would you go on zero Aztecs?" I said, and she smiled.

"Will you go to Zaachila, and tell Cosijoesa exactly what you've told me?"

I'd been thinking about trying to have a talk with Cozy Joe.

"We can get you there," she said, and clapped her hands. The door opened and in came attendants, and served me the richest cup of cocoa I ever drank in my life. "You go now."

"Will I see you again?"

"You will see me again in Achiutla," she said, but I had no idea what she meant, for hadn't she claimed never to leave her tomb?

9.

They had lunch in Huahuapan, quesadillas made with beautiful green tortillas and sharp cheese, and, though Brill considered ordering cocoa, cold Dos Equis beer.

Sandoval was still a little formal, but Brill thought he knew a simple way to restore the good feeling with which they'd started the trip. He let the Mexican reach for and pay the check. That made them host and guest, so that Brill could say, as he himself resumed driving:

"That was quite a ride, Tomás. I feel as if we'd hit the beach at Iwo Jima together."

Sandoval, relaxed, laughed at that, and Brill was able to speak of something which had finally crystallized for him; he realized it had been on his mind since he'd visited Giengola, way down by the Isthmus.

"This road, Tomás. I've been thinking about it ever since I came to Mexico, hearing about it. Seeing it today with you. Along it there are several huge sites, like Monte Albán and Mitla and Cholula. And there must be two or three dozen more, as large and attractive as Yagul, say, which haven't been dug."

Sandoval agreed.

"And there must be literally hundreds more small ones, like the one we're working at. And down at the end, Giengola. The battlefield. What I've been thinking is, the road itself and what's along it, is like a great cross-section of times and cultures, isn't it? Simply because it's always been the road? And it could be, I don't know, a great archaeological park. Hundreds of miles long. The Route of the Pyramids. I know what I'm talking about would seem to be mostly for tourists, but suppose you could demonstrate the whole cultural sequence—including Spanish Colonial and revolutionary Mexico—in terms of a road. People could do what modern tourists do—that is, get in their cars and live in it for a few days. And in deciding where to dig, where to reconstruct, things like that—well, to use Newman's favorite word, it could be interdisciplinary. Interinstitutional. I mean, you could select some places for their scientific interest, some for historical reasons, some just because they were pretty . . ."

Brill talked on. It was a vision, and he did not find himself comfortable trying to describe a vision about whose details he knew so little. But Sandoval said, being practical:

"You know why there is so much money for classical archaeology, in Greece and Italy? Because it's good tourist business. This is not so bad. To create things for travelers to see is a way of teaching, my friend."

10.

Coming out of the U.S. Embassy in Mexico City, his document officially dated, stamped, and acknowledged, Brill crossed the wide street and bought a bottle of absinthe.

According to the tale that went with the sale, the great Pernod absinthe-making family of France, having bought the formula from Dr. Ordinaire in 1797, had got its feelings hurt when their beverage was made illegal after more than a century in France. Melancholy, wrapped in cloaks, they had come to Mexico where a new and tolerant people permitted them to keep the secret distilling methods at the service of humanity. Since Brill knew that Pernod anisette was still a going item in France—and Illinois, for that matter—and had heard that the firm could make absinthe legally enough in Spain, he doubted the romance; but, never having had the stuff before, treasured the bottle which he opened in his hotel room.

It looked, smelled, and tasted like Pernod, and he had one with ice and considered his remarkable resemblance to Toulouse-Lautrec in the mirror. Then he took the nap which had eluded him in the car while Sandoval was driving, and slept for over an hour.

When he woke, his hand went like a snake for the bottle. He watched it move sinuously across the covers, its clever fingers opening just in time to seize the bottle by its neck, its coils constricting tight enough so the hand could bring the thing to its master.

"Good work," Brill said, wanting to reward a hand like that, sat up and thought he would do a little determined absinthe drinking. He knew no one in Mexico City, had nothing much to do but eat supper sometime—or not eat it if he so decided. The places one might see or shop at were closed by now, he supposed. So he had a couple.

Set down the third on the cover of a blue and white, paper-covered book on the bedside table, which someone must have left in the room: *A Pocket History of Mexico*, by J. Patrick McHenry.

Who?

Brill rose, saluted, and cried: "Give me McLiberty or give me McDeath!"

And dived laughing onto the bed, rolling onto his back, accepting the enthusiastic applause of the ceiling.

The phone rang. It was Sandoval.

"Roberto," he said. "Let's take a bath."

That was a pretty nutty invitation, but when Sandoval interrupted his laughter to add that after it, they might go to the fights, and have some supper, Brill accepted, and directed his hand to close off the absinthe bottle, firmly. He couldn't have said whether it was liquor that turned him on or the legend.

It was right around six when he went out onto the street, and he was wrong about shops: they were all open and all sparkling. The street was jammed with people, smartly dressed, the waifs and beggers of the afternoon gone home now, to rest perhaps.

Brill met Sandoval at the Hotel del Prado, and they went together to the basement.

"You would like a shave?"

Brill didn't feel he needed one, but then neither, as far as he could see, did Tomás. So he said, "Fine. Why not? Let's have a drink first."

They had gin fizzes, made with egg white so they really fizzed, and carried them into the barbershop where Brill had the first barber shave he could remember since one he'd had in 1946, to celebrate being out of the army.

On the way to the steam room, for it was a Turkish bath Sandoval had meant, they picked up a couple more gin fizzes, leaving the glasses behind in the stream, and went to the center of the operation. Big, gloomy-looking Indian men in tee-shirts waited there at wooden tables, with coarse sponges.

"Always, when I have been in the field, I come here to get cleaned," Sandoval said, as if it were some sort of car-wash. "Here. You get here and you will have Manuel, El Guapo." A preposterously big and ugly man suddenly hovered over Brill. "When young, he became a picador," Sandoval said. "But the horse fell on his legs."

"Okay," Brill said, and stretched out naked, face down on the rubbing table, his pores open and his skin soft from the steam.

"Yow," he yelled, when the coarse fiber sponge started lathering into his back, yet it wasn't bad, after a moment—the scrubbing, the pummeling, the jerking of his arms, fingers, toes.

"Yeah," he said, sitting up when it was over, somewhat dazed, and followed Sandoval, his body glowing, into another room, where he was pushed without time for reflection into a small, indoor pool of ice-cold water.

"No," cried Robert Brill, but in an awful way it was exhilarating. Got out.

"Now," said Sandoval, struggling out to sit beside him on the tile. "You feel fine."

"Okay, Wow. Yeah." He was allowed to relax for a moment and he watched the other patrons going through, Mexican businessmen, he supposed, and professionals, putting themselves in shape for Friday night out. There was no one else around with conspicuously white skin like his, and he supposed that for the first time he realized that he was in an Indian country. Indians. It pleased him.

"Let's find our bartender," Brill said. "I need more egg white."

When they arrived at the fights, Sandoval whipping the little rented Ford through traffic and laughing like a madman, the preliminaries were already on.

Two rather large, slow men, hit at each other, while the bored crowd yelled at them as if they were homosexual burlesque dancers. The next bout, the fighters were smaller and the crowd pleasanter to them.

Each pair, as they went through the three-rounders, was smaller, lighter, and faster than the pair before.

"Is it always this way?" Brill asked.

"Which way, Roberto?"

"The big men are first, the small ones in the main events. We do it the other way around."

"But the big men are not athletes. They are not fast. They are not special men. Anybody can move as they do."

Brill thought about soccer. It was dexterity people wanted to see here, not power.

After the main event, Sandoval inquired if Brill was hungry. Brill was ravenous, but made the error of saying he would be happy to eat whenever Tomás was hungry.

"Good. We go to the fronton."

Brill hoped that was a restaurant; it was not. It was the jai-alai court, where Sandoval, hardly even willing to stop for a fast tequila, entered wildly into the betting. Bookies circulated in the stands, taking bets after each point, as the odds changed. Sandoval bet nearly every time.

The bookie, ten rows away, would cry his deal, Sandoval's hand would go up, and the bookie would toss a tennis ball, with a slit cut in it, into which Sandoval put folded money and from which he took a slip recording the transaction.

The action on the court, to which the crowd paid very little attention, was curiously fast and beautiful, and Brill at least watched, not understanding how to bet. It seemed to him Tomás was losing quite a lot.

During the second game, the last of the evening, for they'd arrived quite late, Brill excused himself to find a men's room and found, in addition to it, a café which was part of the fronton. He got a tequila, a menu, and a beer, ordered, in a whimsical mood, squid "cooked in its own ink," and found it delicious.

Walked back to the stands, past the parimutuel windows, carrying a beer for Sandoval, and arrived in time to see his friend tearing up a double handful of bet slips.

"Ay," he said. "It cannot happen but it did. Six points ahead, and we lose."

"I'm glad," Brill said, with a smile. "I was betting outside, at the window, and won. So I can buy supper."

The squid was only the beginning of what he felt like eating.

At the Gran Taxco, a restaurant with three waiters to every table, they ate miraculous shrimp fried in batter with a green, foamy, garlicky sauce, and after them red snapper.

"This is huachinango," Sandoval said. "This is the best, which comes from the west coast, not the east. When my family has important guests for dinner, they do not serve meat or turkey. The cook makes huachinango from the west coast, baked in orange juice and onions."

"A Mississippi catfish," Brill said, "is pretty good. But not what you would serve important guests."

Huachinango was the best fish he'd ever eaten.

"For late supper, you must have turkey mole. You have had mole?"

Late? It was after eleven, and Brill said: "Sir, consider me wined, dined, and ready to recline."

"No." Sandoval wouldn't hear of it. There was a place, wherein he held a membership, had had a charge account for years, wherein the girls were so beautiful, would not 'bberto wish? Here was the thing: Sandoval's friends went there, and he did not wish to see them tonight, for certain reasons, for then he would have to spend tomorrow with them, surely 'bberto understood? But he would phone this place, a sort of club, and leave 'bberto there to enjoy himself as he wished?

'bberto said he really was a little tired really from Oaxaca, and Tomás said he was a dog, and winked.

Brill, swallowing a yawn, drank some black coffee, a cognac which he hadn't ordered. Another coffee. A cognac that he did order, and the two men walked out on the street. Something in the cool night, the thin air, the feeling of festivity in the city, revived him; besides which wouldn't Tomás be hurt if he really insisted on going to bed so early? Only midnight.

They were in the car, not returning to his hotel, of course, but going to the Lomas, and Brill held, without quite wishing to, confidential information: there was a young lady. They were going to pick her up. She worked as the hostess for an elegant restaurant in the Lomas, but more significantly, Tomás Sandoval M., archaeologist, communist, general's son, father of two, and sports fan, paid her rent, in a *casa chica* in the San Angel Inn district.

Brill was fascinated into some degree of wakefulness. He'd never known a man who actually kept a woman before. He supposed they existed, in the States, in cities; in Rosetta and places like it, it was neither possible nor necessary, certainly not for a young, trim, lively man like Sandoval.

So: now 'bberto understood things Tomás' brother did not even know. That Tomás and his Maria Eugenia would spend tomorrow at the *casa chica*, and therefore Tomás' friends must not know he was in town. Sunday, Tomás would go to his parents, would be driven by his father to Cuernavaca where his wife and the boys were staying now; and would come to Oaxaca, by bus, on Sunday evening. 'bberto would not be asked, but should he be, by some Mexican acquaintance (Brill had none), he was to say that Sandoval rode here with him and back as well?

Por supuesto.

Brill expected a caricature. Brill met a lovely girl.

The restaurant in which Maria Eugenia worked looked like a Chicago cocktail lounge; the menu, which Brill looked at out of curiosity, featured in capital letters: EL NEW YORK STRIP STEAK, and the music was genuine Muzak. And as at the baths, Robert Brill was the only gringo there.

Brill hated it. So did Maru. Except that Tomás said that nickname was old-fashioned, call Maria Eugenia "Ginny"; she called him Sandy and both used, frequently, words of U.S. slang. U.S., thought Brill sadly, imperialist, jet set, slang. No; don't be sad. They have energy. They are young.

Ginny was an actress, Sandy said proudly, in Mexican movies, but not successful yet. Brill guessed that success was just exactly as far away as it must be for the pretty girls, dressed becomingly in evening clothes, who seated people in restaurants in Hollywood.

The top of a tall building, Brill wasn't sure where, was the next place they went to, another lounge, more Mexican somehow, to drink whiskey, which meant Scotch, and eat enchiladas of turkey with mole, a dark brown, bitter sauce. A trio played music that wasn't New York or Mexico, but anywhere music—a little jazzy, a little European, a little Latin, Gypsy, film score. Rather pretty, and quite soft.

It put them all three in a rather pretty, soft mood—jazzy, European, Latin, Gypsy, film score. An anywhere mood. Melancholy and close, and how the hell could Sandy (Tomás) have heard a remark from another table about Ginny (Maru) through the companionable haze?

Brill's guess was that he didn't. Maru's was that he was just a Mexican man, so many drinks and he yells a *grito* and wants to fight.

"It is not a call of joy, the *grito*, but hysterical," she said in her husky, melancholy, Latin, European, Gypsy, oh to hell with it—Brill had to get up, and see what the boys were doing out on the balcony. The boys were fighting, Sandoval's opponent in evening clothes, small both of them, like the men in the main event fights earlier.

Big, slow, nonathletic Brill, a dumb preliminary boy, collared Sandoval and pushed the other guy away, smiling. Smiling he stood between and would not let either hit the other any more—let them even pop away at his big arms—until his friends came to lead the man in dinner clothes away.

"Now, Sandy," Brill said. "Why in the world would anybody go out drinking and want to get in a fight for?"

Tomás Sandoval M. apologized, stiffly first, then with warmth, an embrace, thanks. He went to the washroom to straighten out and clean his face.

Brill, still on the balcony overlooking Mexico from the top of a skyscraper, saw Maru standing in the doorway. Sandoval went by her. She came to face Brill, and they turned together, but a foot apart, and walked, with the international sound of the piano, guitar, and alto saxophone fading behind them, to the railing overlooking the lights of the city.

After a time she asked, very quietly, in soft English: "What is it you can see, Mr. Brill? Bobbee. Out there, what do you see."

He thought and looked for a time before he answered, "I see New York City in 1910, Maru."

Sandoval joined them, and Brill said he would drop them off in San Angel.

11.

At breakfast, setting aside J. Patrick McHenry's *Short History* as being too full of absinthe to make sense, he read instead from Willey and Phillip's *Method and Theory,* one *muy* in *libro por los* swingers *que* do their thing *en la anthropología:*

> The temples, palaces and other public buildings of the Classic are of great size and elaboration, attesting to the planning, skill and labor organization of the builders.

Go, Willey, go.

> The Classic stage is also characterized by the appearance of great art styles . . .

Cool.

The Postclassic, . . . too, is urban, perhaps more so than the Classic . . .

Groovy, Phillips, let it all hang out.

There are evidences of population shiftings and migrations, of war and troubled times. A decline in the aesthetic level of the Classic and in religious architecture suggest an increasing secularization of society . . .

. . . a militaristic cast to many of the Postclassic cultures . . .

A mi me gusta escuchar ustedes funky Harvards rock *y* roll.

12.

Saw the museum again, shopped, and started for Oaxaca, and in his mind the formulations of Willey and Phillips were gradually replaced by formulations of method and theory by the great Berkowitz and Minnegerode:

"Name some other big-time theocratic civilizations, besides the pre-Columbian Classic down here. Go on. Name one."

"What do you want, Berko? Zoroastrian Persia. You want me to say Gothic Europe, don't you, you pump handle?"

Brill, no Theoretician and certainly not a Methodist, turned south for Sugartown.

13.

"Cozy Joe will see you now," the young priest said. "But make it quick, will you, Zap? He's getting married tomorrow and he's got a lot on his mind."

"Okay," I said, and went in.

He was a heavy-shouldered young guy, with a looping Zapotec nose that gave him a pleasant ugliness. I liked him right away.

"Tell it your own way, Zap, and don't pay any attention to the damn priests," he said. "How's the Olmec Queen?"

"The Queen of the City of the Dead?" I grinned, he nodded.

"I always meant to make it up there. Too busy. I guess it's quite an experience." I nodded, he grinned. "Now I'm getting married, I guess I'll have to pass it up."

"I've had another experience or two," I said, and told it all to him, starting with when I left Grandad's village to guide the so-called merchants. I didn't have to tell any of it twice. Cozy Joe caught the intricacies, and knew almost all the personalities.

Every now and then he'd interrupt to say something encouraging, like: "Hey. You got a grand slam through the ring? I wonder how they kept that news away from here."

And finally he filled in the thing I hadn't quite figured out: "The Aztecs' idea was to get as many of the new Mixtec allies as they could past here and down to Mitla, Zap, before we caught on. They could go there on pilgrimages, or by night, and be hidden in Mixtec houses till the time came to move against us from two directions, you see? The man you call Fudge is the bag man; he'd arrange things and make the payoffs. And Nose, of course, was going to take the southern command."

We talked all afternoon, and the last thing he had time to say was that the situation in the Tlaxiaco district was a bitch. "The other three parts of the Mixteca you can figure, but the boys around Tlaxiaco—shitfire. It's a bitch and always has been. How do you get along with your cousin—no, he'd be your uncle, wouldn't he?—Windy?"

"We used to be good friends," I said, and about then the young priest came in and said it was time to go to the great patio.

"You come on and sit with me, Zap," Cozy Joe said, and I did, wearing my troupial cloak for the first time publicly. With that, and a good snootful of royal pulque, I was feeling pretty elegant when the matchmaker came across the threshold with Cotton Ball on her back.

She was perfectly lovely, even if she was an Aztec, and I could see from the way she looked at him that she was crazy about Joe.

There were a bunch of speeches, and they took Cozy Joe's green feather cloak and Cotton Ball's white one, and tied them together.

Old men and old women started getting up then, one by one, dressed in stuff they hadn't had out of the trunk in years, and gave long speeches of advice. The more pulque we drank, the longer the speeches got. Cotton Ball seemed to listen seriously, or at least submissively, and Joe good-naturedly, but every now and then he'd whisper another question or observation to me that continued the conversation we'd spent all afternoon with; his mind kept working on it.

At the end Cozy Joe stood up, smiling, and took time to say to me: "Zap, I get put away for four days now before I can see her again. After that, it's apt to be a day or two before I start functioning much like a king. But I don't see how I can let the Tlaxiaco situation go for another week. I'm going to try to take action, and if it works, I'm going to want you to make a trip for me, okay?"

"Sure," I said.

"Maybe you'll wind up with 6-Rain for a bride after all."

"I'll do anything you say," I said.

"The young priest who showed you in today. He'll be coming to your quarters. Trust him. Don't trust anyone else."

It was five days after the wedding before the priest came, and I was restless. I'd been working on my jade, to pass the time, and not showing myself much on the streets of Zaachila, and not at all in the Mixtec part of town.

On the fifth day the priest came and said that everything was arranged, I was to dress like a pilgrim, leave immediately for Achiutla with a group of genuine pilgrims, and on arrival send word to Windy to meet me there.

"Windy?" I asked. "Are you sure?"

"The man you called Grandad is dead, and so is 1-Smoke, your rival," the young priest said. "Windy's in charge."

"Assassination?"

"Zaachila Indian Agency," the priest said. "ZIA. Windy's in charge. But I wouldn't go any closer than Achiutla, if I were you, until you've talked to Windy."

I joined my bunch of pilgrims, and we reached Achiutla in two days. When I got there I wanted a sure way of telling Windy who it was waiting to see him, so I hired a courier and sent my Bobala jade back home again. All the rabbits were finished.

While I was waiting, I thought I'd better keep on looking like a pilgrim, so early in the morning when the sun had cleared the mountain, and everything was sparkling, I went on my knees with the others, up the red plaster street, to see the Heart of the People.

The whole Mixteca knew it was the greatest of our jade carvings, and though I'd always wanted to, I'd never seen it before.

I'd heard it was like the great, secret heads hidden in the jungle, somehow, which none but the greatest priests have ever seen, made by our father's farthest fathers, long before we were born as Ñusabi, People of the Rain. And of course I'd seen the smaller clay heads which are made in the western lowlands and derive from the great stone heads (somehow).

People would say: "The Heart of the people? Perhaps it is like the heads in the jungle, and perhaps it is like what is in your own pocket—the little green stone figurines all boys and girls in the Mixteca carry for good luck, and most men and women, too."

I didn't know what the hell it was that made trying to describe this jade get people talking like they thought they were soothsayers, but they all did.

The figurines are those little stones, an inch or so high, that look like smooth sections cut from miniature columns. Halfway down there's generally an indentation, depending on the skill of the man who made the one you carry, indicating shoulders. Above this are features in relief, eyes and mouth, seldom any nose, perhaps an indication of headdress along the top. Below shoulder level hands may be indicated, folded across the breast, and sometimes—not too often—there are feet. I've made them for kids myself.

They make nice pocket pieces, and some of the older ones, polished by a couple of hundred years of handling, are really pretty, but you have to inherit those. They came from a time when this region was itself, before the flow of soldiers and the flow of trade.

We pilgrims reached the temple, paused, and still walking on our knees, and some bleeding from the knees now, went up stone steps, following a masked priest who led us very slowly. There were many steps, at the top a stone platform, and in its center a red plaster building with an intricately thatched roof. It looked like basketwork, and the wooden door frame was carved in geometric patterns.

We were allowed to go in, on our knees, one at a time. I had been waiting on my knees for seven bars before my turn came.

The Heart of the People.

First, the stone itself, from which it was made, was dark green almost black, yet light seemed to dwell in it as it does in crystal, and gleam from it as it does from obsidian.

It was neither a column, nor a great head, but both and more:

"You will see me again in Achiutla," she had said, and it was so. It was the Queen of the City of the Dead, my Olmec queen, but as a flawless girl, not in her personal girlhood but in the beginning of our race, the head thrown slightly back, the turquoise nose restored to flesh, the face expressing that terrible kindness faces show when laughter is suddenly stilled and grief not quite begun.

"I am Sorrow's sister and my brother was Joy."

I gasped. I did what I am certain every pilgrim did: the figure exalted me, and I rose to my feet, as if without volition.

I felt like a different man when I left the temple of the Heart of the People, and was still in a silent, wondering, exalted state when lunchtime came and Windy with it.

He seemed different, too, if for different reasons. Subdued.

" 'lo, Zap."

"Windy."

"I guess we're allies now, buddy."

"Are we?"

"I got my instructions," Windy said. "You're taking over 1-Smoke's town."

"I heard Smoke was dead. I am, huh?"

"That's right."

"And you've got your town."

"Yes. But I would have, later, anyway."

"I didn't have anything to do with Grandad being killed," I said.

"It doesn't matter, does it? He let you go. You were supposed to be the one to get it."

"Yeah. Politics."

"Well, he's gone. And I've got a town. And you've got a town. Only . . ."

"What?"

"We aren't going to be enjoying leadership much. Just long enough to train our damn troops and march their ass out of there."

"What's up?"

"Your friend Cosijoesa, buddy—he must know where everybody's golden toads are buried. He's put the whole Tlaxiaca and most of the rest of the Mixteca together in a new alliance. With the Zapotecs this time."

"Against the Aztecs? God, Windy," I said. "That suits me. I'd rather kill Aztecs than Zapotecs."

He looked at me. "So would Grandad have," he said. "Only Grandad didn't think we could. He figured going with the Aztecs was the only way to save anything. They're the future, Zap. Everybody will be speaking Nahuatl by the time your kids grow up. At least that's how Grandad read it."

"He didn't know Cozy Joe."

"You think he's the boy who can beat the Aztecs? Tlaxcala couldn't do it. The Coast couldn't do it."

"Maybe they're over the hill," I said. "What's the plan?"

"We go south," Windy said. "All of us. Get the Aztecs' supply line stretched out thin as we can. Down to Tehuantepec. Zap, you've fought defense on fortified hilltops—Cozy Joe's going to fortify a whole damn mountain."

"That sounds great to me," I said. "Come on, Windy, smile. We'll get our boys trained and see if we can't stop this Aztec shit, once and for all."

"Sure," he said.

"How's Rain?"

"Rain killed herself," Windy said. "You'll never believe this, Zap, but she wanted to marry Smoky. That's why Grandad cut you off really, if you want to know."

14.

Back in Oaxaca, a letter from Cal at his new training camp: all well at home, when he left. Trinket fine. Mom about the same. Cal was close enough to go home weekends. His father was to take his time, and not worry about things in Rosetta. Maybe Cal would make a trip to Mexico, to see what he was doing. What would Dad think of Cal and Trinket coming down there, if Dad was still there, for Trinket's spring vacation? Trinket's idea, Cal said, but Trink was too shy to ask.

It was a pleasant fantasy that his children might like visiting him here, touring the ruins and the monuments.

He reread the affidavit he'd got fixed up for Tommy, and still couldn't decide whether to send it or not.

15.

On the dig the center of interest was the round building now. Sandoval felt he'd won the belly-bumping round with higher authority in Mexico City, and Pederson would be permitted to dig through part of the superimposition. They were hoping for written confirmation.

"It'll take time, though," Gary said. "I'm going to clear and consolidate all the latest structure first, so we know exactly what's there, while we're waiting."

At Mound 3 the masons were also consolidating, shoring up the tomb itself so that it wouldn't have to be filled in; it had been decided to finish clearing the inner rooms, but not the outside, all around the building. And on Friday, in Brill's absence, a second and third tomb had been found. Tomb #2 had been rifled, in contemporary times, but Tomb #3, which Newman was supervising, gave promise of producing their first primary burial, since the mound in which it was located was hardly a mound at all—thus the building containing the tomb appeared not to have been rebuilt.

Brill had some sense that he was beginning to be useful. Berkowitz and Minnegerode were on a new mound now, with a pair of diggers, and Brill worked his pair alone at completing the work on Mound #3. He began to do some architectural drawings, projections of the buildings each group had partly uncovered, and Gary felt these could be published as part of the report which the students would prepare later in the spring.

Brill was beginning to be curious about the laboratory techniques, especially those used in pottery classification, and in the middle of the week, riding back after work with Pederson, Gary said:

"Bob, what would you think of taking an MA with us?"

Brill said, "Huh?" and Gary explained that he, Newman, and Sandoval had talked about it. Brill had, after all, the academic degree from law school, and a good variety of undergraduate courses. He had done much of the reading that anthropology students specializing in archaeology did, had a fair command of Spanish, and the beginning of field experience.

"I wouldn't suggest a PhD," Gary said. "It takes too long, and in any case I assume you wouldn't be interested in teaching. But you may want to do more of this, you seem to have a feeling for it. I think you could pass our MA exam with another semester and some directed reading, and that would give you status to work down here when you wanted."

"I'll be damned," said dreamy Brill. "I thought the day of the gentleman amateur of archaeology was over."

"There's room for a lot of work down here, by all kinds of people," Gary said. "Besides I . . . well. It's meant something to me to have you with us. I'd like to think it could happen again."

Brill smiled: would have the short cut then, sidekick and confidant, *compadre*, of an established man to whom large doors were open.

"Sandoval's told me about your idea. The Route of the Pyramids," his *compadre* said.

"Oh, for God's sake," Brill was embarrassed.

"Archaeology here conceived as a park, three hundred miles long, to be visited by car."

"I was just making conversation," Brill said. "To pass the time on the trip."

"Nevertheless," Gary said. "It'd be a way of talking to some foundations, and some other institutions. You wouldn't have to limit it to the Mexico-Oaxaca-Tehuantepec road. It could loop back along the east coast, through Veracruz."

"Colonel Mazzard going to get an MA?" Brill asked. Walked old Gary to his quarters, talking things over.

He'd come quite a distance in his feeling for Gary in a few weeks. Gary's public image in Rosetta as a bright, persuasive, intellectual promoter with a sly flair for publicity was silly. Essentially Gary was second-rate at those things, uncomfortable with people, overcoming shyness with the surge and stammer of a smart high-school student speaker, with stage fright and a memorized speech. Gary was a complicated, essentially a withdrawn man, poor at relationships except the one where authority went with the position of teacher, floundering when events broke through position to the man. But he was a good teacher, and a hell of a man where his passion focused, the dirt and rocks and cactus, ancient buildings and mute history of the field. At last Brill liked him.

He might, Brill thought, walking next to his hotel, master enough of the scholarly detail at that to become at least an anachronism, the sort of amateur whose help would be welcome.

When he thought of the alternative, back home in Rosetta, Mexico seemed more attractive than ever, and he wondered who you wrote to in Hong Kong for suits.

So musing, he moved through the lobby of the hotel, up the stairs, saw the door of his room standing slightly open, smelled perfume, and said, with some annoyance:

"Nancy?"

"You bastard," said a husky voice that nearly stopped his big fat heart. "You might at least try to sound glad to see Nancy, whoever *she* is."

He grabbed her hands and tried to say her name, but how can a man say even the two syllables, Gabby, when he can't get his breath?

"You are the dustiest man I ever saw in my life," she said. "Who is this Nancy, anyway?"

"I'll . . . I'll wash."

"You artifact."

"What a sneaky trick."

"Want me to leave?"

"Sure of yourself."

"Yes, Mr. Brill. No, hey. Stop right there, until you're clean . . ."

And of course he would not have stopped, seeing suitcases, with presumably enough clean clothes in them, except that Sandoval and Newman came dashing into the room with a letter, Newman crowing:

"It came. Tomás wins."

"Permission to dig the observatory," Sandoval cried, and Newman:

"Hey! Gabby, Gabby."

"Madmen," Gabby said. "Rusty, dusty madmen," and to Sandoval, "Are you a Mexican madman?"

"Ay-yiii." For no particular reason that Brill could ever figure out, Sandoval gave the *grito*.

"Beer, tequila, brandy," Newman cried, and Brill fled to the shower.

Good God, he thought, stripped off, turned on water, feeling the chill of gooseflesh in physical anticipation of the warmth and wet of it: *I'm among friends, and my love is here.*

The flesh of his arms, legs, thighs, chest, back, swelled and tingled with the pride of that thought, and drops of water bounced right and left.

Tried, in order to make the happy minutes pass while he scrubbed sufficiently, to think where the hell he was in his mental history.

Could not remember wind and rain and smoke.

In the exuberance of the evening which followed, Brill tried, from time to time, to measure his happiness: I am as happy now, he thought, as, tired and glowing, I felt when we won a football game and Felix and I would drink and boast, and make young Gary Pederson laugh himself sick.

"Let's do a cave dig, damn it. Origins of ceramics." (Newman)

"Southern Veracruz." (Pederson)

"I'll get the damn money." (Brill)

"Cloud forest." (Sandoval)

"The road?" (Pederson)

"Rain forest." (Newman)

"No. South of Tampico. Totonacs. The coast." (Gabby)

Gabby?

Or the evening of his thirty-second birthday, when the partnership with Tommy was young, Pat her old self, and the partners had won a case. The two couples deeply, intricately, woven together in criss-cross emotion, and he held the thread to keep it from unraveling—Martha Rebranch was the thread, her eagerness to couple with him that night and whenever else he would, and yet at the same time it was clear that that was not the kind of closeness Tommy felt or Pat—so that Brill was in control of it all, and the hurting happiness of finding a way of saying gently no to Martha so she would not be offended, yet not being stuffy, not diminishing her, though he quite desperately wanted to feel her body under his, but was loyal to his wife and his young partner—out of that tension and those kinds of love had come a boisterousness for all of them that was happy as anything could be.

"Mr. Brill, darling, you absurd man. I will stay right here in Mexico with you, forever and ever, or until *mañana,* Plowboy, whichever comes last."

"Ay-yiii."

Or certain perfect evenings with Martin at the duck shack, mornings on the river.

Night with Gabby in Oaxaca, when their rowdy friends Newman, Sandoval, Berkowitz, Minnegerode, and even rowdy Pederson, had all gone home.

Mr. Brill and Mrs. Light embraced to a point just short of madness.

"No, Mr. Brill," she whispered. "You do not remind a girl of her pudgy-handed little five o'clock worry drunk of a father. You're a very physical man, like a black athlete or I suppose a white one, or something else that doesn't come strutting my way every day, Mr. Brill, and a peculiar and interesting man . . ."

And went off to sleep.

She did. Halfway along to sleep himself, in pleasurable drift, Brill's left thigh kicked out in vigorous spasm, and it shook him totally awake.

The old insomnia, his familiar for so many years that it was strange he hadn't noticed its passing here in Oaxaca, was back again. He got up, and after a time felt sure enough of the depth of Gabby's slumber so that he turned on the lamp on the dresser across the room.

He stood at the foot of the bed, looking at her, soft face encircled by soft hair spread out on pillow, and whispered:

"You think I don't know a goddamn last chance when I see one?"

Then he crossed the room to the lamp again, and reread the letter from his strange, cool son, with its implied postscript from his shy daughter. Looked at the document, the affidavit for Tommy. Thought of Pat.

Realized he had made all the old bargains human life is based on: to give the cool or angry young a father, the target that won't shoot back. To stand by a friend in trouble, even when the friendship ended, because what being friends implied had been there when Tommy first began to cheat the tax lords. To carry the woman, if she failed, because she'd carry you if she could. Not to take advantage of a child's love. And something, too, an equally old bargain about the land.

In the morning Robert Brill flew home.

16.

Over the waters of the Gulf, where he'd once flown himself, but in the other direction, he remembered without difficulty where he'd been in the history:

On the first terrace at Giengola, with Windy, holding the center. All along in front were rocks, piled to form walls, but the walls themselves were weapons: you could push rocks off the top layer and roll them down at Aztecs trying to climb up, after you'd shot your arrows and thrown your spears. Before the hand to hand with the maquauhuitls and the knives.

It was the third week of the siege, and Cozy Joe had done his work well. All along behind us were the big jugs, sunk into the ground, of corn and water and oil.

Women stayed just behind there, to grind the corn and cook. Sometimes we raided at night an Aztec camp to steal turkeys and dogs for meat, and destroy whatever weapons we could get to before they woke and ran us off.

I'd seen Joe that morning with Cotton Ball, lovely and sad as Rain by now, when her people and her husband's people were slaughtering one another.

"Aztec attack in the morning," Joe'd told me. "Probably your sector."

So Windy and I had our men up early, and Cozy Joe's intelligence was right. They hit us just after daybreak.

We were ready. Their first rank we broke with arrows.

The second rank we let come close enough so that we could damn near smell them: then we rolled the rocks. It was great.

They were caught in what amounted to a small landslide, caught around the ankles, and down the hill they went, scrambling and screaming as the spears found them, too.

A few came through.

One Jaguar knight reached me, just as his ankle broke, and was lying just in front of the wall, moaning.

I jumped the wall to finish him, ripped off his headdress. It was Silent Sam.

"Hell, Sam," I said. "I'm sorry. Ankle pretty bad?"

"Hurts, Zap. Really hurts," he said.

"I thought you were an eagle knight?"

"I changed. The . . ." he moaned, "eagles were getting too many old guys. We Jags . . ." moaned again, "are getting the action."

"Yeah," I said. "I'm sorry, Sam."

"You taking me up the hill for sacrifice, or what?"

"No," I said. "We got no food to hold captives, Sam. Cozy Joe's orders . . ."

Brill looked down at the waters of the Gulf. He couldn't decide whether to let Zap kill his old friend and adversary, Silent Sam the Aztec.

At that moment, Brill thought, strange, pale, gold-starved men with hairy faces were landing on the coast, three hundred miles from Giengola, bringing new gods and new kinds of death, so that who won this siege would never matter after all. And the hair-faced tribes, in a few more hundred years, would themselves be suddenly confronted with new kinds of death. And new gods?

It might be a kindness to Silent Sam the Aztec to let Zap kill him after all, but suddenly Brill was struck with and diverted by something he hadn't realized before: it was a matter of resemblances in the images of his cast.

He had known all along, really, that Zap looked not like himself, but like his cousin Felix. What he realized with a sharp interior snort was that Silent Sam looked like Robert Brill—and that Rain, 6-Rain, before her self-destruction, had looked not like Gabby or Louise or Beth, but like Pat after the plane crash, like his mother, like Libby Franchot, even like Maru—all the slim, lost, troubled, brown-eyed girls.

"Would you like a drink, sir?" said the stewardess.

"*Tlasokamati*," said *Wewetkeh* Brill. "*Yutokammitikeh, itiatyoweh.*"

He didn't, of course. Brill never learned Nahuatl. And anyway, all of that means "No, thank you," more or less, whereas what Brill said was,

"Yes, please, miss."